Companions in Femdom

Two Novels of Female Domination

D1785624

Book Seven

"The Inferior"
By
Kurt Steiner
&
"A Wife Takes Control"
By
Rebecca Tarling

Contents

THE INFERIOR

PROLOGUE

Cornwall

Naked, back against the smooth painted plaster of the living-room wall, legs sprawled out before him on the chill parquet flooring; he looked on as she entered from the dining room carrying a chair.

Panic provoking hysteria, he watched her position it over and to either side of his feet before taking the single step required to bestride his body. Powerful legs, clad in the sheerest black hose, towering above his shivering frame as her eyes bore down into his own to intensify his terror.

Levels of empathy and warmth remarkable only for their complete absence.

Unlike him, she was fully dressed. Outfitted in a somber, severely cut, two-piece suit in charcoal grey - crisp white shirt and matching accessories completing the ensemble. A uniform, of sorts, imparting an impression more redolent of authority than service; out of keeping with the position she held in his household yet apposite at one and the same time.

"Authority", he thought, loss matching terror, that had once been his; certain, as he watched hands rest on hips and an insolent tongue slither across somewhat inflated lips, it would never be gifted to him again.

As she stared down upon him, brown features implacable; yet unable to quite disguise their delight at the depths to which she had reduced him; his whole body became a film of perspiration. The subconscious divining her intention and reacting accordingly. Fear -along with levels of humiliation even he as a writer would be hard-pressed to describe– adding a perverse urgency to the throbbing at his groin.

A reaction to his situation, and another source of shame, he found difficult to reconcile with the man he had once believed himself to be.

Though not restrained in any way, movement was impossible - as was intelligible speech. All he could do was watch as she seated herself and slipped her feet from the spiked black court shoes that had pecked their way across the parquet towards him a few seconds earlier. The smell of moist nylon assailing his nostrils heightening a disgrace already functioning at high altitudes.

The position, gender and race, of his tormentor an unholy trinity in the mind of the man on the receiving end of her intentions

To allow this woman… this… girl… this… flunkey, to manipulate him in such a fashion was unthinkable and had to be… had to be…

So what, the above being true, he asked; self-castigation truncated by silent interrogation; explained the way his breath caught in his throat as she slowly slid her skirt over powerful young thighs to bunch it at her hips?

Why did the expanse of shiny black pantyhose, clinging to her legs so tightly, command his attention with more urgency than a nearby oasis dominated the thoughts of a thirsty nomad?

Why, as she undid the buttons of her shirt to reveal even more of the full breasts he had only recently noticed and developed such an infatuation for, was he unable to look away?

And why, finally; when the soles of her nylon-encased feet came to rest on his bare thighs; did his restricted breathing suddenly find release with a sigh that sounded, for the entire world, like a swoon?

"You want them?" she asked; the English in which she had an advanced degree of fluency unable to prevent the linguistic corruption resulting from the accent of her mother tongue. The cold implacability of her tone breaking the silence and belying her youth in a way he found utterly terrifying - even as his masculinity berated him for reacting in so spineless a way to someone so many years his junior.

With a supreme effort, he managed to nod, eyes halted on their unavoidable upward swing by a glimpse of her cleavage and remaining there. Astounded two such beauteous things could co-exist with the less than stunning visage above them.

And then, suddenly, his attention was elsewhere. Eyes lowering as the friction of her pantyhose against his manhood diverted his gaze to her feet. His tormentor's surprisingly dainty peds sliding along his penis, sole of each turned inwards, as the column betraying him found itself trapped between the high arches of her instep.

"Look at me," she demanded; the unfamiliar frisson of nylon against foreskin and the undeniable submissiveness inspired by the situation overwhelming him.

Her command, however, jolted him from his preoccupation just long enough for a modicum of spine to assert itself. It was one thing, after all, to debase himself in front of her in such a way. Quite another, he knew, to actually look into her eyes and see his disgrace and humiliation mirrored back at...

His body jack-knifed with agony as both his thoughts and his "Spine" vanished.

Suddenly; before his mini rebellion had any chance to morph into full-scale revolt; he was screaming.

Silently – unable to give voice to his pain.

His very life force sucked from him as his body spasmed involuntarily and he voiced soundless anguish towards the heavens; the same foot that had seconds ago been bestowing such intense and perverse pleasure upon him stamping down on his testicles; intent, it appeared, upon mashing the cylinders defining his masculinity into the wood of the parquet flooring itself.

"I warned you what would happen if you disobeyed," she said, eyes mocking as his agony increased and threatened to void his stomach of its contents.

Had it held any.

"Perhaps," she suggested with much relish; "you will find it easier to obey as a eunuch."

He could only watch with terror; eyes bugging from his head as she increased the downward pressure of her foot; soundless entreaties rising in intensity and going unheeded as she stood to gain more leverage in order to neuter him. Malevolent brown eyes finally displaying warmth as the pleasure she took in his unmanning went into overdrive prior to taking orbit as his masculinity and the testicles symbolising it, was crushed beneath her pretty young feet.

Any second now, he knew he would hear that inevitable "Squish!" sound as those same testicles burst outwards and flattened themselves to the floor; reducing him to something less than a man and something no more useful than a... than a...

Uncharted territory, pain levels soaring off the graph, that finally allowed him to give voice to his agony as he screamed and screamed and screamed and…

CHAPTER ONE

Anya

In the studio quarters allocated to her above the garage, Anya Jalav studied the five feet of her diminutive but full-bodied form in the bathroom's full-length mirror; pleased with the progress she was making with her older employer in the main house.

Entering the seventh month in her new position, she knew she had some way to go still, both youth and the sheer power of unfulfilled desire making her more impatient by the hour to reach her desired destination. Even if, with the help of a new friend, expectations of success for her endeavour grew at a corresponding rate.

As the Indian girl only recently turned twenty took in the shapely, if prematurely matronly, contours of her firm body and its magnificent breasts -those same breasts that, amazingly, had yet to know the caresses of a lover- she cursed the somewhat equestrian features of her face. Features, with large cheekbones and prominent overbite, she had to thank for the neglect extended to the rest of her body thus far. Accepting that the face her "Friend" described as: "oozing character", made what she had in mind for her handsome English "Master" so much more difficult.

Though not, she prayed, impossible.

For, despite her concerns at what rested atop her neck, the body below gave her little pause for thought. That, she was now assured, in no way presented a problem.

A loner by nature -and a preference confirmed by experience- her confidence in the body staring back at her from the mirror was both shared and bolstered by Rajiv, her aforementioned, new –and only- friend.

"Patience, my dear," her Internet mentor had told her earlier that evening, via the wonder that was Skype; connecting Cornwall to Calcutta in no more time than it took to take a sip of ice cold kucchi lassi. The same "Mentor" whose idea it had been to suddenly start addressing her employer with the old-fashioned form of respect.

A form of respect -as he had assured her it would- the man employing her would find curious to begin with but soon view favourably as his all too obvious vanity and self-importance kicked in.

"I have scrutinised the photos of yourself you attached to me," he all but leered. "Scrutinised them, very, very, closely – if you take my meaning. Trust me, my young friend, your charm may not be of a conventional nature but it is undeniably present and all the stronger for not being of the bland and uninteresting kind."

Anya felt her cheeks flush: criticism she was used to and could deal with; compliments called for a response alien to her experience.

"I speak," Rajiv was continuing, "of that bastardisation of womanhood represented by the bulimic stick insects the moronic magazines of mass culture label: 'Physically beautiful'."

As ever, the words of her new friend had instilled welcome assurance - much needed after yet another inspection of the looking glass and her: "Equestrian" features, as she had once heard them described. That same friend's on-screen face a visual corroboration of his existence and a compliment she had yet to return with the setting up of a webcam of her own.

"Your appeal to this man," he went on, the expression on his aged and fleshy, if still appealing, features giving witness to his seriousness; "must lie in more than just the allure of a pretty face, anyway."

"In that," she answered ruefully; features reflected back at her from the window behind the computer, "I hardly have a say," ending her complaint with a derisive snort.

Rajiv was sympathetic but firm:

"Do not despair over that which you can do nothing about," he advised her; sounding at times like this as if he were a venerable Japanese sensei rather than a sixty-something former clerical officer with the Indian Civil Service. "A discerning man will always take quality over prettiness alone and, trust me on this, your face suggests nothing if not character and moral fibre."

His words of reassurance on the subject winning him only a cynical:

"Hmmph!"

"Remember, Anya," he went on, neglecting to mention the

perverseness of that 'Moral fibre': "to rush the process will be to invite failure. If he once suspects the nature of your intentions you will lose him and the journey will be over - for you as well as me. Be assured when I tell you that the opportunity to place your brand upon the tender white buttocks of such a creature is one that comes along all too rarely –perhaps only once, if we are lucky – in a single lifetime."

Though he was telling her no more than she had told herself on numerous occasions, Anya nodded at the screen containing her mentor and his habitual jogging-suit as if she were hearing his counsel on the subject for the first time and he was actually in a position to see her do it.

A favour he had extended to her and, as he frequently reminded her, waited with impatience to be returned.

"Keep in mind," he continued, "the nature of the prize lying in reward for the self-control I urge upon you."

"I seldom think of much else," she assured him.

"Yes," he could do no more than agree. "It is a heady prospect – especially for one of your tender years. A fellow human being as your chattel. Your creature. Complete control over an older man who once employed you. The same man who, at this moment, regards you as no more than a substandard form of life; placed on this earth with no greater purpose than to make his worthless existence more comfortable. A man, moreover, from whom you will have obliterated all traces of pride, masculinity and self-dependence until he looks to you for everything – even though he may hate you as he does so."

He gave his words some thought; sensing she was doing the same.

"As well as your possession, Anya, you must also think of him as your... creation."

He paused for a few moments more, knowing he had her full attention.

"If you do as I suggest," he began again, deadly serious, "your power over him will become total and irrevocable. He will look to you for everything and regard the smallest, most infinitesimally minute gesture of approval from you as if it were a gift from mother Kali herself.

She remained silent; sure her somewhat verbose mentor was

not quite finished.

"More," he continued, not disappointing; "though he may continue to detest you for bringing him to such a pass, he will never possess the strength to deny you anything – even though he will, at times, make pitiful attempts to try. Each unsuccessful effort leaving him worse off than before."

At the last of his claims, an image had formed behind Anya's eyes.

She saw her still clothed body, hands-on-hips, as she stood in the large en-suite adjoining the main bedroom; her naked employer crouched on all fours at her feet as she stepped over his legs to bestride his back - his eyes, much to her gratification and in obedience to her instructions, lost in contemplation of the terra cotta floor tiles. Her employer supporting himself with his arms to remain in position while she raised her skirt and pulled her panties to one side; the shaking of his shoulders indicating he knew what was to come.

Lost to the desire inspired by her fantasy, Anya smiled as she saw a stream of hot, warm, urine gush from her pussy to saturate his hair and neck before trickling down his face towards nostrils and mou…

"How would you feel, dear Anya," her mentor's words cut into her daydream, "to return here to your hometown with a handsome and obedient English servant in tow?"

Coming back to planet earth with a thud, she allowed herself a smile at his words and forgave him his intrusion into her daydream. Ill-timed or not, the welcome nature of the prospect he dangled before her ensured she forgave his intrusion and made touchdown less anti-climactic.

"Consider," he urged, "the reaction of the sewer-stupid shits you told me made your time here in Calcutta such a torture. Imagine how their dismal and fixed little lives would be put in perspective to see the object of their taunts; elevated so far above them she is capable of commanding the obedience and devotion of such a possession."

Considering that "Reaction" gave her much pleasure.

"Tell me honestly, Anya," he pressed, "is the winning of such a prize not worthy of some small application of patience?"

Despite the familiar excitement his words instilled in her –not to mention flaunting her power in the faces of those "Little shits" who had indeed made her early years so miserable- Anya's hackles, as they always did whenever she was criticised unjustly, rose instantly.

"My impatience, Rajiv," she protested loudly and heatedly, correcting her fellow countryman and native of 'Kolkata'; "shows only when I speak with you on the subject of my prospective chattel."

The raised decibel levels, filling the room as she put him right, of no concern to her; knowing that -even in the unlikely event of her employer venturing near her quarters from the main house where she served as his housekeeper- he had no knowledge whatsoever of the Bengali in which their conversation was being conducted.

"I would not dream of ruining things at the crawling stage by attempting to run," she assured him. "Fate and good fortune have conspired to place me with the right man at both the right place and time. If you think I will allow such a gift to slip through my fingers you are a very deluded 'Mentor'."

It was a reprimand he accepted graciously and one she was sincere about, her earliest sexual memories having been of control. Power over another human being so strong it was unanswerable. The same thrill of dominion over an unwilling man of greater years she had been able to experience up to now only through her dreams and the wonder of the net that fuelled them. The same "Dreams" she had now committed herself to knowing in the first-person.

"That is reassuring to hear, my sweet," the strong male voice told her. "You are, after all, at a very delicate stage. Though do bear in mind it will serve you well to disregard your baseless concerns regarding your features. You have far, far, far, more than an appealing face in your favour – at least if the pictures you attached to me do not lie. I assure you, were I of the opposite sexual mindset in such matters, I believe I could very quickly become obsessed with the power inherent in that young body you have kept under wraps for so long."

Despite her distrust of flattery –possibly from not having much experience of the phenomenon– Anya felt her face flush with pleasure at the compliment - even as another thought occurred to the "Sensei":

"Tell me, Anya," he asked, "do you ever question why you are the way you are?"

Her response was as instant as it was emphatic:

"Never."

"Really?" he asked. "Are you not curious at least?"

"To what end?" she answered – a little dismissively he thought. "What would be achieved? Does fire burn any less brightly for our knowing how it finds its heat? These are feelings and desires I have known for as long as I can remember. Rather than question satisfaction I prefer to enjoy it. We are what we are, after all. You as much as me."

The head on the screen could do no more than nod agreement; for though he considered her naïve in ways befitting her age, Rajiv knew also she was wise beyond those years in many others. Her articulacy -and the somewhat old-fashioned manner of speech contradicting her lack of a formal education- the result, he knew, of having been taught her second-language by a retired Professor of English Language and Literature at Calcutta University, for whom she had skivvied as a very young girl.

"A good answer," he laughed. "As Santayana insisted: for true barbarians such as us, the simple existence of our passions is reason enough for their being."

He waited for her to respond; pleased with himself.

Giving it up when praise for his cleverness-stroke-memory remained withheld; her "Professor", it transpired, having left the "Literature" side of things unexplored.

"But to hell with useless philosophy," he broke his own pause. "I should like to return, if I may, to the subject of the visual. When, my dear, are you going to return my favour and set up a webcam so we can view each other as we speak? Call me old-fashioned but, when at all possible, I like to see the face of the person with whom I converse on matters so… intimate."

Now it was her turn to laugh:

"Just my 'Face', Rajiv?" she teased; a certain discomfort in his on-screen reaction emboldening her further: "Or do you wish me to provide you with visual stimulation even more intimate in nature? Am I to believe the photographs I sent you of my pure young body are no longer enough for you?"

"No to the first and a resounding 'Yes' to both the second and the third," he answered instantly; "Discomfort", had she not imagined it, already on the backburner.

"As I may have mentioned before, Anya," he reminded her; "and excepting the beasts of the field: the mind is the gateway to Nirvana. Physical pleasure becomes ecstasy only when mental stimulation is at requisite levels. As nature underpins everything natural and organic; so the cerebral underpins all things human and sexual. That said, however, it is also true that in the same way as academic learning improves the quality of intelligence, so do pictures, in situations such as ours, take the text to higher levels."

Had he been in reception of a signal with which to view it, he would have seen Anya was already nodding agreement - having acknowledged to herself on many occasions how limiting she found the absence of: "Learning".

Frustration, for both the above lack itself, and her mentor's long windedness, making his assertion one with which she could only agree.

"But enough of me," he said, returning to business. "I would – again- like to hear about the welcome your Master extended to your new wardrobe and his response to you since. Run his initial reaction by me once again, Anya… If you would be so kind."

Anya smiled to herself at his request, finding in it no hardship. Her Master's "Response", after all, having been of a kind she savoured. Boding well for her future plans in his regard.

Those "Plans" involving nothing less than the complete enslavement of a handsome Englishman.

A "Handsome Englishman", moreover; who was not only her employer but –making the scenario in prospect that much sweeter to her- almost three decades her senior.

The nature of that "Scenario" changing almost every time she closed her eyes to fantasise about it; fantasies so numerous and powerful she had actually given them numbers to be able to summon them up more readily.

CHAPTER TWO

Anya's First Fantasy

"You have to ask me," she reminded him, standing in the kitchen where he had sought her out.

Her raven black hair hung loose over the smooth brown skin of her shoulders and her expression as she regarded him was one she had heard described as: "Haughty"

She could tell how taken he was with the grey woolen dress and sheer nylon pantyhose as it tapered down and disappeared into black shoes with pointed toes and sharp heels.

"Please, Anya," he began, "can I..."

"No!" she barked, enjoying the way the handsome Englishman flinched. "You should be naked and on your knees before me. Do it now!"

His haste to do as she asked would have been touching had it not been so pathetic.

"Look at you," she sneered. "Tying yourself in knots to obey a young girl - and you so much older than she. A brown girl and your servant too, and you an Englishman; what would your friends say?"

Almost before her jeering had finished, he was kneeling at her feet on his haunches, servile and anxious; the need etched upon his features a joy to behold.

"Ask me then," she reminded him again, as if he were little more than a half-wit rather than a mildly successful former writer some thirty years her senior.

"Please," he begged.

"Please, what?"

"Please, Master, let me... let me masturbate for you."

"What?" she snarled, feigning outrage; "Are you a pervert? You want to touch yourself in front of me? In your own kitchen?"

"Please, Master."

"You are a pervert, are you not? Let me hear you say it."

"I... I'm a pervert, Master."

She smiled.

"I just wanted you to be clear on that point;" a hand coming around from behind her then, to dangle something before his eyes. "Do you know what these are?"

His eyes sparkled hungrily:

"They... They're your panties, Master," he told her, lips dry.

Without a word she took a single step towards him and draped them over his head; sure to position the gusset over his nose.

"I have worn them for the past three days so they will be nice and...ripe for you."

Below her, she watched with amusement as his tongue darted out to taste her stale secretions.

"I expect a thank you when I give you something."

"Thank you Master," he obeyed through the fabric covering his mouth.

Turning to her side, she hitched up her skirt to present him with her right leg, the pressure on her calf muscles from the high heels dimpling their length on the upward rise to her sleek and powerful thighs, rippling beneath the sheer black nylon containing them.

"Here, on the kitchen floor, in your own home, you are going to hump your servant's leg like the animal you truly are," she told him. "Then, when you know yourself for the dog you most resemble, you are going to clean your man-juice from her nylons with your tongue. Understand?"

"Hmmm," came from below her, her slave too immersed in the sensations provided by her soiled underwear to find words.

"I do not think, after this, we will have any more confusion concerning just who is in charge here."

She reached out to pinch the lobe of his ear with her free hand.

"Up!"

Instantly, he rose from his haunches to his knees.

"Do it!" she snapped.

After a moment's hesitation, he wrapped his arms around her hips and pressed his erection against the side of her pantyhose-clad leg, the rasping of the nylon against his foreskin bringing a muffled gasp from him.

"Hurry along!" she ordered him. "I have things to do."

He did as she asked immediately; the taste and the smell of her soiled underwear continuing to assail his senses as he thrust against her leg in an unholy imitation of a rutting canine.

It couldn't have been more than five strokes after he began humping, so strong was his excitement, that he let out a massive gasp and exploded against her; jet after jet of white semen covering her thigh; his body sagging against her hips as she looked down with contempt.

"There," she told him, mockery unmistakable; as was the sheer fulfillment she received from such control: "not such a cruel master after all, am I?"

Stepping from his grasp, she surveyed the semen soaked nylon at her thighs and tutted before tearing her panties from his head.

"Well?" she said, after a few seconds, tone expectant: "Don't just kneel there like an imbecile,

His stared up at her, eyes that were more than just a little beaten showing puzzlement also.

With a huge sigh of the type one makes at the shortcomings of a half-wit, she again took him by the ear and leaned down to glare into his eyes:

"Get your unworthy tongue to work and clean me up, you animal."

CHAPTER-THREE

The "Master"

For the third time that week, Bernard Lambert found himself waking to the sound of his own screams.

The fact it was still only Tuesday hardly offering itself as a reassurance.

Nor did the fact he came awake in the surroundings of his own study. The brown leather of the comfy sofa upon which he was taking his usual afternoon catnap, clammy against the skin of his bare forearms. Neither time, place, nor sofa, doing anything to lessen his concern for experiencing such dreams at all.

By way of confirmation, his hands went to his groin; relief at what he found there joined by a frantic banging which, though startling, at least hastened a full return to the land of the living.

And, more crucially: the intact.

"Master Lambert?" came the cry. "Is everything as it should be?"

There was no mistaking the deference in the heavily accented voice and old-fashioned English usage. Both, he considered, chiming nicely with the anachronistic form of address she had only recently started using when speaking to him. A form of address that was yet more evidence of the respect in which she held him and from which he took so much pleasure - despite the increasingly disturbing nature of his dreams in her regard.

Respect and a form of address that went a long way towards restoring his self-esteem after his recent setbacks; while, at the same time, reassuring him the status quo continued to hold sway – despite the worrying nature of the new fixation holding his subconscious in its grip.

That it was a somewhat recidivist and despised status quo – dead and buried with the British Raj some three-quarters of a century ago- not preventing his self-congratulation for having revived the tradition in his own home. The achievement of such a rebirth in a new; "Politically correct" and enlightened, millennium lessening his self-approbation not a penny piece.

"Anya?" he had asked her; shortly after she had started using the honorific. "Why are you suddenly addressing me in such an old-fashioned way?"

Still in her saris at the time –and, consequently, of no interest to him- his housekeeper had surprised him with the answer that, unbeknownst to him, she and Rajiv had pre-agreed should such a question be asked. The change that would ensure the surprisingly magnetic pull of his eyes towards the powerful and shapely legs with the pronounced calf-muscles -legs she had not seen fit to reveal until then- still some weeks in the future.

That subsequent attraction one that had demeaned him as much upon first sight as it did now. It being an attraction he found increasingly troubling. As if the swapping of sari covered bare legs and sandals for pantyhose and heels; combined with his reaction to the change; made her seem a different person in his eyes.

"Because you are a man of substance and it is deserved, Master," she had answered him, delivering the untruth without a trace of the self-consciousness normally guaranteed to betray liars with a limited talent for the ways of deceit.

There being no trace, either, of the amusement she had taken from his obvious delight in such outrageous and fraudulent flattery.

Going on to flatter him still further when she saw her initial success:

"I have been here almost six months now," she continued, "and you have proved yourself thoroughly deserving of your position in the world. Firm but fair. In my country there is no shame in acknowledging such a worthy man as 'Master'."

Then, as the script she had devised with her mentor demanded, her look had become troubled.

"However," she said, expression still thoughtful; "if by addressing you in such a way I cause you embarrassment, I will use a different…"

"No, no!" he had disabused her. Swiftly. "I'm all for tradition. If that's how you wish to address me then so be it."

And so it was. As Rajiv had assured her it would go; so had it gone. Her "Master" and his already inflated ego -puffed up further every time she addressed him in such a way- being groomed for what would come later.

Back in the moment, though, the man himself wondered what

his servant would think of her "Worthy" Master were she to divine, somehow, the contents of his dreams. Acknowledging thanks as he did so -to whomever atheists acknowledged such things- that mind reading was not included in her seemingly endless array of domestic talents.

"Master Lambert?" came the cry a second time; a double reassurance he was back with the living as the door flew open and she stepped inside; expression a mixture of curiosity for a room she was entering for the first time and feigned concern for the man it contained.

"I'm fine, thank you, Anya," he told her, clearing his throat mid-sentence as the unlikely leading-lady of his recent dreams came towards him – clad, coincidentally, in the self-same outfit he had pictured her in as she had gone about destroying his testicles.

Adopting a critical expression intended to let his servant know he wasn't happy she had entered his "inner-sanctum" at all; Lambert pushed the imagery to one side. It was a domestic incursion –despite the mitigating circumstances- he found extremely annoying. He had, after all, explained at length, from the commencement of her employment with him, that his study was "Off-limits".

And at all times.

He could only hope the boldness of her intrusion was not some statement of emancipation to go with the English fashions replacing the discarded saris and traditional Indian costume she had worn on first taking up employment in his home.

An adoption of anglicised dress that had disturbed him for some reason.

A change -though her attitude towards him was no less deferential- that made her seem, somehow, less… He groped for the word best able to convey his meaning and found it…

Submissive.

The above being a quality in a woman he had always found extremely pleasing.

"I heard you scream out, she told him," aware of his discomfort – even if that discomfort was not acute enough to prevent him stealing glances at her hosed legs and full breasts. Nor her from noticing that -though the interest he seemed to take in her body below the neck was, if anything, growing more pronounced-her face, as per usual, remained neglected.

"Nothing to worry about," he assured her, a little tetchily; irritated at her persistence and drawing himself up authoritatively; snatching an eyeful of her, somewhat: "School-teacherly", legs as he did so. That they were ever so slightly bowed making them seem, somehow, more… powerful. These being, he recalled, the same legs and feet he had seen above him not seconds before as they stomped his testicles to mush and went about supplying his dream the ultimate terror.

"I was just acting out a scene from the new book," he lied, unable to prevent the catch in his voice her presence inspired. His growing preoccupation one he was at a loss to explain to himself. An interest in his horse-faced housekeeper stemming from the very moment she had decided to shed the costume native to her homeland and wear the more familiar designs and fabrics of his own.

Not to mention the absence of a woman in his life for the first period of any real duration he could recall.

"You can continue with whatever you were doing, and allow me to get on now," he told her, manner made terse by recent memory. Eyes, even as he dismissed her, wandering down to the full breasts he could see straining against her shirt and imagining them unfettered.

In truth, the nature, frequency and intensity of his thoughts in her regard were becoming a real worry. No matter that sexual fantasies were as everyday and run of the mill to him as they were to any other man. After all, the odd dream concerning the same person was certainly nothing to be concerned about.

But this was different.

Not only were the dreams and unbidden images becoming more vivid; but their capacity to disturb seemed to be multiplying exponentially also.

"Dreams", that left him mystified as to their source; as well as mortified to admit –given his horror at their content- the excitement he took from them.

Though by far his biggest concern in their regard was the identity of the girl taking centre stage as they played out.

Being totally candid, and without wishing to sound harsh, he had told himself -and as good as she had proved herself at the menial chores for which he had hired her- she was, when it came down to it, no more than an ugly and badly educated Indian girl from a low caste background. What she was now, he had assured himself, was all she would ever be. Single or married –especially the latter- what she did for him now was what she would do for others throughout the remainder of her life.

"I am making tea, Master," she informed him by way of corroboration, making no impression on his preoccupation.

So why," he told himself, if she was so easily dismissed, was the girl having such an effect upon him – her image popping into his head at any time or place? Why, at any moment, would he picture the two of them in situations revealing her in any number of erotic positions and poses as they interacted with each other?

And why, more worryingly, were these "Interactions" becoming so…

There was no other word for it.

"Weird."

Though he had always enjoyed being top-dog, both physically and domestically, in his relationships with women it had always been more a case of vanilla-with-edge; rather than the more blatant BDSM scenes of strong masters and subservient women depicted on his computer, Scenes he knew –no matter how appealing he found them- he would never indulge in.

So, that being the case; yet to be indulged tastes running in this direction; why was it that every time she invaded his sleep it was he, Bernard Lambert, her employer and "Master", who was designated the unenviable role of second-class citizen?

And why, if these "Scenes" were reserved for his sleep, was he picturing one now?

CHAPTER FOUR

Master & Servant

The smooth, unblemished brown skin of her buttocks hovered above his face as she crouched over him, her own face –when he could tear his eyes away to look at it- a mixture of high excitement and cruelty at having reduced him to such a position. Then, suddenly, she began to lower herself; hands pulling apart her cheeks to expose her anus that he may better see what was intent upon engulfing him. Already the smell was indescribable and he wanted to move, but couldn't, her arse settling on his face until his nose found itself inserted deep inside her and…

"I am making tea," Anya Jalav told him for the second time; the tyrant of Bernard Lambert's slumbers standing before him in her now customary heels and hose as he sat on the sofa hosting the most recent of the dreams in which she was involved and, now, imagery of a more conscious manifestation.

"Sorry?" he asked, looking up at her; a lingering image of her lowering arse still filling his thoughts. A tiny germ of knowingness in her expression he hadn't noticed before making him instantly suspicious; as if she knew what was going on and felt contempt for him. Though, given how mediocre he found her -in all but domestic matters, anyway- it was an impression he shrugged off immediately as totally implausible.

"Tea, Master," she repeated. "I am about to make some. Cake too."

The mundane nature of her statement prompted self-mockery for his worries in her regard. She was, after all, no more than a highly efficient young servant, grateful for the opportunity he had provided her to escape the deprivations of her background and live in England.

Nothing more sinister.

Any, off-the-wall, thoughts he was having in regard of her, he considered, had more to do with the recent changes in his circumstances and the way his subconscious reacted to them than the girl herself. The opposite side of the bed he had rarely known unoccupied throughout his fourscore and more years, playing its own part, he was certain, in his risible preoccupation with such a person.

That the same reasoning power could apply to his servant -and he might not be the only one grappling with an idée fix- not a possibility that occurred to him.

"Just tea will be fine," he assured her as he considered his still trim figure and made silent assurances of his own in respect of both his dreams and the nature of them.

Adding after a few beats:

"I'll take it in the living-room."

Nodding politely, she had turned on her heel to leave.

"Oh, and Anya?" he began in a stern tone; asserting his position; despite the competition provided by the back of her hosed legs as they made for the door. The arrogance that had seen the collapse of his marriage –as well as an inability to accept advice which might just have kept his writing career on track- goading him to take a higher ground with his retainer in the here-and-now he found impossible to reach in his dreams.

Turning, she regarded him quizzically; horse-like features and large brown eyes made even more prominent by the black hair she had swept from her face and tied at the back:

"Yes, Master?"

Eyes rising from her legs, he hesitated as his attention was transfixed yet again.

This time it was her tight, knee-length, grey skirt; doing its best to provide decency to a provocatively protruding mound; that caught his eye. His tongue snaking from his mouth at the sight in an abortive attempt to moisten lips made dry by a sudden image of that same appendage as it gently lapped at the folds of her labia. Oral worship becoming more and more frenzied as he knelt before her and…

Screwing his eyes tight to banish the image, he feigned a yawn to disguise his excitement and hoped she had noticed nothing untoward; professing unspoken gratitude when he opened them and realised that was indeed the case; berating himself for endowing the girl with a perception and intelligence alien to both her mindset and position in life.

"Do try to remember what I told you, Anya," he reminded her;

bolstered by his own condescension; voice harsher than her crime merited.

An expression of confusion crossed her features.

His hand indicated the interior and its contents, sweeping over them by way of a rebuke, as if she were unaware of her exact location.

"My study?" he reminded her.

For a few seconds she feigned incomprehension, then; light apparently dawning:

"Apologies, Master. I was concerned when you cried out and forgot your instruction. It will not happen again."

"Please see that it doesn't," he told her with a benign smile as she nodded and turned for the door.

The Lord of the Manor had conferred absolution - despite the fact he was having trouble facing the recipient of his forgiveness after the events of his dream. It being, he accepted, a mild, though unjust, taking to task of his young Indian servant. Though seeing it at the same time as a necessary taking to task that restored equilibrium and order to his new world and was, therefore, justified.

As she closed the door behind her and her footsteps receded towards the kitchen; he rose from the sofa and stretched; reassured and grateful to be back in the here and now; even if he had to admit the fact this was the latest of a number of similar dreams he had experienced during the past week or so –his young housekeeper taking centre-stage in each– was less reassuring.

And yet, he reminded himself, after the study was his and his alone once more -and putting aside the disturbing content of his dreams- he was, for the first time in a good while, feeling more than a sniff of much needed optimism.

At forty-eight he was still a vibrant and handsome man - an opinion actually held by people other than him; even if they did stop some way short of endorsing his, somewhat tiresome, belief in his own superiority. Along with his air of assurance, a youthful complexion and a full head of hair camouflaged his years and went a long way to explaining his success with the opposite sex down the decades.

Though, and despite his aforementioned: "Superiority"; even he had to admit the well, in that respect, had run dry since his relocation to Cornwall.

Still, there were other compensations.

The presence of that same housekeeper, so troubling to his subconscious; along with the absence of the trifling responsibilities of domesticity and marriage –despite his ex-wife's efficiency in such matters- but one of them. The small voice at the back of his head -warning him it was not healthy to devolve too much responsibility for one's life, trivial or not, to a young stranger from a different country with different beliefs, customs, and background- mostly ignored.

"Just the same, though," he told himself out loud, picturing a certain room, in a certain Bayswater hotel; "perhaps a call to Gianni and a trip to London is in order."

A prospect receiving a positive nod.

"Yes," he told himself, head continuing to affirm his intention. "That would do the trick very nicely. Just the tonic to put this ridiculous situation into perspective."

CHAPTER FIVE

Rajiv

Switching off the television, Rajiv eased himself from the sofa he had been slumped upon for the past five hours -toilet breaks too numerous to mention- to hitch up the bottoms of his jogging suit.

An exercise aid worn more for comfort and practicality than its eponymous purpose.

It not being too often he left the apartment these days and, when he did, physical exercise could not be said to rate high on his list of priorities.

Though still an imposing looking man as he passed his mid-sixties, the physical activity missing from his day-to-day went some way to explaining his aches, pains and physical lassitude. The three companions of his twilight teaming up to win a huge groan as he stretched underused arms towards the ceiling and moved towards the window.

The aforementioned "Five hours" having been whiled away – killing time until he Skyped his protégé halfway across the world-with a selection of dross brought to him by the wonders of satellite and a little light masturbation triggered by his twice daily contact with his protégé in England and the prospect of the latest upcoming tête-à-tête.

That he was little more than a voyeur -albeit on speaking terms with one half of the couple he pumped his meat over so regularly- bothering him not in the slightest.

Anya had already told him of the mans troubled dreams and his reaction to her in the new wardrobe he, Rajiv, had suggested, and her retelling of Bernard Lambert's first sight of his housekeeper in more typical English clothing was something he couldn't seem to get enough of hearing - the genesis of a new conquest always, with hindsight, the most exciting point of the process.

Explaining his insistence she repeat the episode for him.

The image of this conceited Englishman seeing his

disregarded young housekeeper in skirt, nylon, and heels for the first time one he could not get enough of. Imagining his reaction to the hourglass, Junoesque, body he had yet to be privileged to see in its uncovered glory –as he, Rajiv Singh had been so privileged; albeit in the form of a computer slideshow. The power inherent in the girl's womanhood no less diluted for her only standing an inch or so over five feet. His reaction when it was finally unveiled to him, if only the Englishman were astute enough to know it, being the seedling that would soon develop –if Rajiv and his protégé proved adept enough- into an overwhelming craving that would, as young Anya desired, see him flat on his back as she perched above him and emptied the contents of her bladder into a mouth as eager as it was disgusted.

"Tell me, Rajiv," his protégé had asked shortly after he had received the photo slideshow of her: "were we not separated by two oceans, and I were suddenly of a mind to give a man permission to place his cock in my virgin cunt, would you like to be that man?"

"My dear, Anya," he had laughed, playing down the disturbance at his groin caused by her use of such language for the first time, "were we not separated by two oceans, I assure you I would neither ask for nor need your 'Permission'."

It had been her turn to laugh then:

"Then I must make sure we do not meet until I have you... tamed," she told him; something in her light-hearted tone warning him she was not being quite as flippant as she would have him believe; her mentor taken by surprise, just the same, at the eager way his penis reacted to her assertion in his regard.

Replaying the conversation as he reached the window, he groaned again; aware that, despite his aches and pains; he had another erection to give witness to the fact the one he had experienced after her stated intention of having him "Tamed" was no fluke.

Though he remained, as said, a striking looking man, the stiffness in his legs and upper body provided one more reminder of the passing years to go with his closely cropped silver hair and recent desire for companionship. The same need making his daily contact with Anya Jalav of such importance to him.

Past retirement age, he was comfortable enough in a financial sense. His civil-service pension and the contents of his late partner's will had seen to that. But no abundance of material possessions could fill the void the loss of Ilse had created. Such a meeting of minds, sexuality and compatible temperaments came along only once in a lifetime.

The gap created by her departure from his life one he hadn't even bothered to try and fill.

Few people, he thought, would understand how any man who had treated a fellow human being so unjustly, so cruelly; so disdainfully and autocratically; could protest to having finer feelings for that person. There being nothing in their mundane lives -lived out, as they were, to the specifications of church, government, or trashy magazine- to promote the understanding that not all "love" resulted in the simulated achievement of marriage, mortgage, babies and grandchildren. A toeing of the establishment line resulting, finally, in the advent of the greatest catchall of the lot.

Death.

Gazing out from his twentieth floor apartment at the sunbaked panorama of Calcutta, stretching westward towards the Hooghley River and the Sarangabad Government Complex –the same complex where, many moons ago, he had worked as a clerical-officer- a hint of moistness around his eyes gave further evidence of the changes the years had wrought and brought a shaking of the head for such, previously inexplicable, sentiment.

From the sill he picked up what had once been his former partner's collar; the thick and heavy band of leather he had locked around her neck to signify she was his.

The very same collar she was not allowed to remove without his permission and now took pride of place upon his windowsill as a reminder of what he had lost and so missed - so much so, in fact, he had begun the blog in her memory that recounted their life together.

The same "Blog" that had been seen by his young protégé and had led her to seek his assistance.

Eyes still fixed on the panorama beyond his windows; even if the view he was seeing was of a different kind; he recalled the moment Ilse had begged for the leather he now found himself stroking with such tenderness.

Guessing, and not for the first time, at the nature of her thoughts as she waited for him to put the final piece of her submission to him in place…

Chapter Six

Ilse

Knees to the rug and hands clasped in front of her, the German businesswoman waited in silence.

Just as he had instructed.

Her soon-to-be "Owner" not wishing, she knew, to have the rear view he so loved and abused obstructed.

The indignity of the position, in her own home, before a younger man who rented an apartment from her across the city, was not lost on the forty-year-old Bavarian and only her fear of disappointing him kept her in place.

A fear, nonetheless, she both welcomed and thrived upon; the levels of submissiveness her Indian master revealed to her as surprising as they were terrifying. The masterful young man intent on owning her peeling away layer upon layer of what she had thought were hardwired personality traits; stripping them away as if she were no more than a German onion with an outer skin he found of no use to him. Her would-be master intent on paring her back until she came face-to-face at last with the real Ilse Dressler.

Her helplessness to prevent his domination of her -if the reaction of her body towards him spoke true- was something she both despised and thrived upon. The intermittent and familiar sparks of anxiety and anticipation, tingling the length of her exposed spine, becoming charges of pure electricity as they reached her shaven pussy heightening that arousal she fully expected to saturate the rug below her at any moment.

As the smell of her sex pervaded the room and her arousal ran in rivulets down the smooth hard thighs she worked the gym so hard to maintain, she heard a sigh and knew he was behind her; savouring the view he had demanded she present to him. Insisting she pull her lustrous blonde hair from either side of her face and twist them into pigtails.

"The perfect look for a nasty German frau-slave," he had laughed when delivering the instruction, her nipples; jutting from impressive breasts; becoming, if possible, even harder at the recall.

"So," he began, tone of voice arrogant and condescending, entertaining nothing other than complete acceptance of the terms he had set for her; "it would seem a month without my superior Indian cock in your substandard Teutonic cunt has brought a change of attitude."

He waited for a reaction to his taunts; ready to punish the infraction if her temper got the better of her and reward her obedience if she behaved.

A win-win situation.

At least for him.

In the event, it was "Reward" that won out – had he been of a mind to extend one.

"Do you want me to repeat myself," he asked, tone dangerous.

"N-Nein," she said quickly; not having realised a response was required; believing her lack of reaction alone enough to win his approval.

" 'No', what?" he snapped. " 'No', you don't want me to repeat myself, or 'No', the absence of my cock in your hungry little goody-box has made no difference to your attitude of a month ago?"

"And remember your manners when you answer," he reminded her before she had a chance to reply.

"N-Nein… Meister," she began, realising she had never felt so defenceless in her life. Exposure of both her hairless sex and equally smooth arse heightening an already frightening sense of vulnerability and providing evidence that, for the first time, someone else was in control of not only her body but her mind also.

"Ich… Ich…"

"Say it," he commanded. "And look me in the eyes when you do."

Raising her eyes slowly to gaze into his, the inflexibility and strength of will she saw staring back at her was all the confirmation she needed. If she had ever thought that what they were doing with each other was a game, the expression on his face told her –and with emphatic finality- it was not a view he shared.

"Say it now!" he demanded, eyes becoming more intense as he sensed her final capitulation. "And say it in English. I will have no German. It is far too bold a tongue for my submissive little slut."

He waited.

"Y-Yes… Master," she almost whispered finally; desperate and needy and wanting to come so badly. His orders having expressly forbidden her from touching herself until he arrived and gave consent. Orders she had obeyed; rather than accept the alternative and lose the promise of paradise - of which he had, so far, given her two brief, but addictive, tastes.

Then, looking into his eyes:

"I… I miss your… your superior Indian cock in my… my substandard Teutonic cunt."

This time she was the one who waited; eyes lowered to the carpet.

Finally:

"There," he gave praise, manner almost friendly, overlooking for once the absent: 'Master'; "that was not so hard, was it?"

Naked and on her knees in the home she owned, Ilse Dressler expected a hand to pat her head then throw a bone for her to chase at any moment.

Instead of that, he came around to stand before her.

Arrogantly.

Hands clasped behind his back as if surveying his property.

The jeans, tee shirt and loafers he wore, making her nakedness all the more humiliating. Not lessening any when a smile transformed his stern face. Her young "Master" taking a cruel delight in his mockery of the older woman below him as she knelt in tribute to the superiority of both his gender and his race.

Finally, after what to her had seemed a long pious Sunday, his hands came around from behind his back and -even with eyes lowered- she sensed what it was he dangled from one hand.

"Do you know what this is?" he asked.

"Ja, Meister… I mean: yes, Master. It is a collar for a dog."

"Wrong!" he snapped.

She jumped, startled at the correction.

"Try again," he ordered; "different gender."

Attempting to swallow non-existent saliva, she marvelled at her supine response to such treatment as she realised what he wanted to hear.

"It," she began, throat dry, "it's a collar for a… for a bitch, Master."

This time a half-smile greeted her answer by way of a reward.

"Better," he said, taking a step forward to bring her eyes level with the bulge in his jeans and offering up the dog tag attached to the pink leather of the collar. "What does the engraving say?"

Ilse read it and knew the point of no return was only moments away.

"Say it aloud," he ordered.

For what were only a few seconds but to her seemed an eternity; she asked herself if this was what she really wanted. If she once committed to what he had in mind she knew with certainty the power of the need she already felt for him would grow stronger and stronger. So strong that any return to the life she had now and had thought herself happy with would be impossible. Could she truly handle being a chattel to a young man of a different race almost half her age? To give up her individuality and live as the extension of another's will? Never again to be allowed to make a decision of any importance again?

Did she truly want that?

As her eyes flickered from the German lettering he had insisted be engraved on the dog-tag, to the sight of his hard cock as it attempted to burst the restraints of his jeans; her decision was made for her:

"It says," she began; voice unrecognisable as her own: "Property of Rajiv Singh".

Adding; a few heartbeats later:

"Master."

As her eyes lowered again a self-satisfied chuckle reached her from above.

"That's right," he agreed, withdrawing both collar and dog tag; delighted to have heard her say it out loud. "That means, if you wish to be filled once more with the cock you cannot seem to tear your eyes from, you have a decision to make."

"But I thought…"

"Which," he cut her off sharply; "is exactly what you will cease to do from this moment on. If you must think at all then think of how you may best serve your master. All other 'Thinking' will be my responsibility. Your only responsibility will be to obey."

Before she could respond, she found herself groaning with

need. A hand going to the back of her head to press her face to his groin. Allowing her both a sniff and a feel of the paradise denied were she to have second thoughts.

Then, thrusting her head away, he undid his fly to release his penis; gratified at the lust instantly transforming her features – even if he knew the fear she felt for his intent.

"A month ago," he reminded her; "when you were simply a horny German businesswoman being fucked by the young tenant you had deigned to –with much superiority, I recall- lease one of your properties; you informed me you would never suck a cock. The very thought of doing so, you assured me, repulsed you."

Ilse felt her body tense.

The act of Fellatio one she had never quite managed to bring herself to perform.

The thought that where semen flowed so had urine before it, guaranteed to trigger her gag reflex whenever her lips came close to an eager penis.

"If you wish to wear my collar and experience my superior Indian cock as it does your hungry German gash the honour of satisfying its needs, you are going to take it from my jeans, wrap your painted Bavarian lips around the head, and suck it as if your life depended on winning its approval."

He waited for it to sink in.

"Then," he went on, "and only then; when you have finished your act of worship; you will grovel before me and beg most abjectly and respectfully to have my collar attached to your neck."

As his cock danced before her eyes and his words rang in her ears, Ilse found herself in the unbreakable grip of a demonic triad she knew to be fear, revulsion, and –the most powerful of all- lust.

"I shall count to three," he told her when she made no response. "If my meat is not surrounded by biddable German dentistry by that time, I shall leave and you will never know me again.

She looked up at him with horror.

"One…" he began.

"Master," she implored him. "Please!"

"Two…?"

"Anything but this, Master. Anything."

"Three!"

She continued to stare up at him, tears streaking her face now; but making no move towards him.

"Very well," he told her, hands reaching towards his fly. "You have made your decision and I…"

The words of exit dying in his throat as he felt his throbbing erection surrounded by the soft flesh of her mouth…

CHAPTER SEVEN

Rajiv Again

…Still in place before the window, Rajiv wondered at the strength of his current erection for an incident from his life almost forty years distant. The power of his deceased partner not diminished by either the passing of the years or the new adventure –albeit passive- he was in the process of planning with his protégé in England.

Replacing a woman such as Ilse something he described to himself as:

"An impossibility".

When Ilse was alive he had, at least, gotten out to restaurants, cinemas, and business functions from time to time. Now, without his partner to drape on an arm and give these interludes meaning, he far preferred to stay at home in the company of Johnny Walker.

And - when his old friend wasn't available?

Well, then there was always his long-time mistress to fall back on.

A consolation with the exotic name of: Bombay Sapphire.

To his left he could see the large balcony where he used to so love taking Ilse from behind; her pendulous breasts overhanging the balustrade, twenty-floors up, as she clung to the rail while he explored her beautiful anus; their naked forms visible to anyone with either binoculars or, for the more committed voyeur, helicopter. The breath leaving her body in a series of animalistic gasps groans and grunts as he battered at her stage door with growing power. Leaving him feeling godlike for both his ability to satisfy her cravings and to take exactly what he wanted, and, more crucially, exactly when he wanted it, from his frau-sklavin.

It being the same balcony upon which he had kept her tethered by the collar for hours upon end whenever she proved disobedient or recalcitrant; until allowing her the opportunity to show her remorse by begging to wrap her sensuous German lips around his eager, if disdainful, Indian meat.

Now, with all the above conspicuous in his life only through absence; it was no surprise Anya Jalav's request for him to mentor her had appeared as a Godsend. Providing him, as it did, with a small respite from the bottle. Along with a friend, a sense of importance and, praise be to Buddha, a purpose.

The above triad of missing elements all the more welcome for coming in one package.

A: "Package", with an hourglass shape and superlative tits, she had kept sari-wrapped for far too long and for which his regularly exercised cock was very, very, grateful.

Even if he was at pains not to let her know it.

Yet, gratitude notwithstanding, he knew that, despite his desire for complete control in his relationships, it was where similarities between them ended. Unlike Anya -who had no time for such: "Irrelevancy"- he would always need the presence of the romantic, the spiritual and the emotional, to complete any relationship. A necessary correlative for the offsetting of those darker needs that, from time-to-time, demanded satisfaction.

For Anya, however, control meant 24/7.

Unquenchable and unrelenting.

And -as long as there was a breath in her voluptuous body- total.

Returning Ilse's collar to its place on the sill -almost reverently- and returning to his workstation, he felt a little sadness for the girl who would never know the tenderness of true affection that lent foundation to all relationships worth having.

The man known as Bernard Lambert, he considered; punching in his password and waiting for the welcome screen to appear as he reviewed the man's situation; was not in a good place.

Even if his surroundings did remain the same.

Sooner rather than later, Rajiv Singh knew, he would find himself with no study, no Indian housekeeper, and; most importantly of all; no say in the matter.

Were he blessed with the gift of second sight and able to read Bengali, the man known as Bernard Lambert would be sure to notice the nameplate soon to be found hanging outside the dwelling he had once ruled over.

A nameplate engraved with a single word.

"Hell".

And, in "Hell"… he would be the servant.

CHAPTER EIGHT

Lambert

A week on from the incident in his study, Bernard Lambert was still pondering the pros and cons of giving Gianni a call to arrange a visit to London; giving it serious thought as he took in the panorama stretching out before him beyond the large bay window of his study.

The room at the back of the house he had designated as his workplace had some of the best views in the house and, drinking them in now, he once again had the feeling -despite his inexplicable attraction to his young servant and those dreams- he was gaining some small measure of control over his life.

A fresh burst of optimism ensuring the element of threat he found in his dreams of the girl was temporarily placed aside; allowing him to see the new look parading her previously unsuspected assets as no more than a very welcome bonus of eye-candy.

On which subject, only that morning, he had been given yet further evidence of her ability to... stir him...

...“Good morning, Master,” she had said, placing his breakfast tray across his lap, “I trust you slept well?”

Propped against the headboard, the inevitable erection caused by her appearance each morning threatening to unbalance his tea, toast and boiled eggs, he scanned her expression for any trace of irony and was relieved to find none; her heavy lips devoid of anything he could have taken as... contempt.

But then, how could she possibly know he had masturbated to an image of those lips as they surrounded his cock and sucked him to completion before swallowing the resulting eruption?

Even more impossibly: how could she know that, when he did finally manage some sleep, their roles were reversed and this time it was his own naked form kneeling between her legs in supplication?

“Sniff your owner's cunt,” the dream Anya had commanded

him; the strength of will implicit in her equine features far more powerful, he knew with certainty, than he could muster at this time or any other. "Sniff but do not attempt to touch," she reminded him, totally confident he would do exactly as she asked - despite his desperation to do exactly the opposite.

"Watch my finger as it slides into the beautiful Indian box denied you," the dream Anya had continued. "Observe the evidence of the pleasure it takes in owning you as it runs over that finger and onto my knuckles."

His eyes locked on in a way that would have been the envy of any tractor-beam from science fiction.

The sight had made her laugh:

"Yes, my old thrall. Impossible to look away, is it not? You have become a slave to pussy. And a servant girl's pussy at that."

Her laughter seemed almost demented as she added:

"My so-called master is now my pussy-slave."

Eyes riveted, exactly as she had said, he could make no argument.

"Shall I be kind and let you suck it?" she said, tauntingly, holding up her finger. "Shall I do that? It would be an incredible honour for you would it not?"

"But then," she said when he could make no reply: "are you worthy of such a gift?"

Her finger dangled before his eyes and he could smell the secretions won from her arousal; eyes closing as he felt that delicious weakness he always experienced when he knelt before her in such a way; erection arrowing upwards toward the brown goddess who was, inexplicably, taking over his existe...

"Shall I pour, Master?" she said, hands still on the tray as she leant over him; large breasts, restrained this time by another white cotton shirt. This one however, being of the sleeveless variety and giving him, for the first time a glimpse of smooth and hairless armpits.

"No," he snapped, more tersely than intended, annoyed she had interrupted his reverie and even more put out by his recall of the dream and, more importantly, its nature.

His servant had affected a look of contriteness.

"Sorry," he said guiltily, knowing his outburst had been uncalled for and staring now at her underarms; taking advantage of gravity's pull upon the shirt at the opening where a sleeve should have been attached to take in the smooth and hairless skin of her right armpit. "I was miles away. Yes, please pour, Anya."

With a toothy smile, as if grateful to be forgiven, she had done just that; leaning in closer as she did so to give him a whiff of the armpit his eyes darted to when he was sure she was distracted by the filling of his cup.

Taking advantage of her preoccupation, he began to breathe through his nose; praying she wouldn't notice as the fresh yet un-deodorised and earthy smell of her underarm hit his nostrils and injected fresh life into an erection hardly requiring it anyway.

"Honey or sugar today, Master?" she had asked, eyes remaining on the cup.

"Hmm… er… Honey," he said, completely off-guard, attempting to collect himself as she served him his tea, unfolded his Daily Telegraph and, with her usual smile returned to the door and let herself out…

…Back in the moment once more, ensconced in his study, Lambert could only marvel at the effect this girl was having upon him. More and more, he found himself seeking her out wherever she happened to be working in the house to snatch glimpses or, if unobserved, drink in the five-feet or so of matronly but perfectly proportioned body. Wondering at the magnificent tits that seemed ready at any moment to burst the confines of her now habitual white shirt and the powerful but shapely young legs as they tapered down to a pair of the sexiest feet he could remember seeing. Tiny but perfectly formed toes, with immaculately clipped nails and varnish of the deepest ruby, the perfect platform for the whole lust-inducing edifice.

Even if, for him at least, appreciation stopped rather abruptly at the neck.

His curious and seemingly growing fixation on his young housekeeper being the one inexplicable blot on the new wave of optimism he was currently experiencing.

In this new mood, even his writing career –the same career he was in despair over not long before- no longer seemed the lost cause it had seemed barely a few weeks ago. A measure of optimism explaining the tentative start he had made on a new crime novel he had decided to approach from a more modern point-of-view.

As he perched himself on the arm of the sofa and savoured the view beyond the glass, his concerns regarding the effect of his housekeeper upon him receded somewhat. The south-westerly vista; along with the bright and breezy afternoon accompanying it; doing nothing to dilute either his new purpose or restored humour. It being, if anything, the kind of day guaranteed to raise even the lowest of spirits.

Even if images of his servant from the subcontinent with the incredible breasts and powerful legs still flashed before his eyes intermittently as she went about massaging his feet, sucking his dick or submitting to his all-powerful cock while he thrust into her tight rear-opening. Images of male supremacy he knew would undergo a complete reversal the moment sleep took hold and wakeful volition found itself at the mercy of the subconscious.

Shaking off the latest, unbidden, images of his unlikely lust object, he continued to take in the view outside from his position on the sofa. That autumn was his favourite season only adding to the pleasure he took in the panorama beyond the window. The dazzling, if less puissant, rays of the October sun refracting against the blue swells of the sea as the breeze swirled in and brought the salt of the briny with it. Weather, resulting from the confluence of English Channel and Atlantic Ocean, stirring autumnal leaves into a million, musical and soothing, sighs for the passing of their youth.

Heaven.

Even the Cornish fishing village he had disliked when he'd first visited as a child; nestling below the cliffs upon which stood his house; seemed, somehow, less... plebeian - despite its lack of either a decent wine-bar or bistro – though there was a pub, at least.

Even if a clientele unworthy of his interest supplied yet another negative.

With a small start of surprise, he felt obliged to admit that - now his own individual style had been stamped upon it- even the house his aunt had willed him and he had left London for was beginning to grow on him.

Not, of course, that he'd had a choice in the matter.

The death of his mother's reclusive older sister –and last remaining relative– had, of course, been sad. He was not a heartless man and, in his own way, had been fond of the old dear; always remembering –or at least ensuring his publisher did– to send her a copy of his latest work. The same work that –along with his marriage to Siobhan- had gone to pot over the past four years as the audience for his, somewhat "Antique", crime novels had either moved on to other, more realistic and gutsy, practitioners of the craft; or joined his aunt wherever she now found herself.

"Time locked and socially antediluvian" – Time-Out.

"A literary dinosaur for the new millennium" – London Review of Books.

Reviews and reviewers of the same ilk the cause of much sourness on his part.

Bastards!

A: "Sourness"; not lessened any by the subsequent neglect of both publisher and agent.

Never having been a "Clubbable" type, the friends he did have had been made through his marriage. And they, to a man and a woman, and for reasons he understood only too well, had sided with Siobhan during the divorce – the fact he had fucked so many of her Girlfriends" making it extremely likely, and perfectly understandable, their husbands or partners would not bust a gut trying to bond with him. There were no children and, with both his career and home: "Down the toilet", the house on the cliffs above the Cornish fishing village was nothing short of a godsend.

"Who knows?" he'd told himself before decamping west; "I'm not in bad shape and London doesn't have a monopoly on attractive, willing and available, women. Anything can happen."

After three months in his new abode he had still to meet one.

After six, he had started to question whether they existed at all and wondered if, without his knowing, Cornwall had passed legislation outlawing not just casual sex but beddable women themselves.

For him, anyway.

His one weekly pleasure coming on a Wednesday when he drove Anya inland to a town with a shopping mall, drinking coffee and people watching as his housekeeper busied herself buying provisions - there being no shortage of women of the kind he was drawn by to be found in such places.

Even if the large majority of them were pushing prams or on the arm of a husband.

Another thing he hadn't reckoned on when first upping sticks to Cornwall had been the house itself. Loving order and hygiene as he did –a by-product of his upbringing- the work required to keep the place to the standard he had insisted upon from Siobhan was not something to which he himself was prepared to commit. The hypocrisy implicit in his own idleness so obvious it skimmed under his radar completely.

Which was when: cleaning, laundry, dishes and household accounts in disarray; the idea of a housekeeper had first occurred.

Turning to Google he had been pleasantly surprised. Both in terms of personnel and cost. One of the first sites to catch his interest extolling the virtue and cheapness of domestic help from abroad.

Which was how Anya Jalav, a young, uneducated girl from Calcutta, barely in her twenties, entered the life of a divorced, middle-aged and out-of-favour, English author.

And decided to make it her very own.

CHAPTER NINE

Rajiv & Anya

Almost seven months on from taking up her employment in his home, Anya Jalav was at her computer in the quarters above the garage; deep into the lunchtime half of her daily "Progress reports", as Rajiv described them; though, and as per usual, it was old news her mentor seemed to enjoy making her relive:

"When I entered his bedroom that first morning," she began; her mentor's most recent instigation of this umpteenth revisiting of the memory, prompting restless fingers to work her cunny through the fabric of her panties; "you would have thought from his expression that a stranger had entered bearing toast and tea."

"Did he comment?"

"No."

"How did you dress?" Rajiv probed, prior awareness of the answer not diluting his eagerness to picture it coming from the thick and, to him, sensual lips he had seen in her photographs - self-taken snapshots that had revealed the incredible young body below her less than beauteous face to his gaze for the first time; the memory of which flashed before him now.

Even that face she was so scathing about –as evocative of horseflesh as she had assured him it would be; was full of character; even if it was character of a cold, diamond hard, nature.

But it was the body; despite her shortness of stature and belying the equine icing with which nature had seen fit to top it; that grabbed the attention. Locking and shackling his eyes onto the screen as surely as if they had been glued there. A body, he knew, no loose and shapeless sari –no matter how revered its designer–could possibly serve justice.

Reaching for himself for the third time -and within an hour of receiving the slideshow- it had struck him that the mass of her naked figure seemed almost caricatured - so compact and heavy did it seem. The exaggerated hourglass shape, with copious amounts of unblemished brown flesh, was not so much… fleshy… as firm; needing to be in order to support two massive and impossibly perfect breasts with bullet hard nipples that stood proud above…

"What did you say, Anya?"

His return was greeted with a laugh, as if the location of his brief excursion had been faxed to her beforehand.

Though his expression was impossible to read, a slight breathiness in his enunciation led his protégé to believe her employer was not the only one developing feelings for her.

The fact she had not yet spoken a word in answer to her mentor's request giving her another small clue.

"I dressed very simply and exactly as you had advised," she spoke now. "In one of the outfits you had me purchase."

The outfit in question one of a number, similar in type, she had bought from a number of charity shops in the town she visited with her employer to make the weekly shop. Lugging provisions back to the car while he sat, read newspapers, and drank coffee in a Starbuck's on the lower level of the town's mall. A wardrobe she had picked up cheaply and paid for from the small monthly salary that was paid into her account and she hadn't, up to then, drawn upon.

"A crisp, white shirt," she went on, "top two buttons undone to reveal a hint of superior Indian cleavage. A black skirt to just above the knee. Black nylons. And a pair of matching open-toed sandals with low spiky heels."

The recital made her marvel.

Had it really only been a month since she first discarded her saris to wear the clothes guaranteed to gain her "Master's" attention?

Such progress!

"It was the same outfit," she went on, picking up where she had left off; "with minor variations, I now wear every day and find so… liberating."

"A picture of which you promised to send me," came the accusation, a certain quivering in the voice of her, back from orbit, mentor betraying excitement to match anticipation.

"And you say I am the impatient one," she taunted him, before continuing:

"My lord and English master made no comment on it - though comment was hardly required for me to tell he had noticed. The redness upon his cheeks, when I caught his eyes lingering upon the painted nails of my feet through the nylon of my hose, was evidence enough I had gained his attention. His first sight of my legs in pantyhose and heels seemed to transfix him. Explaining also, perhaps, his terse: 'Thank you', as I gave him his tray and made to leave."

She paused, allowing her mentor to savour the imagery before continuing:

"In short," she went on, "his behaviour was as predictable as you had told me it would be."

She paused again then; knowing he would be forced to ask her to continue; savouring a small moment of power over her older mentor; enjoying also the fact her "Master" –unusually- had gone into the village for a lunchtime drink. His absence meaning she would, for once, not have to rush her "Mentor's" insistence on a mid-day "Progress report".

More worryingly –though she had not mentioned it to Rajiv- Lambert had spent the whole of yesterday in London. Her tentative attempts to discover his reasons for going having seen themselves dismissed; though his agitated demeanour left her convinced he was going to meet a woman; even if his crestfallen demeanour when he returned late that evening seemed to indicate any such assignation had not gone well.

The above a comfort ensuring she at least slept well.

The last thing she –they- needed, after all, was her "Master" introducing a "Mistress" to the household.

"That was not all," Rajiv came in, on cue and eager; tone accusatory - making her smile as she made him wait.

"As I reached the door," she told him finally, an unseen and somewhat mocking smile curling her lip, "I turned back quickly and caught him staring at my legs with a strange look. He tried to turn away, of course, but by then it was too late."

"What kind of a strange look?"

"Lustful," she informed him without hesitation and with much pride; a condition she could not recall inspiring too often.

If ever.

Until now.

"Of course, I said nothing; acting as if all was as usual and asking him if he would like some marmalade with his toast."

Her mentor mulled it over, chuckling to himself, until:

"Good. Very good. And what of his reaction to you since that first time?"

"More of the same; but still more intense. Though I can tell he is resentful of the attraction my body below the neck holds for him, he finds it impossible to prevent himself watching my every move. Who would have thought such a handsome and worldly man could be so easily swayed by a simple pair of legs and breasts."

Rajiv chuckled:

"Trust me, Anya, there is nothing 'Simple' about your breasts. And do not leave your feet from his growing fixation upon you. His reaction to your pretty painted toes is equally as encouraging. More so, in fact."

"He does seem…" she searched for the right word "…taken with them," she agreed.

"As he should be… Now, having gained his attention for the first time, you must take the steps necessary to imprison it."

Anya was silent – having already determined she was going to do exactly that as the fingers frotting her clit picked up pace.

"You say that since his move from London he has become increasingly isolated," Rajiv went on, almost as if to himself. "This is also good. Something that will work very well in your favour."

"From what I can gather," she breathed; "apart from the ever decreasing royalties from the sale of his previous work; his writing career is all but over. I have listened through the study door as he attempts to contact his agent and rages into the telephone when he is not put through. To my knowledge his calls are never returned. He has periods of intense depression, which explains both his lethargy and the readiness for me to take over more and more of the responsibilities that should be his."

"Which is something all well and good on your part," Rajiv reminded her.

"Of course," she agreed. "Though he has seemed a little perkier recently"

A thoughtful silence followed.

"What of the ex-wife?" Rajiv asked finally.

"I have read some of their correspondence with each other when he leaves the house to walk," she told him. "From the recriminations she cannot help but let slip, it seems he was rather free and easy with his cock in respect of her friends."

At her mention of the word: "Cock", Rajiv's attentions toward his own beneath the computer desk intensified. Something about hearing the description from lips that had yet to experience one and -much as his Ilse before her had done the same- insisted they never would- pressed his own buttons.

"Trust me," she went on, "she hates him with a passion. I can only imagine how grateful she is their union was childless."

"No contact between them whatsoever?"

"Apart from the cold correspondence I have just mentioned, tying up the loose ends of their marriage, none."

"Friends?"

"Not one has contacted him since my arrival here. If he has any friends then they are at pains to keep their regard anonymous."

"What of female contact?"

"See above. And, were he to have any, I would know, believe me. The house is quite isolated and our nearest neighbours are over a mile away. Near impossible for anyone to visit him without my discovering the fact. As you know, he used to drive me to the shopping mall and supermarket some ten miles away for provisions and other weekly necessities; but now even this has stopped and he sends me by taxi. Apart from walks along the coastline and the odd stroll down to the village itself; he is at home the whole of the day; locked in his study as he attempts to write the novel he says will change the tune of his agent and publisher and:

"Put me back on the literary map".

They had laughed together, both at her imitation of her employer and such an implausible notion - having previously familiarised themselves with the work that had seen him removed from this "Map" in the first place.

"I could have sworn the other day," she said by way of an afterthought, "that he was trying to sniff my armpits as I served him his breakfast in bed."

An afterthought bringing more laughter from Rajiv before he grew serious:

"Does he socialise with anyone from the village itself?"

Anya shook her head emphatically as she answered: "As I pointed out, he uses the village only when he wishes to stretch his legs. There is a path leading down to it from the cliffs; but he is rather dismissive of it… The village, I mean. Not the cliffs."

She gave a snort of derision before finishing.

" 'Too rustic' for his tastes - as he puts it in his pompous and pretentious way. Which, translated, means: the local peasantry are not at all impressed with him. Plus, he has yet to see anything to fuck – or, more to the point, anything available to fuck that would fuck him back."

Again, Rajiv felt a fresh surge of blood to his manhood.

"Well," he began, urging control upon himself; "it is all most promising for you, Anya. The longer you become the only female in his life – albeit in a menial capacity – the more his interest focuses upon you. Between the two of us, it will not be long before we have this superior Englishman where he belongs; begging to lick the day's dust and sweat from the feet of his young Indian servant."

The expulsion of breath she tried to suppress without success told him his words had breached the dam coming between his student and her latest bout of self-satisfaction.

A not unusual occurrence during their chats with each other, he knew - though his own release would come later. Experience having taught him that delay served only to take ecstasy to still higher altitudes.

After waiting for both her thoughts and her pulse-rate to calm, he went on to deliver his warning:

"I have no doubt that you can achieve what you wish with him," he continued. "But –and this is terribly important– you must always keep in mind that the man you have chosen is not looking for the relationship you have mapped out for him. In fact, from what you tell me -and despite certain underlying characteristics- quite the opposite would appear nearer the truth."

"But what I intend is not impossible?" she asked; a hint of petulance at the prospect her wishes might not be achievable betraying her youth.

"Not in the slightest, my precocious girl," he reassured her. "You already have the knowledge that will hand you the keys to his innermost being. Your task now is learning how and when to use them once he has been made to realise his only option is to entrust them to your keeping."

He paused then – fondly reflective.

"It was much the same for me and my beautiful Ilse before she passed away; remember?"

Anya did indeed. The blog she had stumbled across during her nightly trawl of the net, the same blog that had led her to contact Rajiv in the first place, had spoken of just the kind of triumph over another human being of which she had long dreamed. For as long as she could remember, in fact. That it had been a man, triumphing over an unwilling German businesswoman from whom he rented a home, did nothing to prevent her applying the situation to her own. Fantasising herself into the male role while the unwitting Bernard Lambert took on the part of Ilse.

"Of course, it was a little easier for me with Ilse," he had continued.

"Easier in what way?" she asked; curiosity piqued.

"Though I was loathe to use force with her, there was, with my greater male strength, always that option. There were many, many times when nothing but a severe bare bottom spanking – amongst other physical punishments- and time spent in the corner would answer her disobedience. The humiliation of being forced into such childish penance as painful to her in its own way as the spanking itself. And a decision, once I had made it, she could do nothing of a physical nature to alter."

"I take your point," she told him, reversing the principals in order to take some enjoyment from the retelling; seeing that point, however, as a not particularly challenging one and wanting to move on.

"Your tone betrays boredom, Anya," he said, picking up on her dismissal. "But it will interest you to know that Ilse's advanced age in comparison to my youth made her feelings of dishonour and mortification all the sharper and made my own reactions both sweeter and longer lasting."

Her silence was revealing.

"Something, sweet Anya," he went on, reading her mind; "you will soon experience for yourself –albeit with a slave of different gender across your lap- from the same end of that spectrum I myself occupied at the time. "

As she listened, and in spite of her disinterest, in his point at least, Anya was again teasing her virgin cunny through the fabric of her panties. Images of the Englishman –despite his "greater male strength"- draped over her lap as she tanned the pale skin of his backside with a hairbrush; the imagined cries for mercy filling her head acting upon her after the manner of a particularly uplifting symphony and stirring her lust to motion yet again.

"For you, though," he went on, "it is a little different. Physical persuasion is not an option - at least for the moment. The female-male dynamic being, I must confess, somewhat more complicated."

"How so?"

"By that I mean: in order for a woman to inflict a beating upon a male victim of choice –and the fantasy world of dungeons and shackles absent- consent is necessary for the beating to take place.

"Is that all?" she scoffed. "From your words I thought you had a more complex dynamic in mind."

"Bear with me here, Anya; all I say is that, in the absence of consent, a woman who desires to inflict physical punishment upon a physically stronger man must go about her business in a more, shall we say, devious way."

He allowed a few beats to pass.

"Do correct me if I am in error," he began again, sarcasm obvious; "but isn't "Consent" the one thing guaranteed to play no part in your desires?"

"Do not tease me, Rajiv," came her instant response. "Why ask questions to which you already know the answer. We are alike in this – as you well know."

A chuckle greeted her accusation.

"You are right, young Anya; as always. We have much in common. Even as I sense your finger teasing you once more towards completion, my trusty right hand again caresses my engorged cock beneath my desk."

"Filthy old beast!" she snapped, feigning shock; continuing to rub herself through the soaked panties. "And what makes you think I would behave in such a fashion?"

"Because," he laughed; not taken in; "while you enthuse my ageing body with your willingness to listen and the vitality of your youth, I bequeath you my years of knowledge and experience in order to make your dream possible. We are partners at a distance and, as such, are perfect for each other.

"I cannot speak for you," he went on, "but it is, for me at least, sufficient. My pleasure is taken in guiding you towards the fulfillment you seek through the enslavement of this Englishman. For my part, I wish nothing more than to allow you to experience the same heady euphoria of ownership I knew with my Ilse."

Now it was his turn to pause for a few moments.

"Though I suspect," he began again, "that your personal feelings towards your erstwhile "Master" share nothing of the tenderness I felt towards my sorely missed slave."

Anya's frottage of herself through the, by now, saturated fabric of her panties slowed as she considered the truism.

"Your suspicions would give credit to your perception had I not assured you of such many times previously, Rajiv," she served gentle rebuke; drawing another chuckle from the sub-continent.

"Even taking my relatively few years on the planet into consideration," she went on, "it is difficult to imagine encountering such pomposity, self-delusion, misogyny and a belief in one's own inherent superiority, in a lone man. He is a composite of everything I loathe and is the beast awaiting a collar I have dreamt of since such desires first made themselves known to me. As you are aware, Rajiv, I detested him and his easy assumption of racial, physical and intellectual superiority on sight and will do all and everything in my power to bind him to me in as abject a manner as is physically, mentally and legally, possible."

From Calcutta, silence greeted the end of her outpouring, then:

"Anya, I find it hard to believe your former poverty and lack of a formal education. Your articulation of your purpose truly takes away my breath."

His subtle assertion of his own superiority in terms of class and learning were not lost on her.

"And your inability to concede me a brain because of such a lack deprives me of mine."

Another chuckle greeted her rebuke and she laughed along with him - instantly forgiving the small eruption of male ego.

It was, when it came down to it, the opponent with whom she lived to do battle.

Not for the first time, she offered self-congratulation for seeking his advice after having visited his blog; telling herself, once again, that the relationship she shared with him was as normal –close inverted commas- a relationship as she was ever likely to have with a man.

Even if it was not her intention to allow it to remain that way.

"You find him handsome though?" he asked, expression intent.

"You know this already," she told him – scenting a hint of jealousy in the question.

"Just making sure your passion burns as brightly," he assured her.

"Really?" she asked, growing bolder. "Or is it that you see yourself in the role I intend for him?"

No answer came from her hometown.

"Tell me, Rajiv, now you have reached your dotage, have you finally decided to take your courage in both hands and taste life on the receiving end of the whip? Even as we speak, are you picturing yourself naked before me, my collar about your neck? Knees to the porcelain and obedient mouth wide as I fill it with my waste?"

There was silence from her hometown and she realised Rajiv had moved away from the screen.

An absence that made her think, for a few indecisive moments, she had gone too far.

When all was said and done, she reminded herself, this was not some milksop English writer she was dealing with but a proud Indian male.

More pertinently: an Indian male who had once reduced a proud, arrogant and commanding, German businesswoman to abject slavery.

A man, more to the point, whose experience she not only valued but needed.

Just as she was about to apologise, his face filled the screen and he spoke:

"Ten years ago, my little Anya," he began; tone darker than his usual when conversing with her, eyes blazing into the screen; "I would have taken such an assertion as a challenge."

Eyes still blazing he fell silent, until; to her relief; the face on the screen broke into a broad grin:

"However," he went on; "we are friends. Partners in a mutual venture – even though you will be the one to reap the majority of its rewards."

With a start, Anya realised she had been holding her breath; having gained some small idea of the power he must have been able to call upon in his prime.

"Also," he went on, still grinning, "and despite your tender years, I know the real thing when I converse with it. Should we have met during my pomp -and our paths taken the route of conflict rather than mutual regard- I have no doubt you would have proved a worthy opponent for me."

His young protégé could do no more than nod agreement – not letting him know she considered herself to be far more than simply: "Worthy".

Far, far more, in fact.

"So, my wise mentor," she led with some flattery of her own; "where do we go from here?"

CHAPTER TEN

Anya's Second Fantasy

He must feel awful, she knew, her smile smug. The sensation of having his head buried under the duvet between her powerful young thighs, as she relaxed into the soft, freshly laundered pillows, enhanced by the certainty his lips would stay at her pussy and his nose remain buried in her anus the whole night if she chose.

A decision in the affirmative more often the case than not and a position she demanded he maintain; no matter how hot, sweaty and stinking close proximity to her netheregions became.

This position in her bed something she insisted upon; the consequences for not complying ones he knew very, very, very, well. Yet one more humiliation for him and all the more precious to her for knowing how degrading he found it; his excitement at being close to her intimate parts soon fading before the reality of having to inhale the smell of her arse and pussy the whole night through.

After all, she told herself: what employer would spend every night with his nose buried in his servant's arse and his tongue in constant contact with her labia?

But then he was hardly her employer any more now, was he?

Barely recognisable as a human being, in fact, let alone a man of any substance at all.

And certainly not a human being of any autonomous variety.

Pf course, his inability to maintain this nightly vigil at various times had led to some equally delicious punishments.

Delicious for her, that is.

Even if she had trained him well enough in the short time since his fall from grace to make such interludes few and far between.

"I want your mouth on my pussy and your nose up my superior Indian arse," she had told him that first time; going on to warn: "By the time I am through with you your subconscious will be so well-trained that, even if you somehow manage to fall asleep,

your face will not deviate from its position."

Adding then; the look on his face inviting yer more cruelty rather than the compassion it sought to inspire:

"You will not move. Not even to relieve your tiny English pee-pee. Disturb my sleep and you will experience real pain."

In truth, she didn't care if he slept or not – so long as his head remained in place. He could snatch an hour or so during those growingly rare times of day when she had no use for him. It was a nightly ritual, she considered, that was the perfect way to ensure his continuing submission. It being, she reckoned, nigh on impossible for pride, superiority, and that famous British self-respect, to find any purchase on the smooth slopes of her buttocks and the drenched folds of her cunt.

"Long worshipful strokes," her voice through the duvet reminded him as he flattened his tongue to lave at her pussy in accordance with her command - careful to keep his nose in place as he obeyed her instructions. "That's it. Just the way I like to drift off to sleep. But I do not hear you sniffing. Deep breaths through the nose now, you know the rule."

Of all the indignities to which she subjected him this was her favourite –even if making him lick her armpits clean of the day's perspiration came close. That she could actually condition him into actively seeking that which he hated yet another source of entertainment and satisfaction from which she took an immense and –she could do no more than acknowledge- perverted pride.

There being in her life now no shortage of such entertainments and satisfactions.

All the above, along with making him sniff her malodorous feet through the exacerbating confines of her hose; actually making him petition her in a humble voice to be granted the privilege of debasing himself; forms of worship and obeisance she had made a part of his daily reality.

She never tired, she told herself, of hearing her former master beg for his own dishonour and, as his breath began to rasp through his nostrils in accordance with her demand, she remained utterly convinced she never would.

Luxuriating in his tongue's ministration as she felt herself beginning to drift off, she was already anticipating waking in the morning and using the toilet.

Another source of delight close to the summit of her perverse tastes.

"From now on," she had told him, "you will be helping me when I need to piss or shit," his horror at such a prospect one more development she relished. Yet another building block in the formation of the perfect servant, she had told herself righteously; insistent there be no inhibitions before him on her part and he be conditioned to look upon the responsibility given him for even the most basic of his young Indian master's physical ablutions as not just a gift but an honour.

"Whenever, I say: 'Toilet', you are to stop what you are doing and crawl after me on all fours. You will then kneel before the toilet bowl and place your upturned hands upon the seat as a cushion for your Indian master's lovely brown arse.

"Then, after you have done this and I have taken my place upon my throne, you will place a reverential kiss upon each of my thighs before placing your head between my legs to better observe your queen's fountain as it fills the bowl below."

His face at her flowery depiction of this most foul of acts had been a picture of abject misery.

"When it is complete," she had gone on, "I will stand and you will use your tongue to clean me."

For a moment, she thought he was about to laugh; not believing, despite the cruelties she had inflicted upon him until then, that she was serious.

The thunder building behind her expression and the words she had spat out next cured him of any such delusion:

"Get used to the taste very quickly, my peon, for very soon I do not expect to have to use the bowl at all…

CHAPTER ELEVEN

Lambert

Over eight thousand miles away from where Rajiv Singh sat at his computer pondering his future, the unknowing object of those musings was sat outside a pub in the fishing village he usually steered clear of, sipping a pint. His nearness to the sea and the sound of waves gently lapping against the harbour walls making no headway with the despondency they were usually so successful in banishing.

Or at least diluting.

Bernard Lambert's current mood, however, was made of sterner stuff. For, though he put it differently to himself –ego based denial a powerful mitigator- his decision to get out of the house owed more to a need to escape the proximity of his young housekeeper than any need for a warm lager in a tatty public house.

Mind-numbingly banal conversation of the regulars a given.

"Regulars", who looked and sounded as if the nearest they ever came to an original thought was the supply of an erroneous answer on Quiz-Nights.

His presence outside a pub he didn't like, with a beer he didn't want, in a fishing village he couldn't stand, owed to reasons he was loathe to admit – even if he sensed a time was coming when he would have to bite the bullet and do just that.

Much to his dismay -and rather than easing off- his fascination with the young Indian girl was growing.

Dangerously so.

Not two days ago, as a matter of personal record, he had done something that, under normal circumstances, would have made his skin crawl.

A mere recollection of his transgression doing exactly that right now.

The large swallow of unwanted and warm beer, triggered by a memory of the deed itself, spoke volumes for the shame he felt at having committed such an act.

The previous Wednesday, to be precise. Acting rather than writing, for once. In order to feign sickness and forego driving Anya to the mall inland for the weekly shop.

Insisting on getting her a cab and telling her to make an afternoon of it while he rested at home.

That "Rest" involving the use of his spare key to let himself into her quarters above the garage while telling himself he made the intrusion only to: "Familiarise myself with the living habits of my servant".

Justifying his actions further by telling himself she was someone who lived in his home and it was his right to know something of her private life.

A flawed self-justification a small section of his conscience recognised as a crock of the very worst grade shit – even if it wasn't of sufficient strength to make itself heard.

Upon letting himself into the "Quarters" themselves, it came as no great revelation to find they were immaculate. Surprise at what he saw absent – despite a sneaky suspicion the diligence, efficiency and love of hygiene she displayed in his home might lead to a slacking off and slovenliness in her own.

The order and cleanliness greeting his eyes as he slipped up the stairs at the side of the garage to let himself in making him wary - careful to touch very little and to leave whatever he did make contact with in exactly the same place and condition in which he'd found it.

Taking in the sofa bed, television and computer; along with the tiny but well equipped kitchen with breakfast bar; he actually congratulated himself on his thoughtfulness for having provided her such a pleasant living accommodation.

Having told himself beforehand that his reason for entering her quarters was simply a means of finding out something more of the way she lived, it was something of a wake-up call to find the subconscious reason for his intrusion awaiting him in the compact bathroom.

For some reason, being in her bathroom induced a strange sensation in him. One he hadn't experienced before and something of a puzzle to him; as if his insides had suddenly swooned; actually having to sit on her lowered toilet seat as he waited for equilibrium to return. The knowledge he was resting on the same spot upon which she perched herself to go about her business doing nothing to help him in that sense.

"This," he thought to himself, taking in the small but immaculately kept en-suite, "is where she performs her most intimate bodily functions."

Placing, as always, that equine face to one side; he had pictured that powerful body as it released a stream of golden piss into the bowl and imagined those strong shapely legs, spread wide and calf muscles tensing, as what had once been nourishment was squeezed past her anus to "Plop" into the water below.

Which was when the laundry basket took his eye.

Almost involuntary of himself, and while a part of him looked on; unable to quite believe he could stoop so low; another, less squeamish, less… moral part of him was already delving into her dirty washing.

His search becoming feverish until, finally he retrieved a pair of black panties and held them up in front of him. Hesitating only a few moments before he brought them up to his nose and inhaled.

Deeply.

The pungent and musky odour of his housekeeper's young pussy buckling his knees.

"This" was her smell, he told himself: "virgin, uncorrupted… intoxicating."

Her: "Master"; only stopping his exploration of his servant's most intimate private scents to turn the panties inside out and lave his tongue over the soiled gusset. Tasting her secretions second-hand and continuing to do so as he fished out what he had always thought was seven inches of erect cock and now seemed like ten. Stroking himself like a madman while her name resounded in his head as if it were a mantra; until, finally, his whole body spasmed and jet upon jet upon jet of his essence scatter-gunned across the bathroom to land on the opposite wall as his knees buckled beneath him and he sank to the tiles.

After a minute or so, when both his heart rate and his thoughts had lowered to manageable levels, he could only look at the evidence of his arousal as it slithered down the ceramic tiles and acknowledge it was the most powerful orgasm he had ever experienced in his forty-eight years.

A quick glance at his wristwatch gave him pause and he set to cleaning up the evidence of both his intrusion and -now his need had been temporarily gratified- disgrace from walls and floor. It being only an effort of will; coupled with the fear of her returning early and catching him in the act; preventing a repetition of the process.

An even greater effort required to stop himself stealing the underwear itself.

Now, sitting outside a pub he didn't like in a fishing village he liked even less, the full disgrace of his actions dampened his spirit.

Swallowing back his unwanted pint as the memory sickened him to his soul.

"What in fuck's name am I becoming," he said aloud, forgetting where he was and quickly looking up to see if he had been heard; grateful the tables around him were empty.

Though he did win a second look from the sixty-something barmaid; dressed too young and sporting a big perm above unnaturally symmetrical teeth; smiling in his direction as she collected the dead-men of previous punters. Artificial dentistry and the waft of Ammonia from recently transfixed hair doing nothing to prevent the old trout being one of the more appealing examples of the village's: "Attractive and available", women.

It was the same remorse for his action –masturbating as he licked soiled panties, that is; not swearing in front of an old trout- that had led to his phone-call to Gianni and yesterday's trip to London. That he could have a sexual need of such intensity for someone of his housekeeper's type baffling enough; but, for it to go beyond that, was nothing less than… nothing less than…

Memory failing him -and his thesaurus on the shelf in his study where he had last left it- he gave up and seriously considered asking Anya Jalav to leave his employ.

It was, he knew, becoming too much. Bad enough to have the life he knew –a life with a dutiful wife; willing and available women; and mini-celebrity- wrenched from him. But; to start over again; only to find himself obsessing over an ugly domestic help young enough to be his…

Not bothering to finish the obvious and equally depressing thought he rose from his seat and headed off in the direction of the path that would lead him back to the house.

"Thanks for calling," the be-dentured matriarch of the salmon family cried after him; sarcasm made all the more obvious for the authentic Cornish in which it was delivered as she snatched up his empty mug.

By the time he reached the path and began his upward climb, he had convinced himself there was no other option but to let the girl go.

By the time he was halfway up and had stopped for a breather; images of her legs and feet –along with those incredible breasts and the scent of young pussy that had triggered the most momentous orgasm of his life until then- were giving him second thoughts.

By the time he had reached the top, staring down at the tiny village and harbour below while his breathing returned to normal, he had done a complete volte-face and changed his mind; telling himself the problems were his and not hers and berating himself for acting like a pre-pubescent:

"Grow up, Lambert, for fuck's sakes!"

A self-motivational pep talk, which had the desired effect of perking him up as the house rose into view. There were, after all, many positive aspects of his life he had to be thankful for and went some way towards jolting him from his depression. Positive aspects, left to run their course, which might even have been capable of going the whole hog and banishing his woes completely.

Had, that is, his thoughts not returned to yesterday and his attempt to escape his mushrooming obsession with his housekeeper.

Travelling to London to rekindle memories of the man he had once been via the replication of an interlude from his past.

CHAPTER TWELVE

Bayswater

A gust of wind through the open balcony windows billowed out the curtains as a naked Bernard Lambert lay on the bed in the very same Bayswater hotel room he had once used for his lunchtime trysts.

A scene of many sexual conquests –and one in particular- providing a timely reminder of his former prowess in such matters he was sure would put his current mindset in regard of his servant in perspective.

At least that was his intent.

The young woman, barely out of her teens, at the foot of the bed, kneading the soles of his feet as per his requirements, was around the same age as Anya.

Which was where any similarity ended.

In contrast to his housekeeper, the skin of the girl's naked form was pale and natural; a refreshing change from the peroxide hair and Essex-girl-wannabee spray tan he found so deeply unattractive.

Sheep-like implied.

One of the reasons Gianni, his long-time guide in these matters, had introduced her to him in the first place.

The obvious and tasteless playing as little part in the Concierge's predilections as they did in his.

With her short blonde hair and pale skin, the girl gave off a sense of the Nordic reminding him of Siobhan. At least until she opened her mouth. The estuary English emerging from it something he had always found… grating. His ingrained snobbishness ensuring he gave thanks to the certainty that, on the few occasions during the next hour when she actually opened that mouth, it would not be to speak.

"You have a good body for an old-… older man," she said, correcting herself in mid-sentence as he withdrew his earlier appreciation of 'Certainty'.

"Nice cock too," she told him, moving sinuously up over his

legs to bring herself closer; lowering her pert breasts to either side of his dick and pushing them together to trap it there.

"Are tit-wanks your thing?" she asked with a smirk.

Prone on the mattress, Lambert wished she'd shut the fuck up. Bad enough to have to listen to that grating low-grade accent without having her run through her repertoire of what she considered: dirty talk.

"What in shit's name was Gianni thinking?" he asked himself. Was this what he thought he wanted nowadays? Had it ever been what he wanted?

"I've some Viagra in my Louis Vuitton," she told him, barely bothering to disguise her contempt as his still flaccid prick plopped out from between what were, he admitted, and despite his disinterest, impressive tits.

"I don't need Viagra, thanks," he told her; neglecting to say that if he did he'd probably need a truckload if his blood flow were to make it past both voice and patter.

"Could have fooled me," she said, a thought occurring to her: "Tell you what, just so it's not a total wipe-out, why don't you suck my toes for a while then I'll let you eat me? Sound good?"

He looked at her as if she'd just crawled up the toilet duct.

"You, want me? To eat you?" he asked; impressed, at least, by her pluck.

"Yeah, you'd like that, wouldn't you?" she told him, totally unfazed. "I can always spot a pussy boy."

"You can?" he asked, a hint of his former temper kicking in, voice dangerously low; though she was either too dumb or too feisty to notice or be bothered.

"Stands out like a sore thumb," she nodded. "Bet you'd like to drink my piss too. Pussy boys always like a bit of urine in my experience."

"You reckon do you?"

"Tell you what, do a nice job on the old fanny and I might give you a taster – but only "Might", mind."

In spite of himself and the bromide effect of her voice, there was a small twitch downstairs.

"There we go!" she squealed. "Am I good. Or am I good? A pussy boy and a piss freak, all in one package. Bet you lick arses as well."

"Not yours sweetheart," he thought instantly; the fact he didn't say it out loud, before tearing verbal strips off her and proceeding to fuck her overused cunt numb, firm evidence he was undergoing a sea change.

Out of character behaviour bringing the male-menopause instantly to mind.

Even as that same mind dismissed it.

Bernard Lambert knew exactly where his problem lay.

And, if there was one thing he could be certain of, it was the knowledge that problem wasn't in the room with him.

"Sorry," he told her, "but it's not going to happen."

She shrugged her shoulders and slid away from him.

No look of regret, or hurt, or recrimination.

No nothing.

He might just as well have told her he wasn't in the mood for a hand of whist.

She could care less.

By the time he'd pulled a sheet over himself and sat up she was already half dressed; placing her nylons in the "Louis Vuitton" for speed of exit and slipping into her Jimmy Choo's.

"I'd say it's been fun but…"

"You're an honest girl. Right?"

She smiled and he smiled back; suddenly seeing her as human; a person in her own right rather than a necessary convenience he could use for his own…

The "Convenience" and its accent cutting into his thoughts:

"It makes no difference, you know?"

He nodded, knowing exactly what she meant.

"Good," she said. "I'm glad. I wouldn't like it to get nasty."

"No problem," he told her, reaching for his wallet to take out some notes and pass them to her.

"A deal's a deal," he agreed.

Accepting the notes she made as if to count them.

"It's all there," he assured her. "I promise."

She stared at him for a few moments, considering it; then:

"Yeah. Course it is," she conceded. "Gianni said you're the real deal."

Then, with an air-kiss and a twirl, she was gone, leaving her punter to reflect on the past twenty minutes and what it signified for him.

The fact he had been attempting to picture somebody else the whole time he had been with the call girl was sobering. Knowing it had only been a grating Estuary English accent and some, by the numbers, slut talk preventing that picture from supplying the erection he needed if he was to do what he had paid for and fuck her.

A resigned smile greeting the realisation.

He had never considered himself close with a buck, but at least then he would have got something more for his money than a desultory foot-rub.

Flopping backwards on the bed he groaned.

The whole idea had been a fucking –or; dependent upon one's point-of-view: fuckfree- disaster.

A complete waste of his time and cash that –if the way he felt now was any guide- had left him more despondent than when he left Cornwall to come here. Having it confirmed he was so fixated on his servant he couldn't manage an erection without first summoning up her image, had not been the result he had in mind.

A non-event placing him in even more of a quandary over what he should do about it.

As he lay flat on the king-size-double and listened to the traffic from the street below, he considered the whole piss-puerile situation with his housekeeper; allowing the breeze from the open window to cool his fevered brow until the inevitable happened.

His despondency not lessening any when an image of a naked Anya imprinted itself on his retina; beginning with her pretty feet and up past those powerful hosed legs, continuing on over insolent hands-on-hips to zoom in on her commanding breasts and….

Lo and behold…

Lift off!

CHAPTER THIRTEEN

Anya

It had only been seven months but, to her, it seemed a lifetime ago; the sights and sounds of Calcutta no more now than distant memories – and pretty depressing ones at that. Recollection made all the easier to jettison given its dispiriting nature. Any intention she might have entertained to create a database of a fonder and more recent variety; at least in the near future; non-existent – even if taking up a position in England had been a massive step for a young Indian girl of minimal education and deprived background.

But then, what was there to keep her in Calcutta she gave a fig about?

The cramped room she rented above a sweatshop?

The family she neither had nor wanted?

The friends she had yet to make and couldn't locate interest enough to try – not to mention the social life dependent upon such interaction?

All the above, taken together, making it a decision she had made without fear.

For Anya Jalav was –along with the gift of a native, if twisted, intelligence, and as her friend Rajiv had come to realise- made of sterner stuff.

"A virgin forged in steel," her mentor had declaimed, confirming her own thoughts in regard of herself.

Pitiless, in fact.

A force of warped nature.

Determined no mere animal of a man, whatever his position, would ever storm the citadel of her womanhood.

Quite the contrary, in fact.

If there were any storming to be done then she would be the one sitting atop the weaponry of siege and woe betide the ill-fated fortress upon which –or upon whom-she set her sights.

Of course, there had been no problem with a visa as she already held a British Passport – the selling point that got her onto the agency's books in the first place. As a point of fact, she had been born in Bradford. Daughter of an arranged marriage the male half of which -and the father she had never known- had suffered a massive coronary not two months after her birth. Leaving her mother; knowing barely a soul and with little English; with no choice but to return to the home of Anya's widowed grandfather in India and the grinding poverty she had travelled to England to escape.

What had finally clinched Anya's acceptance had been the photographs of the home overlooking the Cornish coastline she would be expected to take care of for her new employer. Her imagination triggered further by the fact that home would contain only one occupant other than herself -a middle-aged English crime writer by the name of "Bernard Lambert". Isolated home by the sea and lone male occupant combining to seal the deal for her.

Imagination that had run riot when she researched her prospective employer and saw, despite his years, how handsome he remained - almost a composite, in fact, of the men she pictured in her fantasies. Near enough, anyway, to convince her fate was working its magic and have her packing her meagre belongings to wing her way to a new life on the English Riviera. Sea, writer, and an isolated house atop the cliffs suiting her reclusive temperament -and, later, her purpose- perfectly.

Understandably, her first few weeks had been spent learning the foibles of her new employer: likes, dislikes, habits and routines, et al. An employer –see above- to whom she was instantly attracted; despite there being no sign, or likely to be, of any similar regard coming her way; quickly realising the initial route to his attentions was through respect, attention to detail, and obedience.

From the old computer he'd supplied her with and access to the net she had already discovered the salient facts of his background -career in reverse, private life a mess, something of a womaniser- and quickly assessed him as a man who would respond positively to anything that heightened his own self-image.

On her very first night above the garage –alone in a strange country and despite all the new experiences she was coming to terms with- she had manipulated herself to orgasm.

Several times.

By the time exhaustion and Morpheus had forced her own

submission, the man she had travelled to England to serve had – amongst other humiliations- eaten from a dog-bowl, been urinated upon and, finally, been branded like a pig with the evidence of her mark he would carry until the end of his life.

Never, she mused to herself, before the god of sleep finally took her, had she reacted to a man in such a powerful way. So powerful that; upon waking the following morning; before beginning her first full day of work; she repeated the whole euphoric process. Her new employer, she told herself, filling all the criteria of her post-pubescent fantasies –and a few of the earlier variety too.

Undeniably handsome.

Pretentious.

Racist.

Egotistic and vain.

And, more importantly she sensed: weak.

Very, very, very, very, weak.

The above obsession with her new "Master" one she would duplicate every evening when she was alone from then on.

Sometimes, even, during the day itself.

The fact he was as transparent to his new employee as water and she had seen through his pomposity and superiority immediately, made her burgeoning intentions in his regard easier. Those twinned character flaws bolstering her in the intention that he see her as no more than the perfect, attentive and obedient, housekeeper.

Something she sensed he would find very appealing and, more relevantly, unthreatening.

It was a feat she achieved with remarkable dexterity and a feat he allowed her to go about achieving with minimal interference; entrusting more responsibility –as trivial and menial as it was- to her each day.

Within a week, she had the house spotlessly clean and looking immaculate.

Within two, she was familiar with every detail of his routine and anticipating his demands before he made them; providing a sense of care and security he couldn't fail to find welcoming; even becoming adept at the Northern European and Mediterranean cuisine he insisted upon – coming to enjoy it herself and, if truth be known, grateful not to have to serve up the spicy and pungently aromatic fare of her own country that only served to remind her of the drudgery from which she had only just recently escaped.

In short, she ensured he wanted for nothing; his most minute and most trivial need anticipated and served – sometimes before he realised he was in need of anything himself.

With the help and advice of her new, and first, friend from her hometown she had set in motion the process of dependency; encouraged by the small signs that seemed to indicate her unknowing -and increasingly purposeless- "Master" was responding to her agenda in a way that could only bode well for the future she had in mind for them both.

But it wasn't until the anniversary of her fifth month in his employ, during their weekly trip to a shopping mall in a nearby town, that a seemingly small discovery would lead to the coming change in both their roles and her wardrobe.

Normally on their outings –the one time she would leave the house apart from walks into the village and along the coastline- he would drive her to the mall and allow her a couple of hours for the weekly shop while he sat outside a Starbucks drinking coffee and reading the day's papers.

For her, after she had lugged the shopping back to the car – alone– it would be a tour of the high street shops and anything else she had the time and the fancy to do.

On this particular day, however, she found herself distracted from her usual routine and found herself observing his.

Exiting a shop on the upper level of the mall, she happened to look down to the shops below and realised she was directly above Starbucks.

There, back towards her, sipping a cappuccino was the familiar wavy brown hair, streaked with grey, of her employer, newspapers strewn on the table before him. Newspapers, she realised, that were being completely ignored as he people watched.

Deciding to truncate the tour of the shops that was fast becoming a bore to her, she made the decision to observe her handsome employer from above; secure in the knowledge he could not see her without twisting in his seat and gazing directly upwards.

A seemingly small decision that would change both their lives.

The very first thing to take her notice, his head swivelling as he people watched, was the way his head swivelled to follow the passing women.

Not just any women, you understand?

And, to his young housekeeper's disbelief, not the obvious, ten-to-the-dozen, fake blonde, fake breast variety she had convinced herself would be his type.

These passed his table without eliciting a flicker of interest.

No. That interest was reserved for examples of womanhood occupying a category well removed from supermodel, model, or even just plain attractive. Examples, she realised -after it had happened too many times to be coincidental- possessing at least one common denominator.

An insight into his mental make-up that could do no less than inspire her horse features to a smile as she continued to watch.

Each of the passing women who gained his appraisal, she observed, had figures that could, most accurately, be described as matronly.

None of Rajiv's "Stick insects" these.

However, the ones most guaranteed to rivet his attention were those with powerful legs. Short or long, young or old, bulky or plain muscular, it made no difference. So long as they were of a certain shape and clad in heels and hose he was drawn to them; legs and figures normally to be found on the more authoritative nurse, governess or any female in the more prosaic positions of power.

Any woman, in fact, she realised, experiencing a surge of pure exhilaration for her discovery, with the kind of legs she had seen mirrored on someone else.

Someone with whom she was extremely familiar.

CHAPTER FOURTEEN

Rajiv & Anya

Later that same evening, after the events at the mall, she had Skyped Rajiv; thinking he would play down her discovery and, instead, finding herself delighted to hear him confirm her suspicions.

"It would appear," he told her, the smile filling her computer screen leaving no doubts in respect of the encouragement he took from her news; "that you have stumbled upon his heel." His pleasure, she noticed, undiminished by the almost empty bottle of Johnny Walker she could see at his side and the fact it was deep into the small hours Calcutta time.

"Pleasure", matched by her puzzlement.

"His what?" she had asked.

"His Achilles Heel, Anya," her mentor explained. "A demi-god. Son of Thetis. Held by the heel as he was dipped in the waters of the Styx to make him invuln…"

He stopped in mid-word, giving it up. For all her attributes and individuality, the girl shared much common ground with her youthful contemporaries. A narrowing of personal references but one example of mutual ignorance.

Impatience being another.

"What I mean to say," he tried again, "is that you have found his weakness."

Her reprimand was instant and, he told himself in recognition of his penchant for unnecessary literary allusion, probably just:

"Well why didn't you just say that in the first place?" she carped, having yet until then, despite her articulacy, to have even heard the word: "Metaphor".

Still less understanding the literary allusion accompanying it.

"As I have explained to you before, Anya: when you are fortunate enough to have a man's desires signposted to you, and assuming a reasonable level of intelligence –or at least a low and basic animal cunning– it will not be long before you also find yourself gifted with the key to the cage you would fashion for him.

All that remains after you have supervised its construction is to lead him to his captivity and engage the lock."

"You make it sound simple."

"In relation to the keeping of a woman, my dear girl, it is. My belief –and you will allow I have some small experience of that which I speak– is that a woman can never be entirely tamed. There will always be that spark of rebellion deep inside that must keep a master upon his guard - unless, of course, he is prepared to have his situation reversed - or, worse, ended."

Anya smiled to herself at the truism.

"With a man," he continued, "it is different. Men are simpler and less complex - as well as being all the more predictable for the absence of the hormonal. When a man is broken, he is broken for life. Never –rare exceptions acknowledged- will he raise hand or head again. His owner takes possession of his deeds and keeps them until either the slave is sold or dead."

Again he paused.

"With a woman, however, and no matter how harsh and intensive her training; she remains forever on leasehold. Believe me, to underestimate that fact is to invite problems that are fully deserved."

"I trust what you say," Anya told him truthfully, "though I am not totally convinced. But, even if I were, how would this help me break the man of my choice?"

The laughter at the end of the connection was indulgent without being mocking:

"You already know the answer to that, my dear."

"I do?"

"The management of men is hardwired into the mindset of females from the womb onwards. As well you know. To break the spirit of the chosen creature is to simply take what comes naturally to your gender. Put simply, it is a matter of taking a few steps further forward than the more vanilla of your sisters – as many, to be precise, as the situation requires and you desire. What you witnessed at the shopping mall gives you knowledge; which, in the right hands, equates to power."

The silence greeting his assertion told him he had his protégé's attention.

"If the man of choice attempts to kiss your lips?" he continued in the high-rise-terminal fashion so popular with youth the world over. "Show him your cheek. The next time he heads for the cheek? Offer him your hand."

"And if he refuses?"

"Shun him. Then, when he returns and attempts to kiss the hand he insulted? Show him your pretty foot. Or in your case," he laughed, "a muscular calf."

In Cornwall, his laughter was matched.

"From such a lowly position," the sub-continent continued, "it is a brief journey to the anus, the armpit, or any other orifice and appendage upon which you wish him to lavish attention. He must be familiarised with each and every one of your most intimate smells and feel honoured to be on worshipful terms with them – even if he may, at certain times, find them… disgusting."

"Yes!" she breathed into the phone, unable to help herself; her mentor's take on the subject in complete accordance with her own.

"Animals such as these," he finished, "can only truly be said to be broken when it is a physical pain for them to be denied access to their owner."

Silence again reigned as she took it all in, until:

"You are making me wet," she rebuked, light-hearted but truthful. "And not for the first time."

"It is a talent," he agreed; laughing along with her; the two of them partners in a crime at the planning stage.

"This is all very encouraging," she said, "but I still have a long way to go."

His reply, given his usual downbeat approach, surprised her:

"Perhaps not so far as you think," he said encouragingly. "What you saw at the mall was more than just a simple discovery of his tastes giving you a chance to finally gain his attention."

"I'm not sure I understand."

"Anya, the physical aspects to which a man is drawn in a woman and, more tellingly, the design of those aspects, reveal his sexual nature in a way that can sometimes be clear to all but the man in possession of them himself."

"What are you saying?"

"I am saying, my dear, that; given his fixation for certain legs and feet, and the undeniable fact the design of the legs and feet he finds most attractive match yours –which; though undeniably shapely and erotic in their individual way; are not what most men would consider to be catwalk material- I am willing to wager that your employer, ignorant or unwilling to recognise the fact as he may be, is a latent masochist."

"You make no sense," she said; his assertion puzzling her; no matter how pleased she was to hear it. "How is it possible for a man not to know himself?"

"For men of my age," he told her, remaining patient, "and, I would guess, your employer's, the notion of manhood and what constitutes the condition was extremely rigid during our formative years. Even today, when men are encouraged to make contact with their…" a tone of contempt transformed his voice: "…'Feminine' side, certain manly aspects are both encouraged and, more to the point, expected. Hardly surprising that a man with a need to submit to a woman would suppress that urge rather than face the contempt of father, friends and colleagues. Far easier to submit to the social stereotype and become the man's man society expects than risk ridicule and be true to one's own inclinations. Sexual behaviour, once this stereotyping is in place, is known as 'Sublimation.

"One has only to study the characters in his bland novels to realise he sees women as a threat. The main reason they are always fragile, helpless, and in need of a strong man to both rescue, care for them, and give their lives meaning. The longer his true needs are suppressed and sublimated the easier it is for him to convince himself those needs were out of character in the first place. The good news for us is that, when they return, they do so with their power multiplied a hundredfold.

"When he does finally submit, his early conditioning will ensure any pleasure his masochism derives from your command and control of him is mitigated by his hatred of you – along with a deep and lasting shame for having submitted at all. Making every day a fresh triumph for you as he concedes yet more ground - hating his owner and despising himself; even as he feels compelled to do your bidding."

"The sooner I know such a day," she assured him, "the better I will like it."

"Yes," he agreed. "It is, Anya, a very happy anomaly – for you at least. One that will supply a longevity of sensation ensuring your ownership of him remains always to your taste."

Savouring his words; Anya Jalav knew the taste of "Ownership" was one she could scarcely wait to experience; optimism for actually doing so buoyed by the knowledge it was an experience her mentor seemed thoroughly determined she should have.

"Now," he began after allowing her a second or two to absorb his words, "blessed with this new knowledge of his tastes, I believe it is time we became a little more creative with both him, our strategy, and your wardrobe."

"I am all ears, O wise mentor," Anya assured him.

"Tell me, my dear," he had asked, taking her gentle mockery in good part; and as if in afterthought; "are you religious, by any chance?"

"Not in the slightest," she told him. "Why do you ask?"

"Just a thought that strikes me…Give me some time to think it through and I shall explain in more detail tomorrow lunchtime. In the meantime however, make sure you return to your sari's."

Anya started; nonplussed:

"But why would I do that when he is…"

"Humour me in this, my dear," he came in, "and I promise you will not be disappointed."

Chapter Fifteen

Lambert

"Is there something wrong, Master?" she asked.

It was two weeks on from his disastrous trip to London and, if the memory of his failure to perform was not quite buried it was - with the help of his servant and her recently acquired Western dress-sense- camouflaged. The same servant with the body of a Venus and the head of a Gorgon becoming of more interest by the day.

Her question arriving as she placed a breakfast tray on his lap and unfolded his newspaper for him.

"Wh-What makes you say that?" he answered with a question of his own, a little uncomfortable, not to mention miffed, at having his thoughts read so swiftly – and effortlessly.

"You seem… well… surprised," Anya replied, understanding now why Rajiv had pressed her to return to the costume of her homeland. Had it needed confirming, the look of anticipation-thwarted by the absence of what she had come enjoy describing to her mentor as her Uniform", would have been exactly the tonic required.

The words of their intended victim himself yet another affirmation they were on the right track.

"No, no," he assured her, indicating her sari. "I suppose I've just gotten used to you wearing more… Western fashions."

"Oh, I see," she smiled, unfolding his napkin and pouring his tea; waiting for him, as she knew he would, to go on.

A clearing cough indicated he was about to do just that.

"I suppose the sari's are more comfortable," he offered finally.

There was a palpable air of disappointment to him, she thought with no small satisfaction, as he realised the sight of her in the type of clothing he enjoyed so much was to be denied him – at least for the day.

"It is true, Master," she agreed; hesitating purposefully, "and yet…"

"Yes?" he prompted when it seemed she had finished.

"If you will excuse me sounding so bold," she went on, "European fashion just feels so much more… so much more… womanly."

She could have sworn his face lit up.

"And you enjoy that?" he asked – hopefully, she thought.

She nodded – shyly. As if the mere mention of such a prospect made her seem wanton; playing in to his perception of himself as both wiser older employer and superior man.

"Then why stop?" he asked. "You are in England, after all. There's nothing to stop you from dressing exactly as you wish."

So far the conversation was going exactly as Rajiv had said it would go – a case of setting a pervert to catch a pervert, she thought to herself; managing to stifle a smile before returning to naïve subcontinent servant mode.

"You do not think I look…" she allowed her voice to trail off.

"Go on," he urged – impatiently she thought.

"Well… silly," she said, averting her eyes and waiting.

Confirmation of what Rajiv had told her would follow came swiftly.

"Of course you don't," he assured her. "Western clothing suits you very well. In fact, I was wondering why you would even consider returning to your old clothes."

"Actually, Master," she began. "I only intended to do so for today – if that is acceptable to you. I do not have much in the way of Western clothing and I need to wear something while the clothes I have are being cleaned."

"Of course that's acceptable, Anya," he assured her, a thought occurring to him then: "In fact…"

"Yes, Master?" she prompted.

He seemed to think about it some more before reaching a decision.

"In fact, Anya, as you have been wearing the clothes to work in the house, I think it's high time I gave you a clothing allowance. That way you would have enough outfits – let's call them "Uniforms" – to wear while you're on duty and you could save your own clothes for private use."

Anya widened her eyes at her employer's largesse, as if such magnanimity were beyond her wildest hopes.

"Would you really do that, Master?"

He was already nodding, her reaction playing in to his perception of himself as some bountiful latter day Viceroy beautifully.

"We'll set you up with an account at the department store in town and you can buy some work outfits along the same lines as you've been wearing recently."

"I do not know what to say, Master," she said, still in thespian mode.

"Shoes too," he went on, warming to his theme, growing excitement all too obvious to her. We'll go into town after breakfast."

Anya allowed a huge smile to transform her toothy features: "Master, you are too generous."

"Nonsense," he said, flowering under the cultivation of what he saw as her growing idolisation of him; certain it wouldn't be long before he gained more intimate access to the parts he was intent upon clothing – and upon his terms. "I expect you to be ready to leave for town the moment I've finished breakfast and showered."

"Yes, Master," she agreed deferentially, already heading for the door. Turning back when she reached it to add shyly: "Thank you, Master."

When the door closed on her magnanimous employer, his searching hands were not reaching for their morning repast.

On the other side of that door, his devious young servant listened, ears pressed to wood, the better, she knew, to hear the unmistakable sounds of his growing preoccupation with her.

"Yes," she muttered to herself when a final gasp from the other side indicated crisis had been reached and passed, "I play a part in most of his every waking thoughts now."

Breaking into a smile then:

"It will not be long before I dominate those thoughts completely.

CHAPTER SIXTEEN

The Religion

When he surprised her in the basement it had not been three days since he had taken her to town and bought her more clothes than she had ever owned in her life. Clothes, she instantly realised, that chimed in with the look he was so taken with; the same "Look" she had watched him ogle as women dressed in similar fashion had passed his table at Starbucks. Clothes filled with the matronly and substantial rather than the bimboesque and inconsequential.

"How are you this morning, Anya?" she had heard from behind her as she loaded the washing machine with whites, breath catching in her throat at the sound of his voice.

During those "Three days" she had sensed his interest in her growing - it taking all of her willpower; along with Rajiv's admonishments not to do anything rash in order to facilitate the coming role reversal more swiftly; to prevent herself from doing just that.

"He will come to you, Anya," Rajiv had assured her. "He must believe himself the instigator. That way he is more easily led."

If she had not been totally convinced when Rajiv first suggested her course, she was now.

Not once during the time she had worked for him –apart from showing her around on her first day- had he ventured down into the basement that doubled as a laundry room.

And here he was.

"You startled me, Master," she told him, feigning more surprise than she felt. "It is not usual for you to come down here."

"Just thought I'd see how you were getting on. You know? Now I've more time on my hands," he told her in what was obviously a rehearsed reply.

"Now that your agency barely acknowledges you and your publisher acts as if you do not exist; along with your wife and friends; you mean?" she was tempted to ask, laughing inwardly.

Contenting herself instead with:

"Everything goes very smoothly, thank you, Master."

There was an awkward pause then – for him at least – as Anya closed the machine and set the wash; his servant sensing his eyes upon her capacious rear as she bent to the controls; roaming over the grey cotton of her skirt as it hugged her contours before travelling down to her legs and…

"Is something not right, Master?" she asked, jolting him from his perusal.

"Wh-What makes you say that?" he snapped, suddenly on his guard.

"Just that it is most unusual for you to be down here," she told him, careful not to sound as if she were uncomfortable with his presence. "You do not –if I may say- seem yourself."

"Truth be told," he went on, eyes flickering from her face to her legs and back again as she pretended not to notice, "I'm at a bit of a block with my writing. Not used to having time on my hands, you see?"

Anya nodded understandingly and recalled Rajiv's advice:

"Boost his ego. Flatter his misplaced pride in his superiority. Bolster his own self-regard until he basks in your obvious recognition of his superior status and seeks you out as a means of gaining yet more approval. The more that approval is missing from the other areas of his life the more he will look to you to supply it. Soon he will start to behave in ways guaranteed to make you happy with him and before long this behaviour will become ingrained without him being aware of it – or, if he is, dressing it up as something other than the weakness it is. But at no time –no matter how servile his behaviour becomes– must you act in any way other than his obedient and respectful servant. By the time he has an inkling of the changes taking place in his life he will find he is too far gone in his dependence upon you to help himself."

It was advice she had found –as indeed she found most of his advice- sound.

"Suppose I'm a bit bored, if the truth be told," he had gone on, finishing with a snort of laughter meant to tell her he was none too serious.

"It must be difficult for you, Master," she agreed, only the prize lying in wait at the endgame enabling her to control her growing contempt for his all too obvious weakness and self-pity.

"But I am sure it will not be long before your work is back in demand once more. All men of great talent such as yourself must endure trying times."

It was all she could do not to laugh at the way he nodded agreement with the nonsense she had just spoon-fed him. Just the same though, it was the nearest they had come to a conversation with each other since her arrival – and the fact he had instigated it underlined the wisdom of her mentor's advice and was a heartening indication of the progress she had made with her intended victim in such a relatively short period of time.

"So," he went on, still maddeningly superior but at least trying to engage with her on terms not too many light years from equality, "how have you settled in? Everything to your liking? Accommodation good?"

"It is very much to my liking, Master," she lied, picturing that day when he moved her belongings into the big house and took his own to…

"That old computer of mine I let you have working okay?"

"Very well, thank you, Master. It enables me to stay in contact with my spiritual advisor so much more easily than the exchanging of letters."

"Spiritual advisor?"

Anya nodded, as if that were information enough for him.

"I had no idea you were religious," he told her.

"My beliefs are fundamental to my life," she told him, preparing the ground for the stroke of genius Rajiv had dreamed up a while ago.

"I had no idea," he said, a little disappointed she thought, thinking, no doubt, that any piety on her part could prove an unreceptive counterpoint to a growing lechery on his.

"It is not a mainstream religion such as Islam or Hindu," she was quick to explain. "It is many, many, centuries older than either; though, like them, it is based on the teachings of a great prophet. We do not worship a God so much as we pay tribute to the individual soul – or, as my advisor puts it 'The godlike in others'."

"I'm not with you," he said – a difficult admission to make to an ill-educated Indian servant but one he felt obliged to confess nonetheless.

"I am sorry, Master," she went on, as if caught in a sin, congratulating herself on her own aptitude for the thespian as she did so. "I should not really be speaking in such a fashion. My religion is peculiar to the region of my origins and – though we are many thousands of miles distant – its teachings and obligations are not meant to be shared with..." she hesitated; deliberately.

"Go on," he urged, coming in exactly where she had intended, the growing belief that she was managing this handsome and older white man, her employer, setting her senses afire.

"I... I am sorry if I transgress, Master, but you are... you are..."

"Yes?"

"An outsider and..." -she dropped her eyes- "...and a non-believer. My apologies, Master."

Anya stared at the floor, a penitent, forced by honesty into giving offence; praying her Lord and Master would understand and show mercy.

A pose she knew the man she was intent upon owning could do no less than find arousing.

Lambert felt tempted to laugh, so – there was no other word for it – "Primitive" was her behaviour. Never of a religious bent himself, only the prospect of her "Beliefs" interfering with his lustful intent in her regard prevented him showing both disdain and ridicule.

"What is the name of this religion?" he asked, a soupcon of his scorn making itself evident in his tone, despite his diplomatic intentions.

Anya allowed her eyes to rise to meet those of her employer and found herself jubilant to find his own eyes had taken the opportunity of her lowered head to take in the legs and feet covered in the black nylon pantyhose he had purchased for her previously.

"It is a name only to be shared between believers," she told him, amused at the startled way his eyes leapt from their appraisal of her painted toenails beneath the nylon to find her own. "We are a very small sect and the strictness of its requirements ensures the numbers remain low – though we are no less devout. More so, perhaps."

Lambert was intrigued, despite his disdain.

"And you are bound not to speak of it?"

"No, Master. I speak of it all the time. But only with my spiritual guide and other believers. With –I am sorry– non-believers such as you I am only allowed to speak of it in the most general terms. Names, places, and history are forbidden to be shared with any but those favoured with inclusion."

"Then tell me about it in 'General terms'," Lambert insisted; insistence predicated not so much by any great interest in her beliefs themselves but by the magnificent breasts he could see heaving beneath the white cotton work shirt he had chosen for her and the legs below he found so strangely compelling.

Worth listening to some mumbo-jumbo if it kept one in their close proximity for a while longer, he thought, amused by his own cunning.

"Master," she began, tone becoming serious, as near to being assertive with him as she ever been. "My religion is everything to me. Were it to be ridiculed I would find myself unable to remain within the place or with the person where or with whom such a thing happened."

For a moment, Lambert just stared at her, taken aback by her sudden infusion of backbone, though by far the most surprising thing was his reaction to the prospect of her leaving.

He had actually felt afraid.

Just the same, shame at the fear instilled in him by the prospect of losing the flunkey, ego-massager and unlikely lust object prodding his pride into action, his expression became stern.

There were, after all, appearances to be maintained.

"Are you rebuking me, Anya?" he asked, injecting some severity into his tone.

His reminder of their respective positions having the desired effect.

"No, Master," she assured him, expression earnest. "I would not dream of doing such a thing. And besides, my religion forbids such disrespect to a person of higher standing such as yourself."

Her contempt of him knew no bounds as her flattering –and totally fallacious- description of him had the desired effect; two patches of colour actually suffusing the cheeks of her "Master" as her words had their intended effect.

"I was only trying to explain how seriously I take it and how impossible it would be for me to remain somewhere where I found my beliefs ridiculed."

Mollified, Lambert was now –and exactly as he was intended to be- puzzled.

Then, finally; still puzzled:

"How do you mean: 'my religion forbids it?'"

Chapter Seventeen

Progress

"It was amazing!" Anya told the eager face on her screen, her mentor's hands, as usual, out of range of the webcam, a slight faraway look telling her all she needed to know by way of explanation for their absence.

"He bought it then?" Rajiv pressed, eager, again as usual, to hear of her progress with the intended prey.

"Every single word," she answered, her own face, had he been able to see it, full of pride for the way she had pulled off the deception. "Though he is unable to disguise his contempt for your non-existent religion neither can he hide his delight at the primitive philosophy we have tailored to meet his superior pomposity."

Rajiv was nodding, knowingly.

"It is as I explained," he began. "This is a man to whom self-esteem is everything – whether it be deserved or not. A world where the weak serve the strong and look to them for everything is something that would appeal to such a man immensely."

"Even when he finds himself the one doing the looking?" Anya asked.

Rajiv laughed.

"When we are finished with him, my dear, it will not matter a jot whether it appeals to him or not. We will have him at a point where your presence in his life and what he must do to preserve it is hardwired into his own mindset. Your treatment of him –though he will despise himself for enduring it- will not only come to seem natural but just. Though he will hate you, his desire for you and growing sense of inferiority will serve to keep him coming back for more.

"As the addict considers himself one half of a whole man and justifies the actions he takes to satisfy his needs -while still considering himself a decent individual- so will Bernard Lambert continue to seek you out for his base gratification. And each time he does so his self-esteem and sense of himself as a strong and independent man will die a little more; though, perversely, his need to believe himself still worthy of the description will ensure he continues to look to you for verification. You are going to break him both mentally and physically until he is at as low an ebb as a man can be."

"Rajiv," she sighed, smiling, the usual sensations flooding through her at his words.

"Then," he continued, "you will be in a position that will enable you to allow him to rise as high or as low as you choose."

He chuckled.

"My guess is that his second coming will not be a particularly elevated rebirth."

As was always the case during their discussions of the ongoing situation, Anya was becoming increasingly aroused. The more evidence she saw of her employer's unlikely infatuation and growing dependence upon her sensitizing her at the very core. Making her wonder if the pleasure brought about by his eventual capitulation would ensure her thumping heart made a surrender of its own.

A possibility that fetched another smile.

What a way to go!

"Tell me," Rajiv was asking: "does he seek you out more, now he has you dressed after the fashion he desires?"

"More and more with each passing day," she answered. "Yesterday, when he came down to the basement, I sensed he was girding his loins to make a seduction – even though I also sensed the distaste his desire for me instills in him."

"Then you chose the perfect time to introduce our Religion," Rajiv congratulated her.

"I thought you would be pleased," she said, a little smug.

"Oh, I am, Anya. I cannot believe the progress you have made with this… this… poseur. He may be a weakling but his sense of racial and educational superiority is strong. That you have burrowed under the defences of his age, race and pride in so short a time –and without him suspecting a thing- is something at which I begin to marvel; his continued underestimation of you can only make his eventual fall all the harder for him –and all the sweeter for you."

"Yes, yes. That is all very well, Rajiv," she reprimanded him, suddenly tetchy, tone not at all playful, "but I am losing my patience with talk of what might be. What I want right now is to see him kneeling before me, to feel his servile tongue lapping at my young Indian cunt. Knowing he knows he is there because I demand it and he can do no more than act in accordance with his owner's wishes. I want to see his cock struggle to come erect in the cage to which I have consigned it and look to me with pleading eyes to free him; all the while careful not to voice such a demand for fear of displeasing his young master with the ugly face."

The head of her onscreen mentor began to shake by way of a reprimand –even if the warped pleasure he took from such a prospect was equally as visible. His voice though, when it came, unmistakable for anything but a rebuke:

"Again, you make reference to yourself as ugly when in truth your features denote only strength at the expense of superficial and ephemeral prettiness. I have warned you many times now, Anya: believe yourself unattractive and there will always be those only too ready to cement you in your prejudice."

"Yes, yes, I remember," she scowled, still irritated.

"Please, do not lose patience now, my admirable girl," he warned sincerely, warped pleasure tinged with amusement now for what he saw as her understandable eagerness. "You have insinuated yourself inside the barbed wire surrounding his base camp - move slowly and with cleverness and you will soon take command of the compound itself."

A sigh greeted his assertion.

"!It is all very well for you to urge caution, Rajiv. You have, after all, experienced that which I have yet to know. All very convenient for you to take pleasure in the situation and massage your manhood from thousands of miles away, but I am here. The situation is before my eyes and must soon be resolved before my patience gives out."

Despite the depraved nature of both their discussion and their intent, Rajiv's chuckle was fatherly:

"I understand, my sweet. But trust me when I say you are very, very, close."

"So you keep telling me," she replied; her tone, still tetchy, serving to remind him of the youth her articulate, if culturally challenged, exposition of her needs and goals could at times disguise.

"Unless I am much mistaken –and you will warrant I have been accurate up to now- the next few days will bring you closer to your goal and go a long way to easing your understandable need to bring the situation to a head."

There was silence as Anya considered this; the look of concentration and nodding head as she came around to the idea unseen by her mentor and, thus, leading him to take that silence as ominous.

"Are you still there, Anya?" he asked; tone, she thought, a little worried – needy, in fact; a prospect that made her smile. Though his involvement was only that of a voyeur with communication privileges he was equally as committed as her; the reclusive nature of his personal situation and the desires that age insisted he could no longer gratify for himself remained undimmed.

Her "Mentor's" dependency upon her as a sexual outlet – albeit by distance removed- a reassuring one.

CHAPTER EIGHTEEN

Lambert Again

It hadn't been Bernard Lambert's habit to take to bed at nine in the evening and masturbate.

The past tense crucial in the construction of the above sentence.

Now, however; rising earlier and earlier each day that he may spend more snatched time in the presence of his new obsession; such an occurrence was an everyday event – and, more often than not, was repeated more than once – a routine his disastrous interlude in London had exacerbated rather than disrupt.

It was, in fact, occurring now.

Some days after his discussion with Anya concerning her religion and three weeks on from that disturbing dream in his study, the writer's optimism concerning his new life and recently started novel had been consigned to history. Not only had the chapters he had sent to both his agent and his one-time editor been returned dismissively but his agent had informed him she would no longer be able to represent him owing to the claims placed on her time by her: "More in demand", clients.

If the dashing of his hopes in respect of his writing was not enough by way of despair, then his growing fixation with his young Indian housekeeper was intent upon making good the shortfall. A fixation her strange "Religion" and her "General" explanation of its functions had, if anything wetted rather than dampened.

He had found himself growing bolder with her; seeking her out wherever she happened to be working in the house and engaging her in conversation; though mindful of his superior status and careful to keep it intact when speaking with her; assuring himself she would see his sudden interest in her as no more than simple boredom on his part. After all, what else could she possibly take it for? If that short and general explanation of her religion and its insistence upon weak serving strong and unintelligent serving intelligent had confirmed his opinion of her low intelligence then it had also assured him that she knew her place in regard of him.

Though, he had to admit, the little she had permitted herself to tell him of her beliefs indicated a weird religion indeed and, no doubt, explained why it was so obscure and little followed.

"Can I ask you a question, Anya?" he began as she had served him tea in the living room, the sea beyond the windows glittering in the autumnal sun, his tone that of a man sure not to be refused.

"Yes, Master?"

"When you go into town for the weekly shop," he began, "do you use the time you have to yourself to have a pedicure?"

Anya feigned mild surprise at his inquiry when her true response was elation; allowing her eyes to lower to her feet, legs bare for once, the smooth brown skin ending in delicate long toes with vermilion painted nails; before adopting an expression of puzzlement intended to draw more from him.

Successfully as it had turned out.

"It's just that your feet and nails are always so beautifully turned out," he went on.

"Thank you, Master," she said, pleasure not feigned, many steps ahead of him and prepared to respond accordingly as she placed the tray containing his mid-morning tea on the coffee table. "I realise I am not what is known as a 'Beauty' but I see no reason not to take care of what nature has seen fit to give me."

"A sensible and laudable attitude, Anya," he congratulated her with his habitual condescension. "We should all do the best that we can and be the best we can be."

"I knew you would understand, Master," she smiled, overbite prominent in an equine face she knew was the best it could be; growing, with Rajiv's assurances in regard of the rest of her body and her employer's reaction to it, less and less concerned on its behalf.

"You remind me very much of my spiritual advisor," she went on, lying as if it were second nature to her. "Like you, he is a man of great talent and understanding. A strong man who does not reserve praise where it is merited. Were you of my race and so inclined I am sure you would, like him, rise to high position within our religion."

Lambert felt himself flush at her praise. As ludicrous as he found organised religion and the credulity of its followers –not to mention the puerility of his servant's own beliefs- his vast self-esteem could no more deny taking pleasure from a compliment than his lungs could deny themselves the sustenance of air.

"In my country," she began, pouring tea into a cup, "it is most unusual for a man to notice a woman's feet. It makes the care I take with them all the more worthwhile."

Now it was Lambert's turn to feign surprise:

"What are you saying: that you look after them yourself?"

She nodded, not trusting herself to speak, sensing something momentous was about to happen between them. Something albeit tiny, that would, nonetheless, alter the changing power dynamic between them still further.

"But this is terrible, Anya," he began with the words he had rehearsed for exactly this situation.

"I do not follow, Master," she said in a worried voice. "Do I do wrong?"

Lambert laughed benignly by way of allaying her fears.

"No, no. You misunderstand. I was simply trying to say that no woman or young lady should have to undertake such a task for herself."

Anya felt her heart begin to thump, seeing the direction in which he was attempting to lead her – and only too willing to allow herself to be led there.

"If I am truthful, Master," she told him wistfully, playing his game, "I have often thought how nice it would be to have such a task performed for me. Back home I was always envious when I watched my employer's memsahib have her feet bathed and pampered before having her toenails painted. It was something she took very seriously – almost a ritual, in fact."

"Well then," he pounced, opening spotted and taken, "why not have it done for you?" the tightening at his groin, he realised, evidence of the excitement he was taking from their, supposedly, innocent conversation and making him grateful for the long tee-shirt he had neglected to tuck into his jeans that so conveniently hid the tightening itself.

"I am afraid it is too expensive, Master," she said with regret, adding milk to his cup as he pictured a non-existent servant holding the foot of a non-existent memsahib.

"Are you saying I'm not paying you enough?" he teased,

manner light.

"No, Master!" she answered quickly; pretending to take him seriously. "My pay and lodgings are very generous. But finding a person in England willing to perform the task as my former memsahib insisted it be performed would be impossible."

She paused, as if concerned about what she was to say next.

"Though, if I am honest, it has always been something of a dream for me to have my feet looked after in the same way as the memsahib. But I have always known this is not likely to happen to one such as me. In truth, I would far rather take on the duty myself than settle for some pale imitation of service from a person only interested in the money to be gained from performing it, rather than taking pride from the task itself."

Lambert sipped at his tea without tasting it and nodded understandingly at her words, despite his contempt for their inherent stupidity. What other reason would a person have for performing such a task than money?

Such was the strength of his denial and hypocrisy; the increased tightening at his groin was not an answer he was willing to address quite yet. And, anyway, something else was puzzling him.

"Why do you say it would be impossible to find someone to perform a pedicure in this country?" he asked. "Surely there are any number of high street practitioners willing to do it for a charge."

"That is exactly my point, Master," she told him. "It was a duty the memsahib had performed for her with respect and deference.

"A pedicure?"

"Yes, Master," she nodded, completely serious despite his obvious mockery of her assertion. "There were two of us servants: myself and an older man –also of my faith- by the name of Rajiv."

She fought back a smile as she relegated her "Mentor" to the minor role of flunkey.

"As I explained to you before when you asked," she went on, "my religion believes in the weak serving the strong and the strong caring for the physical and spiritual needs –whatever they may be- of the weak. Rajiv took no shame from the service he gave the memsahib as he recognised her as a woman fate had decreed should be his superior - despite the fact she was not of our faith and was extremely demanding when it came to both her personal needs and her grooming."

Lambert thought about it; eroticised despite the fact "Rajiv" sounded like a weak-willed wimp who was getting his rocks off, rather than a devotee following the disciplines of a religion. The fact he himself was angling to get his rocks off in just the same kind of way not troubling him. He, after all, had a different endgame in mind. Seductions, when it came down to it, took many forms. If humouring his housekeeper a little was what was required to gain the desired end result then she would find him more than willing to oblige.

"And besides, given my religion," she continued as Lambert groaned inwardly; having feared that "Religion" was about to put in yet another appearance; "I would rather send money back home to help my family than waste it on something I can quite as easily do for myself. Of course I would like to be pampered in such a way as you describe but, if it means I have less to send to those who need it more than I, so be it. Money and material possessions are frowned upon by those of the faith."

It was exactly the type of response Lambert had hoped she would give – impossible to have been better, in fact – leading him, as it did, into his proposal.

"You know I used to do it for the former Mrs Lambert?" he told her, both pompous and a liar.

"I am not following, Master."

"The former Mrs Lambert's feet, Anya," he told her, erection now raging beneath the tee-shirt camouflage. "Whenever possible, I always took it upon myself to ensure they had the best of care."

Anya placed a hand over her mouth as if amazed by the prospect; hoping it wasn't too hammy.

It wasn't.

"Does that shock you, Anya?"

She allowed a few seconds to register, then eventually:

"I… I must say, Master, that it does a little."

"But why? What could be more natural than a man taking a pride in his woman's appearance?"

"Nothing at all, Master," she answered, still in pretend shock - even if such a desire chimed exactly with her own thoughts on the subject.

Though not too shocked.

She didn't want to scare him off, after all.

"I am sure it is natural here, Master," "But in my country such a thing is unheard of."

"Well, Anya," he began, maddeningly condescending, stating the obvious: "You are not in your country now. We take a far more relaxed view of such things here and so should you."

His voice carried just a hint of threat, she thought, and that suited her perfectly as she dropped her eyes and acted as if chastened.

"Yes, Master. You are right. I work in England now and the culture is different. If I am to stay here I must adjust as much to your ways as my personal beliefs and my religion allow."

She waited, then:

 But, just the same…"

"Anya, Anya," he came in, tone meant to be soothing, an intellectual calming the fears of the unschooled. "I'm not reprimanding you. Not in the slightest. I realise our cultures are different. What I was about to say was…"

He paused a moment, unsure even at this late stage, despite his all-encompassing sense of superiority. He had done nothing but think and, more importantly, fantasise about what he was going to suggest for days now but despite the fact he wanted it so badly he also knew he had to be careful. Though he felt sure she knew her place in his regard, he did not want her thinking he had romantic ideas about her. That would be just too ludicrous. Were it somehow to prove the case then she would have to go – even though he truly hated the thought of losing someone who made his day-to-day run so smoothly; the prospect of finding a suitable replacement highly unlikely he reckoned.

"I was about to say," he picked up where he had left off, a little nervy, despite his comforting sense of superiority over her, "that: instead of paying out the hard earned cash you send back to your family to have your feet pampered, "why not let me do it for you?"

She pretended not to have heard properly; partly in order to make him sweat a little; but mainly to give herself the space to bring her own feelings of elation under control.

"I'm sorry, Master," she said eventually. "I think I misheard you."

"It was a simple enough statement," he told her, manner offhand, as if what he were suggesting were the most natural thing in the world for an employer to pose to his young employee. "I was asking if you'd like me to give you a pedicure and paint your nails rather than do them for yourself."

She had remained silent, wanting him to make the running.

"Did you hear me, Anya?" he asked, a spot of colour high on his cheekbones indicating the beginnings of irritation.

"Yes, of course, Master," she replied quickly. "Forgive me if I seem rude, but it is not an offer I have ever expected anyone to make me, let alone so great a man as yourself."

Lambert waved a hand airily:

"It's not a proposal of marriage, Anya," he rebuked her. "I will still be your employer and you will still be my housekeeper. Nothing will have changed or be about to change."

Anya fought back a smile. Had he been given a printout of her thoughts at that moment he would have not have been so sure of his assertion in that regard.

"Master, it is a very generous offer," she said instead. "But you are a busy man. You have more important things to do with your time than… look after your servant's feet."

"Nonsense," he said with largesse, her use of the term 'Servant' placing any thoughts of her acting above her station to one side. He might consider her religion deluded and warped but - for his purposes- at least it had the advantageous effect of keeping her in her place.

"Things are on the quiet side for me at this time," he told her truthfully, neglecting to mention they were likely to stay that way, "and it will give me something to do. Something to keep me occupied until things get frantic again. I really am very bored at the moment."

"Master, I am confused," she told him.

"It was a simple enough offer to grasp, I would have thought," he sniffed, becoming tetchy again.

"Yes, Master, I understand your offer –though I must admit I am amazed you have made it- but…"

She deliberately allowed her voice to tail off, waiting for him to come in.

"But what?"

Anya hesitated a few moments before drawing herself up to her full five feet, as if steeling herself to deliver an unwelcome truth:

"Are you saying…?"

Again she hesitated and again he came in.

"Go on."

She nodded, as if apologising for wasting his time. "I… I am sorry, master, but are you saying you would look after my feet the way Rajiv took care of the memsahib's?"

Lambert hesitated himself now. Was that what he was saying? And just what exactly did "Rajiv" do for the "Memsahib"?

"Forgive me, Master," she came in, pretending to interpret his silence as a negative. "I knew I must be mistaken. That you should offer to reward your humble servant in such a way at all" –she laughed at herself for the way her language was becoming even more anachronistic in appeal to his presumed supremacy- "is beyond my wildest dreams; but to offer to do so as Rajiv did is simply… simply… unimaginable."

"Unimaginable?" he paraphrased, eyes flickering to the perfection of her feet that was so out of sync with its counterpart of the higher altitude.

"I am sorry, Master. I allow my childish dreams to get the better of me. It is ridiculous I could think, even for a second, that a man such as yourself would bestow such honour on a person like me."

She bowed her head deferentially, preparing to take her leave.

"I will not allow my daydreams to get the better of me again, Master. I shall return for the tray when you have finished."

She had almost reached the door when he stopped her.

"Anya?"

She paused for a few moments to collect herself before turning, not wishing him to read her excitement.

"Yes, Master?" she asked, face masking her feelings; even if her Master was having trouble doing the same.

"Do I take it you would you like me to give you a pedicure in the same way Rajiv gave your former employer a pedicure?"

She stared back at him, askance, as if unsure of his

seriousness.

"Well… Yes, Master," she agreed, finally, feigning befuddlement, "but…" for the first time in his presence she delivered a nervous giggle. "Master is teasing me."

It was exactly the right tack – not enough surprise to make him feel she were mocking him and enough expectation and deference to make him believe he was the one driving the bargain.

"Not at all, Anya," he insisted, comportment that of a great man dipping his toe in the waters of mediocrity; certain those waters would not rise high enough to cause either him or his reputation concern. "We all have dreams and yours seems a particularly harmless and easy to gratify desire. If you'd like to experience a Rajiv type pedicure I can't see any harm in being the one to gratify your wish."

Anya was all wide-eyed anticipation mixed with a large dash of admiration for the handsome employer intent upon making her fantasies a reality.

"But, Master," she drew him in further, "you do not know what Rajiv did for…"

"Really, Anya," he snapped, impatient to seal the deal now. "How much can a pedicure involve?"

His next words, however, were just what his devious servant from the subcontinent wanted to hear.

"Whatever Rajiv did for your former mistress I'll do for you."

Anya was exultant, already anticipating Rajiv's own excitement when she Skyped him later that evening.

"As I said before," Lambert lied again: "I'm at a loose end and it will be good for me to have a purpose to focus on. If it helps fulfill the long cherished dream of a valuable employee, all the better."

As he returned to his tea she dropped her eyes, as if flattered at being described in such terms as: "Valuable". Her voice, when it came, was thick with gratitude for the largess of her esteemed employer:

"Thank you, Master. You are truly a special individual," her laughter again threatening to bubble up into the open as he gobbled up the ludicrous praise.

"My religion," she assured him, "also teaches us never to insult a person who offers to do something nice for us and, if caring for my feet is something that would help break the monotony of your days, I am very happy to accept your offer. As my spiritual guide said when I described you to him: you are truly a man amongst men."

"Then it's settled," Lambert told her, elated, taking her compliment as no more than his due rather than the oleaginous means to an end for which it was intended. "Until things start getting busy for me I'll take care of your feet and nails for you as I did for my ex-wife and Rajiv did for your ex-mistress. Be ready when I have finished my tea and I'll drive you into town to purchase everything we need."

An intoxicated Anya had nodded and was already at the door when he called:

"And Anya…"

She turned.

"Call it my treat."

CHAPTER NINETEEN

Anya's Third Fantasy

She was seated behind what had once been his desk in his study; wearing the severely cut two-piece suit in charcoal grey she knew he loved so much; skirt rising up to mid-thigh as she sat to reveal her powerful young thighs she knew he loved even more.

"Come," she said, at the sound of the two timid knocks upon the door; the knowledge he was having to ask permission to enter his own study in the home he owned, she knew, would not be lost upon him and would increase his feelings of shame and helplessness.

"You, er wanted me, hmm, master?" he asked having great difficulty forcing the word out, his whole face aflame with blood made molten from humiliation and self-disgust.

"Very good," she applauded him, "you remembered to show me the proper respect – verbally at least. This tells me you are getting used to the idea you are no longer the master of this house or, equally importantly, yourself. "Now, come around to this side of the desk," she ordered, pointing to a spot at her side where she wanted him to stand.

As came around to stand before her she swiveled to face him, a navy blue high heel dangling from one foot.

"You look uncomfortable," she pointed out, her eyes roaming over the front of the track-suit bottoms she insisted he now wear about the house to facilitate 'Ease of access'; the bulge she saw there all the more exciting to her for being unable to come fully erect. "Are you uncomfortable?" she pressed.

His face was a picture of abject misery and the thoughts behind it easily guessed at:

"Why am I allowing myself to be treated this way?"

"Why have I allowed this to happen?"

"Why don't I just rip the chain with the key to this damned belt from around her neck and kick her arse back to the shithole from where she came?"

She shook her head as if disappointed:

"I read you as easily as a children's book," she told him. "You still believe this is some kind of game you can bring to an end the moment you tire of it. But you do not tire of it, do you? And, should it come to pass that you do, by that time I will be such an integral part of your life the mere thought of not having me in it will cause you a pain worse than the physical. Imagine, my older English peon, how devastated you would feel to know you will never again experience the taste of my toes in your mouth and feel the trickle of my urine as it makes its way over your docile face. Never to see these legs you adore so much and the breasts above them you have yet feel or place lips upon. I am in your blood now and I will stay there, of that you may be certain."

A groan escaped his lips as his cock responded to her words and tried to expand inside the titanium encasing it.

"But," she went on, swinging foot lowered to join its companion on the carpet; *"I am a little puzzled. I thought I made myself plain on the subject of how you should present yourself to me whenever you enter my presence – even if you had only left it seconds or so before."*

The fear transforming his features as he pondered the penalty for his forgetfulness almost made her smile as he dropped to his knees and lowered his face to her instep, the black nylon rough against his lips.

"Do not forget to count to ten," she reminded him.

When the time had elapsed he knelt up, careful to keep his eyes upon the feet his mouth had just left.

"Which leaves the small matter of punishment for having forgotten to adopt your position of respect in the first place."

She saw him take a nervous swallow.

"Stand up and take your pants off."

His eyes came up at her, horrified, knowing her intention and appalled by it.

"I warned you of what would happen if you were disrespectful," she told him as if her were an infant rather than a forty-eight year old man employing her. *"Now take them off."*

Again he hesitated.

"This instant!"

Rising to his feet he reluctantly began to comply.

"Much better," she said as the tracksuit bottoms came off to

reveal his chastity in full glory; the lack of the underwear she had proscribed him revealing all to her eye.

"Look at you," she smirked, as he stood before her in shame. "I wonder what the wife you cheated on so frequently would think of you now. A conceited and disloyal fool dependent upon his servant for his sexual release."

She could see the barb had hit home; a simple mention of his ex-wife enough to bring home to him what he had once been and what he now was; his thoughts on his fall from grace interrupted as she reached into what had once been his desk and retrieved what looked to be a Ping-Pong paddle.

Tapping the wooden paddle against her palm, her eyes indicated her lap.

He stared at her, not quite believing she would go through with it, despite the evidence he already possessed in regard of her inflexible will."

"Anya…" he began, forgetting himself, "…I mean: Master; please don't do this. It… It's wrong. You… You have to leave me some self-respect."

Self-respect is for humans who have proved themselves worthy of such treatment. You are nothing but an animal."

He hesitated again, eying the paddle she was tapping against her hand as if it were the guillotine itself.

"The choice is a simple one," she told him. "Either you drape yourself across my thighs and accept my correction of your lack of respect…"

She watched his eyes lower to her strong legs in mention of her thighs, knowing a large part of him wanted nothing more than to lie across them and submit.

"…Or," she went on, "I leave this house and your life this instant and will never return to it. Taking…"

A hand went to her neck and brought the key of his belt to her lips, her tongue darting from her mouth to taste it.

"…the key to your cock with me as well as the combination for the lock it opens. It's your choice, You being a big strong man I am sure you could get the key from me, but the combination? Never!"

Her words she saw were making him even more nervy.

"Still," she continued; "I am sure you will find someone talented enough to cut through the titanium of the belt and release *you – even if the sophisticated cutting equipment does remove half of your manhood as it does so."*

For a few long seconds he considered it: be spanked like a little boy by an Indian girl young enough to be his daughter; or accept he would never see her, or the key and combination, to his chastity belt again.

"Yes," she said as he draped himself across her lap and she placed a proprietorial hand upon the older man's pale white buttocks; "I sensed that might be your decision.

"Now," she told him, "let's make ourselves comfortable and we can begin.

Making them 'Comfortable' was a matter of making him place a wrist beneath the sole of her foot and sliding her legs apart to trap his metal encased penis between her knees, trapping it firmly.

"Give me your other hand," she said; twisting it towards his neck and bringing from a gasp of pain.

There was a silence then and he could sense her gaze upon him, savouring the depths to which she had reduced him and was about to lower still further.

Then the paddle came down upon his naked arse and he shrieked with pain.

The above action repeated for ten minutes until he was a blubbering and beaten wreck, all fight taken from him as she rolled him from her lap to the carpet and placed a foot on his neck.

"There," she told him, breathing heavily after her exertions; "I do believe we have reached something of a watershed in our relationship. Let us have no more delusions from you that you can refuse me anything from now on.

He was sobbing like a schoolboy still; probably the first time since he had actually been one that he had cried; but she knew he had heard her words.

Then:

"You have precisely one minute to pull yourself together," she told him, "then I want you under my desk…"

CHAPTER TWENTY

Rajiv Reflective

Sprawled across his sofa, the Bollywood pot-boiler playing itself out on his new flat screen television no more than an unacknowledged montage of sodium images, Rajiv found himself picturing the drama being played out across the world in Cornwall and imagining the events unfolding as he waited –with no great patience- for the nightly Skype session with his partner in perversion.

As was his custom, he had insisted Anya omit nothing when describing the moment her "Master" bent the knee to serve at the feet of his horse-featured young compatriot and, as always, her powers of description –in terms more prosaic than lyrical; though no less… exciting for all that- did not leave him wanting.

Just as they had agreed after she had Skyped to let him know of Lambert's offer, Anya had not mentioned her Master's offer again.

"Make him come to you," he had advised her. "He must make the running. From this moment on; despite your outward demeanour remaining utterly respectful and deferential; everything you do must place him in the position of supplicant – even if he initially views his actions as made of his own volition."

It was a course of action she had agreed was sensible and acted upon but, after two days without any mention of the offer on her Master's part -despite the fact he had, on the very day he had made it, driven them into town to purchase what would be necessary to make good on his proposition; unaware that what he required was already in his possession- Anya had been deflated.

"What is he waiting for?" she had asked Rajiv. "Should I remind him of his offer?"

"No!" he snapped, a little harsher than he intended, correcting himself immediately:

"Forgive my tone my young friend. But to do that will be to cede him the higher ground. He must ask you. That way there is no possibility of his suspecting he is led. Be patient a while longer and all will fall into your lap, my sweet – or should I say: at your feet."

Unconvinced, but amused, Anya had laughed with him; despite knowing her breaking point was fast being reached.

On the third day, however –and just before Anya did something of a similar nature herself- Bernard Lambert cracked.

"Well, Anya?" he had asked, approaching her as she polished a table in the front room –manner accusing, as if she had let him down.

"Sorry, Master?" she had asked, rising from a crouch to her full five feet -some eleven inches below the gaze of her employer- bearing, as always, respectful.

"Do you want this pedicure or not?" he snapped, as if the responsibility for instigating it were hers, the unjust recrimination serving only to highlight his own impatience.

For a few moments she had stared back, expression uncomprehending, then:

"I am sorry, Master. When you did not mention it these last two days I thought you were not serious."

She lowered her eyes to the floor in a parody of maidenly abashment.

"I thought you did not mean what you had…" She raised submissive eyes to his: "If I am truthful, Master, I was disappointed."

Lambert's head shook from side to side at this, as if she had somehow let him down; his own expression becoming stern as he delivered a mild rebuke:

"Anya, you will do well to remember that when I give my word on something I see that something through. Why else do you think I drove you to town to purchase the necessary items?"

"Forgive me, Master," she began, instantly reverting to the penitent mode she knew he found so pleasing and, more importantly, non-threatening. "I should have known you would not go back on your word."

Lambert's eyes had narrowed:

"Word?"

Was that how she interpreted it? He thought he had offered to give her a pedicure, not a notarised pledge of…

"If I offend," she went on, interrupting his thoughts, "it is only because I am unable to believe my good fortune in finding a

Master so respect worthy and considerate of his servant's feelings."

He extended her the usual dismissive hand wave, as if his largesse were nothing; despite his obvious pleasure at her having pointed it out; momentary misgivings dismissed by her obsequious words.

"It's a small matter Anya, no more."

Going on quickly then, impatient to begin:

"Now, when you've finished what you are doing, we'll get started. Where do you want to do this?"

Anya pondered this, as if she had not given it a thought.

"Excuse me, Master, but first I must…

She paused, as if about to say something indiscreet.

"For heaven's sakes, Anya," he barked. "What is it now?"

"Apologies, Master. But I must remove my…" again she hesitated.

"Remove what? Spit it out girl."

Her eyes lowered to her pantyhose and her Master's followed in the same direction.

"Oh!" he gasped, light finally dawning. "Of course. Yes," he agreed, a tad thwarted but knowing it would be asking too much for her to remove said hose in front of him – at least this stage.

"So, where shall we do it?" he went on quickly, camouflaging his disappointment.

"I think the kitchen would be best Master," she said. "We can lay some paper in case of accidents."

"Very well, he nodded agreement. "I'll go and get the necessary things and meet you there."

With a last glance at the hosed legs beneath her knee length grey skirt, legs he was becoming more taken with by the hour, Lambert went off to fetch what he needed for their coming session, totally missing the beatific smile on the face of his young servant as he did so.

When he entered the kitchen a few minutes later, Anya had removed her pantyhose and was already waiting for him, seated on a high backed wooden chair in the middle of the room, newspapers spread before her on the tiled floor.

Placing the creams and varnishes he had purchased on the floor, Lambert was in the process of pulling over a chair for himself when she stopped him.

"What is the chair for, Master?"

"Excuse me?"

"Apologies, Master, but I was wondering why you needed another chair?"

"Well…" he began, nonplussed, considering it obvious. "I'll need somewhere to sit."

"Master, please correct me if I seem forward, but you said you would perform the task as Rajiv performed it."

"Well, yes, I did?" he agreed. "But…" the small voice of concern at the back of his head found itself unable to compete with the magnificent young breasts he was gazing down upon as they strained against the confinement of her, by now, habitual white cotton shirt; not to know that she had undone another button in his absence that he may have a less obstructed view of her décolletage.

"But surely I need somewhere to sit?" he asked, tearing his eyes from the rise and fall of her full brown tits and finishing his sentence

"If you sit, Master," she told him, careful to maintain deference despite the somewhat humbling nature of what she hoped he was about to do for her, "I will have to raise my feet in order to rest them in your lap."

"Yes?" he replied, still at a loss. "So?"

"I am afraid that is not a good way to apply varnish as it may run," she answered, hoping he would believe her. "For the pedicure to be perfect the soles of my feet must be placed as near to the floor as possible to minimise the effect of gravity upon the varnish. That is the way the memsahib insisted it be done."

Having, despite his assertions in regard of his ex-wife, no experience in such matters, Lambert found her explanation reasonable.

"Perhaps then it would be better if you just directed me in what you want," he suggested.

"You will not be offended, Master?"

"I just suggested it, didn't I?" he reminded her, impatient to start, the erection beneath the long blue tee shirt he had been careful to wear outside his jeans –decision made with concealment rather than fashion in mind- becoming more urgent.

"Forgive me, Master, but it is not usual for me to be in such a position. I do not wish you to think I am telling you what to do."

"Well, unless I can somehow divine what your fellow servant actually did for the memsahib, I can see no other way," he said, the need to make contact with the young woman's flesh –albeit at such a low level- becoming stronger by the second. The surreal –not to mention warped- nature of the situation he had engineered doing nothing to lessen either his need or his impatience to see it gratified.

Which was when an idea struck him.

"I have it," he began. "How about if we role-play? I'll be Rajiv and you can be the memsahib. Would that make things easier for you?"

Anya clapped her hands together excitedly after the manner of a seven-year-old being told she was to be the princess in the school play – had she gone to school as a seven-year-old that is.

"Oh, Master!" she exclaimed, looking up at him with admiring wide eyes he would be sure to take as reverence and adulation, the prospect a lowly flunkey such as she, could have an agenda of her own, she knew, playing no part in his reckoning. "Can we really do that? My religion teaches that –so long as it does not intrude upon our everyday situation and responsibilities- that imagination is the tool of consolation and can make the life of even a lowly person such as your servant a pleasant one."

Lambert groaned inwardly, having wondered how long it would take for her "Religion" to rear its unwanted head; praying her strict adherence to her puerile beliefs was not going to interfere with his intentions in her regard.

Piety, of course, being something that had no role in the entertainment his imagination was in the process of devising for his young housekeeper.

"Very wise," he agreed with a touch of dismissal – though not too much. Knowing how seriously she took her beliefs he did not wish to impair his progress with her by belittling them.

Taking on a lighter tone he set the game in motion:

"So, memsahib, how should we proceed?" ending his words with a smile of encouragement intended to make her more comfortable in her role, unworried about the servile part he was about to play in the scenario so long as it gave him access to her. They would, after all, when done role-playing, return to their respective roles. Life would resume as normal and stay that way.

At least until the next time they played.

And the more they "Played", he thought, images flashing before his eyes, the more he felt certain the sexual barriers placed between them by her weird religion would come tumbling down.

For her part, Anya knew that the time to play the submissive servant was over for the time being. He had given her carte blanche to act a certain way and if she managed to go too far and offend him then she at least had the excuse that he had been the one who insisted she do so in the first instance.

Emboldened, she began:

"Fetch a bowl of lukewarm water, some soap and a towel, Rajiv," she ordered.

"Yes, memsahib," he said, still smiling, looking about him."

"What is the problem, Rajiv?"

"I'm looking for a towel, Anya."

"Do not be familiar," she snapped, startling him a little, her tone suddenly autocratic, watching as he bit back a response before her smile of complicity reminded him of the nature of the game he thought they were playing.

"Forgive me, memsahib," he said, paraphrasing the words and manner she herself used when in servant mode. "Where will I find a towel?"

"Upstairs in the hallway closet," she told him with a shy smile intended to allay any misgivings he might be experiencing.

Her own thoughts on the same subject allayed when he returned her a smile of his own.

A smile of encouragement, she thought.

Duly persuaded, she continued on:

"Hurry now, Rajiv."

Warming to the game and taking amusement from her obvious relish in stepping outside of her role as flunkey, Lambert nodded his head respectfully and hurried upstairs to give Anya the opportunity to hike up her skirt and feel herself beneath the, by now, sopping black panties she had worn for the last two days; the smell of her excitement –as intended- pervading the close proximity.

A smell she knew he would be unable to miss when he came close.

And a smell he was going to become very familiar with.

Only now he would not have to delve into her laundry while she was out shopping to do so.

When he had returned with the towel and filled a bowl with water and soap he placed them at her feet.

"Shall I fetch a flannel?" he inquired.

"Shall you fetch a flannel, what?" she asked, the tiny smile intended to reassure him still in place.

He missed a few beats until light dawned.

"Shall I fetch a flannel, memsahib?" he repeated with an indulgent smile.

"Better," she observed, granting him another smile of her own, as if acknowledging their secret game and its temporary nature.

"You must show respect at all times, Rajiv," she reminded him, careful for now to keep her tone playful. "I am granting you a rare honour and you should be careful your behaviour merits it or you will find it withdrawn."

"Yes, memsahib," he said, amused, lowering his eyes to enter into the spirit of their diversion; consoling himself with the knowledge their role reversal was temporary and the true nature of their relationship as servant and master could be restored at his whim.

"Lay the towel before me and place the bowel upon it," she ordered. "There is no need for a flannel when you have hands perfectly capable of doing the job, Rajiv."

He nodded and did as she asked, excitement rising as he realised he was about to touch her; something in her new and autocratic manner –even if he knew she was just aping the actions of her former memsahib- striking a chord at his netheregions. "I could get to enjoy this game," he told himself without thought there could be consequences.

"Now you must kneel down and make sure your hands are wet and soapy," she went on, marvelling as he did so while raising her skirt to thigh level and making his first whiff of her fragrant Indian pussy imminent; the young Indian delighted at the way his hungry eyes followed her actions.

"Cup the heel of my right foot with your hand," she instructed him when his hands were soapy, "and wash them."

Erection raging, Lambert tore his eyes from her powerful legs and the glimpse of black cotton panties her movement had exposed and reached out from his kneeling position to take her foot in his hand; the perfectly formed toes and the smoothness of the brown skin taking his breath away and, if it were possible, heightening the response beneath his tee shirt still further. The sensation of her warm flesh in his hand for the first time –albeit under such lowly conditions- made the constriction at his groin even more uncomfortable.

"Pay attention to the skin between my toes," her voice came from above him as –to her wonderment and exultation- he did as she asked; fighting to retain control as he did so; wanting nothing more than to smother her exquisite foot and matronly brown legs in kisses before taking her upstairs and…

"That is enough, Rajiv," came the voice of his pretend memsahib from above him after what seemed like seconds but had, in reality, been a matter of minutes; Anya delighted at his absorption in the task and only too willing to stretch it out.

"Dry my foot and repeat the procedure with the other then dry both and apply the varnish remover," she continued, easing her thighs apart enough to allow him a glimpse of her panties and, more importantly, to smell what they covered.

In a new and quite different world, Bernard Lambert did exactly as she ordered, the desire to simply sweep her up in his arms, take her upstairs and pound her young pussy until she screamed submission, unbearable. Only the knowledge he would be losing an irreplaceable servant as well as a fantasy object held him back; convinced as he was that her adherence to the beliefs of her weird religion would insist she leave his employ and deprive him of a valuable housekeeper as well as a…

What happened next made restraint even more difficult for him.

That first whiff of her young pussy through the unlaundered fabric of her underwear, as he finished drying her foot and reached for the other, reacted upon his senses in the way of a gunshot; pervading his nostrils and heightening still further the sensations coursing through him from the strange and unnatural position in which he found himself – game, or not.

"Is there something wrong, Rajiv?" she asked as he hesitated, the sole of her left foot cradled in the palm of his hand, the adrenalin coursing through him all the more potent for the physical sensation of smell that had added itself to the metaphysical aspects of role-playing.

"N-No… memsahib," he answered with an effort of will, attempting to maintain the temporary status quo; senses scrambled by the smell itself and the fact its presence indicated his servant's own excitement for the game they were playing. Something, a small voice told him, which boded well for the other, more traditional male-female pastime, he had in mind for her.

"Then get on with it," she ordered when he hesitated, voice simulating that of an authoritative English lady; rewarding him with a jocular smile when he looked up questioningly in order to take the edge from any qualms he may have been experiencing. Not wanting him to think the situation was going beyond his initial intentions.

"That journey," she had told herself with an inward smile of fond anticipation, "I shall save for later."

"Of course, memsahib," he responded, fears -if he'd had any- allayed; lacking the necessary imitative skills to mimic the voice of an Indian servant but reassured in their game by her smile; even as he was driven on by his lust.

After washing and drying her second foot –taking discreet pains to breathe in and savour the growingly pungent smell of arousal, emanating from between her legs and no more than a foot above his head- he looked up at her again, questioningly.

"Should I apply the nail varnish now, memsahib?"

Anya shook her head and gave him a dismissive stare, as if she were dealing with a particularly dim witted retainer.

"Really, Rajiv," she scolded. "How many times have you performed this task for me?"

Lambert could only wait, unsure of his response.

"What is it that has to be done before the nails are ready to be varnished?"

He was at a loss.

"Oh, Rajiv," she breathed. "What am I to do with you? You really can be terribly stupid."

"My apologies, memsahib," he began, the slightest of smiles as she berated him keeping him committed to their game and winning from him a smile of his own. "Remind me please."

Anya sighed. "Oh, very well. But I warn you, Rajiv, this will be the last time I do so."

"Thank you, memsahib," he said, inclining his head playfully. "You are too gracious to your lowly servant."

With a conspiratorial smirk, Anya nodded agreement before continuing.

"Before you apply the varnish, Rajiv," she began, "the nails have to be prepared."

"Yes, memsahib," he answered, getting into the spirit of the game more and more – enjoying himself, in fact, certain now it would end in a way he would be sure to find enjoyable.

"And what is the best unguent to use when preparing a lady's toenails for the application of varnish?" she asked, tone now replicating that of a teacher towards a particularly clueless pupil.

Again, Lambert could only stare, as clueless as the schoolboy she seemed to imagine herself addressing.

Anya tutted impatiently, outwardly in control but heart fluttering within; praying all her preparatory work would not be in vain and he would go for what she was about to propose.

"Saliva, Rajiv," she told him, pausing for it to sink in. "Nothing improves the lustre of a lady's nails more than good, old-fashioned, masculine saliva."

Lambert's jaw had almost dropped to the floor.

"Sa… Saliva?" he repeated, wondering if she meant what he thought she meant, hackles rising above his uncertainty as he recalled a similar proposition, put to him a little while ago in Bayswater from the lips of a profit driven Essex call girl.

"That's right," she told him, a playful expression imploring him to continue the game.

"B-But, memsahib," he began, already telling himself this was a different –and totally unthreatening- situation, "how will I…"

"The same way you have always done it, Rajiv," she told him, holding his eyes with her own, gratified when he could not meet her gaze and averted his own.

"I don't understand," he said, even though she knew he did.

Taking her courage in her hands, Anya took a breath and said it, convinced that if he caved in to the demand she was about to make he would gradually cave in to just about anything else she insisted upon.

"You must place each toe in your mouth and suck until each toe is coated with your saliva. It is the only way to achieve the desired result."

Below her she saw him give an almost imperceptible shake of the head and wondered if –as Rajiv had warned she could- she had gone too far too soon; staring down at the top of his head as it continued to shake until she felt sure he was about to rise to his feet and tell her the game was over.

For what to her seemed an eternity they remained in this position until, wonder of wonders, his hands, head still bowed, surrounded her right foot and lifted it to his lips.

For another eternity he just knelt there, head lowered with her foot in his hands.

Then, just as Anya had convinced herself he would rise to his feet and walk out; she watched as he separated her big toe from the others and slowly placed it in his…

…The credits rolling at the conclusion of the Bollywood potboiler went unseen by Rajiv as he returned to earth from his latest retrospective of the accounts given to him by Anya; it taking a great effort of restraint not to pleasure himself there and then; only the knowledge he would soon be speaking with his protégé and hearing of her latest exploits with the growingly enthralled Lambert preventing him from lowering his tracksuit bottoms and…

"Control and moderation, Rajiv," he admonished. "Lest you wish the law of diminishing returns to dilute the power of ecstasy."

As if in perfect sync with hard won self-discipline, the bleep of the computer heralded an incoming call.

Switching the television to stand-by, Rajiv smiled and quickly took his place before the console; certain that the latest update from his Skype partner abroad would reward his temporary denial.

"Anya, my sweet," he began. "How do things progress in the war zone?"

CHAPTER TWENTY-ONE

Bayswater Again

Some months back –when his lack of female company had first endowed her with some small sexual interest- Lambert had imagined taking his young Indian servant in ways she would be sure to find utterly humiliating.

Ramming home to her his power and her lack of such.

Whenever and wherever he wanted.

Oblivious to her objections and comfort.

She was there for his convenience and comfort, and his convenience and comfort –at least in his head- meant exactly the opposite where she was concerned. His disgust at himself for entertaining such thoughts in regard of one he considered so… "Lowly"… self-mitigated by the bestial acts his imagination forced her to endure as he entertained them.

Of course, had he possessed the necessary self-awareness, he would have found it of small wonder she was interesting him more and more. The nature of his feelings in her regard wholly explainable; not just by the fact she was the only person in his life at this time, but also by the respect she extended him which went some way to convincing him he remained a man of substance - despite the humbling nature of the chore in regard of her feet he himself had insisted he perform for her.

Now though, even that seemed to be changing. He couldn't pinpoint exactly when, or even how, but the dynamic between them appeared to have altered in some small, imperceptible, way - though he did acknowledge to himself that having her "Master" on his knees before her while he sucked on her toes could go some way towards an explanation.

And yet, despite the obvious conclusion offered by the above, he sensed the change had been triggered sometime before he had led her into accepting his offer of a regular pedicure.

Troubling him more, however, was her growing facility to trigger his libido - simply by dint of her presence. When he rose above his self-disgust and actually took pause to give it what passed, for him anyway, as in-depth consideration, he was hard pressed to recall the last occasion when the fantasy figure prompting him to wrap a hand around his overworked cock had been somebody other than his young housekeeper - though he found it of some consolation that the simple young Indian woman had no idea of her attraction for him - even if the arousal wafting down to him from her young pussy as he bent to attend her feet indicated nothing if not the reverse.

An attraction for him he had so far been unable to translate into a physical relationship of the kind he'd initially wanted from her – her religion, he considered, no small barrier where progress was concerned.

Into the bargain –as if his obsession for such a person wasn't degrading enough- his fantasies concerning her had undergone a complete turnabout since the sight of her legs and body, covered in clothing that was not a sari, first gained his attention.

Of course, he had already been the recipient of dreams where their situations had been reversed and she had been the one in control.

These had been disturbing enough.

Now, though, since he had taken it upon himself to take care of her feet on a regular basis, it was his conscious mind, as well as the sleeping variety, which weaved scenarios and fantasies where he, rather than her, was taken in ways sure to humiliate and degrade. His waking –and sleeping- daydreams were beginning to exercise an ever-multiplying sway over him and -though it did occur to him that spending a twice-weekly session on his knees, attending to his own servant's pedicure, could be contributing to his fantasies in respect of her- he was loathe to admit, even to himself, that so young, uneducated, and facially unappealing a specimen as his young housekeeper could have gained such a hold over his imagination.

All so different, he considered, to the reality holding true for him a short time before.

An image from the time of his former pomp forming behind his eyes as he made yet another attempt, having failed on one recent Bayswater occasion already, to remind himself of what, and who, he had been. Conjured up in the hope he might once again return to that sorely missed state of grace.

Or at least exercise his cock to a different image…

…A light breeze wafted through the balcony doors of the Bayswater bedroom Gianni had prepared for him; cooling his body with light caresses as he gazed down at the adoring face of his wife's closest friend; blonde hair spread across the pillows as her eyes implored him to continue with what he was doing.

"Not so fucking smug now, are we?" he had snarled down at her. "Feel like teasing me now, do you, slut?"

No answer was forthcoming as her mesmerised eyes took in his still engorged cock as it waved before her eyes.

"Remember?" he snarled. "Flashing your legs and pussy at me whenever Siobhan's back was turned? Not to mention your pussy-whipped husband. Or does he know you enjoy a good fucking from a real man? Perhaps he enjoys attending to you after you've had a man-sized load deposited in your greedy little cunt."

Ineffectual moans of protest escaped her lips.

" Is that what you do, slut?" he went on, mining the seam. "Put your tight little cunt over his mouth and let another man's cum ooze into his mouth?"

With pleasure, he saw his abuse of both her and the unknowing husband was exciting his wife's friend still more; feeling, he had to admit, a certain pride that this, so, so, superior, woman was submitting to him in ways guaranteed to make him feel like a Titan.

In control.

Superior.

The whole world was his playground and the bitch below him -the same "Bitch" who had thought herself such a cock-tease- had become nothing more than one of the rides.

His throbbing cock continued to pulse a few inches from her fascinated eyes and he watched as her tongue protruded in anticipation of taking the monster in her mouth. The same monster that, not moments before, had drilled her to a teeth-shattering release while delaying its own. Pounding away at her still snug twat to drill itself so deep inside her she fancied she heard her uterus beg for mercy. Drawing out his meat after he'd repeated the pummeling a few times until only the head remained inside; before ramming it back in with all his force; his own lust beyond measure as he watched her buck writhe and scream.

And boy, did she scream!

"Do you want to suck me?" he asked; sliding up her chest; legs astride her stomach as her breasts heaved and struggled to make comedown in the aftermath of the ecstasy he had just supplied.

She had stared up at him, eyes wide; unable to quite believe he was still erect after having pounded her to such an orgasm. Eyes with a new look to them. A look he had seen before after other sessions of such a nature and knew to be adoration. The smug, superior, bitch who'd thought she could treat him with the same lack of respect she reserved for her pantywaist husband screwed into an oblivion for which she would always hanker after and seek to replicate.

"Do you want it?" he demanded; waving his prick before her mouth tantalisingly; the smell of her own recently fucked cunt assailing her nostrils and, to her shock and self-disgust, inflaming her desire even more.

"Beg," he ordered.

Her eyes closed at the command, body covered with a sheen of perspiration lending her skin a shininess that made her helpless position beneath him all the more erotic.

"Say, please," he demanded; adding: "or I'll take my cock away and you'll never see it again."

The threat was enough and her eyes opened; need and a soupcon of fear joining her adoration.

As their eyes locked he could feel her resistance begin to crumble; until, in a voice one would expect to hear in that aforementioned playground, his wife's former bridesmaid, friend and confidante, placed a kiss on the head of his victorious cock and said the magic word before wrapping her lips around his cock and...

TWENTY-TWO

Lambert

…The Bayswater hotel room morphing into his own bedroom once more, Bernard Lambert considered the empowering, if brutal, interlude and many more like it –if not the most recent disaster- and knew with certainty his world had undergone a change that might just be permanent.

Indeed, it felt to him as if he were looking back on the exploits of a man he had never actually known.

That lunchtime session with Carly, his wife's closest friend – the same one he had recently travelled to London for with the express intention of replicating with Gianni's blonde of choice; and the one that had turned out so disastrously- had not only been the catalyst for the end of his marriage when Siobhan discovered their tryst, but had also been guaranteed to stir him to rampant erection whenever he took the time to revisit it.

But that was then.

Before the girl from Calcutta had arrived.

Before his seclusion and lack of female company had ensured he would look at his retainer in a different –more interested- way.

Now though, there was nothing.

Everything had changed – and not just his address. For reasons he felt unable to guess at, he was in the grip of a strange obsession regarding a young woman from the sub-continent who was -to put it bluntly when compared to the line of beauties he had bedded; Carly included- plug ugly.

So why was he continually beating himself off to her image?

And why was he humbling himself simply to kneel before her and wash her feet before wetting her toenails with his own saliva before painting them?

And for what?

Apart from his contact with her feet and the smell of her ripe young pussy he was getting nothing from the deal in return.

Worse, at every subsequent pedicure session his "Memsahib" seemed to introduce a new and more humble way for her "Rajiv" to serve her – and, still more disconcertingly, he was acceding to her demands:

"Really, Rajiv," she had tutted during their third session, indulgent smile still in place but seen less frequently during their sessions, "do you truly expect me to remove my own shoes?"

"It's no more than a game," he had told himself as he knelt down to slip black courts from hosed feet, the smell of her sweat soaked hose, far from repulsing him, scattering his senses in a different, more positive, way.

The removal of her footwear from then on becoming an integral part of their "Role-play".

"Should I really have to remove my own pantyhose when I employ a servant to do it for me?" she had asked on another occasion, previously indulgent smile not so indulgent now, testing her power a little.

From then on he had knelt before her and –reverently, as instructed, making sure his hands did not linger- removed her pantyhose.

By the time of their fifth session, he knew she was more comfortable in her role as the smiles used to reassure him during their earlier encounters had vanished completely to be replaced by a horse-face that was both implacable and autocratic.

"She's simply making the most of the fantasy I'm allowing her to experience," he consoled himself; assured by the knowledge he could call a halt to their game at any time and reassured by the deference and respect she showed him at all other times – even if he suspected her earlier awe of him was not quite so prevalent.

But of course, with all such role-playing, there comes a time where the make-believe of fantasy blurs into the stone cold fact of reality; repetition and acceptance reinventing the previously unthinkable as something normal and routine until it found itself ensconced as everyday behaviour and, therefore, extremely difficult, nay impossible, to jettison.

What other reason, he thought, would explain his behaviour of recent weeks? For what other reason would their sessions together have evolved in such a fashion? And why, more importantly, would he have allowed such a degeneration of their respective roles – fantasy or no?

The strangest part of the whole unfolding scenario being the way he actually looked forward to their twice-weekly sessions.

Why else would he have agreed so meekly to polish his servant's shoes after removing them and before pampering her feet?

Why else would he be sucking the brown toes of a young girl who was not only his employee but also a person he considered of sub-standard breeding and intelligence?

And why else, only today in fact, had he agreed when the "Memsahib" insisted, yes, insisted, he wash her pantyhose?

"By hand, Rajiv," she insisted. "They must be given the best of care."

Lambert's head shook as he marvelled at these recent developments, a stirring beneath the bedclothes as he recalled the feel of her pantyhose in his hands lending an irrefutable answer to his questions. The owner of the disturbance immediately throwing back the sheet covering him to stroke the evidence resulting from his obsession; images of the horse-faced and vertically challenged Indian flunkey dancing before his eyes. His resentment at the seemingly inescapable and, he thought, unknowing hold she had on his libido doing nothing to diminish the raging erection triggered by his thoughts of her.

Even if, of course, and totally in keeping with his character, he had again laughed his reaction away as no more than a temporary wormhole of abnormality from which he would soon emerge.

Unscathed.

It was all too ludicrous; he had tried to convince himself with his usual vanity and self-deception -and no more, he considered, than one of the dangers for those in possession of a heightened writer's imagination.

"Think about it," he had urged himself. "She's the only woman –the only person- you have day-to-day contact with."

Hardly surprising, he thought –more so for a man used to female contact and now deprived of it; and despite her ugliness– that he would come to look upon her in a more sexual way; especially given the "Game" they now played with each other. A "Game", moreover, he himself, with an agenda of his own, had angled to bring about.

As a fair man, though others who knew him would hardly describe him in such terms; he could hardly blame a cerebrally challenged Indian serving girl if his attempt at seduction hadn't turned out exactly as he'd planned. A failure for which –given the attraction he knew her pussy felt for him- he pinned squarely on her "Religion".

Also, he was bright enough to know that, as he devolved more and more responsibility to her for the running of both the household and himself, there would be the possibility he could become too reliant on her.

Dependent, in fact.

Worse, he had the impression she was aware of his growing dependence and was not dismayed by it – even if her outward behaviour towards him was as exemplary as ever.

The more she did for him, in fact, the less he seemed able –or was prepared- to do for himself. The escalating depression and demoralisation, coupled with his aforementioned isolation and lack of the female company he was so used to, had set in train a cycle of events he felt quite unable to halt – and worse, found comforting enough to leave as they were.

But then, he would reassure himself:

"Why wouldn't he?"

She was a young girl, for crying out loud!

And none too bright into the bargain.

Her ludicrous religion evidence enough -even if she was capable in the domestic sense- of her intellectual shortcomings.

Hardly feasible to believe she could be a threat to a mature and knowledgeable man such as himself. The house belonged to him, after all. All decisions made inside it were ultimately his. If, for the moment, he chose to give her more responsibility while he licked his wounds, so be it.

Ditto their "Game".

Despite its somewhat perverse nature it changed nothing. It was diversion, nothing more. The girl took pleasure from it and, amazingly, for the moment anyway, so did he.

"And if it ain't broke…?" he questioned aloud, leaving the cliché unfinished.

Satisfied he was under no threat and having once again convinced himself he remained in charge of both the house, his employee, and himself, content to let the situation ride, his hand encircled his cock and pumped.

Furiously.

An image of himself between his servant's legs, tongue lapping feverishly at the folds of her pussy, fetched a gasp from his lips. The thought of himself as he worshipped at the shrine of an ugly Indian girl young enough to be his daughter, pressed buttons consigned so long to the vaults of memory he'd forgotten they ever existed in the first place. The same buttons, he was unable or unwilling to realise, that were taking him on a journey from which he, Bernard Lambert, writer and womaniser, would not return intact.

"Anya," he breathed aloud, short stroking and bucking frantically as his fantasy doppelganger drew the girl's inflamed clitoris into his mouth and began to vacuum suck, fast nearing take-off as he recalled the aroma of the pussy assailing him each time he knelt before her; breathing through his nostrils for a few moments then in a futile attempt at reclamation.

"Anya," he sighed, giving up the attempt as he neared the edge.

"Anya…

"Anya…

"An…yaaaaaaaaaaaaaaaaaaaaah!"

With a final convulsion his cock sent spume after spume of ejaculate towards the ceiling as he continued to scream her name. The evidence of his orgasm and its power arcing short of its target to return to earth and splatter over his thighs. Its owner doing nothing to remove it as he waited for the obfuscating demands of lust and desire to recede and the anti-climax of clarity and reality to kick in.

Finally, and at the exact moment he returned his head to the pillow to wait for the dejection he knew would follow, a cough cut into his consciousness.

Which was when, startled into a sitting position, cock still to hand, he saw her.

In the doorway.

Regarding him stonily.

The look of complete disgust on his young Indian housekeeper's face no less disturbing to him for being completed feigned.

"Anya," he began, "I…"

Without a word she turned on her heel and left the room; taking the tray with the tea she had made for him with her.

CHAPTER TWENTY-THREE

Rajiv & Anya

"How cringingly embarrassing for him," an amused Rajiv laughed as he listened to Anya describe the events of the past hour. "He actually cried out your name?"

"Five times, by my reckoning," she confirmed.

His protégé's facility for simple calculation ensuring he laughed harder.

"My timing was perfect," she congratulated herself. "I was sure he took to his bed earlier to do something more than just "Read. Suspicions I confirmed by a few evenings spent listening at his bedroom door."

Rajiv was still chuckling.

"Knowing the time was right, it was not too difficult to sneak into the room unobserved with my tea tray and watch as he reached crisis – not, you understand, that there was tea in the pot anyway."

Had Rajiv been able to see her he would have noticed how her head shook from side-to-side with wonderment.

"It was the most amazing moment of my life," she told him breathlessly. Simply recalling the event threatening to bring her to another crisis. "My older, handsome, oh so superior, Master was masturbating. Over me! What a comedown for such a racist dog."

Her accompanying laughter was downright evil.

In Calcutta too, Rajiv was also amused, though more by the fact a young woman with the body possessed by his protégé could be surprised at such a response from a man - knowing how frequently and with how much fervour he himself had paid her the self-same compliment.

She was still laughing when her mentor's words took the wind from her sails:

"He will, of course, now ask you to leave."

The charged silence greeting his assertion coming as no surprise to Rajiv.

"What are you saying?" she asked, finally, recovering enough to find her voice.

"It is simple enough, Anya," he explained. "Though his spirits are low, his male pride remains intact. It will, in fact, be the last thing to go. The final barrier standing between you and total ownership. But, as of this moment, he remains in receipt of enough self-regard to be shamed by what you witnessed. Believe me, his next move will be to take the easy way out and ask you to leave his home and his employment."

"No!" she protested, appalled and mortified at such an eventuality; that all her planning, hard work and dreams, could go up in smoke so easily. "You are mistaken, Rajiv. He already kneels before me twice a week to polish my shoes and suck my toes before giving me a pedicure. Today I even had him hand wash my soiled pantyhose for the first time."

On screen, Rajiv was shaking his head.

"Do not delude yourself, Anya," he warned. "It is not the shoes, feet and pantyhose of Anya Jalav your master attends but a fictional memsahib who is part of a game you play."

"But..."

"There are no buts, Anya. You have made solid progress, yes, but he remains some way from the servile canine you intend him to be."

"But he depends on me for so much," Anya protested, anger and fear rising in unison. "He does not lift a finger for himself and seems incapable of doing so. I have made myself indispensable to him. Food, laundry, cleaning, even accounts; all these responsibilities he had ceded to me. He wants for nothing. Where would he find another to do the same?"

On the screen before her, Rajiv was again shaking his head ruefully.

"You will find domestic service agencies the world over inundated with the resumes of 'Indispensable" servants, my dear," he corrected her, discarding Santayana this time to bastardise George Bernard Shaw instead.

Not, he knew, that it made any appreciable difference.

The assertion would have angered her no matter who he plagiarised.

Having no understanding of what the word meant cutting no ice either.

"Calm yourself, Anya, and hear me out," he went on, adopting his most dulcet tones in a charm offensive. "I said: he will ask you to leave. Not that you will go."

"How can I possibly stay if he asks me to…?"

"If you contain your anger and listen to your friend without interrupting it is possible your question might be answered."

Cornwall fell silent for a few seconds, until:

"Well?" she snapped.

Still amused, he shook his head at her demand.

"I'm listening," she reminded him. "Or is your silence just an attempt on your part to cover what you know to be a mistake?"

"Anya, Anya!" he chided. "You are not very gracious to a friend who has only your best interests at heart. However, I shall, this once, overlook your ingratitude and…"

"Get on with it, I hope," she finished for him; yet more evidence, if he required it, of the hot-headedness walking hand-in-hand with youth.

"Youth" itself that went on to add:

"I am very angry with you, Rajiv. You mentioned nothing of this when you advised me to walk in on him."

Rajiv waited for the storm to break.

"Had you done so," she railed at him, "I might have had second thoughts before I agreed to such a thing. You are the one, after all, who prattles on and on about the value of 'Patience'"

"Anya, Anya," he tut-tutted, "have you so little faith in your uncle Rajiv?"

"Faith is hard earned," she reminded him; adding, as if by way of a threat:

"But very easily withdrawn."

He laughed good-naturedly at her attempt to intimidate him, knowing -as he did- that this latest "Mini-crisis" would soon be resolved.

"Then I shall restore what you appear to have momentarily lost," he told her, voice assured and even.

In Cornwall, she waited; biting into a lip with growing irritation.

"Within the next hour or so," he began finally, "the telephone connecting you to the house will ring and he will ask you to go over."

"Yes?" she asked. "So?"

"You will," he went on, "find your "Master" waiting for you."

"Obviously… Get on with it."

Rajiv chuckled, genuinely amused by her reaction, prior to becoming serious:

"Before he has a chance to say anything, this is what I want you to tell him…"

CHAPTER TWENTY-FOUR

Siobhan

"Oh, my Lord!" he had cried into the duvet; wishing for nothing less at that moment than the arrival of a lightning bolt to crisp both himself and his humiliation to ashes.

How long had she been there, he wondered?

Had she heard him cry out her name?

Three… no, four… or was it five, times?

His head sunk back on the pillow and he closed his eyes with despair.

To have sunk so low, he thought; the knowledge that not seven months prior to this latest humiliation he had been the husband of an admirable wife –as well as the lover of a host of sexy women- doing nothing to lessen his shame.

Women, in the presence of whom, his Indian housekeeper would have trouble finding, let alone holding, the proverbial candle.

Now though, he would have to face her after she had seen him as he…

And not just seen him.

He had actually called out her name after the fashion of a lovesick third-former.

Five times.

The whole business made him sick at heart; recalling, for some reason, his last conversation with Siobhan – if so one-sided a discourse could be described in such a way.

"I've spent the past seventeen years married to an animal," she had told him, the venom in her voice as dismaying to him seven months later as it had been on that fateful Monday; replaying the scene as she dumped the last case containing his belongings on the front step of the North London home they had once shared and would soon belong to her. Her Nordic features cold with disdain as she made him wait on the step of the Primrose Hill house he had bought before they married and loved so much.

The same house, shortly to be his no longer and necessitating the move to Cornwall.

"What does that say about me?" she raged. "That I could eat, sleep and fornicate with a dog and be none the wiser?"

A question forcing her into a correction:

"Actually," she told him, "I'm being unnecessarily hard on dogs. Canines at least possess the virtue of loyalty. You're only loyalty is to yourself and your faithless prick."

"Siobhan…?" he began, still, even at that stage, believing he could turn things around between them.

"Not enough for you to slip your shop-soiled cock into one of the brain-dead tarts illiterate enough to be impressed with you," she overrode him. "Oh no! You have to give the snake an airing for the benefit of my closest friend."

Her face twisted into an uncharacteristic sneer as she thought it over.

"Correction," she told him; sneer still evident: "my former closest friend."

The memory of lost and irretrievable camaraderie opening up yet another, more maddening, line of thought to her:

"Was Carly the only one?" she asked; face whiter than he had ever seen it. "Or just the only traitorous bitch I found out about? Is there a chance I might have a friend left you haven't actually fucked?"

He was ready to lie in regard of the first option –well, all of them really- when her implacable expression became animated; features below the short, beautifully coiffed, blonde hair twisting into a mask of malevolence.

"You disgust me!"

"It meant nothing," he told her, berating himself for spouting the adulterer's cliché of choice even as he used it.

"It was just sex," he assured her. "I love you, Siobh…"

The power behind her slap stunned him to silence and immobility; preventing either movement or complaint when she repeated the maneuver with her other hand. Neither the imprint of her hands upon cheeks already scarlet with guilt, or pain from the blows themselves, registered with him.

No.

It was the intent written across her flawless features as hands equally as flawless hurtled towards contact that left him feeling sick at heart with the knowledge he might finally have lost her.

The adulterer, in common with the criminally insane -and despite copious evidence to the contrary- credulous enough to believe he would always remain beyond the reach of the law; whether that law be fiscal or matrimonial.

During their seventeen years of marriage neither had raised a hand to each other and it was the fact she had done just that, and with total justification, that so discomfited him as he stared at her numbly, stinging cheeks secondary to the knowledge things between them had reached such a pass and the fact he had no idea how to arrange things so they came through it together.

Worse, however, was the look of utter contempt and undying hatred she had lasered towards him.

A "look" telling him, finally, there was no hope of either appeal or reprieve and that whatever it was they had shared until that moment was now no more than yesterday's dirty laundry.

Taking up the suitcase with the last of his belongings as his own front-door slammed in his face, mustering as much dignity as he could in the situation - knowing her at least well enough to know any further attempt at reconciliation was futile- he had turned on his heel and crunched across the gravel to his Alfa Romeo.

Leaving home, Primrose Hill, and wife, forever.

Now, back in the Cornwall to which he'd subsequently been transplanted, facing a situation he would never have known had he not been so faithless in the first place; the familiar feelings of guilt and loss whenever he thought of the former wife he had treated so shabbily set his spirits on an even more pronounced downward spiral. The self-pity that had seemed his one constant since "Black Monday", as he described it, searching for extenuating reasons that could make his sins more... more…

Finally, giving up on his search for any mitigating circumstances that would, at least, give him a semi-believable excuse and allow him to portray himself as a victim -the usual outcome whenever he considered the cost of the deceit that had taken from his life the best thing ever to enter it- he again acknowledged the blame as his and his alone. Not for the first time, he cursed the stupidity that had thrown away his life with Siobhan for a string of illicit, and mostly unsatisfying, affairs.

The above being a scenario he felt compelled to revisit from time to time,

And one guaranteed to depress him for a decent interval afterwards until his spirits were restored.

This time, however, a more recent shame had relegated the memory of how his former marriage ended into that of supporting player.

A "More recent shame" possessing enough power to cut into what had been, until now, his most abject memory.

Not only had he been discovered masturbating like a schoolboy with a crush on his teacher by the housekeeper he employed –the same housekeeper whose feet he was attending on a twice-weekly basis- but, also, he had actually cried out her name as he ejaculated over her desk.

And more than just once.

Head flopping back against the pillow, he knew there was only one course of action open to him.

He had let the situation degenerate too far and it had to stop.

The sessions with the memsahib –as perversely enjoyable as he seemed to find them- had to end, and…

He gave it some thought and reached his decision.

"Yes," he told himself. "If what just happened were not to be repeated then only one course of action is open to me."

Fighting back the images of fixation that had led him to his current shameful exposure and, if anything, seemed stronger in spite of it, he steeled himself to do what the situation demanded.

His housekeeper had to be sacked.

CHAPTER TWENTY-FIVE

Understanding

It was almost two hours after having discovered him: "in flagrante solo", so to speak; that Anya Jalav took her "Master's" call and made her way to the main house for the first time at such a late hour.

Her "Master", still missing nothing in her regard -despite his embarrassment at having to face her- noting her casual dress immediately. Mortification to one side, he preferred instead to note how the nipples of her –deliberately- unfettered breasts strained against the fabric of a tight tee shirt that ended some inches above the waist. The uncharacteristically contemporary look on her part revealing a flat stomach and –to his astonishment- pierced, belly button, while tight black shorts he hadn't seen until that moment completed the look; highlighting the smooth skin of her powerful brown thighs and diverting him from the humiliation that had prompted him to request her presence in the first place.

But it was what she said –overriding the anxiety inspired by her conversation with Rajiv to take his advice and make sure she spoke before her "Master"- that amazed him:

"…I cannot tell you how ashamed I am for my stupidity, Master Lambert," she told him, not a moment or so after entering his study.

The young servant's nerves and inner anxiety calmed as a look of complete bafflement transformed her employer's face and took both wind and intended course from his sails.

"It was an unforgivable mistake, Master," she hurried on in her role of supplicant. "I should never have entered without knocking. The fact I was bringing tea in an attempt to cheer you from your recent depression –as well as by way of a thank you for allowing me to live my dreams in a small way- in no way condones such an error. I should have better than to intrude upon your private space - no matter how correct my motives."

The look on his face was picture perfect, she thought –if one's tastes ran to cartoons- and made her pause a moment in order to give silent thanks.

Not for the first time, she scolded herself for having ever doubted Rajiv. As he had said it would be, so it appeared to be turning out. With nothing more than the few simple sentences he had suggested, her employer had again been placed firmly on the back foot.

Also again, and as a plus to her relief, the knowledge she was "Managing" her "Master" sent shivers of pure pleasure the length of her spine; emboldening her in the desire to make him submit to her - and not some role-playing memsahib.

"J-Just the same," he stammered, his usual superiority with her absent: "I'm sorry you had to see… You know?"

"You have no need to explain, Master," she assured him, relieving him of the necessity, restoring his self-belief and taking control at the same time. "You are a virile man with a man's needs. It is a wholly natural activity."

"Then…" he began hesitantly, her tolerance placing his intention to ask her to leave on the backburner; her use of the description: "Virile" –and as intended- not only condoning what he'd seen as his shame but, as Rajiv insisted it would, making it seem manly also.

"Then you aren't…?"

He swallowed with difficulty before being able to continue:

"Then you aren't shocked?"

With a look of infinite understanding, she shook her head in the negative; toothy smile tolerant. Being off-duty, as it were, she had allowed her long, raven black, hair to remain loose, allowing it to hang free over her shoulders – a new development he did not miss and she did not miss him not missing. His interest in her, she was pleased to detect, still as strong; regardless of the nature of the situation in which he found himself.

Or, more to the point, in which she had found him.

"As I explained," she began, soothing his anxiety on the subject of her reaction; "it is a perfectly natural activity for a handsome and virile male and did not shock me in the slightest. Though…"

She paused.

"Go on, Anya," he urged, despite his foreboding about what she might actually have to say.

"Forgive me, Master," she began, more than ever the deferential servant, "but I was a little shocked to hear you call my name as you…"

It was a sentence requiring no ending – especially if the instantly reddened cheeks of Bernard Lambert were to be believed – the social standing of the young girl responsible for their reddening as much to blame as her words.

"Look, er, Anya," he began, "I…"

"Do not be embarrassed, Master," she told him, again relieving him of the obligation to explain. "It is not unusual for employers to desire their servants – even servants as ugly as me."

She waited for him to refute the assertion in regard of her face -or to at least soften it- but neither example of diplomacy seemed forthcoming - despite his having, not long before, brought himself to completion with the help of that very same image.

Promising herself she would extract a high and painful price, for both insult and hypocrisy, when he was hers.

"You have been working hard on your book and I am the only person you see," she continued; anger taking a back seat. "It is perfectly understandable."

Her Master nodded his agreement, much relieved. Though, with the situation pretty much resolved -that same "Relief" subsiding and the need to find a new housekeeper and lust object on the backburner again- Bernard Lambert found himself becoming more than a little irritated at being: "Understood".

The suspicion he was being patronised by a person of her years and standing not playing well to his boundless –and still intact- narcissism and self-importance.

"As I hope you have noticed, Master," Anya Jalav continued; "I have attempted during my time with you to become as useful as possible."

Lambert nodded; the truism one he was unable to refute - even if he had no idea where she was going with it. The thought occurring to him that, perhaps, she was going to try and take advantage of what she'd seen and ask for a pay rise.

In the years to come he would wish she had done just that.

"As I have explained," she said, lying through her teeth, "my religion is very ancient and very strict and my adherence to its rules and teachings is to the letter."

Lambert listened politely, if impatiently; unable to work out how her devotions involved him at this point.

"It is, as I have said," she went on, "a religion peculiar to the region of India where I was born. There is no book containing its teachings and knowledge of its origins and disciplines is passed by way of one mouth to another's. Just the same, it is very strict and, because of this, I am afraid many things more sophisticated people such as yourself take for granted are forbidden."

Lambert waited, still in the dark as to where she was going with such a line.

"It prevents any man," she explained, "other than a man of my same religion, from touching me and -given I have no intention of ever marrying or entering into partnership- I have resigned myself to remaining…"

"Anya," he came in, believing he saw her purpose and made genuinely uncomfortable with it; "I really have no wish to hear this. It is most inappropriate."

The smirk suppressed by his servant was as derisory as it instant.

"As 'Inappropriate' as you sucking your servant's toes and playing with yourself over the sight of her panty-clad pussy," she was about to say, biting back the rebuke just in time to hear him protest further.

"I'd really prefer that you didn't speak in such a…"

"Please, Master," she asked, talking over him for what would be the first, though not the last, time; "this will not take long."

Conceding to her request, he waited; miffed at her interruption; but, and despite himself, curious to hear what it was she had to say.

"Nothing is dearer to my heart and my faith than ensuring my employer is as happy and content with the service I provide him," she continued; winning a huge inner sigh from that same employer as she again banged on about the "Religion" and "Faith" he had known nothing on until a short while ago.

"Within my religion," she continued, drawing another inner sigh, "it is a point of no small pride to a conscientious servant. Something, I hope you agree, I have earned the right to be called."

Lambert nodded reassuringly, attempting to bring their discussion to a close.

"That's refreshing to hear, Anya," he told her, as impatient now as he was fast becoming irritated. "But I don't understand the point you're trying to make and it is getting a little late."

"Apologies, Master, I am not making myself clear. What I am saying, is that you need not make love to yourself alone."

At first he thought he had misheard, his jaw dropping downward a spit-second later.

"The next time you feel in need of release," she explained to him, dashing any raised hopes she was offering herself to him her words might have triggered, "simply ask me to come to your room and you will be able to find it in the presence of a flesh and blood woman rather than on your own."

The look on his face was pure incredulity and Anya had much trouble keeping her face straight.

"The constraints of my religion forbid that you touch me, of course," she lied –said: "Religion" not even existing; let alone in a position to "Forbid" anything- "but you will at least have a living presence within sight as you satisfy yourself."

"Anya," he began in a thick voice, unable to quite believe he had just heard what he'd heard and drawing himself up authoritatively - or as authoritatively as one man could who had just been caught masturbating by his housekeeper; "I have no idea what Indian employers expect from their retainers. But this is England. Such things are not done and I'll thank you not to mention it again."

She bowed her head in submission.

An actress playing a penitent.

Even if her efforts were more Cotswolds Am/Dram than Stratford RSC.

Lambert's young flunkey loving the way she was messing with his head and amused he could think it was perfectly acceptable to polish her shoes and hand-wash her pantyhose while, at the same time, deeming it perverse she should offer him a chance to masturbate over her.

"It will be as you say, Master," she said. "You are a proud man and I suspected your answer would be as it is. I shall make no reference to such a possibility again. But, please, do not be offended. My one intention was to try and be helpful to you."

Lambert nodded and she smiled back at him pleasantly; no

trace of mockery or contempt –none that he could detect, anyway- visible on that "Equine" face.

"Now, if we are finished," she began; "I need to return to my quarters and shower. It is late, as you say, and there is much to be done around the house tomorrow."

With another warm smile and not waiting for him to dismiss her, she had gone, leaving Lambert to pour himself a much needed scotch and marvel at what had just transpired; amazed that his prim and equine little servant could have made such a proposition to him – despite her alter ego known to him as the "Memsahib".

Had he really just heard his servant offer herself up as eye candy for him to masturbate over?

Just what kind of a religion was she a part of exactly?

As aware as he was of the fact she came from a region and a country with a culture as different and –stupidity and condescension usual to him kicking in- inferior to his own as beer to wine; what she had suggested left him feeling shocked. The perversity of it –and from the lips of a girl of such a type- was staggering.

A proposition, when considered at greater length, becoming still more shocking.

Could she really have thought he would go along with such a depraved and demeaning proposal?

Given his overweening self-regard, it did not suggest itself to him for one moment that his own lustful behaviour towards the girl could have prompted such an offer; even less that there may have been an ulterior motive behind it. The suspicion she might have pitched it simply to divert him from his original intention to terminate her employment not –given his low opinion of her intelligence- something he gave a second's thought.

Another oversight that, without his knowing it, added another bar to the cell she was constructing for the purpose of incarcerating him.

The same oversight hardly likely to compete with the stirring at his groin that ensured his swift progress upstairs.

CHAPTER TWENTY-SIX

The Envelope

As had been intended by her proposition, Bernard Lambert was soon obsessing over their conversation of a few nights previous, unable to shake a growing desire to experience what she had offered to him.

As demeaning as he considered it to be.

For some reason he found the image of himself, as he knelt before and stroked his cock while she looked on, impassive and untouchable, deliciously perverse; even if he knew it would be impossible to accept such a state of affairs and retain his dignity as master of the household.

An acceptance of her offer he knew was proscribed to him, both by the position he held in her regard and his own self-respect – remaining off limits to him, despite her assurances that what she suggested was a: "perfectly natural activity for a handsome and virile male".

It was as he was about to kneel before her and remove her shoes, at the commencement of the twice-weekly game he had been forced to mention resuming when she stayed silent on the subject –cleverly reversing the norm and placing him in the position of supplicant- that she mentioned the "Gift".

"Before we begin, Master," she began, pointing to a large brown envelope that rested on the kitchen table, her use of the honorific assuring him playtime had yet to begin, "I have something for you."

Averting her eyes coyly then:

"Something I hope you will like," her sudden shyness as he knelt before her triggering his curiosity.

"A gift?" he asked, surprised, his impatience to get to grips with the shapely feet occupying that occupied so much of his thoughts lately put aside for the moment.

"For me?"

"Yes, Master," she said, looking up at him now. "A small something by way of a thank you for all that you do for me."

He made to move towards the table and collect his reward but she stopped him.

"No, Master," she told him, almost forcefully, before softening her tone: "The surprise will be better if you open it when you are alone."

Lambert shrugged, even more intrigued. "Very well, I'll open it in my study before I get down to some work."

"Thank you, Master," she thanked him, tone deferential though she found herself suppressing a smirk at his mention of the study and the non-existent "Work" he made a pretence of doing there.

He was about to lower himself once more, hands already reaching for her feet to begin the game, when she again stopped him.

"If you please, Master…"

Catching himself in mid crouch he raised himself to his full height – a tad annoyed, she thought.

"Was there something else, Anya?"

She nodded, adopting a hopeful expression, as if about to appeal to his generosity.

"Before you attend my feet," she said, choice of words no accident, "I was hoping you would grant me a favour."

"Anything's possible, Anya," he assured her light-heartedly. "What did you have in mind?"

"You have already been so wonderful to me by indulging my little fantasy that I will understand if my request is too much," she went on.

"I will have no right to be offended if you refuse what I ask. You are the Master and all decisions are yours. But it would mean so much to me and I do so look forward to our little…" she lowered her eyes, as if having to overcome crippling timidity in order to mention it "…game."

Lambert waited, wondering what it was exactly she wanted. Of course, being the cynic he was in regard on the subject of people and financial gain; his first thought was an obvious one.

Money.

"What is it you want to ask, Anya?" he found himself pressed into asking when she remained silent.

Seated on the wooden chair below him she hesitated,

conveying to him the impression she was unsure of just how to phrase her request of him.

Finally, with a slight stiffening of her seated posture, she began:

"I just wanted to ask if, instead of addressing me as 'Memsahib' during our pretend time together, you would…"

Anya allowed her voice to tail off as if the enormity of her request were too much; knowing her prey by now and certain he felt secure enough in his patronising superiority to be compelled enough to prompt her.

She was not disappointed.

"Go ahead, Anya," he urged, all magisterial authority now she was in the position of supplicant; still in denial regarding the gradual diminishment of his own role in the house; his conceit bolstered by his contempt for the intelligence of the servant he now lusted after. "No need for shyness now."

"Sorry, Master," she apologised. "Forgive me for hesitating but what I wish to ask is…"

Again she allowed her voice to tail off.

And again he came in.

"Just ask me, Anya," he insisted. "I will not hold it against you and I can always say no if you ask too much."

Anya nodded; her tiny smile intended to let him know her fears had been allayed.

"I was hoping, Master," she began, "that –if you would be so good- you could address me by my first name when performing my pedicure?"

Lambert waited for more.

And waited.

Was that really the big favour she wished to ask?

"Is that all, Anya?" he asked, a little dismissive as she nodded an affirmative.

"Why so nervous about such a small request?"

"I would also like you to…"

"Yes?" he urged, realising there was more.

"I would like you to address me as…" Again her eyes lowered demurely. "As… Ms Anya," she almost whispered.

"Sorry?" he asked, genuinely not having heard, her voice so small.

Her eyes raised and held his, imploringly, he thought.

"I should very much like it, Master, if you could address me as Ms Anya?"

"Ms…" he began, unsure if he liked the idea or not; far preferring the play honorific of "Memsahib", voice trailing off as he considered her petition.

"Yes, Master," she nodded, knowing he was in need of reassurance; her tone becoming more beseeching as a consequence. "It would make the game seem more real to me if I could not only put myself in the memsahib's position but hear my own name spoken when addressed by my servant."

She gauged his reaction to being described as her "Servant" for the first time and, judging it had set no alarm bells ringing with him, continued on:

"That way," she explained, "it would really seem as if it were me who was the beautiful lady of a great and respectable English household."

After a few seconds of thought, Lambert began to laugh, genuinely amused. People, he reminded himself, head shaking with wonder, never ceased to amaze with the monoliths they constructed from trivialities.

If calling the girl by her first name as he performed her pedicure pleased her as she said it would -and, more importantly, gave him access that could lead to greater intimacy- he had no problem in doing so whatsoever.

"I hope I do not cause you offence, Master," she asked, inquiry sincere, unsure if his laughter were an indication of a positive or negative response.

"Not in the slightest, Anya…"

He paused with a teasing smile; before:

"Or should I say: 'Ms Anya'?"

Upon hearing the words signifying his agreement, Anya laughed herself, relieved despite her growing confidence.

"In fact," he continued, about to save her a suggestion of her own and, in the so doing, play right into her hands, "why don't we make it even more real for you?"

"Then…" she began, all feigned and girlish excitement, "then you do not mind addressing me in such a way?"

"Of course not," he said, pooh-poohing her misgivings, before adding with a jocular wink: "Ms Anya."

She smiled delightedly and actually clapped her hands together.

"What possible harm could it do?" he went on. "There's no point to acting if we remain fixed to our everyday roles."

"Thank you, Master!" she gushed.

"And, as I say," he offered, returning to the offer he had been diverted from proposing, "we can make it seem even more real to you."

"How so, Master?" she asked, all excitement and ears.

"Instead of addressing me as Rajiv why not address me as Bernard."

Again she clapped her hands before her Master-cum-Santa.

"Or," she began, fair gushing with her feigned enthusiasm, "if we wished to make our game even more authentic, we could follow the English custom and I could just call you 'Lambert'. "

Silence greeted her suggestion and just for a second she thought she had –as Rajiv had warned her she could be prone to do- gone too far.

"Apologies, Master," she added, swiftly switching to damage limitation mode. "I act above myself."

Her appeal to the "Great man" having the desired effect.

"Nonsense, Anya," he scoffed, the same man who had seldom agreed with even the most minute criticism of either his talent or his behaviour going on to add: "Never let it be said that Bernard Lambert takes himself too seriously."

A sense of relief and, she had to admit, accomplishment for having led him so gently by the nose he had yet to sense the insistent tug upon his nostrils, greeted what he saw as no more than largesse with an agenda and she knew was capitulation.

Yet another brick dismantled from the main building and handed to her for safe keeping; the man gifting it to her totally oblivious to the possibility it might never be returned.

Finally, smiling down at her hopeful and plug ugly face, he lowered himself to his knees, assuring her as he did so:

" 'Lambert' it is…"

Waiting a moment then, before smiling again and remembering to add:

"Ms Anya."

CHAPTER TWENTY-SEVEN

The Gift

Fresh from hand washing her pantyhose after their "Session" - only her presence in the basement, supervising him as he went about the task, preventing her Master from having his way with the nylon that had so recently clung to her shapely, if prematurely matronly, legs- he closed his study door behind him, took up a letter-opener from his desk and sliced open the large brown envelope containing his "Gift".

Retrieving it from the envelope for a first inspection, he wondered, for a couple of seconds, no more, why his servant would make him a present of underwear.

It was only as they were held up for a closer inspection he realised that not only was that underwear not of the male kind but it belonged to his servant.

And worse.

It was underwear he had seen before.

Compounding his sense of foreboding, the pink cotton panties staring back at him were neither new nor, his nose told him, laundered.

His panic instantly went off the scale as he took it as her way of telling him she knew of the crimes he committed in her quarters after packing her off to the shops.

"Oh, my Lord!" he wailed to himself, even more mortified than on the last occasion when she had found him both in flagrante and delicto.

Bad enough she had caught him masturbating over her, he knew, without her suspecting he had been getting his rocks off with the contents of her laundry basket. His growing anxiety ensuring he began backtracking over his actions. An anxiety quieting somewhat when those actions assured him she could have found nothing to make her suspect such an eventuality.

"How could she possibly know, after all?" he asked himself out loud. Unless, of course, she was indeed blessed with that prescience he had previously given thanks to providence for not placing in her possession.

"No," he assured himself. "I'm safe. A domestic goddess she may be; but Nostradamus she ain't." Relief washing over him as he became convinced his horny schoolboy tracks had been covered and this was less accusation than…

He paused in his perusal of the underwear, realising he did not have the first clue what the panties were about - his puzzlement turning to disbelief as he took a closer look at his gift and was immediately thrown into a dilemma. Unsure whether to be outraged or excited as the familiar pungency greeting his nostrils triggered the usual longings. Those same longings he experienced during his weekly intrusion into her quarters and his time in the kitchen, painting her nails from his position at her feet while he sneaked glances between her legs.

His dilemma unable to prevent him going to autopilot and pressing the soft pink fabric to his face that he may breathe in the scent of his servant more deeply – even if the outrage he felt for what he was coming to see as her mockery of him prevented a fuller enjoyment of his self-conditioning.

For the first time, it occurred to him that what he saw as harmless role-playing –an innocent little game he had devised as a way for her to enjoy a long held fantasy of being a lady far above her station- was beginning to get out of… out of…

Too far absorbed in the scent laying siege to his olfactory senses, he found himself unable to complete the sentence.

"And anyway," he told himself in his usual evasive way when dealing with uncomfortable situations and personal truths, "this is not about me."

He had simply tried to do something nice for the girl; pretending to be her Indian flunkey while addressing her with respect and performing the same task she had seen performed for her former "Memsahib". If he were to suspect for one second the horse-faced little ingrate regarded such kindness as weakness on his part, seeing it as a way of becoming more familiar with him in the way of equals, he would –he snapped his fingers- stop it like that.

And the evidence, he had to admit, was not good.

Had he not just come from a session where she had virtually begged him to address her with an obsequious "Ms Anya"?

Even if it had been his idea for her to call him by his surname.

Their "Game" progressing on just those lines before he completed her pedicure and allowed himself to be supervised by his servant as he laundered her hose.

Assessing the above, it became plain to him he had allowed his servant to become too familiar.

"As always, Lambert, old son," he said aloud; chiding himself for the largesse and liberality even those people close to him had been unable to detect; "you're far too soft for your own good.

Fair to say, he placed no store whatsoever in her ludicrous religion, but he was a firm believer in fate - and if fate had decreed she be a servant then it had done so with good reason.

"Some people," he snarled to himself, becoming angrier by the second as he pondered her ingratitude, "take kindness for weakness and try to exploit it."

Throwing the letter-opener to the desk he brought the offending garment to within a few inches of his face and stared at it with fury.

"How dare she!" he hissed; words barely leaving his tongue and about to launch himself into an invective of outrage for his ill use, when, as if of its own volition, that same appendage snaked towards the gusset.

The same gusset, he knew as he closed his eyes to the sight, he could see soiled with emissions from her pussy.

Pictorial evidence he was in the process of backing up with that of taste. An action, it seemed, taken without his being aware of having willed it, separate of his conscious preference; overriding whatever course of action emotions of a less obsessive kind may have intended.

That obsession so strong, it appeared, its gratification could make a case for the most insulting of behaviour.

A case he was making at the very moment the thought occurred to him.

"But was it that insulting, anyway?" he asked himself; self-interest already justifying his servant's behaviour in order to better enjoy it, sure it was in some way connected with her antediluvian faith.

"This 'Religion' of hers might be strange but, in his opinion, what religion wasn't? His anger, an intact, if shriveling, rational side reasoned, seemed to stem more from the fact she had reached the conclusion he was in need of such stimuli; rather than the reasons she had actually put forward for arriving there.

Continuing on in the same vein, it wasn't long before he convinced himself his outrage was no more than misplaced pride on his part.

Continuing on in the same delusional vein.

For all he knew this "Spiritual advisor" of hers might even have been the one to suggest she make him the gift.

And, if that was the case, wasn't it at least an honest faith?

She had said it of her religion herself and he had no reason to disbelieve it was anything other than she described:

"Strict but understanding of human need".

How many of the so-called: "Accepted" forms of worship, after all, could claim to be that? Not only taking needs such as his into account, but, far from ostracising them, actively encourage their gratification in, what was he now acknowledged, a harmless, if off-the-wall, way.

"When all's said and done," he told himself; the same recidivism ensuring his writing remained in the time-warp that had led to its neglect going into full swing; "she comes from a more backward, less sophisticated place and culture than mine. Such behaviour is probably the norm."

Her offer, he considered –no matter how… strange- had been made with nothing but the intention of providing him a service. That "Service" extended as a consolation for his being without a woman for the first time and the understandable difficulties in which such a situation placed him.

Obsession once again having managed to smother objections from the less credulous, less needy of his faculties -convincing himself he had divined her true intention and no mockery was intended- he approached her "Gift" from a different angle.

If she found nothing untoward in her master masturbating over a pair of her unlaundered panties why should he take the opposite flight path?

A question bringing a smile to his lips as he answered:

"No reason at all."

Double-checking he had remembered to lock his study door; Bernard Lambert headed for the sofa.

Trousers unbuttoned and at half-mast before he reached it.

The Master of the house quite oblivious to the fact that, in her quarters above the garage, his Indian housekeeper was consulting her own growing library of fantasies; equally as excited as she lay back on her bed.

Armed with the trusty black dildo that had been FedEx-ed to her by Rajiv as a "Gift" of her own, she peeled off the latest pair of sopping panties she intended he be gifted and picked a number…

CHAPTER TWENTY-EIGHT

Face Saving

"…What could have possessed you to do such a thing, Anya?" Bernard Lambert thundered at her as she stood before him in his study; dressed casually in jeans and tee shirt, her feet bare.

Waving the envelope in front of her, his anger was stoked rather than tempered by the desires instilled in him by her gift and the shameless way he had succumbed to them.

His earlier thoughts of religious tolerance holding sway only until he had pumped his seed into the soft pink cotton wrapped around the head of his overworked penis.

Only afterwards, need satisfied, did the ramifications of what her gift meant for their future working relationship did he convince himself that a reprimand for her temerity in making him that gift was in order.

Now, some two hours after the event, she stood before him as he went about delivering it.

"You are a young girl," he ranted on as she stood demurely before him and accepted it, eyes lowered. "My housekeeper. What were you thinking?"

"It was something I thought you would appreciate, Master," she began, looking up at him for the first time, expression earnest; acting anxiously but in reality quite unconcerned by anger on his part she knew was without substance.

Her confidence in regard of him these days beginning to accept no limits.

Almost.

The deal, after all, had still to be sealed.

"When I explained to my mentor how I had walked in upon you as you…"

Lambert felt his cheeks colour, grateful she saw fit not to complete the sentence.

"He was very angry with me, Master," she said, completing the elliptical. "Even more angry when I told him of the offer I had made to keep you company as you…"

Again she broke off, knowing he knew exactly to which offer she referred.

"That is why he suggested I give you my worn underwear," she added.

"Anya," he began, in control of himself, but only just, "I do not appreciate my personal situation being discussed with a stranger – 'Spiritual guide' or no."

He paused, reining in his growing anger.

"In future," he began when he considered himself under control again, "I would appreciate it if you left me out of your discussions with this… guru."

"But Master, my guide made the suggestion with only your best interests at heart. It was…"

"From now on, Anya," he cut her off, "you would do best by getting it into your head that I am the best –and only- judge of my own 'Best interests'."

"Please, Master, I apologise profusely for any offence and I know my spiritual guide will extend his contriteness also. We made the gesture with no other intention than to… than to…" she reached for the apposite phrase "…than to help you satisfy yourself."

A provocative turn of phrase as it turned out.

" 'Satisfy myse…?' " he exploded; outrage too impatient to repeat the simple two word assertion in full. "Do I look like the kind of old lecher who needs such 'Gestures' to help…? To help…?"

Anya bit back a fit of the giggles as he struggled to articulate just what it was he did need help with; knowing, as she did, that not looking like an old lecher did not preclude one from being exactly that.

"Please, Master," she begged, tone and demeanour as submissive as she was capable; aware she needed to seem as unthreatening as she could at this stage, feeling utterly confident now in her ability to manage him and pull such a feat off.

"No insult was intended and my guide and I had only your very best interests at heart. Please believe me, Master, there is nothing unnatural or disrespectful intended by such a gift. Believe me, quite the opposite was anticipated. It is most natural for a compliment of such a kind to be extended to a non-believer who has conceived a passion for a believer.

" 'Natural!' " he exploded. "Anya, do you hear yourself? I can scarcely believe my ears."

"But, Master, it is no more than a harmless way of relieving the non-believer's frustration at not being able to touch that which he so desires."

He stared at her, askance; a look intended to know by just how much she was overstating his interest in her – even if she wasn't.

"I realise there is no romantic attraction, Master," she reassured him, his thoughts all too obvious to her.

"It is simply a matter of contact."

A relaxation of his neck muscles indicated a softening of temper as she went on:

"I just happen to be the female fortunate enough to be in your presence most frequently." She told him, accelerating that softening with flattery.

"You are, after all, a handsome man who is used to the attentions of the opposite sex – something, if I may be so bold, that is conspicuously lacking at the moment. Your need for solitude in order to write has taken you from London and your usual routine; and the village, I would think, is not exactly overflowing with women of the standard you have come to expect. It is hardly surprising a virile man such as yourself, and in the prime of life, would come to have desires for the only woman with whom he has contact on a daily basis – even if that woman is his servant."

The flattering and face-saving construction of her words cajoled the anger –ersatz as it had been to begin with- from his expression and told her she had taken the right tack by appealing, as always, to his vanity."

"Things have been a little… difficult for me recently, Anya," he agreed, self-pity kicking in.

"Of course, Master," she agreed. "I am with you every day and I see how unjustly a gifted author such as yourself is treated. That you show such forbearance does much credit to you. My admiration for the way you deal with the obstacles life places before you one of the reasons I wished to do something pleasant for you – the many kindnesses you have shown me since I first arrived in your home another."

As she watched him mull over her words she found herself,

and not for the first time, amazed at the capacity for both undeserved self-pity and self-delusion that could allow him to swallow untruths of such a nature without the merest of attempts to consult self-awareness before doing so.

"Perhaps I was a little hasty," he admitted, mollified and with –amazingly, she thought- pride still intact.

"Then you understand?" she asked, hopefully.

He nodded.

"And you are not offended?"

"No, Anya," he smiled, king of his castle again, with all the deference and respect such a position entailed.

Anya smiled back as if she were the most relieved housekeeper on the planet.

"I'm not offended," he went on, conceding the point with magnanimity as he knew he should - the offending garment had, after all, just supplied him with the most powerful orgasm of his life.

"Surprised still? Yes," he told her. "But I realise you were just being a more than usually conscientious servant."

"Thank you, Master," she said with a sigh of relief; her every action pre-rehearsed; gratified to see his eyes flickering downwards to her bare feet and red painted toenails as they peeked from her jeans.

"Am I to take it, Master," she went on, "that you would like such gifts on a regular basis."

His gasp was audible.

"Er, Anya… Look… I…"

She let him stew for a few moments longer before she came to his rescue; loving the way she was able to tongue-tie such a handsome older man despite having had nothing of either his advantages or life experiences.

"My guide said I was allowed to make you the offer," she continued. "He said I should not be offended if you refused but to consider it a great honour if you were to accept. That it was the least I could do after making you the offer that had made him so angry and one I should have realised I had no authority to make."

His servant easily read the expression with which he greeted her statement:

"What the fuck kind of religion is this?" she knew he asked.

"I shall take your silence as a negative, Master," she told him. "I take no offen…"

"No, Anya," he came in quickly. "It is a well-intended offer. A little strange, I can do no more than admit. But I would not insult your beliefs by refusing it."

"Thank you, Master," she gushed. "My mentor was as perceptive as ever when he assured me you were different to the herd of men. I shall do my best to make sure my gifts to you are as fragrant as they can be."

"Anya"…" he gasped, unsure what thrilled him more: the surreal and perverse nature of their conversation, or the prospect of a regular supply of her soiled underwear.

"I shock you, Master. I am too bold," she said contritely. "I sometimes forget that though these matters are normal within our religion they can often disturb outsiders."

"Let's speak no more of it," he told her with what he saw as largesse; even if speaking more of "It" was exactly what he wanted to do. "I accept and appreciate your offer and extend my thanks to your 'Mentor', as you describe him."

She could see him hesitate; something more on his mind:

"I must say, Anya; your religion is a very tolerant one."

"It is as tolerant as it is strict, Master. But please, before you go on, I must warn you again that I am unable to speak of it in any but the most general terms - or, at least, in those directly connected with the situation in which I have placed you. As I have explained before: it is a very insular and rigid religion and I am bound both by duty and my own personal honour to respect its sanctity."

Lambert was already nodding, the panties still lying on his desk warming him to her beliefs more than any burning bush or parting of the Nile. His eyes drinking in her feet with the scarlet nails he himself had so recently painted even as he made agreement, trapped in an appraisal of the balmy Southern tips of her body so in contrast with its Arctic North.

"Is there anything else, you require, Master?" she asked, the perfect flunkey. "If not I shall return to my quarters."

"No, no. I'm fine, Anya," he told her, head coming up, startled. "I'll see you in the morning."

With a smile she turned to leave.

She had actually twisted the door-handle before she turned

back:

"Just one thing, Master. It is a small point but I will have to insist upon it."

Lambert waited; none too impressed with her choice of words, despite the respectful tone with which she framed them.

What right, after all, did she think she had to "Insist" upon anything?

"Before you return my gifts," she was explaining, "could you please make sure they are washed?"

His body jolted. If there were such a thing as a pleasant kick to the guts, Lambert felt as though he were experiencing it.

"Wash her panties?"

Not long ago he'd have kicked her Indian arse from the house for suggesting such a thing; now though, rather than anger, all he could feel was anticipation. He was, after all, already polishing her shoes and hand-washing her pantyhose. What difference could a few pairs of panties make?

And especially when they gave him so much…

"Excuse my forthrightness, Master," Anya interrupted his thoughts. "Do I ask too much?"

"Er… No… No, Anya," he blustered. "Not at all."

A laugh accompanied his disavowal, constructed in such a way as to let her know that what was transpiring between them was no big deal; reminding her she would be well advised to remember that, despite his understanding nature, their respective positions of master and servant remained intact.

"Quid pro quo, eh?" he laughed again. "Least I can do, I reckon."

Her answering smile was constructed along exactly the same lines as his but with roles reversed.

"Thank you, Master," she told him. "You are the kind of man one does not come across very often."

Leaving him then to translate her insult into the flattery he thrived upon, his servant again turned to the door.

This time it was Lambert who forced her to turn back.

"Anya?"

She turned to face him, equine features questioning, the perfect servant at her master's behest.

"Why was your "Mentor" so angry with you for making your

offer to me?"

"As I explained, Master: our positions as master and servant prevent what I mistakenly suggested. Physical interaction of any kind between a non-believer such as yourself and a believer is proscribed unless there is a change in both our working and private relationship."

"Then it's not impossible?" he asked, the possibility her "Spiritual guide" might consider his bathing, massaging and sucking of her toes "Physical interaction" not occurring to him.

She gave it some thought of her own, as if considering such an eventuality for the first time.

Making him wait, before finally conceding:

"No, it is not impossible, Master. In India, and around the region of West Bengal and, more especially, Calcutta, my guide has seen and advised on many instances of interaction between a believer and a non-believer. He is one of the most learned and wise men of the faith and his advice is much sought. As a matter of fact, he told me that, from what I have told him of you and the books of yours he has since read, it was easy to discern you were not only talented, but highly intelligent."

"You must thank him for me," he ordered, buoyed by words and praise for both himself and the work he had not heard described in positive terms for too long.

"I shall, Master," she assented; absorbed at the ready way false flattery from a non-existent admirer was so easily accepted.

"When he suggested I atone for making you an offer I was in no position to make, and make you another instead, I was worried you might take offence at my behaviour. My mentor, though, convinced me otherwise. He assured me you were a creative man of rare imagination and that such men were more tolerant of those activities less favoured and less gifted mortals rushed to condemn."

The unmistakable satisfaction Anya could see written across his face deepened the contempt she felt for the man she was intent upon owning; almost making her own perversion seem... just.

"I like to think so, Anya," he agreed, making only the most ineffectual attempt at modesty.

"But tell me," he asked; the bald fact of having just agreed to wash his servant's underwear not preventing him from trying to sound masterful as he offered up some boldness of his own; "if you could do so without offending your beliefs, would you like a physical relationship with your employer?"

If she were surprised by his question Lambert could detect no sign upon her toothy features - though, had he looked closer, a slight narrowing of the eyes might have indicated the irritation she felt at the way he referred to himself in the third person.

A dead give-away, she knew, in detecting the truly and undeservedly self-important.

"What I want does not enter into it, Master," she told him. "You are a handsome and talented man with the wisdom given only by age; but what I can dream about and what I can have are not necessarily compatible. As I have said: relationships of the kind of which you speak are forbidden between a believer and a non-believer."

"But I thought you just said such a thing was possible?"

"It is, Master. But there are only two ways in which a person not of the faith can be a part of a believer's life."

"And they are?"

"Trust me, Master; neither way is for you."

The self-important one drew himself up, offended after the fashion of pompous hypocrites everywhere. Sucking her toes and laundering her underwear was one thing, but he would not have himself second-guessed by such a person.

"I think," he began, tone adopted that would leave her in no doubt of his displeasure, "you might allow me to be the judge of that, Anya."

The lowered head of his servant assured him his message, and the authoritative way it had been delivered, was absorbed; her demeanour telling him she understood his servant had gone too far.

"What do these two ways involve?" he asked, tone normal again, sensibilities soothed and back in their correct order.

"Master," she told him, looking up now his displeasure had passed. "The reason I was so bold as to venture an opinion on your behalf was that I do not think for one split second of a split second that you would accept either of the two courses open in such cases."

"Sounds interesting," he said, genuine despite his suddenly jocular manner. "Tell me more, Anya."

"I will if you insist, Master. But, though I know you ask only from interest; I feel I must tell you that if I were to explain these ways to you and you were –even in jest or by way of a practical joke upon your servant- to accept one of them, I would consider it as binding as a legal document and would be obliged to leave both your employment and your home if you went back on your word."

"Oooooh!" he mouthed; adding: "Sounds serious."

"It is to me, Master," she told him, putting his guard up as he recalled how she had told him there would be no choice but to leave if she felt her "Religion" were being be mocked.

Lambert performed a mental shrug.

She might well consider any such verbal agreement legally binding but, in reality he knew, it would mean less than a fig.

The most important thing to him at that moment was gaining regular access to the body that was inflaming him so unaccountably.

When she was out of his system she could leave for the outer rings of Saturn for all he cared.

"So?" he asked, expectantly.

She stared back at him, quizzical.

"Are you going to tell me what these two options are or not?"

Anya continued to stare at him for a few moments; then, as if she had reached a decision:

"The first option, Master, is not as drastic or as… final," she explained. "Just the same, it is a decision and a commitment that, once made, that can never be unmade. Even should the non-believer renege on the agreement the believer will always think of him and treat him –or her, she added, catching herself- as the terms of the agreement demand."

"So far, so mysterious," he joked, trying to inject a little lightness. "And what of the second option?"

"The second option requires a far greater commitment and is the greatest compliment a non-believer can pay someone of the faith. It is irrevocable and set in stone. Of course, the non-believer can always choose to go back on his commitment, but that, my mentor tells me, is so rare as to be unheard of."

Despite his amusement for the serious way she treated her Mickey Mouse religion and its mysterious: "Options", Lambert was intrigued:

"And what, exactly, would a commitment to one of the

options entail for a non-believer?"

"I realise we speak hypothetically, Master; but, if you were to commit to the first and less onerous pledging, you would be known to me from then on as my 'Lesser'."

"Your 'Lesser'?" he repeated, trying hard not to laugh and not quite succeeding; diverted enough for it not to register she was now speaking of him as if he were the non-believer in question.

"That is right," she confirmed, ignoring his flippancy. "Though you would be on a less restrictive footing with me than if you were to opt for the second pledge of service you would, just the same, no longer be my 'Master'. Our positions would reverse and I would…"

Stopping, she shook her head, as if marvelling at what she was about to describe.

"No. It is just too unbelievable," she said, letting slip a small laugh. "Even though I know we speak non-specifically I cannot bring myself to…"

She broke off, as if the prospect were just too ridiculous, still laughing.

"What's unbelievable?" he asked, laughing along with her. "How would our roles reverse, Anya?"

Lambert watched as she composed herself, expression becoming serious:

"Were you to petition to…"

"Petition," he thought.

"…to pledge yourself as my Lesser," she went on, "you would have to swear your intention to become useful to me and accept my guidance as your superior."

Lambert snorted sarcastically:

"Is that all?"

"Not quite, Master," she disabused him, ignoring his heavy irony, "but quite enough for you to grasp what is involved without your servant breaching what her religion finds permissible."

"And what about the second option?"

"Ah!" she sighed, as if they had trespassed onto the subject of the truly rarefied. "That is an option of an altogether more binding and serious nature."

"In what way?"

"Let us say that you –and I use the first person theoretically, of course- were to petition me," she told him, deadly serious, "and I accepted you under the terms of the second option…"

"Yes?" he prompted her when she paused.

"You… You would then become…"

She paused again, a sense of the dramatic telling her to make him compel her.

"What?" he asked, finally.

She allowed a few more seconds to pass; then:

"If you were to petition me and I were to accept," she said, holding him with her eyes; "you would then become my… 'Inferior'."

He stared at her, realising that, in spite of his contempt for her asinine faith and its teachings and disciplines, he was actually turned on. Acknowledging, despite his highly developed capacity for denial, that in some inexplicable way the prospect of giving up control to another human being –and a pretty unprepossessing example from a backward country at that- touched on something at his core.

So "Touched" and turned on, in fact, that –after the example of Rajiv's "True barbarian"- the mere existence of his reaction was reason enough for him to accept its being.

And all he needed to be able to dismiss the perverted and dangerous nature of the soil from which it was formed.

The master of the house both unaware and unconcerned that it was precisely his capacity to downplay and mock if it meant he got his rocks off that would –and was- in the process of ensuring his downfall.

"Lessers and Inferiors, eh?" he began, attempting to keep the officer's mess on a light and even keel – despite the insurrection building in the lower ranks. "Not particularly flattering terms, are they?"

"They are not intended to be, Master," she informed him. "They are truthful descriptions of one person's position in relation to another and no more than accurate assessments of the pledge of service taken. The wearing of either title, you understand, invoking responsibilities on both sides - for the followed as much as the follower."

"How so, Anya?"

"Well…" she began, appearing to search for an explanation;

finally hitting on one:

"Should, for instance, the recipient of a petitioner's pledge be found unworthy of such respect then either the Lesser or the Inferior may end their oath of service with no loss of face. The Believer would then find herself under censure for her lapse and receive judgment from her elders."

Lambert expelled air; considering that only in so culturally and socially backward a place as the region from whence she came could such a risible form of worship exist.

"The godlike in the individual," he scoffed to himself, echoing her description of her faith's raison d'exister; only the inexplicable urgency at his groin preventing him tearing verbal shreds from the primitive beliefs of his devout, credulous and unlikely, lust object.

That, and the fact he knew without doubt she had been serious about leaving if she suspected her faith were not being treated with the respect it deserved.

"So," he began, keeping their puerile conversation going by way of keeping that "Lust object" in his presence, "just how does a would be Lesser or an Inferior go about pledging himself.

Anya looked up at him, eyes finding his, as if gauging his question as a genuine inquiry or simply a desire to mock her faith.

And then, decision made, with a horse-face as serious and intent as he had yet to see it, she told him.

It is no exaggeration to say that, when she was finished, the latest of Lambert's increasingly pulsating erections –and to his amazement after what she had gone on to tell him- was as vital and needy of attention as he had yet to know it.

CHAPTER TWENTY-NINE

Withdrawal

It was almost two weeks after their discussion of her religion and the part within it played by non-believers, when Anya, with Rajiv's blessing, began the lowering of the boom.

"May I speak to you, Master?" she asked the back of his head as he sat taking the morning air; absorbed, it seemed, with the panoramic sweep of the English Channel as it made itself one with the Atlantic.

Only just risen from his bed and deciding to take breakfast on the patio, he drank in the breathtaking views as well as his tea. The newspaper unopened on the table before him yet more evidence the day-to-day business of the outside world was interesting him less - the conical breasts and shapely legs of his young servant as she hove into view not leaving him much in the way of a mind for the less personal and relevant flow of world events. What he now saw as her uniform of grey skirt, white shirt, nylons and court shoes, playing no small part in his withdrawal.

The master of the house not suspecting, as he went over the events of the past few days, that a "Withdrawal" of a different kind was uppermost in his servant's mind that morning.

Following the progress of a small fishing boat out of Porth Levon as it fought both currents and catch quotas, it struck him that this was the first stretch of time he could remember since childhood when he had not put word to paper -or symbol to screen, as it were- for at least a short period of each day.

And, more surprisingly, found himself undismayed by the lack.

Moreover, when he actually gave his lassitude in this area some thought, he was unsurprised to find he did not miss the mechanics of a profession that had –sharing equal pride of place with seductions of the opposite sex- absorbed his day to day from his late teens onwards.

If the world he had known -and been, for years, reasonably successful in- could jettison him as if her were no more than damaged goods then he could certainly return the compliment.

That the situation in his home, the same situation he had actively encouraged and gained such an erotic charge from, could be dangerous to his mental well-being -not to mention his position as master of the home itself- barely considered now. So great was the corruptive power of his sexual response to a trap in which, unwittingly or not, he was becoming more and more enmeshed.

These days, it seemed, he was in a constant state of bestial rut; barely recalling the last time he reached completion without the aid of his own hand; even switching at times to his less favoured left in partially successful attempts to trick himself a stranger's hand were performing the favour.

The identity of the "Stranger" in question hardly a conundrum.

In fact, in tandem with the above, he could barely remember the last time he went beyond crisis to an image other than that of his horse-toothed servant from the Third World.

His days passing now in a haze of idle thoughts, imagined screenplays, and ever more exotic fantasies as he allowed himself –albeit unwittingly- to bring about his own demise.

Not prizes on offer for the identity of his leading lady.

In fact, it was rare indeed if more than four or five hours passed before he found himself in either locked bedroom or study with her soiled underwear pressed to his nose.

His current longing and obsession with burying his face between his housekeeper's legs yet another source of wonder for him – especially as not once in their years of marriage had he gone down on Siobhan.

No matter how arctic pure his ex-wife's features and how advanced her adherence to Nordic hygiene; it had remained something he was unwilling to do for the beauty from Gothenburg.

Even if she showed no qualms when it came to taking him past dazzling Swedish dentistry and transporting him to heaven.

So why was the prospect of performing such a task for his dark-skinned servant the only image he masturbated to these days? Taking her most recent "Gift" to his face and breathing deeply through the nose in attempts to assuage a need almost painful in its intensity. Relief hastened by the smell of her providing at least a fleeting escape from the libido she unknowingly held captive.

Her fascination for him -far from lessening- seemed to grow

exponentially. Each passing day ensuring the same macho pride – the same flaw responsible for the loss of both wife and friends-congratulated him on his unimpaired faculty for multiple erections. The existence of such youthful vigour at his age bolstering his own puerile regard; a return to the physical capacity of playground followed by quad blinding him to the dangers inherent in the unnatural fixation prompting it. The same fixation allowing the addictive and unsuspected agenda of the servant bent on taking over his life to work its magic unhindered.

Of course, had he been in a position to ask the two co-plotters from the subcontinent for their opinion –and they were of a mind to answer- they would have told him his behaviour, far from being out of character, was totally in keeping with their assessments of him. They would have told him that, given his supreme confidence in his own sovereignty and the deferential way his young Indian servant still acted towards him, it was no surprise he would quash all thoughts of danger in favour of the depraved scenario devised and tailored to meet this own specific flaws as they saw them.

Entrenched in denial, Lambert's most cherished time of week, without doubt, were the hours set aside for him to kneel at his servant's feet and remove her shoes. Going on to –reverently, and in accordance with her religious beliefs- slide her pantyhose off her hips and down her legs with minimal physical contact, before folding the nylon and placing it next to her shiny black courts. Soaping his hands then and bathing her shapely feet prior to drying them; after which, one by one, placing her toes in his mouth and sucking them that his saliva might provide a more lustrous base for the varnish he would when this specific part of the process was complete.

A spurious premise but one he was more than willing to leave unchallenged; the efficaciousness of which, or lack of such, no longer bothering him in the slightest. His only concern being to take her foot in his hands and place his mouth around the toes guaranteed to set his pulse racing.

By now, of course, -as Anya had expected and he hadn't- their "Game" had evolved into something quite different from the light-hearted role-playing with which it had started.

Back then - even he could hardly help but notice; she had been hesitant and unsure about giving him orders and directions, as if he were the servant and she the master. Now when in game mode, and since they had become "Lambert" and "Ms Anya", she not only seemed more secure but more… peremptory' as lost to the sensations of their shared fantasy as her Master himself. His servant's manner not just assertive but autocratic and imperious too.

A twice-weekly change he found, to his great surprise, he rather enjoyed.

Of course, a part of the game's attraction for him was the knowledge he could dip his own toes in such perverted waters and remain untainted. The true character of their day-to-day kicking in at game's end and returning them, seamlessly it seemed, to the reality of superior English master and subservient Indian serving girl.

"A win-win situation," the deluded and superior, and now professionally marginalized, English writer congratulated himself for on more than one occasion.

Surprisingly, given his attraction for her lower extremities, the only sour note in his household situation stemmed from the time he spent kneeling at her feet.

For though he knew the glimpses of damp fabric, spied between her legs during her more unguarded moments, was evidence of her own arousal, he also knew physical contact between them –other than taking her toes into his warm mouth after bathing them and directly before applying varnish- was proscribed by her religion and the dread "Spiritual advisor". A prohibition, naturally, making such contact all the more desirable to him - even if he was amazed that his greatest desire in her regard now was not the placing of his superior English meat into her uncharted Indian snatch.

The above a predictable male response in the early stage of desire that had undergone a sea change, as his usage of her image to get himself off had become, somehow, less… not brutal, so much as less… assertive.

Now, rather than battering at the gateway to her womanhood until she pleaded for mercy, it was –contradicting a history of distaste for the act- the lowering of her panties and the spreading of her legs as he buried his head between them hastening release. His previous aversion forgotten as he flattened his tongue to lathe her ripe labia, going on to insert that same appendage in her vagina before switching his attentions to the exterior once more and taking an inflamed clitoris between his teeth to…

"I was asking if I might speak with you, Master?" the voice of his oral attentions cut in, bringing his head up with a start.

Lambert was surprised the thud of his return to earth was not heard in nearby Devon, so great was his shock at being intruded upon by the owner of the Indian pussy he had just been in the act of bringing to completion.

"Sorry, Anya," he apologised, collecting himself enough to recover himself and disguise his excursion. "Was just giving some thought to a new storyline."

A likely story, though he wasn't to know it, that would, and did not, cut any ice with his housekeeper.

"What is it you wanted?" he went on, all business, master of himself and his retainer once again; noticing she looked a little more sheepish in his presence –a little more deferential- than usual when she was on duty.

"Looking forward to our little session this afternoon, are you?" he added, knowing he certainly was. "I thought we'd have a change of colour today. I think your nails would look very nice if they were…"

"There will be no session, Master," she blurted it out.

Lambert looked at her as if she were sickening for something.

"What do you mean: no session? Why on earth n…?"

"It cannot happen again, Master," she spoke over him again, adoring the look of sheer bewilderment and, more crucially, frustration stealing over his face. "It is not right."

"But… I thought you enjoyed it?" he asked, spirits already plummeting at the prospect their twice-weekly interludes might come to an end.

Her answering nod confirmed what he already knew; even if it was delivered unwillingly.

"So I did, Master," she said, adding verbal confirmation in the same grudging way. "It was a fulfillment of a dream and I have you to thank for it; but I allowed you to show me this generosity without first consulting my spiritual advisor."

The mention of her "Advisor" brought a curse bubbling up to Lambert's lips where, aware of the regard she had for this fanatical guru of a cretinous religion he was coming to see as the killjoy of all killjoys, it died without expressing itself.

"Then why stop?" he asked.

"When explained what you did for me he was appalled?" Anya began. "I have never known him so angry with me. He said I had disrespected you and gone outside the behaviour our faith expects from a servant to a master."

"This is nonsense, Anya," he exploded, waving a hand, the injustice heaped upon her by this guru nothing compared to the indignation he felt at being deprived of the "Game" from which he took so much perverse pleasure. "I was the one who suggested it to you. How could you possibly be disrespecting me?"

"By accepting, Master," she explained. "By taking advantage of your charitable nature to place my myself in a position above you."

"For heaven's sakes, Anya. It's a game. Nothing more. Your behaviour as a servant has always been exemplary and has in no way altered because of our harmless little interludes. Why don't you explain that to your guide?"

Anya was already shaking her head.

"It will make no difference, Master. He says I have perverted what is natural and wholesome by taking a position over you – no matter we do not take our roles seriously and those positions are impermanent. If I am truthful, he told me he is more concerned with…"

She allowed her voice to tail of as if the subject were too delicate for her, certain the void would be filled.

"More concerned with what?" he demanded, growing angrier by the moment.

"You must understand, Master," she began, almost pleading, as if he were wringing a confession from her. "Like you, my guide is a great man. A strong man. He has seen the effects of vacillation and seen how easy it is to allow setbacks in one's life to weaken the resolve of those who were previously immune to the evils of uncertainty and prevarication."

"Just a second here," he stopped her, miffed at having been discussed and evaluated by some over devout nappy wearer from the foothills of Bengal.

"Are you saying he thinks this is happening to me?"

Anya considered this a good time to lower her eyes.

"I'll take that as a yes," he went on. "What else did this spiritual guide have to say in my regard?"

"Please do not be angry, Master," she begged, eyes still fixed to the decking of the patio. "His thoughts were only for you."

"How selfless of him."

"Truly, Master," she continued, eyes suddenly rising, "he considers you to be a man of substance who has, for the moment, lost his way. That is why he was so angry with me for accepting your offer to become responsible for the care of my feet. He accused me of trying to…"

Again she hesitated, hoping as she again lowered her eyes that he was not finding her limited acting skills corny.

"If you have something to say, simply say it," he demanded, amateur dramatics disregarded.

"I am sorry, Master, but he… He accused me of trying to…" she chose this moment to look him straight in the eye "To enslave you."

The word leaving her over-plump lips hit Lambert like a short left to the guts, chiming as it did with the dreams, both waking and sleeping, he had been experiencing along exactly those lines.

"I know, Master," she agreed, professing to know his thoughts and be in agreement with them.

"My guide is a great man, but even the greatest of men can be wrong. I told him that even if I were misguided enough to make such an attempt it was hardly likely that someone of your talent, looks and education would do anything but treat me as the deluded imbecile he would surely know me to be."

He stared at her, still in a condition of mild shock.

"Look at you," she went on.

He waited.

"And then look at me."

An unnecessary request, given his eyes were already fixed on her; though as their eyes met, Lambert looked away; finding himself unable, for whatever reason, to meet her gaze.

"How could such a thing be possible?" she asked his averted eyes.

"How indeed?" he asked the sparkling blue sea where it met the paler blue of the sky to form a distant horizon.

And yet, though he knew she was right and such a likelihood was impossible, the nature of his thoughts in her regard over the previous months proved, at the very least, her guide's suspicions to be not totally unfounded.

What else would explain his instant sense of blueness in regard of his own weekly horizon and the removal of their game?

"There was much else my guide had to say in regard of your well-being and my behaviour but I am afraid they touch on the innermost teachings of our religion and I am unable to share them with you," she assured him. "But I hope you will believe me when I say nothing was said that did not have your best interests at heart along with a desire for you to be the man you truly are."

Shaking his head at the unread newspaper next to his breakfast tray, Lambert could not decide what he was most put out about: the stupidity and credulity of his servant; the condescending way in which her nappy-wearing guru discussed him with her privately and the imbecilic conclusions he had drawn; or the fact he would no longer have access to the legs and feet now exerting such a sway on his sexuality.

"Again, I apologise, Master," she went on. "I realise how strange this must seem to you and I can see how primitive my faith could seem to one as cultured as you; but it is my faith and I place my faith in it wholeheartedly."

She waited to see if he would respond before going on:

"In my heart I do not believe, as my guide believes, that I set out to enslave you, but, if I did so subconsciously, I hope you will forgive me. Your generosity has touched me and I will miss our time as 'Lambert' and 'Ms Anya' together. But after speaking with my mentor I realise it is over for me. Out of duty to my religion, my employer, and myself I must now concentrate on being the best servant I can be for you. Both my religion and my self-respect demand nothing less."

"Whatever," he told her, waving a hand dismissively, wanting her gone that he might lick his wounds; amazed at feeling so crushing a sense of loss for no great a reason than being denied the opportunity to give his own servant a pedicure.

"Don't trouble yourself over it," he said sulkily, rediscovering his interest in world events and snatching up his newspaper to bury himself behind it; his all too readable disappointment impacting upon the mood of his housekeeper in exactly the opposite way.

"Now, your tea has gone cold," she told him, returning to servant mode by way of a subject change.

From behind the broadsheet there was no response.

"I shall make you a fresh pot while you read your newspaper, Master," she told him, smile utterly demonic for what she had achieved and for what, she was certain, was possible to achieve from this moment on.

With a light step and an even lighter heart, she turned towards the house and almost danced her way towards the open French-doors that would lead to the kitchen.

Things could not have been going better.

CHAPTER THIRTY

Anya & Rajiv

"…You are in his blood," he told a beaming Anya.

Three days had passed since the withdrawal of her "Master's" pedicure privileges -as she liked to describe them. Now, fresh from her shower, she was in the process of sharing the events of her day with Rajiv, knowing he was as eager to hear her news as she was delighted to impart it.

"The offer he dismissed with such disdain not two weeks ago," her mentor was continuing, "scars his subconscious and burns fiercely behind his every waking thought – even more so now he knows the offer is one you should not have made and is no longer available to him."

His head went from side-to-side, mulling it over.

"One can only guess at the nature of his dreams," he laughed wonderingly. "Kneeling naked to pull his pathetic white penis, while you observe from the comfort of an armchair."

He laughed again as the afterthought struck him:

"Fully dressed, I should imagine."

An enchanting image she could do no more than laugh at herself.

"He follows me like a puppy," she told him, laughing still; thrilled with both the new developments and the strength of the bathroom orgasm resulting from them prior to calling Rajiv.

"From being a non-entity in his eyes, I have progressed so far with the dog he is desperate for even a glimpse of my legs, my breasts and my feet – especially now it has been over three days since I informed him my spiritual guide had decided I could no longer allow him access through our twice weekly pedicure."

Amusement creased her horse features as she recalled her actions:

"Those same feet," she smirked, "I am careful to slip from my shoes and rub when I know he is watching and thinks I cannot see."

She laughed aloud, equine features suddenly taking on a look of the deepest malice.

"It is almost as if he has a radar for when I am about to go upstairs and busies himself at the bottom for some trivial reason. Just like a schoolboy attempting to snatch a glimpse up the teacher's skirt.

The latter simile bringing laughter from both as they delighted in the success they were having with their "Toy".

"But then," she smirked, knowing Rajiv had not yet been granted the facility to see her do it, "don't all men remain dirty little boys?"

"I do not pose as a spokesman for my entire gender," he told her, "but there is much truth in your observation. Though some of us do mature into dirty big men."

Again their mirth was shared.

"I truly think he believes," she observed with more gravity, "that I have no idea he does it. From being neglected and dismissed he now seeks me out on the flimsiest of pretexts. I cannot be entirely sure, but I am at least ninety-percent certain he has been letting himself into my quarters when I do the weekly shop to rummage through the basket containing my dirty underwear – though he no longer has a need for this; given I gift him an unlaundered pair every so often."

"And is he still laundering your smalls for you before giving them back?"

"Oh, yes. I am most insistent upon it."

"And he continues to sulk about the discontinuation of your game?"

She was nodding before he had even finished:

"It really is just too delightful," she observed. "I know now how a puppet master feels. The difference being the marionette whose actions I dictate is formed of flesh and blood."

"My marionette too," Rajiv reminded her in a stern voice. "I have an investment here also."

Luckily for Anya, Rajiv was unable to see the curl of her lip that greeted his reminder.

"It is only to be expected, of course," Rajiv told her, treating her silence as agreement; pausing before going on:

"The more his idleness and lassitude has ceded control of the household to you, the more; regardless of your youth; you have become an authority figure in his eyes. Childhood conditioning is re-asserting itself and he will find this variation on the theme difficult -hopefully impossible- to shrug off."

Now, had he been able to see her, he would not have been surprised to find she was nodding vigorous agreement with his words. A response to his wisdom in these matters he would have found very pleasing. Evidence of the kind of respect -less comprehensive but no less welcome- missing from his life since the loss of his beloved Ilse.

"On occasions when he looks at me I swear I see hatred," she told him. "Resentment that someone as lowly as me could possibly have such an effect upon him. There are times when he can barely look me in the eye – though I suspect that has more to do with my face than his embarrassment."

Rajiv's on-screen head again shook from side to side:

"That you are a young woman, from a race and superior civilisation his people once subjugated and he himself considers substandard, adds to his shame for allowing such a thing to happen. You are feeding him a diet of submission and, though he is unaware of it and would hate the prospect were he to discover self-awareness enough to acknowledge the fact, he is feeling a growing need to abase himself."

As always, she thrilled to her older friend's words; his observations dovetailing perfectly with her ambitions and inspiring the usual arousal she was sure to experience at least once during their calls to each other.

"From here on in," he told her; "unless I am very much mistaken; he will gradually enslave himself to you with very little prompting or manipulation on your part – even if he convinces himself he does so for ends of his own."

Her "Good!" was emphatic, eyes staring unseeingly at the walls of her quarters as they dissolved into a location and scene quite different; the vision of which prompted both a smile and an assertion:

"I can hardly wait," she began breathlessly, "until he drapes himself across my lap and his lilywhite buttocks feel the full force of my hand."

The picture described bringing forth another toothy smile as she considered the rightness of the image playing itself out on the back of her eyes before adding:

"And, if what you say regarding his willingness – acknowledged or not- proves to be the case, he will find me more than prepared to help him towards his goal,"

"As you should be, my sweet," Rajiv agreed. "It is, after all, what you have dreamed about the whole of your young life and worked so hard these last few months to achieve."

"I will not disagree with you, o wise mentor."

"And I would not believe you if you did," he assured her, smiling, enjoying her form of address -no matter how lightly it was delivered- his vanity, though not functioning at such an advanced level as that of their victim, serving as an indicator of his own vulnerability when it came to the female.

"Also," he went on, "though I know, like me, you detest the playacting world of the poseurs; in their rubber, latex, and mock dungeons; you might wish to consider the use of a paddle rather than the hand itself. Take my word; such a form of discipline can be very demanding on the one having to deliver it. And believe me, the less yielding surface of a sturdy wooden paddle will get your message across with far more swiftness and discomfort before you send your peon off to place his nose in the corner and reflect upon his wrongdoings."

"Rajiv," she began warningly, "I do believe you are trying to work me up again."

"I will not deny it," he answered without dissembling. "Anticipation is a major player on the course we run - though I know from experience there is nothing quite like the actual sight and sounds of a slave being brought to heel and…"

He cut himself short as a thought occurred to him; tone accusatory when he continued:

"And, by the way, when can I expect you to set up a webcam that I may see you as you see me?"

Anya smiled to herself, knowing he was impatient to masturbate to an actual image rather than a disembodied voice – no matter how thrilling the action it described.

"Soon, Rajiv… Perhaps… I still think about it."

"Then think harder," he warned, a slight edge to both his expression and his voice indicating he was serious. "I grow impatient."

Making no reply as they neared the end of their nightly rendezvous, totally unfazed by both his "Expression" and his "Edge", Anya waited for him to bring the proceedings to an end.

A few seconds later as it turned out.

"Though it is too early to congratulate ourselves just yet," he began, "we have come a long way. Your Master is hardly recognisable to me from the descriptions of him you first gave me."

He allowed himself a fond chuckle.

"Tell me, Anya, how did he react when you gave him your soiled underwear for the first time?"

"The way he reacted the last time I told you, Rajiv," she replied with a sigh, amused just the same; never, in truth, wearied by the reliving of her exploits with the white man in the big house.

"My poor marionette was unable to understand why I was making him a gift at all," she laughed, recalling Lambert's expression. "He looked still more puzzled when I explained why the gift was being made."

"And what did he say later when you said the game –along with his toe sucking and pussy sniffing- was now forbidden?"

Anya shrugged:

"What could he say? I have left him in doubt that, were he to question my religion, I would leave and not return. He was angry, thwarted, dejected. All of those things and more. I think it is safe to say that he now hates both my religion and my spiritual advisor – that is you, by the way- with something of a passion. "

Rajiv laughed but soon became thoughtful:

"Then we have taken huge steps with him. However, you must still take care to move things along with the poseur very slowly. Though I do think we can expect a response of some kind on his part very soon."

"Your thoughts match mine," she agreed.

"If I am any judge he will be missing his interaction with you and your…" a grin lit up his onscreen image "…feet a great, great deal."

CHAPTER THIRTY-ONE

The Gamble

"Anya?" he exclaimed, surprised to see her in his kitchen at that time of night; groin immediately going to red-alert at the sight of her in high-heels skirt and hose and a tight tee shirt, hair hanging loose over her shoulders.

It was not one hour after her conversation with Rajiv and, far from having taken his urgings of yet more caution and stealth to heart, her patience, as she had known it would, had finally snapped.

"Is something wrong?" Lambert asked.

"I need to speak with you," she told him, her previously habitual "Master", for once, not completing the sentence.

Lambert's spirits rose at this development. Could she be experiencing second thoughts for having allowed her "Spiritual guide" to call a halt to the game she had taken such pleasure in?

"I was just making myself a Hot Chocolate," he said, explaining away his presence in the kitchen, the same place he had come to view as her domain – even if he was the one to whom it really belonged.

The master of that house actually looking a little uncomfortable when she did not respond.

Almost as if the silence of his housekeeper was an accusation for his having the temerity to be there at all.

"Would you like one?" he asked when she remained silent.

"Sorry?" she asked, puzzled.

He indicated the boiling kettle and waiting mug.

"No," she said, declining his offer without thanks. "What I have to say will not take long and then I shall return to my quarters."

"There is something wrong," he said. "I sensed it."

"How positively prescient of you," she thought, horse-face severe and intent as she prepared to ditch the advice of her mentor and move things along at a swifter rate.

A gamble, she knew, but a calculated one.

In her opinion, and in contradiction of Rajiv's insistence upon further caution, she had deemed that if Bernard Lambert were not at a low enough ebb for her to manipulate for her own ends now then he never would be. The crestfallen look he'd been unable to disguise three mornings ago when she had told him their game had to end, she thought, evidence enough he was ripe for the picking.

"What is it, Anya?" he asked, expression leaving her in doubt he was hoping she had come to tell him she wanted to resume their "Game".

"Tell me," he insisted. "You know I'll help if I ca…"

"I shall be leaving in the morning," she interjected, encouraged at the way the colour drained from his face as the words putting her gamble into effect sank in.

Even more convinced she was making the right move when his legs seemed to buckle and he slumped down onto a chair, looking for the entire world as if he had just been informed of the demise of a loved one.

"My belongings are packed and I intend to travel to London tomorrow and search for another position."

She watched, a predator stalking particularly ripe prey; her intended quarry attempting to collect his thoughts enough to speak.

Anya Jalav laughed to herself at his uncertainty, almost certain now that triumph would be hers.

And to think, she told herself; that only a few months ago this same weak-willed impostor, now in such a state of indecision before her, could barely bring himself to speak to his young servant except to deliver commands.

Now look at him, she exulted. Distraught at the possibility she might take herself from his presence. The possibility he may never gaze upon her wondrous young breasts and shapely legs again –not to mention handle her slender and soft brown feet- breaking down what was left of his dignity and reserve before his flunkey.

"Who knows?" she asked herself. "Before long he might even reach a different conclusion in regard of my neglected face."

His response when it broke into her thoughts was less than authoritative:

"Why, Anya?" he asked, voice little more than a croak of anxiety and disappointment.

Her own response containing all her master's had lacked:

"You have been given every opportunity to correct your behaviour and prove yourself a man worthy of serving," she told him in a voice of steel, as if that were explanation enough.

"I… I don't understand," he told her sincerely, unmanned by the unexpected turn of events. "What do you mean: 'Correct my…' "

"At the instigation of my mentor," she cut in disdainfully, "I have given you any number of tests devised to prove your merit as a Master worthy of the respect a follower of my faith demands."

"Tests?" he parroted, still in a state of mild shock.

"Not only have you failed each and every one," she told him, a slight curling of her lip and a baring of horse-teeth betraying her contempt, "but you have failed them dismally."

"But… Anya," he protested. "Everything I have done for you has been no more than what any thoughtful employer does for a highly regarded employee."

"Really?" she demanded, becoming more and more assertive by the second, glad to have overridden the sidelined Rajiv and taken the bull by the horns, so to speak.

"Was rubbing your little cock to my image and calling my name as you spurted your disgusting seed the behaviour of 'a thoughtful employer'?" she went on.

"Little cock?" he repeated, sotto voce, almost to himself.

"You have used me. Mr Lambert," she rushed on. "Portraying yourself as a strong and important man in your field when, in reality, you are not only weak but neglected by the movers and shakers of your own profession."

"Now hold on a second," he began, temper finally surfacing as he rose to his feet. "Who the hell are you to speak to someone like me after such a fashion? I have been nothing but tolerant and understanding of your philistine customs and warped religion for the whole of your time here. And yet you have the nerve to…"

"Do not insult me," she spat, the unaccustomed venom in her voice overriding his outrage before it had time to build.

"If you have been tolerant it has been for your own ends," she accused, pausing to let her inference of having known his agenda all along to dilute his outrage further.

"Do you think I could fail to notice how you sniffed the air for a smell of my cunt when you were on your knees before me sucking my toes and painting my nails?"

Lambert's mouth fell open at the boldness of her language and the strength with which she delivered it. Though she was almost thirty years his junior, half his weight and a foot shorter in height, he felt weak before her – the treacherous response he could feel throbbing at his groin doing nothing to bolster his diminishing vitality.

"Did you masturbate to my soiled panties at the point of a gun?" she went on, sensing she was on the verge of overmastering him and making the most of the opportunity.

"Did I blackmail you into polishing my shoes and hand-washing my pantyhose?"

Anya allowed her full fury to rise as she delivered the final nail into his coffin of pusillanimity.

"And was it me who insisted you enter my quarters when I was doing your shopping? Intrusion made simply to use my dirty laundry for your perverted gratification?"

Lambert's heart seemed to erupt into his throat as she dropped the final hand grenade into what he had, until then, considered his secret foxhole.

"She'd known all along," he told himself as his legs gave out once again and he slumped back onto the chair.

"You have shown no control over yourself or your life and I see no sign of an intention to change. I cannot –and will not- serve a man I do not respect any longer."

The sheer rush of jubilation as he lowered his gaze to the floor threatened to overwhelm her.

"You do well to lower your eyes," she told him. "The floor is the only fit place for you."

He was shaking his head now, stunned; her sudden switch from obedient servant to aggressive accuser leaving him defenceless.

"You have used a young girl," she went on. "A young girl who wished only to show you the respect of true service as dictated by a venerable and compassionate religion of ancient origin. Painting yourself as a great man and allowing her to skivvy for you while all you really wished to do was prostrate yourself at her feet and suck her toes."

Lambert's eyes came up at this, a beaten quality behind the

moistness she saw forming in them again threatening to overwhelm her.

Had she really reduced him to this?

"That's not true, Anya," he refuted in a tiny voice, unable to believe he was allowing himself to be treated in such a way in his own kitchen, his own home, and his own country.

"No?" she demanded. "Are you saying you are not attracted to me?"

"Yes… I mean, no… I mean…"

"Look at yourself," she spat, cutting off his feeble entreaties. "So dishonest you even manage to convince yourself you are a real man."

"Now wait a sec…"

"No! You 'wait'," she shouted.

The sheer unexpectedness of her onslaught and the force with which she delivered it –just as she thought it would- had cowed him, stopping him in his tracks; marvelling at the sudden turnabout in her manner even as he found himself backing down from the confrontation she seemed to be seeking.

And through it all, more disconcerting than anything else, his erection raged unabated.

"What real man strokes himself to images of his servant as he sniffs the underwear she has had next to the slit from which she releases piss?"

"Anya, you shouldn't speak in such a way. You're far too…"

"Young?" she finished for him. "Did my age prevent you licking the stale excretions from my used panties?"

"But… That…You…" he expostulated before finally arranging his intended words in the correct sequence.

"It was your idea to give me them," he reminded her, swamped by a number of emotions in direct conflict with each other - hearing such language from her lips but one. Experiencing at one and the same time both aching need and damaged pride; blazing anger and cold fear; abject humiliation and extreme arousal.

For she was right, he knew. He had been having sex with her soiled underwear for over a week –with her blessing- and was hooked on the process. Even the menial process of hand washing her panties afterwards and returning them to her, as she presented him with the next pair requiring his attentions, was exquisitely exciting. Something deep and long buried inside him responding positively to a situation that was not only perverse but…"

As the sought after word came to him he screwed his eyes shut in an attempt to make the nightmare go away; even as his cock continued to thrive upon the warped situation he had allowed himself to stumble into and –worse- develop.

"…humiliating," he finished to himself.

"Simple tests, nothing more," she told him. "To see if there was any manhood in you at all."

She was almost sneering at him now.

"Contrary to my first impressions of you –and my mentor has long been in agreement with me- you are not a strong man. Not a 'Master'. There is much weakness in you that is not to be found in a man of natural command. That is why I have decided I will never address you in such a way again. My religion forbids it and is why I must leave."

Now his anger did manage to break through:

"I've taken enough of this," he told her, rising to his feet in a parody of purpose. "How dare you talk to me in such a way? Who do you think you are? This is my home. I'm still your employer. What gives you the right to...?"

"Is that what concerns you?" she cut in, lips curling with the same disdain he had seen a few seconds earlier –as well as in his dreams. "My rights?"

As he struggled to frame a response, a sneer formed on her face:

" Or is it this?" she asked, raising the hem of her skirt in both hands to draw it up over her powerful young thighs, smooth brown skin seeming to shine as it reflected back the light from an overhead spot.

Breath catching in his throat, he found himself unable to remove his eyes from the vision, the erection that was already spearing a path towards his mid-section becoming positively monumental as she mocked him.

Less than half his age, horse-featured and a foot shorter, it made no difference; he was, he now knew for sure, in her thrall.

"There is nothing more to be said," she told him, smirking as she allowed the skirt to fall back and turned on her heel to leave.

That such a man could be undone by his lust for her as satisfying – and still hard to believe- as she had always fantasised it would be.

Even if she knew her gamble had not been won quite yet.

As it turned out, her hand was upon the doorknob before he recovered enough to find his voice.

"No, Anya!" he cried, amazed himself at the level of desperation all too evident in the entreaty.

"I am going back to my quarters," she confirmed without turning, dismissing him. "Tomorrow I will travel to London and I will not return." Holding her breath then and praying she had not misjudged both situation and man.

She was almost through the door when her own entreaties were answered:

"Please, Anya, you can't go. I… I…"

Maintaining her position, back turned, she waited.

For a few moments there was silence, her lungs refusing to function, so intent were all her other senses on willing his capitulation.

Then, as if a decision had been reached:

"I need you."

The magic words, she thought, motionless in the doorway, once again able to breathe.

Not answering immediately, she allowed him to stew, until:

"You mean that?" she asked, pretending it made a difference to hear it, keeping her back to him that he may drink in the strong legs he enjoyed so much.

She sensed hesitation behind her and waited, knowing he teetered on the edge.

Then, finally; almost a whisper:

"Yes."

Her heart leapt in her chest.

It was all in that one word, sibilant or not:

Need, resignation and… submission.

"Please, Anya," he began. "Sit down and let us talk."

She turned back to him.

"What can you possibly say that will change anything?" she asked.

"Please," he said, indicating the table, "sit down and hear me out. You must understand how difficult it is for me to grasp the meaning of your faith and its disciplines? I am not a devout man but I thought all religions were based upon notions of equality."

"It is that very 'Equality'," she began, Rajiv having schooled her well in the ways of her notional religion, "which remains at the root of all the world's problems. My religion believes in truth and acceptance and sees the unnatural extension of undeserved equality as an evil that can breed only unrest. Some people are superior to others and there is no shame in admitting such to be the case.

Her assertion was not lost on him; having not so long ago had the same thoughts in regard of her himself.

"Know your place, in other words," he said, even at this stage unable to prevent a note of cynicism from transforming his delivery.

"You have it precisely," she complimented him, unfazed by his undertone. "The concept of service is looked upon with contempt when it should be treasured and revered. Our belief is that only in complete acceptance of our failings and the embracing of our true natures can we ever hope to find the serenity that goes with having found our natural position in life."

Lambert shook his head with wonder - despite her beliefs not being a million miles short of his own thoughts on the subject.

At least when he was the one accorded such "Service".

Seating herself on the opposite side of the table from him she crossed her legs that he may hear the rustling of her nylons - the sight of her victim swallowing with difficulty telling her she had not made the effort in vain.

"Say what you have to say," she said regally, amused at the way even something so simple as her panty-hosed legs rubbing against each other could unman him. "I am listening."

Mustering his concentration, he attempted to compose himself, truly desperate that the young girl he had regarded with little but disdain since her arrival in his home remained within its confines.

"Anya," he said, finally, the mere thought of being in the house without her physical presence –not to mention the resulting responsibilities that would then become his- making him feel queasy, so dependent upon her had he become; "I... I want you to...

He couldn't believe he was going to say it.

Drawing himself up in his chair with as much dignity as he

could manage under the circumstances, he decided to simply blurt it out:

"I want you to marry me."

For a few seconds, even Anya was shocked.

She had been expecting something.

But not this.

"I know your religion forbids you marrying a non-believer," he pressed on, despite his own shock for what he was proposing, "but I would be willing to convert."

Still taken aback, Anya mulled it over. So successful had she been in getting into his head, it appeared, that he was actually proposing marriage. And "Marriage", to the ugly young Indian girl he would not have looked twice at a short time before?

What a triumph!

The ugly duckling from the slums of Kolkata?

Proposed to by her employer?

A handsome, white and English, employer?

"Think about it, Anya," he persisted as she pictured the faces of the mediocrities and bullies who had made her time in her hometown such a waking nightmare. "You will have a home, money and position."

Her horse features were beyond euphoria.

For a while anyway.

Triumph and euphoria aside, it was not, after all, "Marriage" she wanted from him.

Not by a long shot.

In common with the discipline of her fictional religion, money and position meant nothing to her.

No, she told herself; only control –and control of the kind she intended to wield over him would satisfy her need. And control of the kind she was committed to wield over him would cede those more material and superficial possessions to her anyway.

"That is very generous of you," she mocked. "But, as I believe I have explained to you, my religion does not accept those not of our race. And, even if they did, it is not my intention to marry."

His face, she decided, aware of no other word in her second language to describe it, was "Crestfallen".

"Now," she began, business concluded –or at least allowing him to think it was; "if that is all you have to say I need to pack my things and…"

"No!" he cried as she made to rise; all he could do to prevent himself from physically restraining her as she lowered the callipygian arse he admired so much to her seat and waited.

"What now?" she asked, unperturbed. "Is it your intention to keep me here by force?"

"N-No… Of course not… I… I just want… Just want…"

He drew himself up in an attempt to muster some dignity.

"What you have seen in the previous weeks and months has not been the real Bernard Lambert," he told her. "Far from being 'Weak', as you say, I am a strong character who has suffered some… some… setbacks. The moment they are resolved I will again be my normal self and…"

"Is that it?" she cut in, completing the rise from the table she had started a few moments before. "Then I wish you all the success in the world. Now, if you will excuse me, I must go and pack."

"No, Anya," he cried reaching out to touch her before, recalling her religion's edict on touching –feet strangely excluded– he managed to pull back at the last moment. "You can't leave."

"My mind is made up," she said, emphatic tone leaving no doubt of her sincerity as she again made for the door.

"Please, Anya!"

"Goodbye Mr Lambert."

She had actually crossed the threshold into the hallway when he almost screamed it out; words shocking him less for their meaning than the fact he uttered them at all:

"If you won't marry me I want to become your Lesser!"

To the horse-faced girl in the hallway, frozen in her tracks by the declaration vindicating her gamble, it felt like the fulfillment of all the childhood fantasies that had merged to become her teenage daydreams; before, finally, maturing into degenerate adult wishes. If she had been beyond euphoria before, she was now in a dimension she found impossible to describe. Her handsome English employer, the same man who had barely given her a passing thought some weeks before, had not only proposed marriage, he was now offering to serve her.

Or, at least, be led by her.

Turning slowly, she re-entered the room, eyes staring up into his and seeing the need, fear and disbelief in them.

Need for her body and the pleasure, sight and smell, it could bring him.

Fear that she may actually leave and deprive him of their proximity forever.

Disbelief he could have fallen so low as to be offering himself in such a way.

"Are you making fun of me?" she asked, playing her hand to the hilt.

"No, Anya, I'm not."

"You are serious?"

His eyes took on a glazed look as this new and unsuspected development, asking himself the exact same question and amazed to find the answer given instantly; the sound of his own voice responding in the positive truly shocking to him.

"Yes, Anya," he heard himself say, voice no more than a whisper. "I'm serious."

Her expression told him she was unconvinced, a slight sneer relaying the message she still thought he was mocking her.

"You... You have become very important to me," he told her, both amazed and appalled by his desperation to convince her of his sincerity. "I can't let you go."

Staring up at him thoughtfully, she took in his words and bearing, as if gauging the source from whence they sprang and asking herself if was pure in origin.

"This is inconceivable," she told herself, head shaking, as if such an idea had not occurred to her.

"I mean it, Anya. I do not want you to leave. If... "

He coughed, mouth dry, finding it hard to say the words he knew she needed to hear.

Rediscovering his voice with an effort.

"...If it means," he croaked, "I have to become your... Your Lesser, then so be it."

Allowing unblinking eyes to hold his –at least until her gaze became too intense- he turned away, sickened at the craven way he was caving in before her but seemingly incapable of taking action to prevent the collapse.

She let a few moments pass; until:

"You make this offer despite our conversation of a week ago?" she asked, inquiry made with feigned disbelief.

Going on when he made no reply:

"You do remember exactly what I told you?"

The mortification and reddening of middle-aged cheeks told her he had as, still having difficulty speaking, he nodded.

"I find this hard to believe," she lied. "You make me this offer despite knowing what it will mean for you if I were to accept it?"

A look of wonderment crossed his face and his expression told her he was asking himself the exact same question. Eyes closing as, despite his obvious misgivings, he again nodded in the affirmative. The once high and mighty Bernard Lambert, she thought, looking more than a little intimidated, unmanned by the swiftness of her transition from dutiful servant to figure of authority.

"No," she said suddenly. "I will not allow myself to be taken in. You play with me. Yet more of your deceit."

"But I said it and I mean it, Anya," he assured her once again, eyes opening once more, the same desperation freeing his vocal chords in the process.

"And how do I know you are serious?" she demanded. "Why should I risk losing face with my mentor and my fellow believers if your courage fails you and your offer is withdrawn?"

"You have my word," he told her, voice shrill now; drawing himself up as she considered it, a ludicrous desire to prove to her she was wrong and he was truly a man of substance –even if it meant committing himself to both her and her philistine religion- forcing him on.

"Please, Anya," he implored her, hating himself for his weakness; even if he justified it to himself as simply a means of getting his way – a chance to sate this baffling obsession with his servant before kicking her ugly Indian arse back to the untreated sewer from whence it came. Convincing himself with his usual talent self-delusion that her power over him was both an abnormality and, far more importantly, transitory.

Anya stared up at him pensively, as self-possessed as he was the opposite, despite her lack of the advantages he had accepted as no more than his right from the womb onwards, as certain as she could be now that she stronger, more determined, and more ruthless than the imitation of a man before her.

Then, as if gauging the depths of his sincerity, recognising his declaration for the artifice it was; she nodded; that lack of sophistication informing her acting skills lending her victim the suspicion something in his proposal was not unpleasing to her.

For a few moments more she held her silence; then:

"If it is possible for me to accept you –and I do not say I will," she warned him; "it will not be some game."

"I understand that, Anya," he told her with some relief; grateful she was at least contemplating the idea; the thought of her being absent from his day-to-day finally placing him on at least a nodding acquaintance with sincerity.

"If you are thinking it will be some amusement you can commit to and then cast aside when the reality proves too much for you to handle," she went on, "I urge you to withdraw your offer now. Games will be a thing of the past for both of us. You will not be Rajiv and I will not be the memsahib. If I am allowed to accept you as my Lesser you will be led and guided by me. It will be total reality and I doubt very much that you will have the necessary strength to see it through."

"Try me, Anya," he dared, attempt at bravado hampered by a croak voice more in keeping with a linguistically challenged bullfrog than a supposedly articulate author.

Anya stared up at him, breathing heavily herself now, coveted breasts pulsing beneath the tight fitting tee shirt as she shook her head with wonder.

"I cannot believe it," she told him. "You truly are serious in your intention to become my Lesser. I begin to view you in a wholly different light."

Lambert swallowed back bile.

"Very well," she told him decision reached. "I shall take your offer under consideration."

If his astonishment at having made such an offer in the first place was great then the surge of relief relaxing his body when she accepted was immense; the voice coming from his own direction as alien to him as the concept of service to which he had just pledged himself:

"Thank you," he heard it say.

Anya nodded an imperious acknowledgment.

"I warn you now, however," she began, tone ominous he thought; "very few, if any, Europeans who have committed to this first level of commitment to a believer have ever returned to the lives they knew before doing so. In fact, all have gone on to the second, more binding, level of service. You must take this into consideration before pledging yourself."

Lambert thought about it, eyes devouring the powerful young body that so inflamed him as he did so; realising with certainty that he would do what was needed to know that body more intimately – even if it meant pretending to let her lead him until her defences dropped.

"Then," he thought, "we will see just who the 'Lesser' is out of the two of us.

Thoughts of payback noted and stored, and mustering as much dignity as he could manage - preferring not to address the matter of being "Led" and what it would entail at that moment- he drew himself up before the new regime and attempted to allay her doubts in regard of him.

An attempt he made simply:

"I don't want you to leave, Anya."

If her pleased expression was any guide, it was an approach paying dividends.

"Perhaps I have misjudged you," she said, seeming to relent, again managing his strings with great dexterity, deciding to lead him to his subjugation with kindness. There being plenty of time in the days, months, and years to come to show him the reality to which he had committed himself.

Encouraging him then with hopes of success for his own, see-through and transparent, agenda where she was concerned:

"There may, after all, still be some hope for you."

Encouraged or not, Lambert still found himself cringing at being patronised by such a person, even if the teeth biting down upon the inside of his cheek kept him silent as she continued:

"When all is taken into account," she went on, almost to herself, "it does take a certain courage to admit one's failings and submit oneself to the authority of one stronger and more capable."

Pausing, eyes never leaving his, knowing the indignation lurking behind them; she waited; until:

"Especially when the person with that authority is so many years junior."

Along with a feeling of nausea at the content of her statement a small explosive charge appeared to detonate in Lambert's gut at her words.

And one in particular.

Was that really what he would have to do to keep her in his life?

Submit?

"I did explain myself correctly before, I hope?" she asked, sensing his thoughts. "Though becoming my Lesser is not as huge a commitment as the alternative it will mean, just the same, that you accept my superiority over you and agree to be led by me."

His mouth was dry again and once more he found it difficult to speak.

"You do understand that?" she pressed.

Her persistence winning him a flash of cognisance.

"What the fuck are you doing?" said a sober, though no less anxious voice. "Are you really going to accept the authority of an ugly young Indian girl and her piss pathetic religion over you?

Slowly, his head began to shake.

"What in shit's name is wrong with you?"

His eyes scanned the terracotta floor tiles for a solution the local DIY centre fitting them had neglected to supply.

"How would Siobhan react?" he asked himself when no response was forthcoming.

With laughter most probably, he thought.

"What would his friends make of it?"

What friends, his inner voice snorted.

"What would his readers say?"

See above that same voice muttered.

His flash of cognisance giving her another chance to torment him.

"I think I have my answer," she told him after a few seconds more silence. "Goodbye Mr Lambert."

Her half-turn towards the door enough to bring him back to his senses – or leave them, as he would later think.

"No, Anya!"

She stopped but did not turn back.

"Wait!"

Remaining where she was, she waited for the magic word.

"Please," came what she wanted to hear for behind her.

And now she did turn back; expression intended to make him think this would be his last chance to win her over and persuade her he meant what he said.

"It's just a lot to take in," he told her.

Again she waited.

"This is all so… so sudden. But…"

"Yes?"

"But…" he went on, tired and crushed she thought, even if she knew there was spirit to be beaten out of him yet, "…I do understand."

Her eyes narrowed, as if gauging his sincerity.

"Truly?"

"Yes," he told her. "I'll do whatever it takes to keep you here. As I said before: you have become very important to me."

Considering his admission, she was amused to see his anxiety as he awaited her decision.

For what to him seemed an eternity she mulled his offer over; her former "Master" standing before her awaiting a verdict; disgust for his own weakness not enough to stop him praying she accepted.

Then; finally:

"Very well," she told him. "I will speak to my mentor."

His all too evident relief was soon tinged with misgivings:

"Your mentor?" he repeated, spirit sagging further down the scale. Nothing good, he knew from thwarted experience, seemed forthcoming when her increasingly reviled -by him anyway- "Spiritual guide" was brought into the equation.

"Unless I can persuade him your offer is sincere and well-intended and he considers you worthy enough to pledge yourself to a believer, it will be impossible for me to accept you."

Closing his eyes to blot out the shame of his request he could see in eyes, and not for the first time, Lambert prayed for one of the natural calamities, that mentor's region of India was renowned for, to rid the planet of both his pestilential presence and the inconvenient religion that had placed him in his current position of influence over his lust object in the first place.

Opening his eyes once more, to assure the bête-noir's disciple of his sincerity, he found himself standing in the kitchen she had made her own.

Quite alone.

CHAPTER THIRTY-TWO

Power Play

"I think it time you moved things along," Rajiv told her when she Skyped him later that evening.

Anya's inner laughter was smug; the feelings of confidence and control she had been experiencing lately –reinforced by her handling of her 'Master' a short while ago- an elixir she found eminently acceptable.

Confidence and control, in regard of Rajiv, whose horizons were about to be broadened.

"I already have," she told him; sure she would get the response she wanted.

The annoyance at the other end of the connection was palpable; lasting for what seemed an age until; finally:

"I thought I advised you to wait?"

"And I decided to go with my own instincts.

"When?" he demanded, as angry as she had expected him to be at the disclosure.

"Not twenty minutes ago," she answered, unflustered by his tone. I told him that, because of the nature of his growing attraction to me, along with his inability to act as a Master should, my mentor feels it would be better if I were to leave his employ."

Again silence ruled; until:

"How did he react to that?" Rajiv asked grudgingly, interest overriding the irritation he felt for her having moved things along without consulting him first.

"Very predictably," she replied.

She made him wait, until; just before she was sure he would explode:

"At first he was angry. Then he tried to reason with me. Then he tried buying me. All very predictable. The prospect of no longer being able to place his nose in the gusset of my panties before licking the soiled fabric clean mad him most disconsolate, I can tell you?"

Rajiv was incensed:

"You have allowed your impatience to run away with you – just as I feared you would. You have placed him in a corner too soon and all our hard work is now at risk."

Anya was amused:

"Do you really think so?"

"I do."

"Then perhaps you could explain," she began with an air of triumph, "why my 'Master' just begged me to allow him to become my Lesser."

Rajiv's onscreen expression was a picture of pure disbelief.

"That's right," she went on. "I told him I would speak with my 'Advisor' this evening to see if he considered my former employer had the potential to pledge himself to me in such a position. I also told him he could have my decision in the morning."

From Cornwall, she watched her mentor mull it over in Calcutta - a heat of his own adding itself to the more constant variety of their shared birthplace.

"And when exactly," he asked finally, voice dangerously low – accusatory, in fact; "were you going to inform me of this?"

"Really, Rajiv," she scolded him in return –her confidence in the ability to control not limited to Bernard Lambert alone; "if you insist on using such a harsh tone with me I might be tempted to end our Internet liaison."

Her words were greeted by another silence.

"Did you really just say what I think you said, Anya?" he asked eventually, a little worried, she thought, despite his air of superiority. She was the one, after all, who provided him with a link back to a world lost to him since the passing of his Ilse -some ten years previously.

Without her, she knew only too well, he was nowhere.

"Not only did I say it but I meant it," she assured him. "I am grateful for your assistance -and the suggestion of my non-existent religion with its rigid beliefs was a masterstroke- but I find myself becoming more than a little tired of this superior attitude you adopt towards me."

"Superior…?" he exploded, losing his composure for the first time in many years. "Why, you ungrateful little…"

"There it is again!" she cut in, her own voice taking on the quality of the whip, allowing anger of her own to surface. "I think, Rajiv, we are at the stage where we must set a few things straight."

"Oh, you do, do you?" he asked menacingly.

"I believe that is what I just said," she responded, unfazed by his tone. "As appreciative as I am for the advice you have extended me, I really believe it to be high time I made you realise and accept your role as a bit player in the drama I play with my 'Master'."

"A 'Bit player'?" he repeated, not sure whether to believe what he was hearing.

"Again: that is what I said. Feel free to repeat anything you are unable to follow."

His face on the screen look fit to implode; so great was his internal rage as she continued on before he could express it:

"The situation to which you beat your geriatric meat is not yours but mine," she reminded him. "Without…"

"My 'Geriatric meat'?" he hissed.

"Be quiet!" she snapped back. "Without me what happens here does not happen at all."

She allowed a few beats to pass, making her next statement more… portentous:

"Without you, however, it goes on regardless."

Watching as the simple truth of it gained his grudging attention, she noted his anger, if not quelled entirely, had already softened somewhat.

From warp to impulse, as science fiction had it.

"If you wish to continue to be a part of what goes on here," she continued, "you will start to show me some respect. In fact, you can start, now, by saying: 'As you wish, Ms Anya'."

"'Ms Anya?'" he repeated, anger restored to warp speed, dilithium-crystals throbbing at full capacity.

"Repeat it as many times as you need," she told him. "Just be sure not to forget. Call it a token of your respect."

On-screen, his outrage was fuelled by a disbelief sending it to new dimensions – the startling effect of uncharted territory putting his insecurity on the backburner for the moment.

"Are you deranged, you buck-toothed ingrate?"

The silence at the Cornwall end was ominous.

Continuing on, and on, in a wordless battle of wills only one of them could win; both of them aware that whoever broke that silence first would be handing the other pride of place in the pecking order.

In the event, it was the one with most to lose and no webcam to view who broke first.

"Are you there still?" he demanded.

Silence continued to reign, unnerving him further, until:

"Anya, are you…"

"I am here. But only for long enough to explain something to you."

"But…"

"Be quiet and listen," she snapped. "Or I will block you as one of my Skype contacts… And I will not restore you."

Her threats had the desired effect; Rajiv knowing her well enough to be sure she did not make them simply for the pleasure of hearing them made.

"Now," she began, confident there would be no further interruptions; "I have something to say. Interrupt just once and it is over between us."

She allowed a few moments for him to realise the seriousness of her threat.

"In a few seconds," she began, "I am going to terminate this conversation and will not take any of your calls from now on. If, however, you wish me to do so again and desire to continue being a small part of my life, you will compose a suitably abject and apologetic email and send it to me with your acknowledgement that I am the dominant partner in this relationship. You will assure me that, despite your age, you are very much the junior and accept my lead."

She allowed him a few moments to mull it over, confident he would do as she said and not interrupt, before going on:

"There is no time limit on this, Rajiv, but, if I do not receive such a message, you will never hear from me again. It is your choice and the only one I offer. Only when you have complied with my commands will I restore your privileges."

Then, before Rajiv had a chance to disobey her and respond, Anya terminated the connection and blocked him as a user; smile as she did so full of satisfaction for the way she had handled him. There was, she considered after all, room for only one leader in a partnership. And he was not it. He may have spent half a lifetime dominating some simpering love struck German, but Anya Jalav, he would find, was neither simpering nor love struck.

And she certainly wasn't from the land of the Frankfurter.

Either he came to terms with the fact she was now his superior and followed her lead, or she would cut him off.

It was as simple as that.

With a broad and contented smile, having scythed one man's legs out from under him, she turned her attention to the prize awaiting her in the main house and how she would deal with him from now on.

CHAPTER THIRTY-THREE

The Lesser

"Are you still serious about what you said last night?" she asked; having made him sweat on both her presence and the decision of her mentor by not putting in an appearance until late afternoon.

Confident, now, her former Master would not complain.

"Or has a night's sleep robbed you of the courage you showed in making me the offer?"

Watching her as she stood in his kitchen, the same kitchen that had witnessed her dismantling of him the previous evening, Lambert noticed she was as precisely turned out as usual. Dressed in what had become her usual daytime outfit of black courts with spike heels, black nylons and tight black skirt with the habitual white shirt, it was easy to see she had slept well herself.

Which was in complete contrast to him.

Bernard Lambert had just endured the most anguished and sleep free evening of his life. Even the night before his divorce from Siobhan could not compete with the twisting and turning, up again and down again, decided and undecided, night of grief he had just experienced. That memory of how easily he had caved in before the girl playing itself out over, and over, and over, until dawn lit the bedroom. The shame he felt for his gutless capitulation no match for his self-disgust at the strength of the erection that led him to make it. Shame raging unabated throughout the night and still going strong by morning; lending physical exhaustion to an equally incapacitating mental variety.

And yet, despite his debilitated condition, what remained of his resolve had prompted him to put an end to the situation and send her packing.

Whatever he may have allowed her to say to him the night before, he assured himself, he remained a man. A description of himself not to be invalidated, he decided, simply because recent events had temporarily weakened him. First thing in the morning, he promised himself, he would give her a taste of the real Bernard

Lambert.

The Indian bitch, he convinced himself, would not know what hit…

"I asked you a question," she cut into his thoughts as he stood before her, expression distant.

"Sorry," he said, a private snapping to attention in the presence of a superior officer from an invading army, resolve vanquished at the arrival of a superior force.

"I was… I was…"

"Yes?" she snapped, relishing the reversal of their roles as she recalled him responding to her in just the same peremptory fashion.

"Let me guess," she answered for him. "You are about to try and wriggle your way out of the commitment you made to me last night. Here, in this very kitchen."

About to tell her that was exactly what he intended to do, drawing on what reserves of strength still remained to him, Lambert had no idea how what left his mouth performed the feat:

"No. Of course not," he heard himself assure her; restored pusillanimity taking heart at her words and the continued and expanded intimacy they implied– as demeaning to him as it would be.

"Are… Are you saying your mentor is agreeable?"

"First things, first," she told him. "Tell me, do you remember all of our conversation of a week ago?"

In his sleep-deprived condition Lambert struggled to recall exactly which conversation she referred to.

"You asked me to explain what the two options open to non-believers meant?" she gave reminder; allowing just a hint of the whip to sharpen her tone.

"I do, Anya," he confirmed, responding for the first time, she thought, like the well-schooled animal she intended him to become.

"And you still want to become my Lesser?"

He nodded, unable to swallow, let alone find words; it was one thing to offer to commit to something so debasing in order to achieve a more devious end but quite another to actually go through with it.

"Then show me," she demanded.

Puzzled, he stared down at her, not sure what it was she wanted to be shown, until their conversation really did kick in and he knew what it was she expected him to do.

"Anya," he began, appalled, "is this really necessary?"

"Can you tell me why else I would ask you to do it if it was not?" she snapped, the crack of the metaphorical lash visible upon him by means of his pained expression.

Lambert was unable to find an answer.

"It is expected of all those who pledge themselves to a superior of the faith," she reminded him. "Though it is considered as no more than a token of intent it is, just the same, non-negotiable. Tell me now if it is beyond your pride to comply and I will leave and trouble you no more."

It might be no more than a "Token of intent" to her and her fellow fanatics, he told himself, but, when she had first explained what a non-believer must do to pledge himself to one of her faith, his unspoken response had incredulity becoming mockery that a human being could be so malleable as to be forced into such an act.

Now, barely a week later, she was telling him that the price for keeping her in his life was exactly that.

"Anya, I..." he began.

"It is, as I say: non-negotiable," she told him. "Either I am convinced of your true intent to follow the guidance of both myself and my religion or I leave this instant. My belongings are packed and ready to go. All that keeps me is the fondness I have developed for you. Both that and the teachings of my faith, compel me to give your life some meaning at last by placing yourself, for once, below another."

"But, Anya..."

"There is no 'But!' " she came in. "Do it or I leave."

Lambert licked at dry lips, unable suddenly to make saliva, knowing he was equally unable to acquiesce to her demand. Were he to do so it would be... would be...

How on earth could he possibly look her in the eye after?

Even if he did have an agenda ulterior to what the act itself represented.

Could he really allow himself to sink this low in order to rise again, simply to have access to...?

As she turned and made to leave he had his answer.

"No, Anya!"

She turned at his cry.

Unhurriedly.

Leisurely.

Expectantly.

Moments suddenly becoming bigger than years as they faced each other down in a battle of wills with only one winner.

Until…

Slowly, almost imperceptibly; in the way of a once grand house in the first throes of caving in upon itself; he sank to his knees before her.

The smile above him he could no longer see was demonic in its gratification, the legs of its owner turning to sweet-water at a sight she had pictured so many times without ever expecting to see.

A handsome older man on his knees at her feet.

And put there without the subterfuge of role-play.

Deceit another matter.

In time to come, neither would know just how long that remained in their respective positions, but, both would be agreed, they would have remained there for some considerable time to come had it not been for the words of the new master of the house:

"Do it!" she barked.

CHAPTER THIRTY-FOUR

Atonement

Halfway across the world; as Anya Jalav began the process that would bind her intended prey to her; another would-be victim –if only at a remove- sipped at a large Scotch; unable to get his last conversation with the girl from his head.

The nature of that conversation and his recall of it stoking his anger and outrage further; her insistence he play second-fiddle to her leaving him speechless with rage.

Rage stoked further as memory played back her demand he address her as…

"In your dreams, ingrate slum bitch!"

So had he hissed after she had cut their Skype connection. Hell would find itself air-conditioned before he demeaned himself in such a way; the revenge scenarios he had started to weave immediately, made more and more outrageous by the swiftly emptying bottle on the table before him.

A depletion not concerning him; there was, after all, plenty more scotch where that came from.

Bitch!

And yet; and despite himself; it had been Rajiv Singh who blinked first.

Then blinked again.

And again.

His original intention to deny the ungrateful young bitch further access to his life and, more seriously from her point of view, the experience and support he had offered her in regard of the Englishman, lasting almost an hour before he composed the first email.

The gap between first and second of a slightly lesser duration.

But it was the third and final missive -not thirty minutes on from the second; after a single sentence response from Anya herself- that proved to him it wasn't the Englishman alone who was having change thrust upon him.

For a while after that discussion, he had stewed on her

treatment of him, devising all manner of implausible retributions for the dismissive way in which she had treated him.

Him!

Of all people.

The one person who had been nothing if not a friend to her.

That the familiar scenario was not lot on him –gifted student surpassing over-the-hill teacher; and finding no further use for him- did nothing to lessen his feelings of anger, outrage and, more revealingly, regret.

The threatened absence of their twice-daily conversations on Skype, he realised quickly –doing much to temper his anger; leaving a hole in his day-to-day no amount of books, television and surfing of the Net could fill.

The only surprise -given his sudden exclusion from both her life; as well as the situation for which he had placed his expertise at her disposal and remained so intensely interested about- was that it had taken as long as it had for his need to overcome his pride and contact her.

"Contact", he was at pains to word carefully:

"My Dearest Anya,

Our last conversation contained both anger and words out of keeping with commerce between friends. Brought about, I suggest, by the difference in our respective years.

Years making it incumbent upon me to make the first move as an opening attempt to repair the unnecessary rift between us.

My experience is that intergenerational friendships –and of a certain nature- such as ours are not only rare but very precious. Far too valuable I am sure you will agree, to throw away over nothing more than a tiny spat.

Be assured, the desire to help you attain your wishes still burns strong within me and all my knowledge and understanding of such matters remain at your disposal.

We have shared intimacies –and without judging each other-

only a very few people can claim and should be beyond playground spats of this nature.

Call me.

Your good friend, Rajiv.

Though short, the email he had composed had been a difficult one; for, in truth, and despite the loneliness, need and curiosity, prompting him to write it; he was still angry with the girl.

Blazingly angry, to be precise.

The time in between their fall out having done little to calm him - even if it did allow him to reflect on the gap she would leave in his life and how he would fill it. An absence -if she were serious, and decided to have nothing further to do with him- that would return his life to the dull and monotonous condition it had been in before her appearance restored it some zest. The same life he had borne over so many years –with the help of books, alcohol, television and Internet, and still more alcohol- regarding which the prospect of a return dispirited him beyond methods of measurement yet devised.

By the time he had girded his loins to compose that first email, he realised there was no way around the fact it would be him making the first move – hence his inference in the email itself that it was a move motivated by his greater age and maturity. Knowing, even as he went about the attempt at damage limitation, she would see it instantly as the exercise in cosmetics it was.

He was the one, after all -and the email proved as much- who needed her.

He could do no more than hope she had the decency to act as a friend should and accept her small victory over him with grace and good sense.

As it turned out, she had the good sense not to accept it at all.

One hour after he sent it there had been no reply; despite his knowing she would be in her quarters and on her computer at the British Meantime of early evening.

Thirty minutes later, and regardless of how needy it made him appear, he was ready to send another:

"Dearest Anya,

I know you are there. Where else would you be?

Why do you not respond to my email? Surely you are not still angry with a friend who has done nothing but promote your cause? Is there not blame for our altercation on both sides?

Despite this temporary setback in our relationship, my regard for you as a valued friend remains undiminished; knowing as I do how partnerships of such mutual frankness and meetings of like minds come along only very rarely throughout the course of a lifetime – if at all.

As always, I am at your disposal.

Rajiv.

It was as far as he was willing to bend he had told himself after hitting the Send button. Even this small willingness to concede face one he knew Ilse would have found hard to believe; unwilling as he had been to extend her the smallest fraction of leeway in any way shape or form – and still less if that concession invited even the tiniest of questions regarding his dominance.

And yet, after another thirty minutes without response, the possibility he may have lost the young friend supplying his twilight years with some sap made the email appearing in his Inbox –albeit an email of a single sentence- as welcome as it was galling:

"You know what you have to do."

The initial hope triggered by the: Receiving Mail, message had turned to elation when her name flashed onto his Inbox.

Becoming outright anger when he took in the seven words and the inference behind them.

That: "Inference", goading him to refill his glass from the swiftly emptying Scotch bottle to contemplate his response.

Having been a player himself, and in possession of a real talent for its mind games and power plays, he knew exactly what she wanted.

They did share similar characteristics, after all.

But, where he was open to a level playing field in their relationship, equality played no part in the union she had in mind. The need to dominate, he was coming to understand, flowed stronger in her veins than his and, though power over the Englishman was her ultimate goal; he now saw she would expect to exercise a lesser form of control over him also.

She wanted –needed- control over anyone she allowed into her life and that person would either accept this or leave that life entirely.

The plain and simple question for Rajiv, at that moment, was whether his need to have her in his life was so great he could –for the first time in his life- play second fiddle to a woman.

Correction:

Girl.

A question: knowing the loss he felt -even at this early stage of her absence from his life- a part of him had already answered; and a decision he conceded he had to make - despite finding it so difficult to accept.

An acceptance, just the same, he was not about to make through the distortion of alcohol.

After splashing himself with cold water to counteract the effect of the Scotch; he had seated himself before the computer to compose his email of capitulation; both head and eyes clear as he readied himself to do what was needed if he was to keep her in his life. Aware that, if he was going to concede power to the girl, then he wanted parameters set and boundaries fixed before doing so.

Both of which, he was certain, were better negotiated with bright eyes and an alert mind than through the befuddling effects of inebriation.

Composing himself before the screen, he decided to get the obvious –if no less difficult- opening out of the way first.

That opening all the more alien to him for having never addressed a person in such a way before.

With a deep breath, his fingers descended on the keys and began to type:

"Dearest Ms Anya…"

CHAPTER THIRTY-FIVE

Demotion

What had happened to him?

Regarding his reflection in the wardrobe mirror as he waited for her to make the short journey over from her quarters above the garage –the "Short journey" it had so far taken her two hours to make after leaving his kitchen and ordering him to wait in his bedroom- the likeness staring back at Bernard Lambert seemed to have more in common with the artistry of the taxidermist than the Almighty himself.

A shell with the guts removed.

An image of himself, as he knelt on the terracotta tiles and went to all fours before her, tore his eyes from the mirror; unable to contemplate what he saw reflected there as his all too recent disgrace continued to wash over him. Watching himself on the backdrop of closed eyelids as, in response to her command, he lowered his head further to place his lips on the toe of a shiny black court shoe. Recalling through his self-loathing the smell of her nylon encased foot surrounded by leather and the excitement it elicited in him. Experiencing for the first time that "Delicious weakness" he had read of in Lawrence's "Seven Pillars of Wisdom" and been unable, or unwilling, to understand.

"It is customary," she had said, through passions inspired by the level to which she had reduced him thus far, "to count to ten when in the position of respect. Do so now."

Nose rasping against the black nylon covering her instep, still marvelling at how he came to find himself in such a position, Lambert had counted; fighting back the urge to cover her feet and ankles in kisses before making his way up to…

"On future occasions," had come a dislocated voice form above, you will repeat this show of respect with the other foot. For now though, I want you to go to your bedroom to wait for me and not leave it until I say."

Imprinted on the backdrop of his eyelids still, he watched as she turned on her heel and marched from the kitchen; leaving behind a former "Master" as weak and powerless as an undernourished foundling. His shame, the watching Bernard Lambert recalled, no less debilitating for her encouraging use of the word...

"Bedroom."

Picture-show over, he seated himself on the end of his bed – dejected, despite the rush of blood to his netheregions inspired by it. A reaction that was both a defeat and a consolation, he decided; indicating as it did that his shameful capitulation had more in common with the kind of battles men had lost to the opposite sex for a millennia; rather than irrefutable evidence of any fibre and resolve he may lack as a man.

And yet, despite his growingly less persuasive assurances that he was only going along with the horse-faced little bitch to achieve an agenda of his own, he could not prevent an out of character self-awareness from calling into question all the qualities he believed stored in his possession.

Returning to his reflection as he sat, deep in thought, everything: virility, self-sufficiency, confidence and pride; the same qualities he had always assured himself were the very least that were required to take pride in one's stature as a man; appeared to be missing.

The man who had pistoned his wife's closest friend to submission in a Mayfair hotel and made her beg to lick the residue of her own arousal from his still erect cock was a memory. As far removed from the image staring back at him, dark-eyed and hollow cheeked, as his ex-wife from the ugly religious zealot from the sub-continent who was probably making her way to his room at this moment; even as he went about summarising his fall from grace to himself.

Yet still, so delusional did he remain, he managed to assure himself his fall would be no more than a temporary blip; convinced that the moment he gained access to her body he would –as he had done with so many others in the past- lose interest and become his real self again.

He was still cogitating along these lines, spirits rising a little, when the bedroom door opened and he rose to greet her.

A sight obliterating all attempts at damage limitation as she entered, careful to leave the door open behind her.

She was wearing nothing but a flimsy and diaphanous nightshirt that reached to mid-thigh, loose raven hair spilling over her shoulders on its journey to her waist. The smoothness of her dark brown thighs and the sheen of her skin as it shimmered downwards towards the feet she –or rather, he- kept so immaculately transfixing his capacity to breathe. A vision ending in the same open-toed sandals she had worn on the first day she had discarded her saris and entered this same room bearing breakfast.

Finding himself unable to speak, deliberately avoiding the equine picture above the neck he had yet to come to terms with, his eyes fixed on the magnificent breasts and erect nipples, last seen heaving beneath white cotton, that were visible through the gossamer of the nightshirt and made all the more breathtaking for the darkening effect of the material itself

On autopilot, he moved forward, instantly erect –more erect, in fact, than he could ever recall being- arms reaching for her; no other intention entering his head besides taking hold of her and…

"No!" she cried, throwing out an outstretched palm to stop him in his tracks. "Stay where you are."

"But," he protested, "I thought…"

"You are not to touch me," she reminded him, breasts still in motion from the stretching of her arm. "You have already signaled your determination to become my Lesser by placing your lips on my feet in the ancient form of respect, but that does not entitle you to anything save that which I wish to allow you. A Lesser is only allowed to touch his superior below the ankles – and only then with his superior's express permission."

"Is that why you come to my room dressed in such a way?" he accused, sensing hypocrisy, bitterness all too evident.

His thwarted expression fetching a smile to her over plump young lips.

"You are right," she told him, elevating his hopes. "I come to you like this for a purpose – though not, I think, the purpose you have in mind."

"Why then?" he pressed, knowing that if he were any kind of man he would not allow himself to be… teased… by such a young girl; knowing also that she would have only herself to blame if he threw her to the mattress and rammed the result of her provocation deep into her virgin cunt.

"I dress like this by way of consolation for you," she went on.

"Consolation?"

"Think of it as a way of lessening your disappointment for your loss."

His brows crinkled in puzzlement:

"How do you mean: my loss?"

Again her horse face contorted into a smile.

"Stand by the bed," she said before taking a chair from the dressing table and placing it near the open door some seven or eight paces away.

Doing as she said he made to sit on the bed.

"I said to stand," she snapped.

Biting back a response –it being, he thought, no time for a confrontation- he did as she asked and watched her take her place on the chair, crossing one leg over the other to give him an unimpeded view of a smooth expanse of thigh. Gently dangling a spike-heeled sandal from her painted toes to capture his attention further and gratified when his eyes focused on the sandal dangled precariously on the end of her toes.

"A beast awaiting his owner's collar," she assured herself, "Utterly unaware of the ring being placed through his nose."

The septum, she reflected, having been pierced already without his even being aware of it.

Standing he unbuckled his belt and unfastened his jeans. They were down to his knees before she could react –the first time – other than his proposal of marriage- he had taken her by surprise.

"What are you doing?" she asked.

He looked at her with puzzlement.

"Well..." he began uncertainly, "the way you're dressed... I thought…"

"Lessers do not think," she told him; using the same autocratic tone she had used with Rajiv earlier.

Her own reminder of her former "Mentor" made her smile. For, while Bernard Lambert had been waiting for her to come to him, she had been reading the two emails Rajiv had finally caved in and sent her. Her first contact with him in the short time since she had read him the riot act.

Rule of three holding fast, she had told herself, the last,

suitably abject, email would be waiting for her when she returned to her quarters.

The single sentence rejoinder she had made to his second attempt at putting things right between them not, she knew, giving him much by way of a choice. His rejoinder, she promised herself, to be dealt with in her own sweet time. That Rajiv had caved in at all though, let alone so quickly, leaving her in no doubt he now accepted who had the real power in their relationship.

A: "Relationship"; she was more than willing to resume.

On her terms.

Returning to the task in hand, she noticed a sullen looking Lambert was still in his position at the foot of the bed, jeans still around his ankles; the tenting of his blue cotton boxer shorts providing evidence of his continuing lust; the strength of her need to see it properly and close-up for the first time urging her to patience.

It would not do, after all, to give him the idea he meant anything to her.

"I dress in such a way," she began, in answer to his earlier question, "in case you are amenable to the conditions necessary to become my Lesser. Should I be persuaded by your sincerity and you are willing to take the necessary oath it is just possible I will grant you your wish to look upon me while you stroke your needy little penis."

Lambert knew he should bring this to an end. He was being insulted and belittled –unfairly, given the size of his cock that had not received complaints until now- in ways he would not have believed possible by the girl seated in front of him; a voice inside screaming for him to show her the exit and remove her from his life. After all, he thought with a flash of cognisance, if this was the kind of power she could wield over him in so short a space of time there was no telling where things could lead.

No, he told himself, reaching a resolution, if he had any manly pride at all he would drag her from his room and kick her capacious brown arse out of his…

And yet, he thought, hesitating fatally.

"What an arse it was!"

Also, though he was loath to admit it, he knew it wasn't just the body below that was responsible for his vacillation. A part of him, he knew, was responding to her increasing domination of him. Lawrence's "Delicious weakness" occurring to him again as long buried childhood experiences at the hands of women of authority; surfaced again with –as Rajiv had assured his own would be Mistress they would- power that was multiplied all the more for being so… abandoned.

It was at that moment, lost for response, that a former suspicion reasserted itself; his face a mask of suspicion suddenly:

"Is this about…?"

"No!" she snapped, having expected the question before now and reading his thoughts without difficulty. "It is not about money," she hissed. "Do not stain either me or my faith with your own sins."

Lambert fell silent, still not entirely convinced.

"You English are so predictable," she spat. "Everything boils down to cash and possessions. It is ingrained within you. One of the reasons my religion will not accept those of your race."

"So…" he began, unconvinced, sarcasm surfacing, "it's not my money you…?"

"Had I wanted a share of your wealth and property," she came in, tone even but eyes blazing, "I would have accepted your offer of marriage. I have tried to explain to you but you seem incapable of understanding something so far above your own petty notions of what constitutes success and position in the world. But then, perhaps, I expect too much of you. My religion is, after all, about honesty in relationships and the dignity of service."

The curl of her lip was derisory.

"Not concepts with which you would have had much familiarity."

As he listened intently to her words, anger rising, she almost giggled at the nature of them; knowing, as she did, that his coming "Service" to her would contain no trace of "Dignity".

"My religion," she insisted, "shuns all material things. Its currency is truth and the peace it brings with it. The embracing of our true natures, no matter what they may be, is paramount in order for us to find the home most suited to our spirituality. You are very handsome," she told him, it sounding nothing remotely like a compliment on her lips. "Were I of a religion that permitted such things and you were a true man, I would not think twice before allowing you the access to my body you appear to desire so much."

The way his eyes roved over her did nothing to make her correct the statement.

"Money," she assured him, "much to your disbelief, would not enter into it. It is my beliefs that bind me, and no man - despite the power of any attraction I may feel towards him. Nothing will make me stray from them. You will do to remember that. Everything else is secondary. They are my guide, my pleasure, and my salvation."

Lambert looked at the girl as if seeing her for the first time; fluency in a language was one thing, he knew, articulacy quite another, and her speech –as deluded as he considered it to be- was nothing if not articulate.

And altered the nature of his situation not one tiny bit, he confessed. The continued tenting of his boxer pants evidence enough to suggest unsuspected eloquence went no way towards lessening a tyrannical and inexplicable attraction running way beyond his control.

"What do want from me?" he asked, almost as a whisper.

She exulted inwardly; he was caving in before her as surely as plywood under the tracks of a bulldozer.

"As I say: I am devoted to both my religion and its teachings and they will always come first. But I am also human. That a handsome male such as yourself desires one such as me is both a tribute and a new experience. I confess it to be one I would hate to pass up – even though I most certainly would and will if it conflicts with my beliefs. The prospect of exercising control over the cock of a mature man such as yourself is one that makes my sadly neglected cunt very excited."

Bernard Lambert felt as if an electrical current had run the length of his body. The shock of such language from his servant's lips made his lust for her stronger. So strong, in fact, her stated intent to "Control" his cock evaded his –admittedly faulty-radar completely.

"As my face has probably made you aware," she continued, ignoring the arousal threatening to make lift-off from his boxers, "such opportunities –even had I been able to take advantage of them- have been sadly lacking in my life thus far. I would hate for one such as this to pass me by."

"Then don't let it, Anya," he urged, about to take a step

towards her when he halted in his tracks.

Sliding the diaphanous nightshirt over her shoulders, she stood before him naked, hands on hips arrogantly; knowing the attraction her body possessed for him and supremely confident in its ability to hold his attention.

A confidence, he would have acknowledged, that was not misplaced as he drank her in; mouth dry and -even had it been moist- unable to swallow. Despite all his many conquests down the years, this was the most erotic thing he had ever seen – made all the more so it seemed by the knowledge of her youth, her status, her race, and the strange religion that, somehow, made her seem both illicit and off limits.

The body before him –face notwithstanding- was a composite of all the parts guaranteed to press his buttons.

And there -as if to underpin his reaction- at the vee of her legs, was the most perfect cunt he had ever seen.

Pure.

Unsullied.

And, most deliciously of all:

Shaven.

The most anatomically beautiful pussy it was possible to imagine; a hairless exclamation mark that pointed up the flat brown stomach and perfect breasts above it; making it all he could do, previous reticence consigned to history, not to slither across and run his tongue over the outer lips jutting towards him in invitation.

"Are you willing to lose this?" she asked, aware she was overmastering him in a real sense for the first time and soaring high on the knowledge. "I do not wish to go. I am now convinced you will make a very able Lesser –even more, perhaps- but unless the demands of my religion are met by both of us I will have no other choice."

Barely hearing her words, so transfixed was he by her glorious young pussy; he made an involuntary movement forward, stopping only when she immediately backed away towards the door.

"What do you want?" he asked rasped, voice again beginning to fail him; a barely detectable quality of pleading in his voice indicating to her his resistance was not so much crumbling as liquidising.

"You must embrace your true nature and acknowledge you are not a Master. It is your only way to regain my respect. You are far too weak."

Lost in appreciation of that perfect and hairless snatch, Lambert barely heard its owner.

"Look at you!" she hissed, triumphant. "The condition of your jewels tell me that you desire nothing more at this moment than to throw me upon the bed and thrust your manmeat inside me until you anoint my virgin pussy with your seed."

Lambert groaned with desire, these being words he did hear.

"A real man would take me even if I were unwilling," she said, inflaming him further. "The shame resulting from Police involvement and the knowledge he would never see me again would make no difference. Yet there you stand, full of lust and impotent to act upon it. Without my permission you will attempt nothing with this smooth virgin pussy you cannot take your eyes from."

He was pretty far gone by this time, she knew, so far gone his hand snaked inside his boxers, eyes riveted upon her pussy as he went to his knees to gain greater access to his ravenous cock and stare up at the object transfixing it.

"No!" she demanded upon seeing his intention, her own excitement at least as great, perhaps greater, than his; determined to prove her willpower was greater than his and bind him to her at the same time.

He took no notice, eyes continuing to drink her in greedily.

"If you do not stop I leave this instant," she warned him to no effect, his hand continuing to pump as his gaze remained fixed.

"Very well," she said, turning and moving towards the doorway – amazing arse almost through it when her bluff paid dividends.

"Don't go!" he all but screamed, removing his hand as she asked; even though it took all the willpower at his command to do so; the prospect of never seeing those breasts, those legs, those feet and the most incredibly gorgeous cunt to bless his vision causing him an almost physical pain.

To his relief, she stopped in the doorway.

"Will you listen to me and do everything I say from now on?" she said without turning.

On his knees on the carpet, staring at the smooth brown cheeks of her arse, he sensed they had reached a watershed.

Her: "Do everything I say from now on", not escaping him.

Nothing, after this, he suspected, would be the same between them. The screen containing master and servant would have been blurred and no fiddling with the vertical hold would return its previous clarity.

"Can I really live with that?" he asked himself; even as his decision was being made for him. Deluding himself still -as was his way- that he could send her packing the moment she was out of his system and that his capitulation was but a temporary one.

Standing, he pulled up his Versace denims, buckled his belt and raised himself to his full five foot eleven to give her a response.

CHAPTER THIRTY-SIX

Another Offer

"What are you doing?" he asked, voice cracking with need as she re-entered the room to stand by the chair she had just vacated; in possession of the answer she had been in no doubt he would give and deigning to find him sincere enough to resume where they left off.

Not answering, she slipped her filmy nightshirt back over her head; encouraged still further by the fear she saw written across his face at what he had taken as an intention to leave.

"I am a little cold," she told him, taking her seat once again; the fear she saw changing to relief placing any earlier misgivings regarding success in perspective.

"You have him on your hook," she laughed to herself. "All that remains is to reel him in."

"Convince me you are truly serious and not playing a game," she told him, retaking her seat, "and I will be willing to accept the responsibility of educating you in the ways of your true nature."

In spite of the urgency at his groin, Lambert felt a certain dislocation:

"My... true nature?" he repeated, almost as if to himself.

Then:

"Educate me?"

"I understand how distressing such a prospect must appear to you," she said soothingly. "How could an ugly Indian girl who is young enough to be your daughter and without formal education be in possession of knowledge you have yet to divine? How could she know that the image you have presented to both yourself and the world is nothing but a façade?"

"But..."

"Exterior camouflage," she went on over him, "of so little substance it can do nothing else but crumble in the face of setback and neglect? How could such a person understand your desire to grovel before her and the needs of the cock that now threatens to explode inside your jeans held in your hands as you wait for her to give you permission to stroke yourself to her image – 'Ugly' face or not?"

"Anya… I… I"

"Allow me to prove a point to you," she said, cutting into his thoughts, voice becoming even suddenly, almost friendly; as if she were asking him to taste her latest attempt at a Cornish pasty.

He watched with a thrill of excitement-stroke-horror as she pointed to the floor before her with the index finger of her right hand; the blood red of her nail varnish aiming at a spot on the carpet a pace or two away from her.

"Wh-What?" he asked, certain of what she required even as he stammered out the question.

"I would like you to take off your jeans and kneel at my feet…"

Though it was a relatively small amount of time in real terms; it seemed an eternity to Bernard Lambert before he could get past his shock at his servant's request and find his voice.

Though he had kissed the toes of her shoes in his study earlier, he had managed to convince himself it was a one-off sign of his sincerity for what he proposed to do for her by way of getting into her pants. Now he was being asked to kneel at her feet as if she truly believed that was his place in life from now on.

"Kneel at your feet?" he said, repeating her words as if half expecting her to tell him he'd heard incorrectly.

"And take off your jeans," she reminded him.

"What on earth for?" he asked, encouraged, just the same by her request in regard of the Versace. "What: 'Point', could it possibly prove?"

The question a needless one, he knew, her intention obvious. Position and pride, however, along with his own sense of himself as a man, besieged as it was, demanding he make some kind of response; despite her intention being clear to him

She gave it some thought, as if she truly hadn't considered her reasons for wanting him there until now.

Then; at last:

"I was about to say: because I told you to do so," she told him. "But it is more to prove the point of which you just spoke. Perhaps to myself. It is, I must confess, just possible I could be wrong about you."

"And how would it prove that?" he demanded, still unwilling to concede - despite the overwhelming compulsion to do exactly as she asked and fall to his knees; taking advantage of the position to bury his face in the provocative and hairless slit he could see across from him.

"By telling me you are exactly where you belong," she answered. "That you accept your position as my Lesser and are willing to embrace your true nature – as well as mine."

By this time, Lambert was having trouble swallowing - air filling his lungs only under protest. Sensing for the first time that if he was foolish enough to enter the approaching watershed, let alone immerse himself in the tank inside it, he would be forever struggling to remain afloat.

Let alone swim.

Her confidence that he was about to do precisely that readable in her equine features in a way he found both ominous and... intimidating.

"It is your choice," she told him. "Either do as I tell you now or I leave this instant."

Seeing his will weaken; knowing there could be but one outcome; she again pointed to the carpet in front of her; sure that, once she had him down, he would not be rising again:

"Kneel."

For a moment, some fire entered his expression as they locked eyes in a battle of wills; then, as she had known it would, the fire extinguished itself and he began a descent to the carpet until he was once again on his knees at her feet – without, this time, the excuse of a pedicure to veil his shame.

As he knelt there and waited, eyes half closed, she could tell he was finding his current position even more demeaning than the one she had forced him to adopt in the kitchen a few hours previously.

He had, she assured herself, seen nothing yet.

"Look at me now," she ordered, noticing, as his head rose and his eyes opened, how distasteful he still found her features.

"English bastard!" she thought.

Gazing down at him, she felt she knew something of the thrill a true queen must experience at the obeisance of a subject, his utter degradation and growing powerlessness at being before her in such a way exacerbating the sensation.

"Does that not feel natural?" she asked finally.

"N-Not really," he lied, resolve receding as, unilateral of conscious thought, his eyes slipped from her eyes to her teeth to her throat, to…"

"Because it feels natural to me, I must say," she told him, a smile crossing her lips as his gaze fastened upon her breasts. "And why, if you protest so strongly does your cock strain so hard against your shorts? Could it be you like the sight of your young Indian servant's breasts from such a lowly position?"

Drinking those same breasts in he could make no reply.

"Yes," she went on. "What other explanation could there be? Hard to take your eyes from them, is it not? How frustrating for you to know they are so close and you can do nothing to satisfy your need to cup them in your hands. To feel their youthful firmness as you lower your lips to the nipples already hardened by the sight of you on your knees in worship."

That he made no answer, just continued to stare at her breasts, was all the confirmation needed she would not be vacating the house that day – or any day come to that.

Though there was still work to be done before he accepted what it would mean if she consented to stay.

"But then," she went on, "it's not just my firm Indian tits you find so enthralling, is it?" instinct telling her such talk, from her lips –and in his language- would inflame him further.

"Is it?" she demanded when he made no reply.

He shook his head, speech beyond him, eyes glued to her Firm Indian tits; besieged manhood; even as his eyes lowered to take in her exquisite shaved pussy; still making subconscious and futile attempts to assert itself.

"If you are the man you say you are why don't you get up from your knees and tell me to leave?"

On his knees before her, Lambert knew it was exactly what he should do.

And yet…?

"Go on!" she urged when he remained motionless. "Do it! You will never see me in the flesh again, but at least you will have a measure of self-respect and some memories with which to beat your English meat."

"Anya, I…"

"Look at you! Trying to convince yourself you remain a man. My 'Master' - even as you kneel on the floor before me."

She sensed him squirm and her laugh was spiteful.

"Keep your eyes on my cunt," she ordered. "Do not take your eyes from it until I say otherwise."

It was, Lambert knew, an unnecessary order.

"At least you have found enough small self-knowledge to offer to become my Lesser," she snorted, allowing herself to become angry. "It is something, I suppose. Though I am not happy to know I have spent the past seven months providing service to a man unworthy of it."

Going with her anger –ersatz as it was- she stood up, towering above him despite her five-feet; looking down imperiously as he knelt before her, head still lowered and shaking from side to side as if it couldn't quite believe what it was hearing; even if, she noted with delight, his eyes remained fixed on her womanhood.

When it came, her voice had an air of finality to it:

"My spiritual guide warned me I should not get involved with one of your kind. Our country suffered from the deceit of you and others like you for too long to allow history to repeat itself on a personal level. Now he has been proved right. Though he assures me that with a firm hand you will become, at least, an adequate Lesser and gives me his blessing to accept you."

She paused to watch him for a moment or two; surprised, despite her confidence, at the speed of the progress she was making - the reason she was now pressing ahead at a faster rate than Rajiv had intended. Noting with intense satisfaction, how his eyes, just as she had ordered, remained riveted upon her pussy.

His sudden docility and the necessary spontaneity demanded by her new intent, sparking an idea:

"Move your face closer to my cunt," she told him; all but coming at the sound of her own command and the instant way he obeyed. "Keep your eyes fixed upon it at all times. But be very careful. You know what will happen if you… touch."

The scene she had engineered was really too incredible, she told herself. There on his knees before her; face not inches from the pussy intent upon dominating him; was the man who had been her employer when she had opened her eyes the previous morning.

His own eyes adoring now the very cunt she intended to be so instrumental in his coming enslavement to her.

It had been exciting to dream of such things, she thought, but to actually…

"You may take deep breaths through your nose if you wish to sniff me," she told him, a need to push him further and the strength of her own passion goading her on.

Without missing a beat, he began to do just that.

"But do not make contact," she warned him.

A slight inclination of his head told her he understood.

"Incredible!" she mused to herself.

To have achieved what she had achieved with him in such a relatively short space of time was, she knew, as amazing as it was unbelievable. Not two minutes ago, it seemed, she had arrived on his doorstep as a menial; now, she was here and he was… down there.

Though, previously, she had consoled herself with the thought her desires were possible; a part of her had accepted such a likelihood was highly unlikely. Now however, she was certain every perverted desire her agile young mind had either read or dreamt of was about to be made flesh through the vessel of choice below her. It requiring a massive effort of concentration and willpower, in fact, to prevent herself from ordering him to eat the overheating gash his whole being seemed focused upon. Only the knowledge she would undo everything she had been working towards if she gave him too much too quickly fortified her resolve to refuse the demands rising up at her in ever-growing clamour.

Below her, nose inches from her shrine, Bernard Lambert was in a similar situation – and powerless to refuse his own demands anything.

He was, he thought –with what reasoning and logic remained to him- in as great a state of rut as he thought it possible to be.

The sight and the smell of that pussy, as he stared and sniffed - swearing he could smell her homeland in the exotic mustiness assailing his nostrils- drove all thoughts of his humiliation and the consequences arising from it out of his head. At that moment, it seemed to him as if he was indeed at the: "Centre of his universe".

Still spellbound, he watched as she slipped a finger into herself and rotated it teasingly before easing it out; glistening and aromatic.

"You may remember," she said, retaking her seat and removing a shoe before wiping the residue of her arousal across the toes of her right foot, "that I mentioned there were two ways in which a non-believer such as yourself can interact with a true follower like myself. The first option, as I have already said, is to become a Lesser."

"It is the option I am told most people in your position opt to take as it is not so… total as the second of the choices available. Though, as a Lesser, of course, you would have access only to my body below the ankle, and only with my express permission."

She waited, gauging his response.

"But, to ease the disappointment I see you feel, you will be pleased to know there is much… excitement… still to be had from so limited accessibility."

If her words reassured him it was not to be seen on his face.

"Nod if you understand," she ordered.

Despite his "Disappointment", he nodded, quickly, allowing her to go on:

"Good," she said leaning back in her seat and raising her foot to his mouth. "Now, I want you to place my toes in your mouth and keep them there. You must savour the taste of me as I explain what I will expect from you and provide you with a small taste of what becoming my Lesser will mean."

Lambert looked at her aghast; his jaw dropping enough for her to place the toes in question upon his lower lip; the smell of her secretions almost making him swoon with need as he opened his mouth and greed took as much of her –thankfully small- foot in his mouth.

"Well done," she applauded as his eyes closed and his mouth surrounded her toes and varnished nails. "But keep your eyes open and upon mine now. I need to know that you understand what I am explaining to you."

His eyes flickered open and found hers; the beaten quality she could see in his gaze, underpinning his euphoria, all the more welcome for her having inspired it.

"Suck now," she told him, almost laughing as he instantly obeyed and his cheeks hollowed.

"Yes," she applauded. "That is good. Very well done."

Below her, on his knees, sucking her toes, Bernard Lambert felt a thrill of pleasure at her praise for his willingness to debase himself in such a way. That praise –along with the taste and smell of her glorious pussy; second-hand or not- enough to side-line the deep, deep, shame he knew he would feel when she left his presence.

Resentment a given.

"A Lesser, you see," she went on, "is permitted to retain his everyday position –with minimal changes- in regard of his Better. For instance: were you to accept this role –as you already have, I believe- I would remain in the position of your employee. You, however, would no longer be 'Master' and, though I would maintain a demeanour towards you in keeping with our respective positions that would enable you to keep face with family, friends and acquaintances –assuming you had any, that is- there would be no doubt in your mind that I was no longer your servant.

"As my Lesser you would not be able to touch me above the ankles at any time –and then, as I have already explained, only with my express permission- while in private you would show me the utmost respect. In return for your recognition of yourself and your acceptance of your new position in relation to me, I would then be able to supervise the sexual needs I seem, for some reason, to inspire in you."

She gauged the effect of her words, unsure how much of what she was saying managed to penetrate the competing sensations inspired by her fragrant foot.

"In short, as my Lesser you would –at my discretion- have a degree of autonomy in your public life; while, in private, and as my religion and beliefs insist, I would have complete responsibility for your behaviour."

She watched closely for some sign of a reaction from him; aware that only hours –minutes- before such a prospect would have driven him to both rage and denial.

Now, there was no sign of either.

"The power of pussy", she mused to herself, as she had once heard it described; "unanswerable - even smeared across a painted toe.

"Nod your head again if you understood what I just told you and continue to suck," she ordered, gratified to find herself obeyed instantly; as if he wanted all intrusions dealt with swiftly that he might return to his chore without further delay.

"Good," she told him, taking her toes from his mouth and almost laughing at his look of desolation for the removal. "I am pleased. So pleased I want to do something for you."

The spark of anticipation ignited within him swiftly becoming an inferno after her next words and the following instructions:

"Lie on your back and spread your legs. And do not speak. If I once hear your voice I will stop...

"That's right. Slide closer now, legs either side of the chair. I have no wish to stretch...

"Hands by your side and no moving. Your eyes must be on mine the whole time. The smallest glance away and your… treat… ends...

"Very good. I like you so much better when you do not pretend to be a man. On the subject of which, we will have to do something about that nasty hair I see on your legs and chest. You have an acceptable body for a Lesser of your age but hair has no place upon it. Also, it goes without saying that your little pee-pee must be kept free of hair too. Little boys do not have hair around their pee-pees now, do they?…

"Is that anger I see? I should hope not. Now, shall we start? Nod if that is what you want…

"Yes, I thought it would be. All little boys like to have their pee-pees played with, I am told. Be patient for a second now while your Better removes her other shoe…

"No! Do not close your eyes…

"There, you can follow instruction. Life can be so, so rewarding if we allow ourselves to be guided by our superiors. Is that nice?…

"No speaking now. A simple nod will suffice…

"My, but you really like the sole of my little Indian foot sliding up and down your stiff little pee-pee, don't you?…

"Should I keep doing it, you think? Have you been good enough to deserve such pleasure?…

"Good Lord, we are breathing heavily, are we not? Is something exciting you? Tell me if it is because I would not want you to have an accident over my…:

Which was exactly the point when, driven beyond ecstasy,

after no more than a few strokes, Bernard Lambert lost contact with the eyes mocking him and succumbed to the exquisite torture of the foot masturbating him to jettison his seed over the red toenails he himself had painted barely three days ago.

"You filthy beast!" she snarled, rising to her feet. "How dare you!"

Still flat on his back beneath her, Lambert felt as if his very life force had been sucked up from his dick along with his semen.

Never had he known such bliss.

Such rapture.

Such intoxication.

Such… surrender.

"My mentor was right I put you to this last test," he heard her voice from above, content not registering for a few seconds, so scrambled were his senses. Only the sight of her magnificent, callipygian, arse as it hovered above him, its owner turning to retrieve her gown, focused him somewhat.

"Test?" he asked.

"He warned me you were unworthy to be a Lesser," she spat, disgust so great it was almost visible upon the air.

"Yet I spoke for you," she went on. "Pleaded with him to ask himself if he could, just this once, possibly be wrong."

Above him, her head shook with anger at herself.

"He said you were no more than a pampered animal."

"Now just a second," he protested, finding his courage now the ministrations of her foot had taken a temporary edge from his needs and his senses were returned to something approaching normal.

"And an animal," she spoke over him, "pampered or no, remains that way until schooled."

Again her head shook with distaste for the man at her feet.

"Had I not seen your behaviour at first hand I would not have believed it. Spurting your stuff over my toes! You disgust me!"

"That's enough!" he warned her, trying to sound authoritative as he rested on his elbows. "What did you expect to happen once you put your foot on my…?"

"Some self-control," she snarled, glaring down at him.

"Are you a man? Or a little boy? Not that even. A dog, perhaps. Who knows, maybe your next housekeeper will allow you to hump her leg as she stands at the sink to do the dishes. It is no less than you are worth."

"I've had about enough of this," he told her, rising to his feet, aware of the mess at his groin and, given the amount plastered over his shorts, wondering just how much could actually have found its way onto her toes.

"Then you are not alone," she agreed. "My mentor was as farsighted and prescient in your regard as he has always been in such matters. For a person such as you there is only one option if he wishes to be accepted by a believer of the faith."

Back turned to her now, using the tissues on his nightstand to make himself presentable, he sighed, post-orgasm bravado making him dismissive of that he would again be needing; waving a macho hand derisively by way of telling her to leave.

And soon.

As he turned and his eyes found those of the young girl whose foot had just made love to him, a certain expression on her face puzzled him. Anya, far from being dismayed by his born again masculinity, was experiencing an epiphany to match the teachings of her bogus faith. Despite his bravado, she was experiencing a huge sense of rightness. Everything had fallen into place. What was happening between them was wholly natural; despite its perversity. The man's greater years, superior education and position, were meaningless in the face of her unquestionable superiority and strength of will.

"He is indeed a dog," she told herself; already thinking of him as something less than human. "Fit only to be of use to a superior master."

Smirking to herself then as her thoughts raced on:

"Even if that 'Master' is a young girl."

Her former employer's change of heart after completion concerning her not in the slightest; knowing that, if he thought so brief a taster would rid him of his obsession, he would soon be begging her to stay should she decide to leave and take any possibility of a repeat performance with her.

Anya certain now he was too weak for a change of heart of any lasting duration as she continued to berate him:

"I should have known. A person such as you is not worthy to be my Lesser."

"Yes, yes, yes. If you say so," he told her, slipping back into his jeans. "Though a change of record might be nice."

Unconvinced and totally unimpressed by his flippancy and new resolve, Anya paused a few seconds before planting the seed that would tell him what she expected when he, inevitably, came to her and sought both her forgiveness for his behaviour and an agreement she continue to live in his home.

Then:

"It is precisely as my mentor assured me. You are not fit to be my Lesser. The only way I would accept a person such as yourself into my life would be as my Inferior, and nothing more."

Not waiting for a response, deciding one would not be forthcoming; she turned on her heel and headed for the door.

"I shall leave as soon as a taxi can get here," she called back over her shoulder. "Goodbye, Mr Lambert."

CHAPTER THIRTY-SEVEN

Rapprochement

"Your emails have been very pleasing email, Rajiv," a still animated Anya congratulated her former mentor two weeks later; the events of the previous fortnight still fresh in her memory; diminished only by contemplation of the greater joys still to come.

She had taken great pleasure in ignoring the growingly desperate, almost hourly, emails and Skype calls he had made in the time since her ultimatum to him; but now, considering two weeks a long enough penance and having used that time to reduce her employer to a level verging on the sub-human, she wanted to share her news with someone else.

"You're welcome," he told her; unaccustomed to the role of second-fiddle, his distaste revealing itself in his tone.

"Now, now," she chided him, determined to provoke a response in order to slap him down; "do not forget your manners so early in our new… shall we say: arrangement."

The face on screen, she noted -not displeased- looked haggard and careworn, as if he had been spent the whole of the two weeks without sleep, waiting for some contact from her, his only company the ever-present bottle.

"Sorry…" he began, then, with an effort: "Ms Anya."

"There," she congratulated him in words he found familiar: "that was not so difficult was it?"

His expression gave the lie:

"No."

There was silence.

"Ms Anya," he added quickly.

"Do not look so disheartened, Rajiv," she told him. "You have had your day and now it is mine. I extend nothing but praise for your teaching abilities and insight into the submissive male mind; but it was inevitable I would outgrow you. Your boundaries - restrained by that sentimentality wholly absent in me- were set long ago; where mine, however, know no end. There is no shame for you to concede power to me… In fact, I should warrant a bet that; despite your sullen expression; you are finding something not unpleasing in your reduced circumstances."

Though eight thousand miles away, the redness betraying the truth of her assertion could still be made out via the marvels of the webcam.

"Is your cock hard again beneath the desk, my Rajiv? Are you thinking naughty thoughts of your new young Mistress?"

Experienced in such matters as he was –had been, anyway- Rajiv missed a breath at her words.

"Is that what you are now: my Mistress?"

"You already know the answer to that, Rajiv. But you must trust me, there is a whole world of difference between having me in your life as a Mistress and accepting me -as my white peon now accepts me- as Master. Now, answer me: are you having naughty thoughts of your Mistress."

"You know I am."

Adding:

"Ms Anya."

"Show me?" she ordered.

"What?"

"Take it out, Rajiv, produce for me that proud cock you have stroked beneath your desk, to both the superior cunt of my photos and the sound of my commanding young voice, without having the grace to at least show me that which I have inspired."

"I… I…"

"Is that hesitancy, I hear, Rajiv?"

It did not displease her that, for once, he seemed lost for a response as she continued:

"But surely not, Rajiv. I recall you made no mention of such hesitancy on your part when you demanded poor Ilse attach her lips to the pleasure stick proclaiming your rampant manhood?"

Still he seemed incapable of a response as she warmed to her theme:

"You were insistent upon it, Rajiv, despite knowing -as you yourself have told me you did- how repulsive she found such an act. Did hesitancy play any part in your behaviour when you listened to her screams and entreaties as you rammed your engorged cock deep into her abused anus?"

"Anya, this is too mu…"

"Did her fear and abject begging as you prepared to defile her womanhood once prevent you from doing as you pleased?"

"It was not like that. We… She…"

"It was exactly like that. Do not insult my intelligence with your puerile protestations of love. "Love", Rajiv, does not intimidate. It does not force the length of its disgusting cock into the unwilling mouth of its subject. It does not bugger and it does not slap, whip or spank the object of its attentions before making that object kneel in a corner as she reflects on the justness of her Master's… worship."

"You are wrong, Anya. Ilse and I were…"

"Do not contradict me!" she blazed, the distance between them doing nothing to detract from the power of either voice or delivery.

"Do so once more and it is over. There will be no second chance."

She allowed a pause; then:

"Do you understand?"

On screen, she watched as he thought about it; before, as she had known he would, he nodded his head.

"Say it," she demanded.

She watched as he appeared to swallow with some difficulty; then:

"Yes," came his voice, Anya detecting, to her delight, a growingly beaten quality within its timbre. "I understand."

Words were not necessary to rebuke him now, she knew; her silence would serve equally as well.

"M-Ms Anya," he added, proving her right once more.

She smiled to herself with satisfaction. It was one thing to intimidate the poseur calling himself a man in the main house; but to do so with a man of Rajiv's stature was a true achievement.

Between the two, she mused, and thanks to the real man on-screen before her, she had the best of all worlds. Explaining, she thought, her fondness for her one-time mentor.

"You are too intelligent not to know what is happening here, Rajiv," she told him, voice almost kindly; more like a friend.

"Our relationship has realigned itself. That is all. The sooner you accept I control it the sooner we can return to being the intimate travellers we were before I decided to control the reins.

Consider your acquiescence in those terms and you will find it easier to do as I ask. In fact, make that: "I am sure" you will enjoy doing so. Look upon it as a symbol of your acceptance of me as the dominant partner and we will enjoy many years as friends."

She allowed him to think it over; the nature of his thoughts as he did so as transparent to her as the Evian she brought to her lips to moisten a mouth made dry by anticipation.

"Will you do that for me, my Rajiv?" she cajoled.

He continued to think on it.

"Will you?" she asked again; a definite question; not an order.

With the groan common to men of his age as they sat down or, in this case, made to get up by way of an answer, he rose to his feet; the top half of his body disappearing from the screen to give her a view of the front of his jogging pants. "Pants", she could hardly fail to observe, with elastic waist put to the test by the erection attempting to burst free from them.

Anya watched, her own breathing shallow and irregular of a sudden, as the tasteless velour bottoms were lowered to his knees and his manhood, minus y-fronts or boxers, sprang to attention, the pubic growth surrounding it still dark; despite his years.

"You have a beautiful penis," Rajiv, she complimented him – sincerely. The seven –no: "Eight", she corrected herself- inches, pointing proudly at the screen, were beautifully proportioned, both in length and girth. A sight making what she would soon be telling him -if he followed her instructions and proved himself worthy- a delight they would both look forward to when the time was right.

He began to stroke himself.

"No, Rajiv," she told him, firm but not harsh, thrilled to see him do exactly as she asked - despite his obvious excitement. "Do not touch yourself until I give permission. Can you do that?"

"Y-yes… Ms Anya," he heard himself answer; the term of respect leaving his lips ever more… naturally.

"Do not be ashamed, Rajiv," she consoled him, "I think no less of you than I did before. You are more of a man than my former employer has ever been or ever dreamed he could be. Just the same though, you are a man."

It was a statement his tumescence could barely refute.

"You said it yourself, did you not," she reminded him:

" 'The management of men is hardwired into the mindset of

females from the womb onwards' ''. I should hate to think you would resent me for taking advantage of your encouragement.

In spite of his position, he was tempted to laugh as he recognised both his words and the truth behind what she said. The erection threatening to make contact with his computer screen a weakness for all men if the correct manipulation was applied.

"In return for your... concession... to me," she went on, choosing her words carefully, "I have a gift for you."

The one-eye continued to stare at her from the screen, rigid and impassive; even if she knew the face above it would reveal curiosity.

"Aim the cursor at "Video" and click," she told him.

Instants later, a deep breath told her she was filling his screen; positioned at her new desk in such a way that he might see both her face and the breasts he waxed so lyrical about; amusement for the increased throbbing of the cock filling transmitted via the wonder of webcam evident in her voice as she spoke:

"Was it not worth waiting for, Rajiv?" she asked, tongue flicking over the thick lips he found so sensuous as she gave a sly downward glance in the direction of her hardened nipples.

"My 'Master' seemed to think so; could barely take his eyes off them in fact - at least until I gave him something else to... sniff at."

"They are... wondrous," his voice reached her.

Adding quickly:

"Ms Anya."

"Good boy, Rajiv," she applauded him. That she was talking down to a man over forty years her senior, as well as being her intellectual superior, only adding to the pleasure she took from doing so.

"Now, you have a decision to make. In a few seconds, I am going to give you permission to show your appreciation of your friend and new mistress by stroking yourself. It is up to you whether you wish to do that as you gaze upon the face you say is so full of character, or the young tits you assure me are: 'The most magnificent I have ever seen''.

Anya waited for his answer; aware she had placed him in a dilemma but sure he would not disappoint her.

Knowing, as he did, her insecurities in regard of her features, he would know there was only one answer to give.

"Ms Anya," he began, all thoughts of the past and his previous relationship as the dominant partner forgotten; "I would like to devote my seed to that part of my friend and new mistress's anatomy that best illustrates her sense of purpose and strength of will."

He paused.

"I would like to masturbate to the image of… your face."…

…It was a full forty minutes later, fully dressed once more, that Anya waited patiently for her older follower, and recently restored friend, to return to the screen from the bathroom after his exertions under her supervision. His new Mistress taking him to the edge before insisting he back away from it, only to repeat the procedure and then repeat it again as he warmed to boiling point. The thick, seemingly unending, strands of creamy white rope finally making a jet propelled exit from his aged –though still in beautiful working order- tackle surprising even her.

Though, given it was only the second such ejaculation she had seen -even if it was the second that day- she could not be said, yet, to be a veteran of such occurrences.

It was also no surprise to her -given the fastidiousness they both possessed for matters of the domestic- that Rajiv would wish to clean himself up after having done the same to his semen covered computer-screen.

"I have another gift for you," she told him when he returned to his seat; counterbalancing his disappointment when he realised a baggy tee shirt was covering the chest he had hoped to see once more after having made tribute to the face above it.

"It is a gift I will give you in the flesh sometime in the near future but, for now, I think we should catch up, as friends do, on what has happened in our lives during our absence from each other."

As intrigued as he was about the gift to be made to him "In the flesh", it was the recent events of which he remained ignorant galvanising him most:

"You've made progress?" he asked eagerly.

Suddenly, the image of her on his screen vanished.

"What…?" he began, realising almost instantly what she had

done and he had not.

"I am sorry. What I meant to say was: Have you made progress... Ms Anya?"

Her face restored itself to his screen.

"I suggest you get used to addressing me in such a way very swiftly, Rajiv," she warned him. "I will not tolerate anything less than complete respect on your part."

She watched him take a huge swallow and knew whatever was making its descent past the gullet it was not saliva.

"In answer to your question," she went on, "yes, I have made progress. So much progress, in fact, I hardly know where to start in order to bring you up to date."

"I am all ears, Ms Anya," he told her, honorific ready to the tongue this time and in no way forced.

Starting from the very moment she had blocked his Skype privileges, Anya did just that until she came to that time when she stood on the gravel of his drive and waited for a taxi she had yet to call to take both her and her belongings to the railway station.

It being –as she had known it would- but a matter of moments before the door to the main house opened and...

CHAPTER THIRTY-EIGHT

Rajiv's Debriefing

…"I don't want you to go," he had told her.

Anya remained by her cases in silence, one dismissive glance enough to tell him where he stood. Her one glance, however, enough to tell her he was freshly bathed from their encounter in his bedroom; a still full-head of grey hair darkened by the waters of the shower along with a baggy tee shirt and casual Calvin Klein bottoms to replace the Versace denims.

Clean boxer shorts she took as read.

"Be reasonable, Anya," he continued, urgency explained, she thought –along with other, equally compelling, worries- by the expectation a taxi might arrive at any second to whisk her away. "What else did you expect to happen when you…?"

His voice tailed off, the image of her foot as she allowed the sole to travel the length of his penis too powerful to contemplate and converse at one and the same time.

At least without descending to gibberish.

Her silence and refusal to acknowledge his presence was beginning to unnerve him. The bravado he had felt when she had left his bedroom; prompting him to tell himself: "Good riddance;" had lasted precisely until the first warm jets of the shower had hit him. The young Indian girl's manipulation of both man and libido replaying itself uninvited as the hands soaping his cock and balls found themselves with a somewhat greater area to cover.

An increased workload accomplished with both speed and alacrity.

His awareness it had been only ten minutes on from his last orgasm that he experienced another not unduly surprising to him.

And hardly likely to be so, given his solo performances of recent weeks.

The above a sobering reminder of the hold she had over his passions, forcing the admission that –despite the degrading source of his response- he had never felt so alive in the sexual sense.

And enough to see him perched on the edge of the bathtub,

head in hands as he sought a solution before she departed his life for good.

"You have to understand," he went on, tone both imploring and self-pitying, simple presence on the drive as she waited, ample evidence of the solution he had reached, "how difficult this is for me. I'm not used to…You are… You are…"

Now she had allowed her eyes to find his, boring into them as if she would penetrate his very soul; cold, brown, and implacable.

"I am what?" she spat, instantly intimidating him, nearly as amazed at the transformation she had made in his regard as Lambert himself.

Nearly.

"Young enough to be your daughter?" she went on. "Uneducated? An Indian, as well as a lowly servant?"

His look was almost apologetic.

"I wouldn't have put it quite like that, Anya," he told her, "but, you have to admit, I am of a different…" he searched for a diplomatic alternative to the word readiest to tongue "…background, to what you have known. You can't expect me to just…"

"I 'expect' nothing of you," she spoke over him forcefully. "Your doglike behaviour in the bedroom was all I needed to see to be certain you are the pitiful specimen my mentor insists you are. I give thanks for his insistence that I test you one last time before accepting your petition to become my Lesser."

Her expression was spiteful as she added the rider:

"Unlike you, he is truly a great man and fully deserving of the devotion and service he receives."

She allowed some time for her words to sink in then:

"Now, if you are quite finished, my taxi will be arriving shortly and I would prefer my own company as I wait."

"No!" he almost screamed, everything else paling into insignificance alongside his need to persuade her to stay.

"What do you mean: 'No'?"

"You are not leaving," he told her.

"My ride will be here any second," she told him. "How do you propose to stop me?"

"Think about it, Anya," he begged. "You have a home here. A beautiful home. Light years removed from the life you tell me you had back in Calcutta. Are you really willing to lose it all just because I haven't lived up to the expectations of this mentor of yours?"

"I would crawl to hell and back, then back again, if he told me my religion expected such a thing of me," she assured him.

"But…"

"As for my life here? How many times must I tell you that money and position mean nothing to me? My faith insists I be truthful, so I will not lie. I have loved my time here until recently a great deal. If there were a way I could remain and still be in accordance with both my own desires and my faith, I would gladly accept it. But, thanks to you and your failings as a man, I cannot."

For the first time, she noted gleefully, he accepted her description of him and his failings without rejoinder, even if the redness of his cheeks told her it was not a withholding he made with ease.

"Leave me alone now," she said finally, tone even but unmistakably dismissive. "Our working relationship is over and I wish to have nothing more to do with you."

Turning her back to him she waited for the taxi she knew would never arrive, which was the exact moment she knew her earlier epiphany of rightness had been sent with fate's blessings.

To their left and behind them, coming from the direction of the village on the comparatively unused road running behind the house up to the old lighthouse and bird sanctuary three miles further on, where the road ran out, a four door saloon moved slowly in their direction.

A four door saloon he could only take for her transport.

Transport that would remove both the girl herself and the most incredible sex he could ever remember.

Albeit at his own hands.

Like a man demented he took her arms and turned her to face him, proscription upon physical contact forgotten and unheeding of her thunderous look. His former servant girl about to berate him, when he sank to his knees; the act itself, and the pure desperation she could see contorting his features, killing her words even as they formed.

His next move impacting more upon the functioning of her lungs than the ability to form a sentence.

As her "Taxi" drew closer, her former Master lowered himself to all fours, placed his lips on the pointed toe of a shiny black court shoe and counted to ten. Only rising to his knees again after repeating the procedure with other foot.

Barely trusting herself to take in much needed oxygen, not taking the chance her own breath might somehow bring him to his senses and interrupt the miracle taking place at her feet, Anya gazed down at him – to distracted to make the count along with him.

It was then, eyes closed to the shame of what he was about to propose, he made the proposal that would inform what life he had remaining to him and what were, for her, the most magical words she knew she would ever hear.

As her supposed transport –the same transport responsible for triggering his collapse- passed behind them, on its way to pursue a perusal of rare avian and automated shipping beacon, no doubt, the words she had worked so hard and so deviously to hear from his so superior tongue, trickled past his lips to be recorded by the ether separating them.

Words, Anya had sworn, she would never allow him to take back.

"Please, Ms Anya," he had begun. "I would like to pledge myself as your…"

Above him, she had waited, willing that final confirmation from his mouth.

Until, shoulders slumping, as if all fight had left him and he was simply bowing to the inevitable; his shoulders slumped and his eyes found hers to finish the petition she had taught him.

"…I pledge myself as your… Inferior."

…Anya gazed at her computer screen with both amusement and understanding as Rajiv slumped back onto his swivel chair, admiration genuine and wonderment immense, after listening in rapt astonishment to her retelling of Lambert's final capitulation and the events leading up to it. That he had been summarily dismissed from any participation in the endgame he had so ingeniously devised no longer provoking bitterness.

"You surpass both your former teacher and his limited imagination," he congratulated his new Mistress. "I bow to your superior talents, Ms Anya."

Anya smiled, delighted. It was no more than the reaction she had expected from him. Unlike the pitiful excuse she had found masquerading as a man of substance, Rajiv had much in common with the composite she had depicted to her former Master as her spiritual guide. The willingness to give praise where it was due and acknowledge superior accomplishment, but one of those qualities; the old man, as she fondly regarded him, as dear to her heart as anyone she had known in her short and difficult life.

Rajiv about to speak when there was a timid knock upon the door and Anya asked the "Old man" to wait, still in their native Bengali.

"Come!" she called, anticipating what was to come and Rajiv's reaction with amusement and pleasure.

As Lambert entered his former study with the tea tray, the arousal only recently subsided after Rajiv's onscreen performance kicked in again with a vengeance.

Though only two weeks had passed and it was still early in their redefined relationship, Anya could not imagine there coming a time when the sight of her former Master, dressed in black serving slacks and collarless white shirt, approached her with eyes downcast. Her Inferior, she noticed with glee –and no small pride- taking great pains to make sure he acted in the deferential way she had taught him to act in her presence.

Approaching the desk that had once been his, oblivious to Rajiv's presence onscreen, Lambert placed the tray down and lowered himself to his knees before going on all fours and placing his lips on the bare toes she presented to him.

As he counted to the mandatory ten, Anya took the opportunity to look at Rajiv and place her finger to her lips. Then, taking the webcam from the top of her computer screen she aimed it at the man on his knees before her. Keeping it trained upon him until he turned his attentions to her other foot before replacing it on the screen.

From Calcutta, Rajiv watched with wonderment, the excitement he had felt only minutes earlier when caressing himself to her order revisiting him with a strength doubled. That she could have brought the man so low in so short an amount of time nothing short of miraculous, he considered, as the man on his knees was lost to his screen and normal service resumed.

It being her voice now that captivated his attention as she looked down imperiously at the man below her:

"Enough!" he heard her command; voice that of a person born to authority, he thought; watching as her eyes rose to follow the movements of her servant as he –Rajiv guessed- regained his feet.

A natural.

"Were you just licking my toes?" he heard her accuse the man formerly known as Bernard Lambert.

"N-No, Master," he heard a voice reply.

A beaten voice, he thought.

Subdued but excited.

Tamed yet... hopeful.

And he had called her: "Master!"

Truly, Rajiv told himself, the young girl is a force of nature.

"Show me your belt," he heard her say, demand accompanied by her departure from his screen as she moved away and to the side, leaving him only with audio.

"You know it's useless to tamper with it?" he heard, puzzled.

"Yes, Master," the man replied.

"Even were you to find someone willing to cut you out of it," she went on, "there would be very little left of your pitiful white pee-pee and tiny balls when the intense heat levels required to do so were finished. As far as I am concerned, it is the best use for titanium yet to be devised."

Rajiv could scarce believe his ears.

In no more than the space of two weeks since his last contact with her she had contrived not just to make a servant of the man, but had encased his manhood itself in a chastity belt.

"Are you making progress with the day's chores?" her voice cut into her musings.

"Yes, Master," he replied. "The yard work is complete and your evening meal prepared and ready for the oven. As soon as you dismiss me I will go to the basement and make a start on your laundry."

"I will inspect it later and make sure it is up to standard. Very good, Lambert, you have my permission to leave."

Rajiv watched as her face came into view on the monitor, her smile –no other word could describe it, and despite the smile beaming towards him- malevolent. His own reaction one of high arousal as he listened to her dominate a man many years her senior so effortlessly – the man's sense of shame and disgrace, he knew, made all the more potent and debilitating for having found slavery at the feet of someone so young and uneducated.

"And Lambert…" she called, waiting.

"Yes, Master?"

"I am pleased with your progress these past two days."

"Thank you, Master."

"You will find your young owner forward when it comes to praise for good service," Calcutta watched her tell the man she had made a chattel.

"Tell me, Lambert," she went on. "Are you beginning to know your place in my life?"

"I… I think so, Master."

"Oh, dear," Rajiv heard her say with mock disappointment. "You do not seem too sure. And after all the time and effort I went to in order to make it clear to you."

"I'm sorry, Master," said the man Rajiv was coming to detest. His Ilse may have been submissive but she was not weak. What she had borne at his hands had not been accepted simply because of an ability to control the strength of her lust for what he had to offer – even if that had played a part in what had attracted her to him; while, with the milksop of advanced years Anya was currently in the process of dehumanising, lust was everything and predicated and accepted whatever indignity his former servant saw fit to inflict upon him.

Despite knowing pretty much the same applied to Anya, it was a concept that did not play well with him – even if he acknowledged the way he himself was manipulated by the girl through the same singular medium.

With Ilse, though, it had all been so different. For the German bottom he missed so dearly, the largest part of the equation in regard of their relationship –just as it had been with him- had been love.

A love not tainted by the sexuality mediocrities everywhere considered twisted as the time-servers went about filling their routine lives with routine days while, occasionally, enlivening their routine nights with routine sex. Twisted or not, his sex life with

Ilse had been built on the mutual foundation of opposites attracting. Ying to the other's yang and fire to the other's water, as important to both that they satisfy as well as being satisfied; which, to his way of thinking, was how love ought to be defined.

Nine-to-five job, dog, kids, house and mortgage in Rajarhat notwithstanding.

With this sham of a man, however, nothing but the gratification of his own base desires mattered. Pride, masculinity, and deeper feeling were simply commodities of use to him as a means of bartering for the treatment he needed.

And that, he considered, was twisted.

Though, his own ever-present and inconvenient honesty could only admit, the same could certainly be said of the ex-writer's "Master". Rajiv again acknowledging it was hardly "Love" on his part that made him so fond of her when, in her own driven, highly focused and uncultured way, she was no better than the man she had enslaved.

Acknowledging also, that the strength of his own need and the way she gratified it would always make him more forgiving of her failings.

"You must know by now that 'Sorry' is not a word I accept, Lambert," his own lust object was explaining was explaining to her other, equally smitten if less favoured, thrall. "Tell me now where your place is."

Though he knew he was made of stronger, less brittle, material than his protégé's victim he could not help wonder how he would handle the girl if their situations were reversed.

His conclusion not flattering to the cowed Englishman his deviant little Anya was handling with such ease as she forced him to perform for his audio audience via the Internet; running him through his tricks as if he were a performing poodle simply to impress her other captive with her progress.

"It… It is at your feet, Master," the poodle's answer interrupted his thoughts.

"Even when I return from town with them hot and sweaty from my high-heels and nylons?" he heard her ask, injecting a note of contempt into the tease by way of turning what might be seen as lightness into a threat.

"Yes, Master."

"But I had to force you to suck my toes the last time I asked. You even had the temerity to turn up your nose at the smell."

"I'm sorry, Master," Lambert replied instantly, Rajiv suspecting this was not a new game for him – even if it was in no way that. "I was new to such a thing. It will not happen again."

"Where else do you belong? How about my smooth armpits? Does it seem… natural… for you to lick the day's sweat from them as a sign of your devotion to me?"

"Yes, Master. I consider it an honour to be offered even the lowliest part of your superior body."

"What?" she roared, feigning disgust. "You would even put yourself at the service of my arse? You would separate the cheeks and place your tongue in my rectum?"

For a moment there was silence and Rajiv thought she may have over egged the pot.

Once more he was wrong.

"Yes, Master," Rajiv heard, a slight quivering of the voice telling him this was not a use to which she had put him yet and one he had -and understandably- doubts in regard of.

"Lambert," she said in congratulatory style, "you excel yourself. You truly begin to grow in your role as my Inferior. Not three weeks ago -had someone told me this was possible with such a mature and worldly man such as yourself- I would have suspected the onslaught of insanity. Now look at yourself. You have finally found your true calling in life."

Rajiv could almost hear the bile as it was swallowed back to enable the man to answer:

"Thank you, Master."

"Get on with your laundry now," she ordered, taking her seat on both chair and screen again before an afterthought took her.

"And Lambert?"

"Yes, Master?"

"You have pleased me."

Rajiv watched as her hands went to her neck and she toyed with what looked like a key hanging from a gold chain before continuing:

It is too early to consider removing your belt," she said, "though you will be encouraged to hear it will, at this rate of improvement, not be too long before I unlock you and allow your cock to hump my panty hosed leg."

Even from a distance thousands of miles removed; Rajiv could hear the pain and disappointment in the former writer's voice – though he appeared careful to remain deferential.

"That is very kind of you, Master."

"You are welcome," Anya smirked, trying to bait him. "But, as a reward for the progress you are making, you may sniff and lick the gussets of my soiled underwear; pantyhose too if you wish to remind and continue to familiarise yourself with your owner's intimate smells."

Rajiv realised he was stroking himself, his hand having gone to his erection without his knowing as he listened to Anya's ongoing demolition of the Englishman.

As the man delivered his thanks and gratitude for having been given permission to perform such a demeaning task and Anya dismissed him from the room, Rajiv assured himself the young girl who had come to him as a novice was not only a "Master" but an artist.

"Are you touching yourself again, Rajiv?" her voice cut into his reverie, a residue of the tone reserved for her real flunkey directing itself at her "Follower with privileges".

"What better tribute can I pay to a true genius?"

"Addressing her with respect would be a start," she reminded him sharply, though her manner had lightened a little.

"A thousand apologies, Ms Anya," he apologised and corrected himself at the same time, buying in to her changing mood with some lightness of his own. Playing her game and, for the first time, glad to do it if witnessing such scenes were to be his reward. The power of what he had just observed all the more potent for stemming from a situation that was real; and, as such, extremely appealing for him – despite his experience as a dominant partner in a previous incarnation.

"It has been an education for me, Rajiv, for which I have much to thank you."

"It is you who are the educator now, Ms Anya," he assured her. "I find it amazing how swiftly you have brought him to such a pass."

Anya laughed, dismissive of her achievement with her ex-Master than the surprise of her ex-Mentor.

"I think he thought that once he had been gifted a taste of my pussy his need for me would recede."

"Plainly, he was deluded," Rajiv himself laughed.

"If anything," she went on, "his desire to kneel between my legs and worship me with his tongue has grown even more strong since I granted him what he desired."

Rajiv laughed again:

"Now that I do not doubt."

"Even more strange," she went on, was that -though his behaviour was becoming increasingly servile beforehand- he seemed to become even more fawning and docile after each interlude serving my cunt."

Rajiv's answer was a single word:

"Copulins."

He watched Anya's eyes narrow.

"They are chemicals released by the vagina when aroused," he explained.

"Yes?… So?"

"It is believed, though scientific opinion is split on this, that when a man performs cunnilingus for a woman on a regular basis and is exposed to these natural female secretions, he becomes more attentive to her wishes. More willing to be guided by her and, eventually, more obedient."

Via the webcam she had finally set up for him, Rajiv could see her thinking about it, her lips curling finally into a smile:

"If what you say is true, and given the time he now spends between my legs," she told him, "I can think my former master can expect unthinking obedience to be added to what is fast becoming a very sore tongue."

The hilarity prompted by her observation was instant and long lasting and continued until:

"So, Ms Anya," Rajiv asked, wiping away tears of mirth, "where do you go from here?"

The smile beaming back at him from Cornwall was full of self-approbation for the way her former mentor had accepted his reduced circumstances in relation to her. Anya accepting his submission at a distance with pleasure that was both genuine and, she considered, deserved.

"Tomorrow, my loyal Rajiv," she began, "will be a big day for my one-time Lord and Master."

"Why? What happens tomorrow, Anya?"

Anya waited.

"What happens tomorrow, Ms Anya?" he corrected himself quickly.

"Tomorrow," she began, deciding to overlook the omission, "the man formerly describing himself as 'Bernard Lambert – Writer' is going into town with the girl formerly describing herself as 'Anya Jalav – Servant'."

He watched as she nodded to herself at something; deciding to keep silent until she was ready to explain more.

"He does not know it yet," she began, "but tomorrow, myself and my Inferior have a very important appointment.

CHAPTER THIRTY-NINE

Power of Attorney

"I am obliged to point out to you, Mr Lambert, that signing these documents and having them witnessed is a serious matter."

In her fifteen years as one of the area's few –if only- Asian solicitors, Sreelatha Chakravarthi had seen, and arranged, many strange things. But then, the English were a strange people as her late husband never tired of pointing out. Just the same, that a handsome writer in his late forties would virtually hand total responsibility for the running of his life over to a young girl from her homeland had to be right at the top of her list.

A "Girl", moreover, she could tell instantly was not of good caste.

"I… I've not been myself lately," he told her; nervous eyes flickering to the girl sitting at his side as if to make sure he was saying the correct thing. Intensely embarrassed, it seemed, at having his deference witnessed by another. "Ms Anya has my complete trust to administer my affairs."

Sreelatha Chakravarthi missed a few beats: "Did he actually address her as 'Ms Anya?'" It seemed a very respectful way to address someone who was not only of a lower social class to him but was also his housekeeper and, therefore, his underling.

She was not even a "Looker" as the English gutter-press had it; so she could hardly extend him the courtesy of believing him ensnared by her beauty. However, for all the buxom Indian lady's surprise at what was unfolding she found something in it not displeasing to her - a "Surprise" undiminished by a certain wetness between her legs.

"I have drawn up, as instructed, a Lasting Power of Attorney," she said, addressing herself to the girl who, it seemed, was obviously in charge; realising she felt no small sense of exhilaration for sideling the handsome Englishman.

"This will mean you continue to administer Mr Lambert's affairs even should his capacity to decide such things for himself be called to question. Meaning the courts would not have to become involved"

In her late thirties, the solicitor found it inexplicable that a man of his looks and standing could possibly be thinking of taking the step he was about to make.

To allow a young woman who was not his equal in terms of age, standing, looks and education to assume control of his life?

What was wrong with him?

He didn't seem incapacitated; either physically or mentally; and, from what she knew of his financial affairs, all was sound; so why this?

The thought had occurred to her more than once that she might be playing her own, albeit legal, part in a blackmail scam – though what the girl could possibly be blackmailing him with was beyond her comprehension.

But then, why else would such a man be going through with what could only be described as: a preposterous arrangement? An arrangement, he had to be aware, that would make him the laughing stock of all those who knew him – were they, of course, to learn of its existence.

Also puzzling was his docility before the girl; looking to her for approval for even the most basic answer he was compelled to give; as if her word were law on all decisions – which, to all intents and purposes, it would be once the relevant documents were signed.

Even more puzzling was the satisfaction she, Sreelatha Chakravarthi, took from the role reversal.

"As of now," she went on, amazed at just how arousing she found the situation; "he is entering into this agreement of his own conscious will and can terminate that arrangement at a time of his choosing."

Her use of the third-person in respect of him was calculated and deliberate; sensing he would not take her to task for her rudeness and the young girl at his side would not disapprove; the feeling they were both dominating this handsome older white man lending her a sense of empowerment she had yet to experience in her relations with the opposite sex.

"However," she went on, "should there come a time when he is regarded by either the courts or the medical profession as incompetent to make such a decision, you will remain in charge of his affairs. Of course, if this were to happen you might want to consider petitioning for legal guardianship to make things less confusing."

Something in the way the young girl's eyes lit up and a certain... horror transformed the expression of the man made the situation even stranger to her – as well as more appealing.

Despite her suspicions regarding legality, Sreelatha Chakravarthi was enjoying the situation and found she was envying the young girl.

The delicious notion of an older man –an older white Englishman- committing himself to the guardianship of a low-caste young Indian girl appealing to a side of her she had yet to explore even in her dreams.

"Well," she went on, not wanting to end their meeting but having others to see and impatient to ease the arousal soaking her undergarments, "unless you have any questions to ask me, I think we should do the deed, so to speak."

After watching the man sign and then the girl, Sreelatha Chakravarthi added her own signature, deposited the documents in her safe and showed her clients to the door.

"It has been nice to meet you," she said to the girl, deliberately speaking in Bengali and ignoring the man; a dismissal intended to show the girl she approved of the way she was managing her older employer.

"It is much to your credit that you would accept responsibility for your employer," she went on, flashing a look at the red-faced man at their side as he fidgeted uncomfortably, unfamiliar with the language but sensing it would be nothing good and eager to make an escape.

"But you must not let his advanced age influence your decision making. Men are born children and remain that way; a firm hand is always the best way with them."

"Thank you, Mrs Chakravarthi," the girl said, pleasantly; not missing the way the man at her side had been sidelined; "I intend to do just that."

"Very wise, Anya – may I call you, Anya?"

A flattered smile and a nod confirmed she could; the girl, despite her air of self-possession, quite unable to prevent the pride she took from being treated as an equal by a professional woman of her own country plastering itself across her face.

"Be careful, my dear," Sreelatha continued, "he is still a handsome man and, in my experience, they are the worst; spoilt as they have been, throughout their lives."

"Those days are over for him, Mrs Chakravarthi. He has had life too easy for far too long. It is why he is so weak and needs the guidance of a strong Indian woman."

"Well-spoken, my dear. And the name is Sreelatha."

As if to emphasise his "Weakness", the girl turned to the older man and reverted to English:

"Go to the car and wait for me while I speak to Mrs Chakravarthi," she ordered, manner peremptory. "I expect to find you there when I am finished."

As an amazed Sreelatha looked on, the man's cheeks turned a deeper shade of scarlet; actually lowering his eyes in –unless she was completely mistaken- what looked to the middle-aged solicitor like a show of deference.

His answer made in the same weak voice with which he had answered the few questions the solicitor had required of him:

"Yes, Ms Anya."

Sreelatha could not help but be congratulatory when the door closed behind him, noting that even his footsteps as they descended the stairs sounded servile and despondent.

"You are a woman after my own heart, Anya," she gushed; envious of the control the young girl form her own country seemed to exercise over such a handsome man.

From Anya's smile Sreelatha could see the girl was genuinely pleased with the compliment and was emboldened to go further:

"I only wish I had taken Mr Chakravarthi in hand in such a way before he died," she confessed, giving it some thought.

"But then, he was not some spineless…"

She caught herself; knowing she had already said too much. The girl may well be kindred to her own sudden conversion to relations between genders but she was still a client and a reputation for indiscretion and speaking out of turn was not exactly career enhancing for a solicitor.

"Excuse me, Anya; I allow my admiration for what you are doing to run away with my tongue."

"Do not trouble yourself. He cannot understand it and, even if he did it would make no difference. As I think you were about to say: he is a spineless Englishman and not the proud Indian I am sure your husband must have been."

Sreelatha smiled a thank you, a little relieved.

"As I say," she listened as the girl continued: "he needs the guidance only a strong Indian woman can give and I intend to see he gets it."

Sreelatha could do no more than be impressed with the strength of character of her countrywoman.

"You have my sincere wishes for your success," she told her.

"That is very kind of you, Sreelatha. If you would please forward your bill to our address I will ensure it is paid immediately."

She had the door open before she turned:

"Should you ever be in the area, do call and arrange to come by. It would be lovely to see you again."

The buxom solicitor's face lit up.

"Some sea air will do you good," the girl told her. "And it will do my charge no harm to show some respect to two Indian ladies instead of one."

Yet more activity between her legs told Sreelatha it was not an invitation she would be likely to refuse.

"I would like that very much," she said smiling. "And if it is okay with you, I think I will take you up on your invitation very soon."

"I will look forward to it," the girl said, still in Bengali. "Though do bear in mind we leave for India next month and will be away for a considerable period of time."

"I will call you soon and arrange it, Anya."

She hesitated, unsure despite knowing the young girl had everything under control:

"You are sure he won't mind? I would not want to…"

The look preventing the finish of her sentence could only be described as contemptuously dismissive as the girl told her:

"It makes no difference whether he does or not."

The contempt and dismissal Sreelatha had seen appeared now to have joined in partnership to create the malicious.

"And, anyhow, when you do visit, you will see a big difference in the quality of his behaviour. Now, if you will excuse me, I do not like to leave him unsupervised for too long."

Having no real idea of what the first part of the girl's statement meant, but excited just the same, Sreelatha nodded and leaned in to kiss each of Anya's cheeks; before, both smiling, they had said their goodbyes.

Waving the girl down the stairs, her next client not due for a further ten minutes, Sreelatha Chakravarthi locked her door and moved to the, thankfully, tinted first floor window of her office to watch her exit. The hand thrusting itself into her pantyhose to ease the arousal that had been mounting since they had first entered bringing a gasp from her glossed lips.

Watching him as he stood by the car and held open the passenger side back door for the keeper of his Power-of-Attorney, snapping to attention at her approach like a corporal before a Brigadier, her fingers became more frantic. Something in the docile and beaten way he acted in the girl's presence ensuring the orgasm she had been threatening to have since they first entered her office exploded upon her senses with a swiftness and knee buckling force she had never experienced from the attentions of the late Mr Chakravarthi.

As her breathing slowed and she moved away from the window to her desk, she was grateful she had some free time before her.

When it came down to it, Sreelatha Chakravarthi was nothing if not a realist.

And one orgasm was not going to be enough.

EPILOGUE

Kolkata

Had a complete stranger, without prior knowledge, been invited into the bedroom and asked to place a bet on the identity of the bald but still handsome Englishman kneeling in the corner, nose pressed to the wall; he or she would have been entitled to consider it a safe bet he was not a financially solvent, mildly successful former crime novelist with a home on the south-west coast of England.

Far from evoking such an image of maturity and self-autonomy, the man sweltering on the hard wooden floor; dressed in black trousers and an ever-dampening white shirt would have taken those with memories long enough -and terms of reference wide enough- back to the more draconian schools portrayed at length in the works of Charles Dickens.

With the benefit of a closer inspection of the man's totally hairless scalp they would have seen the condition was not a natural one; witness given by the crisscrossing of numerous razor nicks left by his most recent shave.

In short, it was a scene most people considering themselves civilised would have found as mystifying as it was abnormal and still more baffling were they to be told it was a view shared by the handsome Englishman.

The same man currently seen attempting to keep his nose pressed to the corner.

At least, that is, until he received the command allowing him to remove it.

But then, Bernard Lambert was no longer "Most people" and had not been of their number for a good while; having had his notions of what was normal and what wasn't blurred for him the past eight months or so.

Twenty floors above ground; from his position in the corner, to the left of the window; peripheral vision was enough to give him a view of the small-hour lights of Calcutta as they headed westward towards the Hooghley River and, eight thousand miles further on, the coastline of Cornwall. Eyes accustomed to tears becoming moist at the thought of the home he hadn't seen for the past six months and knew he wouldn't see for some considerable time more.

"I am Bernard Lambert," he repeated to himself whenever his thoughts were his own and not devoted to pleasing his female Master. A mantra devised to maintain a sense of his own identity. Even as he admitted to himself that "Identity" and what constituted it had been torn from him and replaced with a… with a…

As if by way of a description for the one he was unable – unwilling- to supply for himself, her voice carried across from the bed:

"Does my dog not look natural in the corner of your bedroom, Rajiv?" he heard, his "Master" abandoning the Bengali in which they normally conversed when he was listening and reverting to English – all the better, she knew, to involve him in his own humiliation.

A deep chuckle of appreciation answered her; heightening the deep, deep shame Bernard Lambert continued to feel for the depths to which she had taken him.

Correction:

Depths to which he had allowed her to take him.

The same depths, he was now certain, he would never rise from.

The bitch with the horse-features he had once dismissed as a low caste flunkey had, somehow, insinuated herself into his bloodstream.

Both a sickness and a virus.

And an addiction no medicine, surgical, pharmaceutical or homeopathic, stood a chance of banishing.

"He is such a good dog these days, my Rajiv," she went on, blissful in her cruelty towards him, never seeming to tire of it.

Cruelty both mental and physical.

"And to think, he once considered himself my master."

"He was obviously a very delusional dog, Ms Anya," the male voice Lambert hated so much responded in English - the same male voice she allowed liberties with her patience and his cock liberties with her body he, her devoted servant, would never know.

"His behaviour these days, however, is exemplary and a great tribute to your loving strictness with him."

In his corner, Lambert cringed; the angry red welts striping his arse and chafing against his trousers providing all the evidence he needed or wanted to be sure of her: "Loving Strictness".

"He used to think he was a man, too," she answered. "But that did not take long to educate out of him."

She laughed:

"Can you imagine, my Rajiv; he actually wanted to put his puny white stick inside of me. As if such a worm could be of any use to me or be worthy of such a privilege."

"Why concern yourself with the delusions of an animal," came the reply; "when there is a worm of a larger, thicker and superior, Indian nature impatient to do you such a service, Ms Anya?"

Her delighted laughter filled the room.

"Rajiv, oh my Rajiv! Not only are you the first man to know me but you will certainly be the last. I swear it. If there were a man on the planet with a chance of laying claim to any finer romantic feeling lurking inside me unsuspected, that man would be you. A true man; honest enough to recognise a superior woman when he meets one and accord her the respect she deserves; even if the proud nature of his masculinity prevents him serving her in the same way as that English cur who now cringes in the corner."

The English dog in the corner sensed their eyes on his back and found "Cringe" to be an accurate adjective in regard of him.

"As much as anyone could ever be the love of my life, it is you Rajiv. Your loss to me will be a massive one and I will be here until your frail heart beats its last beat."

"And you, Ms Anya, have my eternal thanks -along with my beloved Ilse- for having made my existence such a delightful journey."

In his corner, Lambert could feel nothing but bitterness and envy for the familiar, almost loving, way the this old Indian degenerate interacted with the same girl who showed him no affection of any kind.

"But now," the degenerate began; "lest we both become too sentimental before your slave, and before my heart takes that last beat, I would consider it an honour if you were to engulf my waiting cock in the most glorious cunt; Ilse included; I have ever had the privilege to serve. Though I fear in my weakened condition

I may not last long enough to give you the satisfaction you deserve."

"Do not concern yourself my valued friend," her words of reassurance wafted across to her chattel, "the pleasure you have given me up to now would last most women a lifetime."

Warmth leaving her voice then as her eyes strayed to the corner:

"Besides, my dog has a tongue and it has been trained exceptionally well."

"I can vouch for that, Ms Anya," he assured her with a laugh, "though I get the impression clean-up is his least favourite task – at least when applied to me, anyway."

"Put him from your mind," she said with dismissal. "He is nothing."

"As always, you are right my superior young goddess. You waste too much of your valuable time speaking of him when you could be mounting your worshipper and taking him to the clouds one last time."

As Anya gave a low throaty chuckle at the retro language they used simply as a means of heightening their captive's frustration and shame she prepared to do just that.

Picturing the activity behind him, Bernard Lambert felt his imprisoned cock rage against the titanium in which it had been held captive without release for over two months. Pain matching frustration as the dying bastard he hated so much was ridden by the same Indian bitch who made him - her totally obedient servant who gave her everything- rub himself off against the soles of her nylon clad feet or hump the outside of her leg as if he truly were a dog.

If he was fortunate.

As the sounds of their lovemaking carried to his corner, Lambert squeezed his eyes shut and wished he could do the same with his ears.

"Oh, Rajiv!" he heard her gasp; my lovely, sweet, respectful, Rajiv."

"Anya, you are a… a true goddess. I pay tribute to… to…"

"Yes, Rajiv, yes."

"Anya, I can't… Anya…! Anya…!! Anyaaaaaaaa!!!

Tears streamed down Lambert's cheeks as the pain of his

restricted erection intensified – advanced self-pity made worse by the knowledge his female Master preferred the enfeebled cock of a dying man to his; wretchedness multiplied further by his certainty of what was about to come.

In the event, it wasn't until a few minutes later that she called to him:

"Dog!" she snapped.

"Yes, Master," he answered instantly; nose still to the corner.

"Crawl over to me and clean Master Rajiv's cream from my glorious Indian cunt."

Dying inside, but obeying instantly, he went on all fours and crawled towards the bed; careful to keep his eyes to the carpet; motivating himself with the thought "Master Rajiv" would not be around for many more days to come.

"Heel!" she ordered unnecessarily; the command a particular favourite.

"Who knows?" he told himself, licking her feet as commanded before slithering onto the mattress to crawl forward and sniff her labia the way she had taught him. As ever; despite his familiarity with the act; fighting back the nausea that assailed him when called upon to lap at her semen drenched pussy.

There being still enough spirit left to him for a spark of optimism to surface; as debased as he knew it to be:

"If she enjoys Rajiv's cock as much as she seems to," he told himself, continuing to sniff at her labia in deference to her wishes, "perhaps she might have second thoughts about mine when we return to Cornwall and it's the only one available to her."

It was a thought -so far had he fallen- that placed his nausea on the backburner.

Temporarily.

Hope translating to disciplined frenzy as he attacked the wondrous cunt enslaving him with new levels of servile gusto in just the way she had trained him.

His desire to please not going unnoticed.

"Oh, yes, my Inferior," he heard from above him as a patronising young hand patted his head in an imitation of affection; the trickle of piss that found its way into his mouth betraying the pleasure she was receiving from his attentions. "You are becoming most... most accomplished at this."

His Master's compliment urging him to even greater levels of service and -almost- allowing him to overlook the great gobs of semen and urine dropping from her pussy into his mouth he found –and always would find- so disgusting.

"You are a good, good, dog," he heard her say and his spirits soared with the ridiculous compliment.

Her demeaning words of encouragement triggering; for some unaccountable reason; an image of Siobhan, his former wife. Her cool Nordic beauty popping into his head for the first time in months as he imagined her standing above him to watch; the sneer he imagined on her pretty face telling him how apt, if unbelievable, she would find it that her once successful husband had been reduced to the role of an ugly young Indian girl's cuntlapper.

"Yes," the: 'Ugly Indian girl", went on as if to herself; unaware her slave had invited company. "That is exactly what you are; and exactly what I intend you will always be:

"A very, very, very, good dog."

THE END

A Wife Takes Control

ONE

"I sense a woman with very special desires, Helen. A woman very much like me."

The black woman uttering these words to the white thirty-something was sat opposite her at a corner table of a busy Starbucks, voice kept low that an adjoining table of boisterous students, doing their best to eke out the one Cappuccino or luxury hot-chocolate to which their meagre funds would run, might not overhear.

"I see so many women of your age – especially white women - who realise just how much potential they have to get so much *more* of what they want, that you must trust me when I tell you that what you're looking for is already partly in your hands."

Helen Drayton, the woman in question, was in her mid-thirties with shoulder length blonde hair and an hourglass figure that, while not fat, could not be described as slim either. Facially she was composed of those sharp angles that hinted at severity and came nowhere close to being described as *"beautiful"*, even if that *"severity"* was counter-balanced somewhat by sensuous and full lips. A *sensuousness* that, as the black woman had already referenced, had decided to kick into life with a vengeance and whose existence had led to their meeting.

Though it had taken many weeks of emails between the two before Helen's coffee companion had been convinced enough by the sincerity of the older woman's need to consent to seeing her face-to-face.

"You already have everything in place," the woman who had introduced herself as Mariah continued. "The failure of your husband's business and the fact it is now your salary as an executive P.A. that keeps him is a massive plus in your favour. As is the fact, and probably more so, that he was foresighted enough to see his company would be going under long before it did and transfer ownership of the house into your name alone. But the one thing you must be sure of before we go ahead is that this is what you want."

Helen had sighed internally. She had already spent weeks assuring the woman via their emails that this is what she wanted – and for good. Now, it appeared, she was going to be required to do so again, even though *she* would be the one paying for the woman's services.

Except she wasn't required to do so again.

"I only mention this again," the woman had gone on, because your husband is obviously smitten with you still and what you want for him is so… drastic."

She paused a moment, then added:

"And irreversible. Once done it cannot be taken back and, whether the outcome be good or bad, will have to be lived with.

Helen gave a *"so what?"* shrug.

Trevor, her fortysomething husband, had long been boring her since those first heady days when his good looks – though they were still intact – had swept her feet from under her when doing business with the man who had been her boss at the time. The fact such a handsome man could find her interesting – even come to love her – both puzzled and flattered her and, for a while, she found herself returning the compliment with a passion strong enough for her to be led down the aisle and into an existence as a housewife she had always insisted was not for her – though she did, in deceitful ways, manage to stay true to her intention *not* to be burdened with the children he had always insisted he wanted. Though, after leaving her job, she had – amazing herself in the process – settled down into domesticity.

And eventually realised it was *everything* she had always believed it would be:

Soul destroying *and* mind-numbingly boring.

Into the bargain, the sex with her handsome, if somewhat selfish, husband soon became tame as the novelty of having such a man desire her wore off and his limitations in the bedroom became more glaring.

Thus her forays onto the Internet during his days at the office and her exploration of sexual desires and situations that were new and… *thrilling…* to her.

Explorations that had, eventually, led her to the black woman's site and their meeting alongside a table of boisterous undergrads in Starbucks.

"What I'm trying to say is, you understand, and to coin a cliché," that same black woman was continuing, "is that there is no going back once you start down this road."

Helen Drayton's expression was mildly impatient, English being her native tongue and having instigated what was going down between them in the first place, it was hardly credible she would *not* understand a facile observation that was at odds with the sound practical sense the younger black woman had offered until now.

The woman's dusky voice was still low and she looked for all the world as if she, along with Helen – who had done just that - had stepped out of one of the finance houses lining London's Leadenhall Street, her professional garb a mirror of Helen's in stark grey and white, even if a pair of unmistakably *huge* breasts were not.

Breasts the undergrads at the next table had certainly *not* missed and could be seen, had the two ladies been at all interested in them, sneaking covert and covetous looks in their direction whenever they felt they could do so without being caught.

"The moment we leave each other this lunchtime, and if you have agreed to go ahead and placed the necessary advance in my account, events will have been set in motion and your marriage as you once knew it will be over. I will not stop even if you have a change of heart."

The woman called Mariah paused and Helen knew she expected a response of some kind.

"There will be no change of heart, Mariah," she said emphatically before flicking a glance at the students and lowering her own voice. I intend to get what I want and, having met you, feel confident you are going to be able to provide me with just that. I've thought it all through very carefully, just the way you said, and I've never wanted anything more in my life."

"Even though you will find it impossible to ever see him as a man again once you get it?"

"Mariah, I have read everything you had couriered over to my place of work and *all* of it was a match with my desires and what I intend my relationship with my husband to be from now on. You of all people should know that my *not* seeing him as a man and treating him accordingly is a massive part of the attraction for me. In fact, and while we are on the subject of doubts, my main concern is not that it will be the right move for me but that you can actually deliver it for me."

The black woman's *"Hmmph!"* was both indignant and dismissive.

"You may be in no doubt of that, Helen. All the questions I insisted you answer about your husband and you found so tiresome resulted in exactly the kind of male profile that led me to take your case on."

Helen waited, a little amused at the way the woman described the undeniably perverse and immoral task she was about to undertake for her as if she had been engaged in the capacity of marital counsellor rather than the catalyst that would lead her into a female-led marriage and her husband into what she intended to be a lifetime of physical and domestic servitude.

A *"servitude"* she knew he would find as hateful as he would find it humiliating.

"Everything, you told me about him," Mariah went on, "from his working and financial situation to his self-regard and the importance he places on maintaining his manly reputation with your joint friends; this, along with his two sisters somewhat… *nauseating…* hero worship of him and his need to maintain it; tells me he is as perfect for what you intend and I can deliver you as the other men I've… *re-educated…* for their wives."

"I sincerely hope you're right," Helen told her.

The black woman's somewhat bored expression told the white wife she was hearing nothing she hadn't heard many times before.

"Let us review the facts, Mariah answered, ticking them off one by one on her fingers as she ran them past Helen for verification:

"One: he has no employment at a time of recession when jobs are near impossible to come by and his age and bankruptcy make it even more unlikely he will be able to land one…

"Two: he has no credit cards and no credit-rating enabling him to get any…

"Three: the home is in your name and if he leaves he has nowhere to go; given his sisters both live in Florida and as a bankrupt with a criminal record – albeit a minor and driving related one - he has absolutely no chance of being allowed entry into the States…"

Helen listened, enjoying the recital of those factors that… *could…* deliver her husband to her.

"Four: You are working and he is taking care of the home while you do so."

"Grudgingly," Helen reminded her. "Until *'something comes up for him'*. And I pretty much have to redo everything he does so, at the moment, I effectively have two jobs."

Mariah laughed:

"Yes. It all follows a pattern. Trust me, his delusions will be the last to go. But, even before you ensure they vanish forever, he will soon be doing his chores and a whole host of other duties you will determine to your complete satisfaction."

"At the moment he acts as if he's doing me a favour," Helen said, almost to herself, expression not a happy one. "As if, despite everything you've just said, he is still the breadwinner and head of the household and me the little wife grateful for his guidance."

Again the black woman laughed:

"*That*, Helen, is a state of affairs that will not exist for too much longer."

"I hope you're right. I can't wait for the day when I can actually *order* him to do what I want rather than have to make a polite request and then have to do it again anyway if, and after, he has been good enough to consent."

"A little more patience and you will not have to wait much longer," Mariah assured her. "And if I continue to repeat myself, Helen, you must understand it is for your benefit and not mine… Though it is true I have no desire to involve myself with time-wasters who like the idea of what I can offer them only to bleat like sheep when they realise it is, utterly and completely, *real*."

Helen gave her an offended look:

"I can assure you I'm neither a time-waster nor some bleating sheep."

At this, the Mariah woman could not help but smile and Helen, after a moment to savour her little outburst, could not help but smile along with her.
Until, finally:

"Then I think it is time we moved things forward," Mariah told her.

TWO

It had been four days after the disastrous tryst in a London hotel during which he had cheated on the woman he loved that Trevor Drayton signed electronically on his own doorstep for what turned out to be *the* pictures from an unknowing and habitually disinterested UPS courier.

To say he was horrified would be to understate big-time.

The pictures of him being… *fucked*… appeared to have been printed from a video and clearly and unmistakably showed him on all-fours taking a massive black cock into a previously virgin arse. What they did not show were the handcuffs securing his wrists and ankles that kept him in place. The pictures were very graphic and left nothing to the imagination.

When he came to the photo of him taking that massive black tool into his mouth and sucking, his face turned white and for a moment he felt he must pass out.

Inside the envelope he discovered a typed note and, placing the sheaf of pictures back, he read what it said:

Trevor,
I know last Monday was a shock to you and this will probably seem worse but, if you value the life you have with your wife you need to read all of this through and come to the only sensible conclusion. I expect my instructions to be followed to the letter and if you don't the pictures of you taking a black-shemale's cock into your arse in a hotel room will go to your wife at her place of work. I don't want money from you – I've checked you out and know you haven't any – but I do want complete obedience if your wife is to remain ignorant of your love of black cock. There is a full video of you taking my erect prick in your arse and I've no

doubt that your wife would be devastated if she saw her pervert of a husband in action.

I really would not advise you trying to talk your way out of this with your wife by showing her this letter as evidence of your being coerced as she will only think you've written it to cover yourself anyway. And, besides, what would she think of being married to a man who could allow another... man... to use him in such a way?

He paused in his reading, mind almost completely numb; though not so devoid of memory he could not remember the pain as that cock was slid into him and the way it changed into…

He cut his thoughts off, unwilling to acknowledge the affront to his masculinity and returned his attention to the letter.

"This can't be happening," he cried out loud, thankful Helen was out doing a job he was now quite incapable of finding. Monday had been but the latest in a long line of disasters that had wrecked a life he had loved and placed him in a position of financial dependence upon his wife. Now this!

That *"dependence"* being something he hated and was careful to keep from his friends, together with his sisters and nephews and nieces in Florida, that they might continue to see him as the successful businessman and strong husband they knew him to be.

A dependence he sensed, from little signs of exasperation in her, that Helen was growing tired of also.

All the above explaining why the email inviting him to the Langham Hotel in Lower Regent Street to attend a job interview had lifted his spirits.

He had been, it seemed, *headhunted*.

The email had informed him that he would be one of a very small number of candidates for the position of Sales Director for a large

German company opening operations in England and that, should he wish to be considered, he should make himself known at the hotel reception from where he would be directed to where the interview would take place.

He, of course, checked the German company out on Google and they did indeed turn out to be *large*. *Very* large. They were, in fact, the largest suppliers of leathers, hides and acrylics to the automotive industry and he himself had done some business with them when his company dealing in the same area had been up and running; the reason, no doubt, he had been contacted he told himself.

Doing his best to conceal his high spirits for this seeming turnaround in his fortunes from his wife, this that he may surprise her with the good news should the interview prove successful, he had once again donned a suit and tie and made his way from their Oxted home in Surrey to the heart of London for the interview that might just end his recent run of ill-fortune.

The *"Ms Hettie Muller"* he had contacted to accept the invitation to the interview had not attracted his undue suspicion, despite having contacted him via a Gmail address – so delighted was he at the chance of employment –and Monday had seen him upon the fourth floor off the Langham being welcomed into a suite by a black woman who looked and sounded nothing like a *"Ms Muller"*.

The woman had, though, possessed an incredible body below a feline face.

And her tits had been truly amazing.

She had also been utterly professional and asked him all kinds of relevant and necessary questions before, at interview's end, stunning him by making an offer of the position.

How could he refuse?

The offer of a glass of Chilean Merlot to seal the deal when, still marveling at his good fortune, he accepted was not be sniffed at either.

Before the bottle had been emptied - and in his elation he had neglected to ask himself why she did not appear to be touching her own drink as he allowed his excitement to let him down his more swiftly than he would have normally – he was naked and shackled and upon all fours on the carpet as his erstwhile interviewer dropped a sober skirt to reveal thighs equally as shapely as the calves below before presenting him with a cock that looked to his suddenly blurry and befuddled gaze at least twice as thick and long as his own.

And felt twice as big again when it entered where no cock had been before.

Not more than an hour later, she had replaced her skirt and left the room with him still in it.

Even if he was not the same man who had entered.

What self-regarded lady's man and heterosexual could have after having just had his arse pummelled to submission by eleven inches of another man's ramrod stiff cock?

That man being a shemale or not.

It had been almost another hour later that he felt able to dress himself, groaning as he did so at the pain in his abused rear, and make a groggy passage from the hotel to the underground and Victoria Station for a befuddled and uncomprehending journey home to Oxted, Any thoughts of complaint or involving the Police brushed aside. The less anyone knew of his ordeal the better he would like it.

Now he was no longer befuddled – though he remained unable to comprehend why this… *thing*… had chosen him as a victim.

That she had known his email address and certain other pieces of his personal information had not occurred to him.

Yet.

His insides were turning over, her hands visibly shaking, as he continued reading:

> *"On Saturday, at precisely 12 o'clock, I will be outside the supermarket at the back of Oxted Station in my red Audi soft-top – if you don't see it immediately I'd advise you to make a very thorough search as I expect you to come to me immediately, get into the car, and do not say a word.*
>
> *I want your eyes low as a sign that you recognise your situation and the power I have to ruin your life. You will be gone for at least two hours so you'll need an excuse for your wife. I would, though, advise you not to tell her or anyone else about this. If I detect even the slightest hint that you have or if you do not follow my instructions to the letter then I assure you that the life you know will become infinitely worse."*

He read message and its instructions again, struggling to believe this had/was happening – even if the discomfort he still felt at his rear and the memory of the shemale's fat cock as it slid into him were too real to be the stuff of dreams.
He felt, in fact, shattered.

Locking the note and photos away in his study bureau, he realised his defiler and the writer of the note was right and, if he wanted his marriage to continue and keep his self-respect in the eyes of family and friends, he had no choice but to do as he… she it?... demanded.

In the time before Helen's arrival home, Trevor Drayton convinced himself that his only way forward was to do as the black freak who had somehow selected him to torment asked and hope to either find a way out of his/her/its clutches or that she grew bored with him. Finding an excuse for his absence the next lunch-time would not be difficult – a phone call to a bachelor friend and an appointment on the golf-course would take care of that – but locating a reason for the how and why of his being chosen by the shemale as a victim was completely beyond him; though he did wonder if his surfing of Internet porn of a different kind to that he was unaware his wife had been accessing herself had somehow put he/her/it onto him.

It would be a few months before he knew but, though he was not aware of it at this time, *know* he would.

THREE

The moment Helen Drayton had come across the female-led and cuckolding sites online her view of life – and more specifically her own – began to change.

There was, she had often heard said, nothing new under the sun and it was quite galling to her that she had suffered the boredom of being a housewife in a conventional marriage for so many years while her husband felt free to pursue the same business ambitions he had spoken of when they had first met and had now seen them vanish into the ether of failure and bankruptcy. And *"suffered"* it, in fact, when the solution had been at hand the whole time. A solution to her boredom made all the more possible when she had noticed the link to Mariah's site on "Cuckold Place", the largest of the web's cuckolding sites.

Having been blessed, or cursed some would say, by an imagination, she was by no means unversed in the less… *everyday…* aspects of sexual desire and its curious off-shoots; but what she found under the simple Google search of *"female supremacy"* simply left her breathless with surprise and… *need*.

That there could actually be women out there who fucked men – and sometimes women – with their partner's full knowledge, even if that partner was unwilling, astounded her. Astonishment that continued to grow when she read of how so many of those… *partners…* became so diminished and docile by the simple exercise of a woman's right to choose. Becoming so docile, in fact, they not only remained in the relationship but took a secondary and, more importantly as well as excitingly to her, *obedient* role.

And some of the degrading and humiliating ways in which the newly docile and obedient husbands allowed themselves to be used was beyond her comprehension.

Almost.

Hardly surprising that not a month after she had started surfing the net and reading such material that she was ready for the next – and real – step.

All she needed to begin with was a willing – and strange - cock.

A *"cock"* that was *not* her husband's.

Severe of features she might have been but the body below that face was still capable of holding a man's interest – it had kept, and still did, Trevor's, after all – and if the looks she saw thrown her way by businessman and others, senior and junior, successful and not so successful, were to be believed, then finding men willing to fuck her in the way she wanted and in ways of which her handsome, older and utterly ineffectual between the sheets husband was incapable would not be any problem.

And so it had proved.

Spectacularly.

The first time she cheated on her husband was with an attractive older executive who made it obvious he wanted her. An extended lunch, a nearby hotel room close to her office, and voila!...

Instant *"Hot-Wife"*.

It had been an eye-opener and, if the executive's pleasure at having pleased her was as much a shock to him, given he hardly considered himself a stud, then her own surprise put into complete perspective what her dud of a handsome husband had been denying her all these years of her marriage.

What *pleased* her most – in tandem with her surprise - was the confident way she, despite his good looks and influential executive position, took control of the proceedings and directed him in ways of her choosing...

"Slowly... Use the flat of your tongue as if you were a thirsty dog licking water from a bowl..."

She discovered a dominance about herself that seemed to make it impossible for this powerful man to say *"no"* to her.

Now, as she watched from the window their detached home her husband load his golf-clubs into his Mazda that was now in her name, this for a non-existent round of golf with a lying and conniving bachelor friend who, dishonesty or not, she had decided to fuck sometime in the near future, Helen Drayton knew the day was not far from coming when she would be exercising her newly discovered authority and dominance on the handsome man whose name she had once taken.

A dominance that would enable her to take *everything* he had left to him.

*****

The following day after receiving the photos and written directions from shemale tormentor came all too quickly for Trevor Drayton. As he had expected, his wife had barely raised an eyebrow when he mentioned golf with Jerry. Though a look of puzzlement did cross her face when she had to call him back to accept the cash she now doled out to him in the absence of and ATM or credit-card.

He had spent a sleepless night and his anxiety had been so strong he felt at times as if he must cry out as his wife slept peacefully alongside him as he snuggled up to her warm, if turned, body that he might find some reassurance there.

The fact she was less interested in sex with him these days had nothing to do with their changed situation in regard of work other than the fact that her job as a CEO's P.A. was quite pressured and the travelling into London exhausted her.

Exhaustion that was not helped, she had assured him, by having to constantly redo simple chores she had left for him to complete and which he had performed, and continued to perform, less than willingly.

All of which, the deluded husband consoled himself, would change the moment his circumstances took an upturn.

Not that he didn't try to instigate sex between them still and was forever complimenting her on how good she looked when leaving the house for the station and then the office. To no effect. She was always too tired.

Though at least she was not so trite as to plead the cliché of a headache.

Now, though, he was on his way to meet a… *thing*… that *did* want sex from him.

Even if he would rather have given him/her/it both barrels of a loaded shotgun.

The instructions were crystal in his mind – how could they not be given the consequences were he to ignore or forget them - and when he located the Audi soft-top and occupied the passenger seat he was actually relived that he had been ordered to keep his eyes lowered.

The drive to wherever he was being taken commenced in a silence that was uncomfortable, but he assured himself that speaking to the *"thing"* would be a sight worse – even if that and other things could not be put off forever.

Their destination, as it turned out would be a Travel Lodge in Caterham some five miles to the north of Oxted.

They were more than halfway into their journey – though he was not to know this – when his driver finally spoke to him:

"I'm pleased with you, Trevor," she told him, tone strong and confident in a way that told him the shemale knew the cards were in her hands; a dismissive confidence that rankled with him, though he remained with eyes lowered that his anger might not be read in them. "I like a man who knows when he's beaten and does as his new female boss tells him."

A lip was bitten so hard he felt sure it must split, but still he said nothing to what he could only take as provocation on her part.

"I assume," she went on, referring to the habitually tasteless outfit not found out of place at a golf-club bar but risible anywhere else, "that you're dressed like a white Harlem pimp for a trip to the dread golf-course?"

Free of whatever it was she had slipped into his wine in the hotel room and which had made him such easy meat for her intentions, Trevor Drayton again tested his lips durability and bit back his anger as she continued:

"We can assume then that you've kept this all to yourself, yes?"

A surprisingly dainty and feminine black hand reached over to stroke a thigh covered by the material of his golf-slacks.

And did so, despite his flinch, confident in the knowledge that she would not be prevented from doing so.

He wanted nothing more than to spit an answer at her before supplying something in the way of physical violence for her to think about, but knew he wouldn't risk it even as the desire occurred to him.

"Yes," was all he allowed himself to say, the situation in which she had him tearing up his insides.

"Good boy,." She applauded him in a tone of voice that did nothing to lessen his humiliation. "Now be quiet until we get to where we're going."

Their arrival at the Travel Lodge was met with no undue attention and before long Trevor Drayton found himself being led into the usual bland room common to the chain, having watched from behind the swaying arse and womanly figure that gave no clue as to the cock lying at its centre in horrific – for him, anyway – contradiction. Not once had she looked at him since they had entered and had taken care of all the booking in details herself and on the way to their room, her carrying the laptop that was the only luggage they had, it was more of the same, her marching purposefully ahead as he followed obediently in her wake, knowing without having to check that he wold be following close at her heel.

Opening the door to the room, she had reached back and grasped his wrist firmly, strength taking him off-guard, to pull him in after her. Only letting go when they were at the foot of the bed. An unnecessary, if symbolic, example of the power she felt she now had over him.

Releasing him, she slid off her jacket to move to the window and stare out, the shapeliness of the bare and utterly smooth black legs that supplied no hint that he was in the presence of anything but a highly-sexed, if highly evil, woman revealed to his gaze as she spoke without turning:

"Trevor, do you understand the predicament you're in?"

His response came instantly, knowing as he did that there was no point prevaricating and that to do so would only extend the length of whatever ordeal she had in mind for him.

"Yes," he told her, acknowledgement made as softly as it was dejected.

"Then I want you to know that I am going to use the power I have over you to do things... Things I feel confident you will not like."

Suddenly, he could restrain himself no longer:

"Why?" he cried.

The shemale turned to face him, feline features amused but unsurprised by his outburst.

"Why me, for god's sakes?" he continued, voice sent to the higher register by his outrage and a rightful sense of injustice.

She shrugged, massive breasts jiggling in response to the movement and revealing they lacked nothing in firmness for being minus a bra.

"Let's just say that your personal situation and the fact I find you handsome and highly attractive made you perfect for me."

Her eyes had fixed upon his with a look he couldn't pin down and he was not to know that she was simply reading his, somewhat, obvious thoughts in response to her reply.

Thoughts that reacted to her admission of the appeal he held for her by wondering if that appeal could be turned to his own advantage.

Thoughts that were soon to be disabused as the shemale laughed:

"No, Trevor. The fact I find you attractive will not allow you to bargain your way out of the situation in which I've placed you."

"I… I…"

"No need to apologise, Trevor," she told him. "It's a perfectly natural reaction and one Ms Mariah fully expected you to supply."

His eyes had crinkled:

"M-Ms…Mariah…?"

"Me, silly!" she laughed. "You surely didn't think I was a *'Ms Muller'*, did you?"

He was staring at her as if she were from another planet, still unable to quite comprehend how she had manoeuvred him into such a position so effortlessly.

"Do I look or sound German?" she mocked him.

He had been about to retort that she didn't look as if she packed a python sized cock in her panties either, but thought better of it.

"All you need to know right now," she went on with what he could only describe as relish, "is that I can ruin what remains of a life that already looks like a ruin if you don't behave in ways I find *totally* pleasing."

The curl of her lip was derisive:

"In fact, I can do it whether you please me or not. It all depends upon my mood and, if you're sensible, you will do your best ensure that mood remains… *benevolent.*"

In spite of his knowing she could do exactly as she said a hint of the spine he had once believed himself to possess had surfaced and his eyes had blazed out at her.
To no appreciable effect.

"I should learn not to stare at me in such a way if I were you, Trevor," she warned him. "*Especially* after what I just told you. After all, it's not just your wife who would kick your sad white arse into touch if she were to be confronted with those pictures of you with my lovely black cock halfway towards your throat – or even *in* it."

The shemale's smile was purest malice:

"Especially as you look to be enjoying it so much."

Trevor Drayton blanched, knowing the pictures had been selected with the purpose of showing him – disingenuously – to be enjoying the defilement of both mouth and arse.

Or, at the *very* least, accepting that defilement.

"Imagine what your sister's and their husband's would think to see their brother and brother-in-law on all fours worshiping the cock of a black shemale… Not to mention the friends of your wife and yourself. Perhaps I could arrange to have a few copies pinned up in the nineteenth-hole of that pompous golf-club you're still clinging to membership of."

He felt physically sick at the thought any and all of the possibilities she had outlined and, spotting this, his tormentor ran with the knowledge:

"How would your adored nieces and nephews react to having photos sent to them at school showing their uncle sucking a big black cock?"

"You…? You wouldn't do that, would you?" he asked, sounding as if he were about to beg for the first time. "They're… They're children!"

Again came the shrug and again the accompanying jiggle of breasts that were, he admitted unwillingly, both wondrous and a contradiction to the gender of their owner.

"It's your choice, Trevor," she told him. "It means nothing to me if you keep your self-respect with these people or force me to have it removed from you. But you should know that I won't hesitate to do just that if you don't behave in a way I find totally pleasing and respectful."

The bile at the back of Trevor Drayton's throat increased in volume and acidity as what had been a pretty horrifying experience – mildly drugged or not – on the Monday began to turn into purest nightmare on the Saturday.

"I understand how new this all is to you so I'll overlook your silence as being disrespectful and take it as a sign that you intend to be a good obedient boy for me."

The pause that followed was charged with an atmosphere from which all positive elements and power flowed from that evil hemisphere occupied by the shemale.

Until:

"Tell me that you intend to be a good obedient boy for me," she said, taking a few sharp paces to narrow the distance between them so that her magnificent breasts were pressed lightly against the underside of his rib-cage and her feline features staring up into his, still some way short of him even in the spiked heels that accentuated her already shapely legs more.

"P-Please," he began, feeling his will desert him in the face of her confidence and certitude that he would be unable to find either the physical or moral strength to deny her what she wanted. "Stop this now. I don't deserve to be treated like…"

The slap that rocked his head to one sand resounded in the room and left him open-mouthed; not so much for the pain caused by its delivery, which was considerable, but because of the strength behind the arm propelling black hand to white cheek and the fact it was the first time *anyone* had laid a hand upon him in such a way since his schooldays.

"Tell me now or I'll take great pleasure from sending those pictures of you taking my cock to those you care for most."

Through the beginning of tears that were also the first he had shed since being a schoolboy; tears he described to himself as unmanly and berated himself as he did so; Trevor Drayton saw the intent in her eyes and knew with sudden certainty that this… *thing*… into whose clutches he had fallen would have no trouble in doing exactly as she said if he didn't do as she wished.

"With your wife first," she added the postscript.

Of course, his first impulse after he had recovered from the slap to his cheek had been to deliver some physical punishment of his own. An impulse that lasted for about as long as it took her to utter her threat and the aforementioned look of fury and intent in her eyes that told him the shemale in whose web he floundered was mentally unbalanced and would have no conscience in doing what she described. Attracted to him or not.

Her next words confirming his assessment:

"Don't think because I find you fuckable that I won't do what I say," she assured him, moving so close he could feel her breath upon his chin as she stared up at him. "You're not the only attractive and *weak* man around."

A few seconds passed before she repeated her demand:

"Tell me that you intend to be a good obedient boy for me," she said.

Her eyes drilled into his and as his Adam's Apple bobbed in a throat parched by anxiety and fear she again felt that indescribable and perverted joy that came from overmastering another human being.

And especially a human being of the white *and* male kind.

Knowing she had him over a barrel and screwing his eyes shut to blot out the vision of the pleasure he knew she must take from her triumph, Trevor Drayton searched for saliva that was not forthcoming before bowing to what he knew to be inevitable; telling himself by way of compensation for his imminent capitulation – and in the age old way of the vanquished - that this way at least he lived to fight another day.

"I... I..."

"Look me in the eyes as you say it," she ordered.

His soul shrivelled inside him, but – images of his wife, family and friends as they gazed upon pictures of him sucking upon a shemale cock foremost in his mind – he did as she asked.

As he thought, the pleasure she was taking from her victory over him was immense as she ordered once again:

"Say it!"

Swallowing back the bile that seemed constant and likely to project unbidden from his throat at any moment, Trevor Drayton steeled himself to say the most humiliating words he had uttered in his life to now and struggled even harder to make sure his eyes remained fixed upon those of his tormentor as he did so:

"I… I intend to be a… to be a good obedient boy for… for you."

Having told himself to rush through it, he had found it impossible to do so; the words and what they meant simply too demeaning to his sense of self-worth and pride to come easily to the tongue.

Something the black woman with a cock who had set herself up as his tormentor also realised:

"Yes, I know how difficult that was for you," she told him, expression darkening as she reached up to stroke the side of his face with the back of her hand and he flinched.

The punch the other hand she had balled into a fist delivered to his solar plexus took every last gasp of wind from him along with any fight that was remaining as he collapsed to his knees at her feet.

"*Never*," she told him, lips pulled back in a snarl, "move away from my touch in such a way again.

Hardly the most athletic or physical of men, despite a well-kept physique and the golf that could hardly be said to qualify as *athletic*, Trevor Drayton attempted to suck air into his depleted lungs while acknowledging at the same time that he had never been hit so hard and with so much power in his life.

"If I decide I want to touch you then I will," he heard her voice from above, his eyes fixed on the pointed leather toecap of one navy court shoe as tapped out an angry and impatient rhythm on the carpet. "In time you'll come to regard it as a privilege."

"The fuck I will," he told himself, able at least to refute and fight her in his mind if not aloud and with physical means of his own.

"In fact," she went on, sounding as if she were giving an idea consideration, "I think this is as good a time as any for you to learn your first lesson concerning the consequences for disobedience."

Breath still hard to come by and unable to form words he now felt too afraid to utter anyway, his eyes remained fixed on the tapping toecap of her shoe and the coal black foot contained within it as she lowered a pair of equally coal black panties and stepped from them.

The glutes of his arse tensed as he sensed what was to come.

And sensed wrong.

At least when it came to the part of the anatomy she would use upon that arse this time.

Suddenly he felt a hand take a hold of his still luxuriant if greying locks and yank him upwards until he was stood before her, breath still rasping in his throat and feeling about as risible, pitiful and defenceless as he had ever felt.

As a black hand went to the belt of his golf-slacks and unfastened it before undoing the top-button a part of him died.

Yet he allowed the assault. An assault upon the privacy he, along with the rest of civilised society, took for granted to take place. An assault, had civilised society been present to witness it, that was being made upon a healthy white man of middle years by a smaller, if well-built black female a good few years younger.

What they would not have seen, of course, would have been the massive black cock that swung free beneath the camouflage of the skirt now it had been released from the captivity of panties.

A massive black cock that was already erect in anticipation of what was to come.

"Better," the shemale owner of that erect cock told him as she sat on the edge of the bed and draped him over her strong black thighs, draping one powerful leg over the back of his own and twisting an arm towards his neck to keep him in place.

As he realised with a thrill of utter horror just what she intended his lips opened to voice a protest.

A protest that died in his throat as the panties the shemale had just stepped from were thrust into his mouth and cut off all possibility of coherent speech.

"The sooner you realise I'm your master in every possible way – physically and mentally – the sooner I can stop having to punish you," he heard her voice from above as he tried to work out what was worse: the fact he was a grown man about to be spanked liked a schoolboy or the taste and smell of the shemale's unmentionables in and coming from his mouth.

From the very first smack of black hand upon unprotected white buttocks, any considerations other than escaping the rise and fall of that powerful hand as it reduced him to a mess of abject pleading behind his humiliating gag were forgotten. He would not have believed a simple hand-spanking could prove so painful and – never the most physically durable, despite his manly physique – he was soon reduced to muffled whining behind the gag as tears began to flow freely.

The shemale was holding nothing back, raising her arm high in the air and bringing it down on his writhing bottom in a relentless rhythm.

And that was not all.

She *educated* him as she spanked.

His life was now hers, she told him – unless he wished not to have a life; or at least not the life he knew. She saw him as no more than a boy and intended to make him… *useful*. If he did exactly as she said from now on she might be persuaded not to tell his wife, family and friends what a cocksucking little pervert he was, but only if she saw a sincere intention on his part to become her devoted manservant.

Through his agonies and the humiliation of being handled so effortlessly as if he were, to all intents and purposes, a child, Trevor Drayton could scarce bring himself to believe he was in a room at a bog-basic Travel Lodge, not five miles from his own home, draped over the lap of a black shemale as she – *it* – turned his arse from white to red and seemed to have every intention of transforming it to an even more ignominious shade of blue.

He tried to struggle but was held effortlessly in position as the hand descended upon his undraped buttocks, the knowledge this… *thing*… could not only ruin his life but appeared to be his physical superior also searing his own sense of masculinity.

And still that powerful black hand rose and fell.

Again…

And again…

And…

Had it not been for the soiled panties that filled his mouth his cries would have had the entire East Surry Constabulary beating a path to the room as that hand continued to descend and strike his arse.

Time, after time. after time.

He would have begged and pleaded now, promising to do anything if only she would stop, but the only sounds he could affect were pitiful little mewling's from behind the gag.

The shemale who had his life at her mercy was relentless and continued on.

Then, suddenly, and mercifully, the rise and fall of the punishing hand ceased and he was rolled from those coal black thighs to the carpet, where he lay mewling piteously.

There was silence above him and it was only after – he knew not how long – when he made to remove the gag from his mouth that the shemale spoke again.

Harshly:

"Leave my panties in your mouth," she barked. "Don't you dare take them out until I say you have permission, you pitiful piece of shit."

The beaten white man in a foetal ball at the shemale's feet wondered how he would prevent himself from vomiting if he were forced to keep the odious item in his mouth much longer.

As it turned out, that was the least of his concerns.

"I want you to crawl on your hands and knees and kneel in the corner – you can choose which," she told him. "I've some emails to send from my laptop and, while I'm sending them, I want you to have a long hard, and *silent*, think about your situation."

The last part of her statement had been unnecessary, of course, given that he had thought of nothing else since she had turned his life that had already been an uncovered insurance claim into an out and out car-wreck.

"When I've finished I'm going to call you over," she went on as remained curled in physical and mental agony on the carpet onto which she had thrust him. "If you don't crawl to me like the good and obedient white dog you intend to become for me, take off my shoes and lick my beautiful black feet, then I'm out of here and we're done and your wife, family and friends – and don't think I don't have *all* their addresses – will soon have the pictures that show you for weak sissy-boy cocksucker you really are… Now get to your corner, put your nose in it and keep it there until I say you can remove it."

Already part-broken from her fucking of him underneath the influence of the drug she had slipped into his drink on the Monday – though he was beginning to sense she needed no artificial aids to keep him in line, the hand-spanking and the effortless way she had forced him to succumb to it had taken its toll and he found himself obeying his tormentor without even giving it conscious thought.

Smiling as the older white man she was turning into a terrified automaton crawled to the corner of his choice, Mariah smiled to herself.

There was nothing she liked better than reducing some macho and arrogant white man into a willing servant and obliging fuck toy.

But with this particular white man – and his wife – the pleasure she was receiving was like none she had experienced before and was as puzzling as it was welcome. There were, she knew only too well, certain men who actually paid for the treatment she had just visited upon the white man who was already on all fours. But *he* was not, she also knew, and never would be, one of their number.

Was that why she felt so… *turned on?*"

"Good boy," she told him when he chose his corner and was kneeling in it with his nose pressed to the magnolia painted wall. "Be nice and quiet while Ms Mariah does what she has to do then you can make your choice."

Tearing eyes and salivatory mouth from the ruin of the white buttocks his kneeling form in the corner presented, the shemale flipped open her laptop and did indeed begin to compose an email.

An email with an address the man in the corner would have been surprised to see was that belonging to his wife.

It was some ten minutes later, progress report completed, that the shemale shutdown the laptop and rose to her feet.

"Okay, white shit," she said. "The time of reckoning is upon you."

Knelt in the corner, she felt sure the man was trembling.

"What's it to be?"

FOUR

"I need to do certain things to you," she had told him.

In the privacy of his study, the latest in a long line of Whiskeys to hand, Trevor Drayton recalled what the shemale had told him after he had…

He swallowed back the twelve-year-old Aberlour he had been saving for better days, and been reduced to opening after the worst - then immediately poured another. Helen had retired to bed hours ago and, apart from asking him why he was so quiet, seemed unperturbed by his troubled demeanour since his return from the *golf-course*. Her *"early night"* a godsend that allowed him to sit in front of his computer and get sloshed.

Not that the twelve-year-old single malt diminished his memory of either the Travel Lodge or the monster who had forced him there.

And certainly not the image of himself as he took his nose from the corner to which she had dispatched him with her panties in his mouth.

The above after spanking his arse.

A mental snapshot formed of himself as he *crawled* upon all fours to her feet and, as she stood above him, removed her shoes and began to lick her…

More whisky went the same way as the last in the hope it could – even if only temporarily – banish the nightmare of his recent experience.

Not to mention the salty taste of the perspiration coating her bare foot that still seemed to pervade his mouth many hours and frequent trips to the bathroom and the swilling of mouthwash later.

"I have a darkness inside me and I'm going to unleash it on you," the shemale who now insisted he address her as *'Ms Mariah'* told him as his tongue lathed at a salty black instep in acceptance of what she demanded from him. "The fact you'll hate me doing it but can do nothing to stop me only makes it all the more… *wonderful*."

He had been aware of her crouching down and running her hands over the arse her powerful black hand had only just blistered, his trousers and underpants bunched around his ankles just as they had when she lowered them.

"Keep licking," she ordered him with a relatively light smack upon his reddened rump as a reminder when he paused in his soul destroying duty, appalled by her words and the knowledge she quite, quite, serious in her intent.

His tongue again found the high-arch of her instep and resumed its lathing of the surprisingly smooth and unblemished foot, steeling himself not to gag at the odour of leather and sweat threatening to make him do just that.

"Good boy," he heard the shemale, his junior by a number of years, offer demeaning praise. "I think we'll soon be coming to an understanding now you have a better idea of what your place is around Ms Mariah."

Trevor Drayton, on all-fours at her feet, arse turning all kinds of weird and not at all wonderful shades after the attentions of her relentless hand and its vengeful palm, found that his mental anguish was more than a match for his physical discomforts.

And her reference to herself as *"Ms Mariah"*, and his certainty it was how she wished him to address her from now on, seemed to take that anguish to new depths.

The whisky having no appreciable effect upon him – though he was two-thirds towards emptying it completely - the forty-something and grudging househusband, bankrupt and, now, creature of a black shemale, poured an even larger tumbler as the image of her hauling him up by the hair from his servicing of her... *feet*... to be presented with the monster of a cock that made his own look so miniscule and had pounded his drug-numbed mind into helpless submission at the start of the week before, horror of horrors, being thrust into his mouth.

Larger tumbler or not, it was almost emptied in a single gulp as the image of himself held in place by the shemale as she ordered him to open his mouth assailed him.

This time there had been no drug inspired lassitude – horrified though he may have been in his stupor – to allow him to mitigate the fact that he had taken a black cock into his open mouth and, under the instructions of *"Ms Mariah"*, begun to suck that part of it he was able to accommodate in this early stage of his... *"training"*.

As the image of the black prick invading his mouth re-asserted itself for the umpteenth time since his return home from the Travel Lodge – together with a recall of what seemed like gallons of sperm hitting the back of his throat and coating his tongue when the shemale succumbed to the pleasure she was taking from her control of him and erupted with a suitably high-pitched scream – he felt his stomach lurch.

The picture of himself at her feet as he sucked at her before being ordered to look up and into her mocking eyes as he did so brought the bile to his throat.

But it was his recall of seeing his humiliation being captured for posterity upon the shemale's mobile phone that sealed his latest bout of... *nausea*.

As he staggered from his study chair to hurry to the bathroom, Trevor Drayton knew that all the Aberlour in the Highlands themselves – of the twelve year variety or otherwise – would not be enough to either banish his memory of the earlier events.

And as for providing a solution?

As his stomach voided itself into the toilet bowl for the fourth time since arriving home, he wondered if there was any way he could somehow come clean to his wife and persuade her that he had been manipulated into sucking a shemale's cock.

A *black* shemale!

And done so twice.

As he voided the last of his stomach's contents into the bowl and took deep breaths to recover something resembling an equilibrium, he convinced himself that, if he wanted to stay married and keep the respect of friends and family, his only option was to do as this abomination of nature demanded of him and hope she tired and moved on to fresh meat as soon as possible.

Trevor Drayton could be forgiven for not realising his marriage was already over and neither the shemale who insisted she owned him or the wife who intended to would *ever* tire of him.

FIVE

"Put your hands behind your head, Helen."

Mariah's words had turned suddenly condescending and, with the sensation of being controlled by this magnificent looking black woman with a body Amazon–like in its femininity while being possessed of a cock that was as beautiful as any the white housewife had ever seen or imagined she would see.

Feeling almost childlike in the man/woman's presence, Helen realized her labia was swollen with arousal.

She could feel it and *knew* Mariah could see it.

The shemale just stared at her, slightly cocking her head as her eyes roamed over the naked white body with a gaze Helen could only describe to herself as: *"proprietorial"*.

She felt hesitant, violated and… *alive*.

And not a finger had had been laid upon her.

Yet.

The housewife and P.A. was still puzzled as to how things had progressed so far and so quickly. One second they had been sharing a bottle of Pinot Grigio in a little restaurant come watering-hole above the piazza in Covent Garden. The next they had taken a cab back to the shemale's stylish and expensive home off Pimlico's Eccleston Square and, two glasses of yet more white later, she had been persuaded to strip naked for the shemale she was paying to deliver have husband delivered to her in a metaphorical gift-wrap of chain-mail and fetters.

She almost started when the shemale, fully-clothed still, walked toward and around her, studying her body so intently it almost seemed as if having a female naked before her was a first.

Behind her, Mariah pulled her arms down behind her back and kissed the nape of her neck possessively.

Helen had always been a woman used to control – even if she had allowed her husband's handsome looks to force her to take a backseat in their marriage. At least until now. In the presence of this black god-cum-goddess who was a mixture of Valkyrie and stud, however, she felt submissive and pliable for the first time in her life and had to admit that the sensations supplied by allowing herself to be... *used*... in such a way were something of a revelation. *Never*, she realised, had she felt so... *aroused*.

Removing her plump and demanding lips from Helen's slender neck, Mariah had reached down and grasped her bare ass.

"Beautiful," the shemale voiced approval of the taut buns clenching against her kneading fingers. "Spread your legs apart, Helen."

The older woman did just that, amazed at the biddable way in which she was responding and knowing it was anticipation of finding herself upon the end of the cock she had seen in the pictures defiling her husband, in first the Langham Hotel and then in a less salubrious Whyteleafe Travel Lodge, that informed her out of character submissiveness.

She also knew that, if submission felt this good, she would not mind dipping into the condition every now and again.

But *only* now and again.

"Wider, Helen," the shemale ordered, not harshly or unkindly, her own voice betraying the excitement she herself felt. "Yes, just a little more.... There!... That's the position I want to see you in."

The white housewife had never felt so open and vulnerable. Her complexion was purest crimson as she pictured how lewd her stance would appear to an onlooker. And cared not a whit.

She had, after all, *never* felt so turned-on either.

"That's my good girl," Mariah told her. "You like this don't you?"

It was and it wasn't a question and no answer was required – especially not when her nipples were so hard and proud and standing straight from her out-thrust breasts.

One of the shemale's strong but shapely hands – the same hands that had recently spanked her husband's naked arse as if her were the recalcitrant charge of a demonic nanny from some piece of underground Victorian erotica - reached down to feel between her spread legs.

Helen realised she had never been so… *wet*.

The shemale chuckled:

"Methinks the future dominant wife enjoys doing just what the lovely black Mariah tells her to do."

Helen didn't answer.

Couldn't answer.

"Unlike her husband," the shemale went on with another chuckle. "Was all he could do not to throw up as Mariah's big black cock filled his mouth and tickled his tonsils."

"Then… Then he'll just have to get used to it," a breathless Helen managed to inform her… *temporary*… dominator, having already given her permission for the husband's defiling to continue at the hands and cock of the shemale who had taken a strangely unprofessional – if enslaving a wife's husband to her for money could be said to be *'professional'* in the first place – fancy to him.

Black fingers insinuated themselves into her arse crack and anticipation of that huge and exquisite shemale cock or not, the white housewife couldn't understand what was happening inside of her to allow such an invasion.

An invasion she hated almost as much as she felt aroused by it.

But…?

Ooooooooh!

It felt… *sooooo*… good.

Suddenly Mariah turned her and bent her over the bed, using her hair to manipulate her into the position she wanted before giving her arse a playful slap. A slap that was nothing like the slaps she had delivered to the husband. Slaps, in his case, that had been intended to break, subdue and demoralise.

"Slaps" that had achieved the desired effect and done just that.

This was different, though, and Helen knew, even as she submitted, that they were indulging in nothing more than foreplay.

The certainty relaxed her.

Mariah might have dominated her husband with complete seriousness and conviction, but she was extending the compliment to the wife simply as a means by which to heighten the pleasure of both of them.

The white wife gasped as, totally willing and in contradiction of her husband's experience, the black cock she had been unable to remove from her thoughts since seeing the pictures of it in Trevor's mouth and arse entered her from behind.

Her scream of welcome was made with a rising pitch as it filled her cunt's width and then assaulted her with its length. She was being used, hard and fast, by a black cock that was penetrating her in a way no other cock had come close to achieving – and certainly not the pitiful husband she was already promising herself would never place his unworthy dicklet inside her again. She experienced submission inspired lust for the first time and simply embraced it; the feeling of being helpless, used, and violated, thrilling her in a way she would not previously have believed possible.

Her release, though it felt incredible, came all too soon for her and all she wanted was for that magnificent pole to keep riding and mastering her.

She was pummelled and violated.

And loved every second of it.

Enjoyment made all the more piquant for the knowledge her unaware cuckold husband – himself pummelled and violated from the same source; if without extending that violation quite the same welcome – was at that moment awaiting her return home after a night of drinks with the girl's from the bank.

As she raised her head and screamed her release to the shemale's ceiling that looked at that moment like nothing less than heaven to her, she told herself he would have some time to wait yet.

And the woman who returned to him would *not* be the one he expected.

Not even close!

Six

"Take off your clothing, right now, Trevor," his wife told him as his mouth dropped open.

"Don't hesitate, and do it quickly, she went on.

Her tone was commanding as he stood before her in their bedroom and it shocked him. She had just returned home from her night out with the girls and, from the moment she had walked through the door, he detected something… *different*… in her manner. True, she had seemed a little distant over the past months but he had put that down to the pressure of her being the one on whom the burden of their finances fell for the first time in their married life and the pressures of the exec P.A. job that went with it. This though, he had assured himself, was different – even if he also assured himself that it could have nothing to do with the humiliations he was suffering at the hands of the black shemale who was taking greater and greater control of him.

This was her third night out with *"the girls"* in as many weeks and after the first two occasions her mood, both in general and with him, had seemed improved.

Something that had given him hope that if he could just find employment and free himself of the ghastly Mariah and the cock with which she dominated him – or perhaps if she grew tired of her new *"white pussy-boy"* – things between himself and Helen could return to an even keel.

He had, after all, not stopped desiring her and was hopeful that, if he could start bringing home the bacon again, she could dispense with her job and, along with it, the tiredness that always seemed to prevent them from making love.

Tonight, however, her mood was not so much improved as…

Strange.

For her part, and though she had imagined how it would feel countless times, Helen Drayton hadn't realized how intense it would be to take charge and issue direct orders to her husband; though there was still, she knew, some way to go before his *"fear"* in her presence reached the desired levels and led to the kind of control her black shemale mentor, and now *"lover"*, had described as hers for the taking.

But tonight she was about to take her own first steps towards making his utter and complete dependence upon her a reality.

The first step being to get him to strip naked before her while she remained clothed and watched him do it.

Whether he kidded himself her insistence he do so was simply the prelude to sex between them or not.

Mariah's words echoed in her head…

"Don't ease him into it, Helen," Mariah had advised as they had relaxed after some of the most intensive sex *either* of them had experienced. "Come straight out with it and go for the jugular. If the pictures you have aren't evidence enough then take my word for it: he's not the strong and proud man you once saw him as and the fact he now sucks my cock and takes my dick in his arse without so much as a murmur of struggle proves it."

"You think he enjoys it then?" she had asked, her hand still wrapped around the incredible black tool that made her white hand look so tiny and was a complete contradiction to the erect nipples upon the full black breasts above it that were sizable enough themselves.

The answer had been instant, as had the shaking of the head and the look of… *disdain?*… upon the feline and utterly feminine features that were also a contradiction of the anomaly residing between her legs:

"Not in the slightest, Helen," the husky, if still female sounding, voice assured her. "If he did I'd be unable to take even the slightest pleasure from… *defiling*… him the way I do. The look on his face as I slide my black meat into his mouth and the knowledge he hates me doing it with a passion is genuine."

Helen smiled, pleased by the fact her husband was being defiled against his wishes and taking no enjoyment from the abuse; not to mention she was the real orchestrator of his torment.

"When it comes to men," that husband's tormentor continued, "I admit it's all about control for me. What I'm *forcing* him to do it is what floats my boat. If I thought for a second he was *'enjoying'* it I'd stop."

"And what if he comes to do just that?"

Again the answer was instant:

"It's not in his nature. Had he been a younger man, in his teens perhaps, then… maybe. But his conditioning was set long ago and nothing will change it. Just because he's weak at base it doesn't mean I can turn his sexual preferences around. If it weren't for the fact I treat him like shit and he saw me as just another woman I'm pretty sure he'd find me attractive. But the curtain's been up on the secret between my legs since my first meeting with him and there's no putting *that* particular genie back in the box."

The shemale gave it some thought:

"Given how you've been cutting him from your own body lately, and the way he was eying my legs during our first meeting for the *supposed* interview, I'm pretty certain he was having sexual thoughts about me though."

"He always did have a thing for a woman's legs. That's why I tend to wear trousers and jeans these days. Just to deny him the pleasure of admiring them."

Helen's smile was evil as she finished:

"Though I do let them loose at certain times to remind and…
torment… him."

The feline and shemale smile was no less malicious as she gave
applause:

"Sensible girl."

They had both laughed until Helen's expression grew serious.

"And you really think he is so devastated by what you have done
to him he will just fold when I start working on him?"

The shemale's chuckle was one of genuine amusement as mockery
was added to malice at Trevor Drayton's expense.

"Like the flimsiest of toilet tissue," Mariah had assured her. "if you
had seen his face when I mentioned sending the photos of him,
with my cock so deep up his arse he was almost giving me a throat
job, to his nieces and nephews at their schools in Florida you'd
know exactly what I mean. Just the fact I knew of their existence,
let alone their school and the city in which they live, terrified him."

For a moment, Helen had looked alarmed:

"Didn't your knowing them make him suspicious? The last thing I
want is for him to think I had any…"

A slim black finger, acrylic nail blood red, pressed against her lips
and cut her off.

"I told him the information was out there on the Internet and
anyone could get it if they just knew how."

After a few moments of charged eye-contact, Helen nodded,
allowed herself to be persuaded. Relief at still being in a position
to take the moral high-ground with her husband great. Knowing as

she did that being able to use the guilt he felt for the weakness allowing Mariah to punish him with even more humiliation of her own would not be possible if he knew it had been her decision to involve the shemale.

Her decision and *her* money.

For a few seconds, as her co-conspirator and now lover shook her head in wonder at how easily she had hoodwinked an erstwhile intelligent and mature man so easily, Helen asked herself why the prospect of taking complete control of her husband's life in such a cruel way thrilled her to the core so much.

And gave up trying less than a milli-second later.

What difference would knowing make, after all?

There was also, she told herself, the prospect that too much insight into her own actions would ruin the incredible pleasure she was taking from the process.

Even at this early stage of her husband's subjugation.

"He swallowed it," the smile was on the sleek black face became as evil as it was feline, "along with some other... *stuff*... without any suspicions whatsoever. He even bought my telling him that my only reason for choosing him was that I get off on dominating handsome and older white-men."

The smile broadened:

"Which is partly true, anyway."

A black hand reached over to take another of a white variety:

"Don't worry., I know how it could mess up what you have in mind if he were to find out. Believe me, he won't discover that what's happening to him was courtesy of his wife's bank-account and her new black lover through any slip of mine."

Helen's relieved look assured the shemale that such a giving away of the game – given that *"game"* was being played so seriously - would indeed *"mess up"* what the single-minded – obsessive on the score, even – white wife had in mind for her husband.

"He has to believe that you're saving his hide. I know that," Mariah reassured her. "It will explain your anger at him for his weakness *and*, more importantly, his perversion that has ensured the lack of respect you'll say you now have for him."

There was an unnatural glow in the white wife's eyes and Mariah – who was already persuaded anyhow - could tell just how obsessed her new lover was when it came to the physical and mental ownership of her husband.

"Both your anger and lack of respect will explain the price he'll have to pay if he wants to go on being married to you and…"

Helen had waited.

"…*not* have his… *secret*… put through the divorce courts where your friends, his sisters and their families, will be sure to see it."

The nod accompanying the *unnatural* glow in Helen Drayton's eyes as she concurred with the shemale's description of what she required was emphatic.

"Don't worry," the owner of the cock that was fucking both her *and* her husband said, arms raised to forestall any further complaints. "I get it."

Helen's look had said: *"I sincerely hope you do"* and Mariah had looked deeply into her eyes:

"By the way," she began, using a forefinger to trace a circle around one of the older white woman's nipples, "since we've become something of an… *item*… as they say, I've decided I'm not taking your money."

Helen had given her a curious look and not responded.

"Don't thank me too hard," Mariah had chided after a few more seconds of silence.

"No," Helen protested. "I am grateful. Truly. But why?"

For the first time since Helen had met her, the shemale seemed embarrassed and, for the first time also, it struck Helen that the… *friendship*… they had struck up was based on more than just sex – at least on Mariah's part.

"I've been with more beautiful women," Mariah shrugged apologetically and Helen, who was realistic on the subject of her looks anyway, did not seem offended by the comparison. "But none of them moved me the way you… *move*… me. There's a certain… quality… you have, a quality I haven't managed to nail down just yet, that… *works*... for me and…"

"Yes?"

"I was just, sort of, hoping that… That, well, you'd let me stay a part of the loop… You know, once you have your husband's balls under lock and key. I thought, perhaps, we could, maybe, work out a way to keep me involved."

Helen had been genuinely surprised – and not just by the unusual hesitance and reticence on the part of her normally forceful and assured lover.

Beneath a calm expression her thoughts raced.

For sure, the sex between them had been – was – incredible. *Beyond* incredible, in fact. But she had thought it was no more than that and would end the moment the shemale had delivered her part of the bargain and delivered Trevor to her as the chattel and sex toy she had long fantasised him as being.

Having Mariah remain a part of her ongoing enslavement of her husband had just *not* occurred to her.

"Mariah, I…"

The feline face looked worried as Helen tried to wrap words around her forming thoughts and, for the first time, the white wife realised it was she, and not the irregularity of nature with the massive breasts and even more impressive black cock who had the real control.

Suddenly, and with that knowledge in mind, the thought of the shemale being a part of her life seemed…

Well…

Desirable.

Thoughts, as growingly attractive to her as they were becoming the more she thought them through, that were accompanied by concerns just the same.

Concerns the shemale who had fallen for her seemed to read:

"I know one of the reasons for wanting your husband under control is so you can have complete freedom to, you know, fuck around – as well as make all decisions for the two of you, but…"

Mariah had paused, surprised herself, it seemed, at the words about to leave her lips.

Then:

"I want you to know I'd be… I'd be cool with that."

A massive surge of arousal swept through Helen's lithe and naked white body as it lay entwined with the more powerful, if no less shapely, form of the shemale in a near monochrome joining.

She was, she told herself with delight and surprise for its timing, experiencing one of the power rushes she had read of in her frequent forays onto the blogs and cuckolding sites of women like herself who described that first experience of power as a partner or loved one acknowledged the right of wife or girlfriend to have sex outside their relationship while remaining chaste themselves.

The fact she could feel such a rush at hearing such an admission from the lips of someone who was neither husband or loved one – albeit someone who had not mentioned remaining chaste themselves – presented her with another question.

How much greater would that rush be when it was her own husband capitulating to her his own rights as both a spouse *and* a man?

Lying there with these thoughts and sensations swirling through head and body, it was not difficult to picture herself dominating not just her husband but this wonderful aberration of nature – even if that domination took a different and more... *inclusive*... form. An aberration of nature and a corresponding cock built, it seemed, and punning on a famous commercial, for the sole purpose of reaching those parts other cocks couldn't reach.

That domination of the shemale she was in the process of imagining, though, one she told herself would be nowhere near as demeaning and humiliating as that she intended for her husband.

A smile creased the white wife's face:
How could it be?

"You would be happy for me to see other men?" she asked.

Her smile was replaced by expectation as she added:

"Other Cocks?"

Looking as hesitant and unsure of herself as Helen could remember, Mariah had nodded, almost as if her own suggestion had come out of the blue and she was as shocked to be making it as the object of her affections was shocked to hear it being made.

"But what if I didn't want *you* to see other women?" Helen asked, testing the depth of the power the black shemale appeared to be handing her, a white hand snaking down to the cock that had only just finished pleasuring her to take a sounding she was sure would prove infallible.

If anything, it was even harder than she had known it to this point.

"Ooooh," she cooed. "I think my lovely Mariah likes the idea of her lover going out to meet men and be fucked while she gets to stay home and… *think*… about it."

The giant black cock twitched in her hand.

"I'd tell you all about it, of course," she assured her, feathering the taut foreskin of a cock that was now arrowed towards the ceiling, having read enough on the cuckolding websites to have some insight into the mindset of the willingly cuckolded – if not that of her husband who, she felt certain, would *never* reconcile himself to the prospect or be in any way willing.

Exactly how, in fact, she wanted it.

"But there would have to be some kind of… *quid pro quo*," she went on, craning her neck to take a nipple as long and as hard as many an under-endowed male's equipment into her mouth that she may suck upon it.

The shemale groaned as the tables were turned and she was the one being played and teased as a whole new world of submission – hers to another, rather than another to her – opened its doors in a way that was as puzzling to the dominant black woman as it was… *exciting*.

"Perhaps," Helen said as she released the nipple from her mouth with a popping sound, "you could babysit Trevor for me while I'm out being fucked by my latest. He wouldn't like it, of course, but that would make it so much nicer for both me and you, wouldn't it?"

The cock thrusting against her feathering hand to gain more friction was all the answer she needed.

"Then, once I'm home, you could bring my husband up to see me so that he can clean me up. I think I'd enjoy that," she said. "Even more so if you had him on a collar and lead and made him crawl upstairs to do so."

Mariah's groaning grew louder and more pronounced as Helen pictured just such a scene.

"Yes. That would be lovely. After all, I can do what I want in the privacy of my own home, can't I?"

The growingly shallow breathing of the shemale assured Helen no answer would be forthcoming anytime soon and she resumed her teasing of that wondrous cock.

"Unless, that is," she went on, voice little more than a rush of air passing her lips, "you'd like to tie him to the hallway bannister and come and clean me up yourself."

The reaction to this amazed them both.

With her hand barely making contact with the shemale's extended prick, semen began to spew from its tip with such force Helen truly thought it must hit the light-shade above.

She could not be sure, in fact, that it didn't.

It was only later, when she was seated in Mariah kitchen, showered and dressed once again in the same clothes she had worn that day to the office and sipping a coffee, that Helen brought up the shemale's suggestion that had triggered her own suggestions in regard of them and detonated, in return, the subsequent explosion of *unnatural* cock.

"I suppose then, seeing as you seem serious about this and are willing to accept I'll be calling the shots if I agree to let you be a part of my life, that we better work something out."

To Helen Drayton's amazement, the look on the shemale's face who had dominated and was dominating her husband with such ease was a mixture of relief and gratitude.

Emboldened, the growingly confident white wife went on:

"We still have an hour or so before I need to get off home, so I'm open to suggestions as to how we should proceed."

A relieved and grateful shemale thought about it for a few moments, then told Helen what she had in mind.

SEVEN

Trevor Drayton felt... *vulnerable*... as he stood completely naked in front of his clothed wife while she stood with hands on hips looking, he thought, *imperious* in the business outfit and heels she had worn to the office and on out for her evening with the *"girls"*.

Despite all the humiliations he had suffered at the hands of the shemale – and taking her cock into both arse and mouth would never cease to repulse him – this was his wife and standing before in a way that seemed... *submissive*... to him somehow was no easier to take – even if the prospect of again getting to have sex with her the way a man and wife should sweetened the pill a little.

There was, though, an overwhelming feeling of self-consciousness as his silent, fully-clothed and, suddenly... *authoritative*... wife watched him strip down in front of her and made no effort to return the compliment.

"Put your hands on top of your head, Trevor."

The words with which she broke the silence were seasoned with no more variation of tone than if she had asked him to pass the pepper and salt and, for some reason, a chill of fear goose-bumped his exposed skin as her changed attitude set alarm bells ringing.

"Put my hands...?"

"On top of your head. That's what I said," she told him, taking a step in his direction that, twinned with the inflexible nature of her expression, seemed threatening somehow – not to mention a certain... *excitement*... he could see in her eyes of a type and kind he had not seen in them up to now.

The verbal postscript to her physical movement underlying just how threatening her move had been and setting warning-bells to ring more alarmingly:

"Just like the dirty little boy you really are."

Her words hit him like a brick and the cock that had come to life at the prospect of being allowed to make love to his wife and feel like a real man again wilted instantly.

"Wh-What do you mean?" he spluttered, fearing the worst and that she had been made privy to his bondage to the... *creature*.

His wife simply stared at him, slightly cocking her head as her eyes roamed over his body with what, even in his wrong-footed condition he could only, describe to himself as contempt.

A variety of thoughts and sensations flashed through his head in the space of no more than a second or two as Trevor Drayton again felt violated. And this time by his own wife. A wife who seemed completely changed from the woman he had taken to the altar and, he realised, had seemed that way for some time now.

His wife was smirking now and, if anything, her contempt was even more marked as she turned from him and retrieved a large brown envelope from the handbag she had left upon the bed.

A cold hand gripped Trevor Drayton's vitals and began to squeeze as she emptied the contents of the envelope onto the duvet.

Even at a distance of a few paces he knew the scenes he would find upon the photos he could see scattered on the mattress.

"How...? How did you get those?" he asked, too stunned to think straight.

"We'll get to that soon enough," she told him, the unnatural calm of her demeanour given what she had discovered unmanning him more than if she had given full rein to her anger. Her eyes bore into his with all the threat and intimidation her unsuspected and welcome talent as a consummate actress allowed. "I thought you might like to try and explain first."

"I… I…"

"Take your time," she told him, making herself comfortable on the side of the bed and crossing her shapely legs in their opaque pantyhose – legs that did not, for once, consume his interest with their usual attraction.

Feeling about as devastated and powerless, not to mention mortified and terrified, as he had ever felt to this point in his forty-something years, Trevor Drayton recognised the picture his wife had taken from the others strewn across the mattress and felt a familiar sense of sickness wash over him as the picture triggered his recall of the event itself…

…Never had he felt so open and so vulnerable. His face had burned with humiliation of the usage being made of him and was made all the worse by his knowledge that camera to the side of him - the same camera the shemale had ordered him to turn his head towards that it might record his features for posterity while revealing only her lower half and the monstrous black cock pistoning in and out of his arse – would have its recording edited judiciously to show him looking as if he were actually a willing partner in his own defilement. Not for the first time since she had entered his life, he had begged the shemale to stop her torment of him.

Only to be silenced by a hand slapping down upon his buttocks by way of a stinging reminder of what had happened the last time he had defied his "Master" and been taken over her knee.

"Keep making eye contact with the lens," she had ordered. "And look as though you're enjoying yourself."

With her thick black cock halfway up his arse, he had still managed to shake his head with incredulity; both for the near impossibility of her order and the fact it was aimed at him.
"Unless," she went on, "You prefer it to be one of my belts that blisters your behind this time."

Terrified of her by now and not sure he could have fought her and won, even if the hold she had over him wasn't in place, he had done as she ordered and turned his head back to the lens with a look that was as near as he could come to "enjoyment"; no doubt the tears in his eyes, he told himself, would be taken to be inspired by gratitude.

"That's my good little boy," his tormentor cooed. "What lovely pictures these will make for my collection of you."

Trevor Drayton felt himself near to sobbing and only the competing distractions of the discomfort provided by the fat cock pistoning in and out of his white arse and not wanting the abomination of nature subjecting him to such an indignity seeing such an unmanly capitulation from him kept him from doing just that.

And there was something else.

Something worse.

Discomfort or not, he was beginning to feel a certain… arousal… at the invasion.

Finally, without taking the invasion to completion – though by now Trevor Drayton knew that completion would not be long in following and also knew exactly how it would be achieved – the shemale withdrew from his arse as he used his hands on the chair placed in front of him for balance and, slowly, moved around him to switch off the camera before seating herself upon the same chair he still balanced upon.

He remained in place, knowing now that to move without her permission would result in punishment – this time with a belt rather than the palm of her hand.

A "palm" that had been excruciating enough on its own.

Staring into his eyes, acknowledging with what he knew was pleasure the capitulation and demoralisation she read in them, she had reached beneath him and taken the manhood that was a lot less impressive than her own in her hand.

Her chuckle was not pleasant, but it was pleasured:

"Why, you little slut. I do believe you're beginning to enjoy this, aren't you?"

Trevor Drayton was too full of bile and desolation at that point to find words to explain why, despite his detestation of what had and was being done to him, his cock was hard. Another strata added itself to the already considerable depths of his despair. All he could do was shake his head in refutation before his eyes had lowered to the carpet in shame.

"Well, your body is, even if what passes for your mind is telling you otherwise," the shemale had gone on, saving him the necessity of a verbal response that was, as noted, quite beyond him at that point.

A small relief that was short-lived.

Suddenly, her hand was in his hair and he was being hauled across to the bed, spirits sinking as he knew he was about to be required to perform an act even more repugnant to him than allowing his arse to be used as a receptacle for the abomination's perverted desires.

Seating herself on the edge of the bed and hauling him across her sleek and powerful black thighs, his shemale tormentor gave the arse she had just finished pistoning five sharp and stinging slaps as an inducement to "pleasing" behaviour before flipping him from her thighs to the carpet and presenting her still engorged cock for his mouth to satisfy.

The eyes that had blazed into his as his own flickered upwards with dread, made a spoken demand unnecessary...

…"Well?" the snap of Helen Drayton's voice had brought him back to a no less pleasing present.

"I'm being blackmailed, Helen!" he cried, realising how ineffectual it sounded as he stood naked before his fully clothed wife. "That… That creature…"

Helen's demeanour as she cut him off was, as agreed with Mariah, icy calm. Such an approach would, the shemale had given assurance before she left her apartment for home, be far more effective. Any histrionics should come from the weaker partner.

"I see," she told him as he stood above her, the cock that had been hopeful of some *normal*, if rationed, attention from the wife he still desired wilted and desolate in the bush of pubic hair she made a mental note to have him shave as soon as she had him fully under her heel. "So, let me get this straight. "A woman with a massive cock much larger than…" her eyes flickered to his manhood, "…*that*… is blackmailing you so she can put it in your arse and mouth. Is that what you're telling me?"

"Helen, you have to believe…"

"Stay right where you are, you cocksucking little pervert," she snarled at him, voice dangerously low, when he took a placatory step towards her.

It was the first time throughout their marriage; despite the upper-hand given her by the downturn in his recent business and employment circumstances; she had used such a contemptuous tone with him.

He would do well, she had smiled to herself, to get used to it.

"Helen, you don't understand," he tried again, desperation washing over him as he pictured what could become of his life if he were unable to persuade her what she could see him doing in those pictures had not been undertaken voluntarily.

"What's to understand?" she asked. "The man I married and who professes to love me enjoys taking a black cock up his arse and then sucking it clean afterwards. Seems pretty obvious to me."

"For heaven's sakes, Helen! You don't think I wanted it, do you? I told you, I was being bla…"

"Blackmailed, yes," she sighed, feigning boredom and irritation. "I know. A beautiful black woman who just happens to be in possession of a cock is blackmailing *you* into sex with her because she/he is too ugly to find anyone else to do it."

"But that's exactly what she is doing," he assured her.

"For someone being blackmailed you don't look to unwilling in those photos."

"She… He… I was forced to smile and make it look that way," he told her, knowing how ludicrous it sounded. "You have to believe me!"

"No, Trevor! I don't have to *believe* you. You have to *persuade* me. You can start by telling me why this person would want to blackmail you and how she could do it. What possible hold could she have on you that she could make you accept such treatment if you didn't really want it?"

"She said… She said she would send pictures to you and our friends, as well as my sisters and my family in Florida."

"Did she now?" Helen mocked. "Has all their addresses does she? Certainly gone to a lot of trouble to get to put her cock in your arse and mouth, hasn't she?"

"You don't understand, Helen. She gets off on having control. She's sick. Having a white man do… *things*… like that for her is how she gets her kicks."

Helen nodded as if considering this, then:

"I see. So tell me, just how did she get incriminating pictures of you in the first place."

"She drugged my drink, Helen," he told her, knowing how ineffectual it sounded even as the words formed upon his tongue. "I couldn't stop her."

"So, you admit meeting up with her then, at least."

"No, no! It wasn't like that. I thought I was meeting her for a job. I had an email from a company I'd had dealings with asking me to an interview at a London hotel and…"

"First I've heard of it."

"I wanted it to be a surprise."

Helen's derisive snort filled the room:

"Oh, I think we can safely say it's that, Trevor."

"I'll show you the email I was sent. It's still in my Inbox."

She pretended to think about it, knowing she had already gone into both his Outlook folders and his Virgin Broadband account to delete Mariah's first contact with him.

"That would be something I suppose."

"I'll show you it now," he told her eagerly, sensing a glimmer of light through his misery and already half-turned to head for his study.

"No," she told him, something authoritative in her tone making him turn back. "You'll show me it – if it exists – when I'm ready to see it. First though, I want to let you know how things stand between us."

Deflated a little, but still hopeful given his belief in the continued existence of the email and the veracity it gave his story, he turned back to her and made to retrieve his trousers.

"Leave them!" she snapped.

"Wh-What do you mean?"

"Just do as I say and listen to me," she told him with a confidence *and* harshness he had not experienced from her when directed at him. "If there's any chance of this marriage continuing – and, at the moment, I don't see much; job offer or not – then you had better listen to what I have to say."

"But…? The email?"

"The email, if it exists, will still be there when I've finished speaking," she reminded him.

Then, more ominously:

"And, if it's not…"

EIGHT

The man turned her docile body and bent it over the mattress in his bedroom, using her hair to manipulate the figure that was somehow matronly and sexy at one and the same time into the position he wanted as Helen Drayton luxuriated in the feeling of being dominated by a powerful alpha-male. Her feelings made all the more potent for the knowledge that she was *allowing* it to happen as a correlative to the control she exercised in her other, more private, life and the fact the Neanderthal who was at that moment controlling her would become a nonentity, never to be seen again, once she had gotten what she wanted from him.

Even if the tattooed mid-twenty-something with the over-developed and hairless body from toe-to-scalp felt he had all the control between them.

As if!

As she stared up at the unlikely poster-boy residing above the bed that was a change at least from the Rihanna or Jessie J pose she had expected – though the somewhat weasel features of UKIP's politically delusional leader did nothing to enhance her physical pleasure - the Neanderthal supporter of home-grown and opportunist xenophobia slapped her ass.

Self-interested *"Farage", with* a missing consonant and erroneous vowel ending or *not*, she seemed to automatically understand that she was meant to arch her back and lift her ass. An action of which the Neanderthal seemed to approve. At least if the dropping of his pants and his speedy entry of her from behind spoke true.

She couldn't help but gasp, but not from the rough and artless entry so much as from the delight she took from being filled by his large cock. A *"delight"* that was a first for the cheating-wife and set her to panting. She hadn't been taken from behind before but, from first impressions, she could imagine it becoming one of her favorite positions.

Though not with her own husband, of course.

His position in relation to her these days was far less... *manly.*

Neanderthal supporter of a self-interested and cerebrally challenged political grouping or not, the panting wife added groaning to her response and realised the body-building alpha was pressing just the buttons she wanted pressed at this point in her faux submission.

Roughly and gruffly he took her from behind and the fact he seemed heedless of her own needs only seemed to enhance the pleasure she took from his simple-minded usage of her.

A simple-minded usage that made it easy for the cheating-wife to pretend to herself she was helpless and used as he violated her rear in a way that eschewed her own needs to the end of achieving his own equally as much as his politics eschewed sense.

Knowledge of which verisimilitude did not prevent her own release as her bog-basic lover found his release to spill his liquid heat into her.

Once again she was flooded, violated, and – *delightfully* - aware of her unfaithfulness to her husband.

That she should think of Trevor at such a time not so surprising really, given it was the abject position to which she had reduced him that made the pleasure she took from making herself available to another man – and especially one as inferior to the man she had married who waited for at home – so… *euphoric*.

As he pulled out slowly, letting her feel every inch of him as he vacated her most private of areas before plunging back in again, any pleasure she might take from the manoeuvre incidental to him, she was aware of her own wetness and the feel of it enveloping his sizable, if not *"Mariah"* like cock.

"Like that don't yer," his harsh and contracted South London accent breathed in her ear, the cold metal of his lip-piercing brushing against her unadorned lobe. "You married cunts are all the same. Look down at us as if we're pieces of shit you've trod in when all the time you're gagging for a portion of the stiff cock we've got and your boring fucking husband's ain't."

Head turned away from him as she received her *"portion"*, Helen Drayton prevented a smile from becoming a full-blown laugh and risking the moron might take it for some kind of mockery of him. She may have ceded him control willingly but the truth was, by dint of his superior physical strength, she could be *really* vulnerable if he became angry. And, moron or not, he had touched on the truth.

Even if it wasn't in quite the way he believed.

He was right, of course, that her husband was not in possession of the kind of stiff cock she required right now, but he could have no idea as to the reasons why or the fact that its dimensions, though smaller, were not so far short of his own.

But then, how many wives had placed a steel-ring around their husband's ball-sac before attaching it to a cock-cage and locking it into place?

Again her smile threatened to become outright laughter and she fought the urge as she thought of all the other women, if the Internet were to be believed, who had done just that with their men.

As his hands roughly needed her full breasts from behind and his Neanderthal grunts turned into shallow expulsions of breath, she knew he was about to spurt his load into her back passage and felt her own orgasm triggered by the approach and the knowledge she still had what it took in her thirties to get a young man off.

Prompting her own crisis more was the prospect of having his *"load"* cleaned from her when she returned home.

Not to mention the abject and demoralising way she expected it to be done.

As Neanderthal man slumped across her back, sated and pleased with himself, post-orgasmic thoughts, such as they might be, taking him to… who knew or cared where, Helen Drayton couldn't prevent her thoughts slipping back in time…

…"How did it go?" the glamorous and utterly undetectable shemale told her as they took lunch in a pleasant but none too glamorous Pizza Express off behind the streets of Gracechurch and Leadenhall in the City of London.

Any number of lunching male eyes flickered across, away, and then back again to their table as the two of them spoke – some of them even giving Helen Drayton the usual male once-over. Their attention, though, was centred mostly on the feline black woman in the skin-tight jeans and thoroughly un-market-floor leather thigh boots with dagger heels. The wondrously full and shapely breasts thrusting against a black bustier beneath her denim jacket not going unnoticed either. In fact, with her long and straightened black hair pulled from her face and tied at the back, the shemale looked the archetypal dominatrix in whose presence many of those men staring at her would have given a month's salary in order to spend a couple of hours polishing her boots or anything else she had a mind for them to do.

Helen chuckled as she answered, unoffended by playing second-fiddle to the shemale and found the looks thrown her way – one of them from a man who worked at her finance house in a junior capacity – amusing. Given she was the object of that shemale's affections and had more than enough attention from suitors of her own, it was easy to be magnanimous. Even more so given what she had achieved with her husband only the night before.

"He is exactly what you described him to be," she told the waiting Mariah, her co-conspirator immediately fixing feline features into an "I told you so," look.

"All those years," Helen continued, voice lowered that it might not carry to adjacent tables, "pretending to be a manly, nineteenth-hole, type when, underneath, he was this weak-willed pussy who folded at the slightest pressure. Just as he did last night when I turned up the heat."

"I had no doubt he would," Mariah smirked. "How did he react when you told him I'd contacted you and we had met?"

"He looked even more surprised than when I dropped the pictures of him…" Helen looked around them and dropped her voice another octave, "…sucking your cock on the bed."

Mariah laughed delightedly and for all the world the two of them could have been sharing a simple mockery of a neighbour's tastes in home furnishing rather than the dismantling and demotion of a man in his forties from formerly proud businessman and husband to no more than his wife's cuckold and flunky.

"What did he say when you explained that I told you I was giving those photos over to you that you might know the kind of man you'd married?"

"Said you were a liar, of course. Same again when I told him you'd said he had promised he loved you and would leave me. Said you had got him to meet you with a bogus offer of a job and drugged him before taking the pictures."

"And, of course, he tried to show you the email I sent as proof?"

Helen nodded.

"Not before I laid out some home truths to him though. I told him it was impossible for me ever to see him as a man again after what he had done with you – blackmail or not – and that, though I still

loved him, I was so angry I was thinking of sending those photos to his sisters myself."

"I can almost taste his fear," the shemale said, sipping from her latte as if to banish it from her tongue.

"I also took the opportunity – as you advised – to tell him how unsatisfactory as a lover he was and how he had never pleased me. That I had sexual cravings of my own he had not once addressed while he felt free to suck cocks and take them up his arse."

Mariah placed her coffee down and clapped her hands together delightedly.

"He tried to tell me I was wrong and that you had really blackmailed him and the email would prove it, but I kept at him. I said that whether you had coerced him or not - and that I frankly didn't believe someone as beautiful as you would need to with a man of his or any age – the bottom line was he had sucked a shemale's cock and allowed himself to be penetrated rather than come to me in the hope we could work something out together."

Mariah nodded approvingly.

"I said you had told me about his fantasies of having a woman dominate him and make him a cuckold, but how he had said I was too dull and buttoned-up to role-play with him."

Helen gave her a sly look:

"That's when I pretended to cry."

The shemale couldn't prevent a laugh:

"You? Cry? Now that's something I'll believe when I see it."

Helen laughed with her.

"Trust me, it wasn't easy. And if it hadn't been for what was at stake I think I would have ended up in tears of laughter as he tried to put an arm around my shoulders and reassure me it just wasn't true."

"I think I can guess what happened next," said the shemale as she raised a latte to her lips.

"I stood up and slapped him," Helen nodded.

Her eyes glazed over with an unholy pleasure nobody who professed to love another person should ever feel from having tormented them as she added:

"I even backhanded him for good measure… And he took it!"

She marvelled at this for a few moments, scarcely crediting she could have done such a thing to the "manly" husband she had allowed to rule the roost for so long.

"The power-rush was amazing."

"Trust me," Mariah assured her, "it gets better and better."

"Oh, I do trust you," Helen chuckled. "After all, of all people you would know, wouldn't you?"

The shemale took a mock bow and continued with her theme:

"You're on the verge of everything you want from your relationship – your one-sided relationship – with him, Helen. No more holding down a high-pressure position while he loafs about at home and does the odd chore when he feels like it. If last night went the way I think it did…"

Helen Drayton's expression could hardly be said to refute the shemale's assumption.

"...then you will soon have him managing all the mundane chores of your life from now on and, if you play on his guilt and weakness the way I say, you will soon be sleeping with whoever you like and when you like – and with his full knowledge. Once you have him at that point – and with the help of moi – you can lead him to accept any humiliation at your hands you desire."

The black man/woman could tell this was not exactly an undesirable state of affairs, even if a warning look did cross her lover's face:

"If... and I haven't made up my mind yet... I allow you to be a part of my life and what passes from now on for that of my husband, there can be no question of anyone else either being told or included. That's non-negotiable. You want to be a part of this it will be on my terms. Completely."

Mariah's answer was instant:

"That's exactly what I want too. The idea of helping you treat a man like your husband in such a way while everyone thinks he's an upright and respectable man who rules his own roost is what makes the situation delightful to me."

The shemale took Helen's hand quickly and just as quickly released it as the older woman's eyes flashed.

"That and... other... things," she added, holding Helen's eyes with her own.

Helen was non-committal and an unusually nervy Mariah pressed on:

"The most common reason a woman doesn't cuckold her husband," she continued, "is that she thinks he'll never submit to it; that he'd rather divorce than be forced into remaining chaste while his wife is free to fuck any available cock that takes her fancy"

"Go on," Helen whispered, breaking her silence and looking interested - much to the shemale's relief as she continued:

"That's why it was necessary to go through the charade of blackmail with him. It doesn't matter if you stumble across the idea of cuckoldry through discovery of your husband's supposed cheating – not to mention the assertion of his 'Mistress' that it's a long-held fantasy of his – and find you like it yourself."

"Refresh my memory again," Helen ordered, knowing fully well what she was likely to hear but knowing also that hearing it again would not diminish the enjoyment she took from the repetition.

"This way you still have the moral high-ground for not being the one who cheated and brought these desires into the open – which is what you want and I agree makes sense. You can have it all. His unconditional submission and obedience to you along with the respect as a woman and housewife in the neighbourhood I know means so much to you."

Helen nodded, almost to herself, hearing her husband's *"submission"* and *"obedience"* to her described once again not losing anything in the retelling.

The look she gave the shemale was serious:

"I don't want people to think of my husband as a wimp," Helen told her. *"Even if that's exactly what he is. They might suspect something like a female-led marriage when they see him deferring to me, and that I can live with, but if they draw that conclusion I want them to be envious that I have such a handsome and well-trained husband and nothing... else. An impossibility if they were ever to find out the truth."*

Now it was Mariah's turn to nod.

"In this," Helen finished, *"and though he doesn't know it, I have as much to lose as him."*

"What happened with the email?" Mariah asked.

The white wife gave a snort of derision and her shemale lover took it to be contempt for her husband's weakness and gullibility.

"I insisted it would make no difference whether it existed or not. That if he wished to stay married to me and keep his sordid sex-life from his sisters and their families there would be changes. That was when he almost lost his temper – almost – and insisted he had been forced into letting you fuck him and then provide a blow-job."

Helen sneaked a look at the tables nearest them but nobody appeared to be paying them any attention so she went on, voice lowered still further:

"That was when I laid the law down. I said that if I heard one more lie pass his lips he was out the door and the photos would be in the post first thing in the morning."

Helen's face became warm at the memory she was about to describe:

"That was when he virtually begged me to follow him to his study and look at the email."

Her laughter, hushed or otherwise, would never be taken as pleasant.

"So desperate was he to show me his evidence he didn't even bother to cover his naked body in his rush to boot-up the computer and go into Outlook."

Mariah was laughing with her now and it was a good few seconds before the shemale recovered enough to observe:

"That must have been something to see when he discovered it wasn't there."

"You have to believe it," Helen told her. "At first he was puzzled, then angry and finally devastated when it could not be found and his Virgin account produced no sign of it either."

"How did you react?"

"I simply walked away and told him to sleep in the spare-room. He followed behind, begging me to believe him, but by the time he reached the bedroom I had it locked and bolted. I told him through the door that I would let him know what I intended to do in the morning."

"And did you?"

Helen shook her head.

"I made sure I was out of the house before he was awake – if, that is, the state of terror I had him in had allowed him to sleep at all. He's been trying to call me at the office all morning and left a string of texts and voicemails on my cell-phone. All of which say how much he loves me and how he needs for me to let him try and prove his case to me."

"And you replied how?

Again Helen shook her head:

"I haven't and won't."

"Good girl."

Helen smiled:

"By tonight he should be ripe to hear what I intend for him. If... when... he agrees to what I have in mind, if he is to stay and the pictures are kept between us, I shall give it a couple of weeks to ease him in and then..."

The cruel and devious white housewife looked at her shemale lover expectantly and waited for her to finish the sentence.

Her lover did not disappoint.

"...You can invite me over to cement his new role in your household."

Both woman and shemale smiled and, as if they were holding up wine goblets, clinked their coffee cups in a salute to their success.

NINE

When his wife had returned from the office the evening after their bedroom confrontation of the previous night – a confrontation that had been followed by the mysterious disappearance of the email that may have at least helped him in her eyes a little; if not totally - Trevor Drayton had, and for the first time, taken care of all the chores.

He had even, with his limited culinary skills, prepared a somewhat basic lamb casserole he hoped would go some way towards repairing the rift between them caused by the abomination of nature who had, for reasons still mystifying him, picked upon his life to take apart and ruin.

It would, he suspected, and along with the laundry and the cleaning, be nowhere near enough to put things right between them and the fact she had ignored his calls and his texts throughout the day underlined his misgivings.

But, then, he had to do something and, given her un-womanly distaste for flowers, the usual token of male contrition was out of the question.

Even had he been in possession of enough cash with which to purchase them.

He had, as she had suspected he would be, been proved right.

His efforts with the house were not commented upon and the food he had cooked so painstakingly, if artlessly, not only went untouched but drew no comment – favourable or otherwise – from the lips he so longed to hear utter words of reassurance, understanding and forgiveness.

Instead, she had marched into the house without a word and locked herself in the bedroom to take a shower in the en-suite before returning back downstairs to shock him with both her demands and the way she looked.

That had been three weeks ago.

Now, as she told him to wait in the kitchen and finish off the cleaning of the floor - this while she answered the door to a guest he assumed to be a neighbour or a wife of a friend - he wondered if he didn't actually prefer his life before the shemale decided, for sadistic reasons of her own, to meet with his wife and give her those incriminating – and quite unjust - pictures.

Then, at least, his humiliation had been limited to a once weekly fucking.

A once weekly fucking from a bitch with a cock.

A bitch and a cock who had ruined what remained of his life and… and…

He shrugged off the other images of what he had been forced to do and, again, went over the events following Helen's confronting of him with the photos and what had happened after she had taken her shower and returned back downstairs…

…The sight of her as she descended took his breath away and he realised lust was not the overriding response he was making to the sight of her as she made her seductive way down the stairs into their spacious and open-plan living area.

Hope was by far in the ascendant.

Notwithstanding the relief he felt for what her coming back down to him dressed in such a way meant, it was impossible not to admire that womanly and hour-glass shape that would never have cut it on a model's catwalk and was all the sexier for it – especially as it had been withheld from him for so long.

To his amazement and pleasure – as well as the aforementioned "hope" - her wonderfully, matronly and erotic at one and the same time, body was encased in some seriously seductive lingerie. Black stockings, topped with a band of lace and a white frilly garter belt below white thong panties while her wondrously firm breast were visible beneath the flimsy gauze trying unsuccessfully to cover her upper body. Her face was understatedly made-up and only served to make the red of her lipstick all the more startling while her hair was loose and hung at her shoulders.

"Hope" or not, the relieved husband realised he had never wanted his wife with more urgency than he did at that moment and, closing the gap between them, eyes moist at the prospect of what would be forgiveness as well as a sexual re-acquaintance, he was about to fold her in his arms when, mimicking a traffic policeman, she held up a palm to stop him and actually placed it upon his chest and thrust him away from her.

"Helen," he gasped, "you look... you look... wonderful," he told her," perceiving her reluctance as no more than a desire not to give in until she had taken her pound of flesh from him.

Not knowing he would need scales of a more... industrial... nature to weight the amount of flesh she intended to take.

"Really?" she asked.

He nodded, erection painful inside his denims, need all but robbing him of coherent thought, let alone speech.

"Better than a big black cock even?" she had asked.

"Helen, please," he began, voice a croak but at least audible.

"Because it seems to me that you'd prefer to wrap your mouth around a silky black dick," provocatively, she ran her hands over her breasts, lingering at the nipples he could see were bullet-hard, "rather than please your wife?"

Suddenly, it was clear to him why she had dressed in such a way and a little of the hope he held out was whittled away.

"N-No, Helen, I..."

"Mariah said you also had a fantasy about me being fucked by other men and wanted me to be more dominant with you."

"Helen, please! I told you. I was being blackma..."

For the second time in the space of a day his head was rocked to the side as his wife slapped him.

"I'll say this one more time," she hissed. "Lie to me again and you'll leave this house in the next hour and those photos will find themselves in the envelopes I already have written out."

"But..."

This time it was her other hand that made contact with his cheek and the stricken and increasingly demoralised husband could almost feel its imprint as she returned it to her side.

"Tell me once more that Mariah was blackmailing you and it's over between us. Understand?"

Just as she had intended, Trevor Drayton stood before her a mass of anxiety and conflicting desires – the least of them at this point, for the moment anyway, being his sexual desire for her. Not only was she threatening to kick him out of the home and send photos of him fucking and sucking a black cock to his nearest and dearest but she was asking him to admit to having sought the encounters out.

"You're not going to tell me that, are you?" she asked, almost orgasmic in the power she was wielding over him and made all the more euphoric by the knowledge her hold on him would soon grow stronger and more inescapable.

She waited, more and more confident with each passing second of manipulating her husband

The pleading look he threw her could have come from a seven-year-old about to be sent away to boarding-school and finding his youthful vocabulary not up to the task of begging with sufficient and persuasive articulacy.

If you don't answer me I'll take it you want to leave," she blazed, impressed by her own acting skills as she placed hands upon hips and allowed her eyes to blaze into his.

His mouth worked but nothing came out and Helen Drayton sensed he needed but a nudge to be tipped over.

A "nudge" she was more than willing to supply.

"I'm going upstairs to put some clothes in a case for you," she told him, turning away towards the stairs and all too aware of the view it gave him of her shapely stockinged legs in their sheer black nylon. "I'd advise you to use the time I'm up there to work out where you're going to be staying tonight and calling a cab to take you there."

She smiled to herself as she reached the stairs, knowing that if he was terrified and miserable now he would be even more so after hearing what she was about to throw back at him over her shoulder:

"Tomorrow, I shall see a divorce lawyer and have you served with papers. The sooner this is out in the open and done with the better... Oh! By the way, I used the passwords you left on the computer to cancel our joint account and your over their limit credit-cards. But don't worry, if you haven't enough cash for a cab I'll be happy to give it to you."

She placed one stiletto heeled shoe upon a stair and added:

"And don't bother yourself about paying me back."

With a wry grin he couldn't see, and wanting nothing more than to thrust a relieving finger – or something more substantial – in her saturated pussy, she had actually taken another couple of steps before she allowed his cry of desperation to halt her.

"No, Helen!... Please!!

She paused in mid-flight and again placed her hands upon her hips, shaking her head slowly to give him the impression she was thinking his plea through, knowing both the effect her scanty dress would be having upon him and the symbolism that was supplied by her being above him as he pleaded.

Finally, still without turning, she said:

"Are you going to lie to me again?"

If a pause could take physical form, she thought to herself as she waited for her husband to capitulate, this one would surely take on that of an electricity grid.

On and on it went, until, finally:

"N-No," came a piteous croak.

"What was that?" she demanded. "I can't hear you."

The anguish and humiliation behind and below her was almost palpable, then:

"N-No, Helen," he said more loudly, clearing his throat of the bile and self-pity that had accumulated there. "I... I won't lie to you again."

Keeping her back to him still, hands remaining on her hips and giving her the impression of a voluptuous, if somewhat matronly and demanding, goddess, Helen exulted in what she knew was the beginning of his surrender to her and nodded her head as if pleased at his decision to play it straight from now on.

"Then you admit you cheated on me with a... girly-boy?" she asked.

"I... I..."

"If the next words out of your mouth aren't exactly what I want to hear we're finished," she told him.

She waited and, if she were to be honest afterwards, was in almost as great a condition of agitation as her husband.

Agitation, though, of an entirely different kind.

What happened next though stunned even Helen Drayton.

She detected movement from behind her and the next thing she knew her husband – the husband she had once taken as manly and strong and allowed herself to be guided by – had flung himself at her feet and placed his arms around her thighs, his right cheek pressed against the smooth skin of a taut buttock left buttock left uncovered by the flimsy thong.

Her husband was abasing himself before her!

Even if he might describe his actions a lot less demeaningly at that point.

He was also, wonder of wonders, sobbing like a chastised infant.

"P-Please, Helen," he begged through his sobs. "You have no idea what it's like for me. First my business and then... this... I love you, but... but..."

Taking the hands clutching her thighs in her own and keeping them in place upon he thighs that they might not inadvertently make contact with the front of the thong and feel the wetness inspired by her dismantling of him, she kept her voice firm:

"Do you love me enough to tell me the truth though?" she asked.

"You... You know I do," he sobbed.

"Then I shall ask you one last time: Did you cheat on me with a girly-boy?"

The pause that followed her question seemed like an eternity to Helen Drayton and all she could hear from behind her were a few sniffles.

She was on the verge of repeating her question when, to her utter joy, the smallest of male voices said:

"Yes, Helen. I..."

His wife had stopped breathing and her heart thumped in her chest as she waited to hear the necessary, and totally unjust, admission that would lead him in to his slavery.

The, just as she was on the point of passing out from oxygen deprivation:

"I did..."

...Coming back to the task at hand and finishing off the kitchen floor his wife, for reasons he considered purely punitive, insisted he clean by hand while on all-fours, Trevor Drayton once again considered the injustice of his lot – even if, being the fair-minded man that he was, he could hardly help but acknowledge the weakness at his core that allowed him to accept it.

What other self-respecting man, after all, would accept his wife being free to have sex with other – *"better endowed"* – partners while he stayed at home and was... *not*?

Her words still haunted him:

"If it's your fantasy to know better endowed men are satisfying your wife the way Mariah tells me, then I'd be lax in my duties to my husband if I didn't realise them for him."

Emptying the bucket in the sink and wringing out the cleaning-cloths, he pictured himself as he had stood before her, wanting nothing more than to tell her the shemale abomination was lying and that he wanted nothing more than to have a loving relationship with the wife he adored. And prevented from doing so by her insistence that she would make him leave if he so much as once more protested his innocence. What with her insistence she be the dominant partner in the household – by way of satisfying *his* desires – and becoming more dictatorial with him with each passing day; though she did not flaunt this in front of the friends and family they still saw on a regular basis - his only consolation being that at least the black abomination with her monster cock was out of his life and the acts the bitch had forced him to do and taken photographic evidence of him doing them were safe from being revealed to his family and friends.

If, that is, he towed Helen's increasingly autocratic line, and gave the lie to her insistence that he had sought out his treatment at the shemale's hands himself.

More tormenting though, was the fact he desired his wife now with more force than ever and had to be content with serving her with his tongue – though thankfully *not* after she had been with one of the lovers he had never seen and, according to her, never would.

This meant he had been forced to continue with the masturbation he had returned to - and for the first time since his mid-teens – prior to the intervention of the shemale and during his wife's seeming lack of interest in him that way.

An act she had, after first ensuring he pleased her orally, insisted he repeat for her while on his knees in their bedroom and one she had been so delighted to witness it had become an integral part of what she laughingly called their *"lovemaking"*.

With his company gone and his assets liquidated, credit-card cancelled and no bank-account of his own and dependent upon his wife for... well... *everything*... and with no chink in the black cloud of his circumstances to lend him even the slightest glimmer of optimism, Trevor Drayton's self-image was about at rock-bottom.

Or so he thought.

He was wringing out the last of the cleaning-cloths he had used to hand-wash the floor when Helen's voice sounded behind him:

"We have a visitor, Trevor. Be polite and say hello."

Sensing something... *different*... in his wife's tone, Trevor was no better prepared for the sight waiting to greet him when he turned.

"Hello, Trevor," said the black shemale who had led him to his current predicament, feline features fairly flushed with anticipation,. "It's so lovely to renew our acquaintance.

Stunned and utterly lost for a reply, Trevor listened with mouth gaping as Helen took it up.

"I've decided I don't like the idea of you being alone while I'm out having... *fun*..." his wife told him, looking calm, collected and authoritative in the grey two-piece costume with matching heels she had worn to the office, the shemale dressed similarly in and outfit of cobalt blue. "Mariah here has kindly consented to babysit for me while I'm out and make sure you do your chores properly and don't get up to any mischief."

"But... But..."

"No need to thank me, Trevor," the shemale came in. "I know things didn't end well with us and, had I known what a lovely woman your wife was, I should never have gotten involved with you in the first place."

Trevor's mortification knew no bounds as this blatant lie was paraded in front of him and his all too credulous wife; outrage heightened by the knowledge Helen would have him on the street and ruin him in the eyes of his family if he were to try and refute the lies of the shemale bitch.

Worse was to come, however.

"It's very good of Mariah to come over and supervise you like this," Helen told him, her look both a threat and a warning, "and I want you to be as respectful to her until I come home as you've learned to be to me... Understand?"

The sandwich he had had snatched an hour ago seemed ready to project itself from his throat as he took in this latest downturn in his personal fortune.

"Understand?" Helen snapped at him, injecting something of the whip into her voice and making his nausea worse as he reacted like the well-schooled animal she was conditioning him to be.

"Y-Yes," he answered in a beaten voice while lowering his eyes, preferring to look at the pointed toecaps of two pairs of shoes rather than meet the threat and mockery waiting for him above.

"Good," his wife went on. "Now, just to show she has no hard feelings and wants to help me make your fantasies a reality and make you the most obedient husband a woman can have, Mariah has bought you a present. Isn't that nice of her?"

Eyes still fixed upon their shoes, face reddened from the blood rushing to his cheeks, Trevor Drayton heard the rustling of a bag and a jangling as something was removed from it.

"Well, at least have the courtesy to look at what Mariah's bought you!" Helen snapped.

Just like the whip cur he was becoming, Trevor's eyes came up and took in what the smiling shemale was holding.

Hell became warmer.

"Well?" his wife demanded yet again. "Aren't you going to say thank you?"

The thoroughly beaten and emasculated husband stared at the metal ring and familiarly shaped cage and padlock dangling from one slender black hand with acrylic talons and reddened cheeks suddenly became deathly white.

"There are two keys," Helen informed him with unmistakable relish. "And I shall keep one."

To his amazement and revulsion, wife and shemale moved into an embrace and kissed.

A *full* kiss.

When they broke off, Helen stared at him and, with laughter and joy in her eyes, told him:

"And guess who has the other?"

Epilogue

The legs either side of him would not have disgraced the most sought after of supermodels – apart from the fact they were more substantial and, therefore, more shapely than the usual stick-insect pins.

Unfortunately, for the naked white man kneeling between them anyway, they came attached with a black cock that would not have disgraced the better endowed porn stud.

A black cock that was, at that moment, halfway down his throat as its shemale owner encouraged him to keep up the good work.

"That's it my little white slut," Mariah told the white husband whose life she had helped dismantle and was in the process of making a living hell. "Don't take your eyes off Mariah when you're sucking her. You know how annoyed she gets when you do that."

The angry red marks striping Trevor Drayton's back assured the shemale she need be no more graphic regarding the consequences involved and, shapely black hands at the sides of his now shaven head, she luxuriated in the control she had over this unwilling white husband she had in her toils.

"Oooh, yes," she sighed, knowing how praise for his talents diminished him as a man and using it whenever feasible. "My little white boy is getting so good at sucking his black master's cock. Wait until I tell Ms Helen. She'll be so proud of you."

The tears in the demoralised man's eyes her treatment of him always inspired worked upon her like an aphrodisiac and she knew it would not be long until she spurted her seed into the back of his throat and held her position until he had swallowed every last drop of it.

Stroking his denuded scalp she delighted in the memory of shaving the lustrous and greying locks from it, exulting spitefully in the knowledge that she – with Helen's agreement – was depriving him of a facet of his personal appearance he took much pride in.

As she continued to ensure his eyes remained upon hers, forgiving the odd lapse when, distaste for her or not, he could not help but snatch a glimpse of her stunning and conical black breasts as they swayed unfettered above his servile head, the familiar ring-tone of her cell-phone sounded off at her side.

"Hi," she said, one black hand remaining at the back of his head to keep him to his task, demanding and terrifying at the same time. "Sorry… No… I'm in the middle of something… Or rather you're husband is."

She gave a derisive snort into the cell:

"Not sure he'll ever be able to get to the end of it, if I'm honest, Helen."

She laughed and then listened, before:

"Okay… No problem. He'll be ready… I'll see you in about half an hour."

Her eyes held Trevor Drayton's with the unmistakable joy of complete – well, *almost* complete – ownership.

"See you then, sweetie."

Triggered beyond recall by the call from the wife of the man currently on his knees *trying* to deep-throat her cock, all it took was one last look into those demoralised eyes below and her seed gushed from her as if released by a team of wild-catters drilling a Texas well.

Her scream surprised her once again as the strength of her eruption outdid the one before it. And the one before that. Never had she known such sexual fulfilment and she knew it was all due to the reality that she, along with Helen, truly owned the white man below her in ways known only to the most demanding masters of the most abject slaves of past times.

The fact he truly hated her usage of him – even if she sensed he was beginning to get at least a frisson of pleasure from serving and being penetrated by her – did the cause of her pleasure no harm either.

For minutes afterwards, neither of them moved. Mariah because she was basking in the aftermath of her arrived crisis. Trevor Drayton because of the crisis he would bring down upon himself if he were to move with the express permission of his black master – even had the shapely but strong black hands at the back of his head allowed him such self-determination.

"Better and better," she told him when she had recovered enough to form a short sentence. "Ms Mariah's pleased with you."

She stroked the bald pate she herself had denuded, knowing how much he hated her doing it and how… *animal-like*… it made him feel.

The shemale smiled to herself.

He had, she told herself, no idea of just how *"animal-like"* he was about to become.

"Now, lick Ms Mariah's lovely black cock clean," she ordered. "And, as you do, I'll tell you about a new treat Ms Helen has for you when she gets home."

She almost heard his inner groan of despair but smiled to herself as the tongue she had trained to do her bidding snaked out clean the length of the pole that had played such a part in mastering him and bringing him low.

"You know, I think you're getting to like being a little white slave-boy for Ms Mariah's big black cock a little too much and…"

Her shrill and angry scream made him jump – not surprising given he knew what her displeasure could mean for him.

"No!... Keep your eyes on mine. You know Ms Mariah likes to see your gratitude when she's letting you make her all nice and clean."

Beaten and dog-like eyes returned to hers and she showed him the pleasure his obedience gave her by running a hand comfortingly and mockingly over his smooth and newly bald head.

"That's my good boy," she cooed. "You do everything your lovely Ms Mariah tells you from now on and life is going to be just dandy for you. That's it, finish off licking clean those lovely big black balls."

With an alacrity the man could never have imagined prior to her entry into his life, his tongue did just that and he felt the full and hairless ball-sac beneath it that *never* seemed less than bursting, no matter how many times it was emptied, the purring her heard from deep in her throat telling him he was doing fine and just might avoid punishment this time.

"Then," she finished, a little breathlessly, pole showing no sign of subsiding, "we'll get you all snug and obedient in your lovely new dog-collar for when Ms Helen comes home with your surprise…"

END

Printed in Great Britain
by Amazon

62723169R00198